The Wrong Abraham

The Wrong Abraham

DAVID S. BRODY

MARTIN AND LAWRENCE PRESS
GROTON, MASSACHUSETTS

Published by:
Martin and Lawrence Press
37 Nod Road
P.O.Box 682
Groton, MA 01450

ISBN 0977389804
Printed in Canada

The Wrong Abraham
by David S. Brody   first edition

This is a work of fiction. Names, characters, places, and incidents are either the
product of the author's imagination or are used fictitiously. Any resemblance to
actual people, living or dead, business establishments, events, or locales is
entirely coincidental.

August, 2006

TO MY PARENTS

IRENE & SPENCER

WHO INSTILLED IN ME
A LIFE-LONG LOVE OF BOOKS

Terrorism Threat: LNG Tanker Explosion

Attack on gas vessel could cause big damage

WASHINGTON — A terror attack on a tanker delivering liquefied natural gas at a U.S. port could set off a fire so hot it would burn skin and damage buildings nearly a mile away....

The tankers, each of which carries up to 30 million gallons of LNG, arrive every few days at four U.S. terminals: Everett, Mass. [abutting Boston]; Cove Point, Md.; Elba Island, Ga., and Lake Charles, La....

In its minus-260 degrees liquid state, LNG cannot explode and is not flammable. If a missile or explosive should tear a hole in a tanker or a storage tank, however, the escaping liquid would be transformed instantaneously into a gas and probably would ignite in a massive fire.

The Sandia report said terrorists, using readily available weapons and technology, could blast a 10-foot hole into the side of an LNG tanker.

The assessment evaluates a range of scenarios that would result in release of millions of gallons of LNG from a transport tanker. The scenarios include a takeover of a vessel by an insider or hijacker, external attacks using explosive-laden boats, triggered explosions or rocket-propelled grenades or missiles....

[This article appeared on the MSNBC.com website on December 20, 2004.]

Terrorism Threat: Anthrax

Anthrax, in many respects, is an ideal bioweapon. It lends itself to aerosolization; its spores can be modified to "the ideal size" for causing lung infection; and the spores resist decontamination and persist in the environment for long periods of time.... [A]nthrax spores could have the same devastating effect on a concentrated urban population as a nuclear device. We therefore neglect the threat of anthrax at our peril....

Early detection and treatment are key to survival following an anthrax attack. Otherwise, the disease, especially the inhalational form, is often fatal.

*[Excerpted from **Anthrax: What You Need to Know**, by American Council on Science and Health, October, 2003, page 5.]*

"The Lord appeared to Abraham and said to him,
I am God Almighty; walk before me, and be blameless."
GENESIS, 17:1

CHAPTER 1

[May]

As he often did when circumstances required bold action, Abraham Gottlieb reflected upon the fable of the dim-witted man who resolved not to go into the water until he first learned how to swim.

Inaction. Cowardly and foolish.

It could never be so for Abraham. It must never be.

He stood on the observation deck of the Custom House tower, a cool, wet wind moistening his charcoal suit and white hair. His liver-spotted hands gripped the overlook's wrought iron safety bars and, squinting through the morning mist, his eyes tracked a reptile-green tanker as it slogged into Boston's inner harbor. The massive vessel dwarfed the city's waterfront buildings, muscling through the narrowing channel like a snake constricting its way through its own skin.

The tanker delivered liquefied natural gas to Boston. Flammable, volatile, deadly. Abraham understood the risk-reward equation better than most—as a young boy he defied long odds and survived the Holocaust, and as an old man he presided over one of the world's largest insurance conglomerates. Some risks were acceptable, some manageable, some unavoidable. But allowing tankers stuffed with liquefied natural gas to slither into downtown Boston once a week was like putting a dragon in a petting zoo and then being surprised at the

smell of charred flesh. It was only a question of time before some terrorist decided that incinerating half of Boston with a giant ball of fire
would make a fine book-end to the Twin Towers attack.

But still the tankers came. It was the kind of head-in-the-sand
decision-making that made men like Abraham incredibly wealthy,
and women like Gabriella Garcia-Ring incredibly dangerous.

Her voice—more like a purr—announced her arrival. "You are
older than I thought."

Abraham hid his surprise, resisted the urge to turn his head. Few
people had snuck up on him over the past 70 years. "And you are
more careless than you should be. My men followed you from your
apartment."

Her shoulders moved up and down in a languid shrug. She lifted
her chin to look him in the eye, arched an eyebrow. "And my men
followed your men. Perhaps they're all still down on the street, chasing each other around the building."

He studied her, perceived her beauty in the way another man
would take note of an overbite or a crooked nose. Full lips, white
teeth, jet-black hair matched by dark, penetrating eyes. She wore a
white tennis skirt and blouse, per his instructions, and carried a gym
bag with a tennis racket handle protruding from one end. Her skin
was deeply tanned, though goose-pimpled in the cold mist; her arms
and legs exhibited a male-like muscle definition that women of his
generation would have thought unsightly.

He lifted a brown canvas tote bag from between his feet, handed
it to her. "Fifty thousand dollars, old bills, not traceable."

She opened her gym bag, dropped the tote in, zipped it closed. She
arched an eyebrow again. There was no playfulness in her eyes. "How
do you know I won't just spend it on shoes?"

He nodded, appreciative of her ploy. Through the banter, she
attempted to draw him out, to get a better sense of him. She knew
nothing about him except that his group was funding her terrorist
cell. Today, for the first time, he had allowed her to see his face. That
was more than enough—his gaunt, angular features and steel gray
eyes made his visage a difficult one to disguise. He would not normally have taken such a risk, but the importance of the operation

meant he dared not pass on the opportunity to look his puppet in the eye.

"You will spend it on supplies and training, as we agreed." In reality, he did not care what she spent the money on—he funded her not so she would succeed, but so he would later be in a position to ensure she failed. It was a delicate balance, a tricky game he played here. "Are your men ready?"

"Soon. Another few months."

"I assume they are Hispanic."

She joined him at the railing, her eyes tracking the LNG tanker's steady progress. "You assume incorrectly. Just because I am Latina does not mean the others in my cell are."

He knew this already, but wanted to test her. Surprisingly, she had not yet lied to him. Even the story about her brother checked out: an equal-opportunity revolutionary, fighting first the Americans in Nicaragua, then the Soviets in Afghanistan. Gabriella either shared her brother's anti-imperialist fervor or hoped to avenge his recent death in the mountains of Afghanistan at the hands of American troops. In either case, as a fixture both on the city's social scene and in its amateur tennis tournaments, she made an unlikely terrorist.

"Have you acquired the weapons?" she asked.

He handed her a credit card-sized manila envelope. "This key opens a storage room at a facility in North Andover; the address is printed on the envelope. Inside the room you will find a large red duffel bag containing ice hockey equipment. Buried under the equipment are two smaller duffel bags, each containing a rocket-propelled grenade launcher, an RPG-7."

Abraham's eyes shifted to the LNG tanker—a single grenade could easily penetrate the shell of one of the vessel's camel-hump-like holding tanks. The compressed vapor would then spew from the tank and ignite, which would in turn ignite the other tanks, causing a giant wave of fire to wash over the Boston waterfront neighborhoods before lapping up against its inland office towers and melting their steel support skeletons. It was a hellish scenario, comparable perhaps to the fire-bombings of Dresden and Tokyo, which created typhoons of fire that killed by sucking the oxygen out of a suffocating city and lifting civilians into its fiery vortex. Abraham's point of reference was a different World War II horror: In his dreams, a fire-breathing dragon circled hungrily above a mob of gaunt refugees as they fled, staggering and stiff-legged, from their freshly-liberated concentration camp. Whatever the nightmarish reality, from the terrorists' perspective hitting the tanker would be an easy shot. The main challenge would be getting close enough to set up and fire the grenade launcher without getting caught.

"You must understand," Gabriella pronounced. "We are not martyrs, we are revolutionaries. We do not intend to die on this mission. I, for one, have no use for 72 virgins, in this world or the next." She smiled again, her eyes glass-like and impenetrable.

She lifted the tennis bag, addressed him as she turned to leave. "We will strike only when we are confident we can do so successfully. The world will see thousands of charred corpses. Mine will not be among them."

*   *   *

The heavy door to the observation deck slammed closed behind Gabriella, leaving Abraham alone on his perch. A Peregrine falcon swooped down, settled on a ledge a few meters away. The two predators eyed each other for a few seconds, unblinking, Abraham's wolf-like gray eyes locked on the dark brown orbs of the bird. The falcon shifted its weight from one claw to the next, then abruptly lifted its beak, flapped its wings, and flew off. Abraham watched it resettle on a neighboring building, its wary eyes glued to his form.

Abraham loped along the perimeter of the deck. He stopped half way around, his eyes settling on a glass and steel office tower looming a few blocks inland. The insurance conglomerate he chaired owned the tower, along with many others in the city. Coincidentally, his niece, Shelby, a lawyer, worked in the building.

He reached inside his suit coat, withdrew a laminated black-and-white photo from his shirt pocket: Abraham and his father held fishing poles; his mother held his baby sister, the baby that would grow to become Shelby's mother. It was early 1937, before his world collapsed. A family picnic, just downstream from a small waterfall swelled by the spring rains. For dessert his father taught him how to toast marshmallows, his large, strong hand on Abraham's, father and son together holding a twig above the campfire flame, rotating slowly until the gummy confection's snow-white crust blackened and curled and melted....

He refocused on the office tower. Once the grenade hit the tanker, it would take less than three minutes for the wall of fire to reach the Financial District. For Shelby and her officemates, there would be no time for escape. They would burn, just as the marshmallows had burned.

Abraham rubbed his forefinger gently over the photo, placed it back in the pocket over his heart. He took a deep breath, continued around to the north side of the building and peered down on historic Faneuil Hall and the surrounding marketplace. Unlike the office tower workers, the thousands of tourists and shoppers and diners on the ground might actually have a chance to outrun the conflagration. Not a good chance, but those that were healthy and unencumbered by children and quick to respond might be able to sprint inland far enough to survive.

Survive, yes, but to what end? Abraham knew many Holocaust survivors haunted by the question: *Why am I among the few chosen to live while thousands around me perished?* Fortune had smiled on Abraham, however. He asked himself that very question once, 60 years ago. And immediately knew the answer.

CHAPTER 2

[June]

Shelby Baskin navigated her way along the cobblestone sidewalk, hopping over puddles, bopping along through the drizzle, timing her steps and leaps and skips to the beat of Alicia Keys streaming from her pocket iPod. Not the typical behavior of a forty-ish Boston attorney. Which was fine with her, because she found many of her professional colleagues stodgy and affected.

She reached a tree-sheltered stretch of sidewalk, glanced up to see a short, elderly man standing rigid in the summer rain in front of her apartment building. The brownstone was turn-of-the-century, the man almost as old. Yet the building's stone façade had benefited recently from the masonry equivalent of a facelift—sandblasted and pointed and polished, the decades wiped away. The man's face, gray and mottled, still bore the pits and scars of the century now gone.

She continued toward her apartment, dodging the puddles but no longer keeping the beat. She was one of a handful of the city's professionals out toting their Saturday morning spoils—hers a fresh apple, theirs a shopping bag from Neiman Marcus, a bottle of wine in a velvet gift pouch, a bouquet of flowers. Yet the old man waited not for them and their fine wares, but for her, the sweaty one in the hooded Red Sox sweatshirt and nylon running pants with an old gym bag draped over her shoulder.

He spotted her, held her gaze. A kind smile unfolded, pushing the wrinkles higher and deeper into his face. As she passed in front of the adjoining rowhouse, he bowed his head to her, droplets cascading from the brim of his hat onto his baggy gray suit. The gesture reminded her of how military officers bowed to ladies in old war movies, their backs stiff and their heels together, more of a bob of the head than a bow from the waist. She had the strange sensation of feeling underdressed. She turned off the music, removed the small earbud headphones.

Through the rain, she studied his face, as he studied hers. She had never met him before, at least not that she remembered, but there was a strange flicker of affection in his eyes as he scrutinized her. Wordless, he bowed again, then reached into his jacket pocket and withdrew a plain white envelope. The movement of his arm released the scent of wet wool into the air, and Shelby flashed back to her childhood, her brother's ice-crusted, woolen mitten rubbing snow in her face. The memory made her shiver, but also warmed her. She reached for the envelope; he released his end only after she had a firm grip on hers. He smiled again, offered yet another bob of his head, then turned and, wordless, walked briskly away along the puddled sidewalk.

Shelby eyed the envelope, her name and Boston address written neatly across the front, and took a deep breath. Two hours at the gym—had the little man been waiting in the rain the whole time? And, never having asked her name, what made him so sure he had made the correct delivery? And why a Saturday delivery? It was probably not work-related—lawyers never hand-wrote anything, and the address contained no "Esquire" after her name. She eyed the letter again, then clutched it and ran up three flights of stairs and entered her apartment.

The condo was on the sunny side of Commonwealth Avenue, which meant that on clear days the sunlight bounced between the polished hardwood floors and high white ceilings of the living area in the front of the unit, flowed into the windowless kitchen and bath in the middle, and even seeped into the two narrow bedrooms perched above the alley in the rear. This occurred on sunny days. Today the apartment was dark and cold.

She tossed her gym bag onto a chair, hung her drenched sweatshirt on a hook. As she pulled off her sneakers, she looked at the antique mirror in the foyer, tried to see herself as the little old man saw her. Family and old friends remarked that she resembled her mom; others said she looked like a green-eyed Jennifer Aniston, though Shelby did not think of herself as nearly that pretty or that bubbly or that willing to spend so much time on her hair....

Her wet socks sloshed and squished against the tile floor as she plodded into the kitchen. She thought about finding a pair of slippers, but reached for the letter instead. Taking a deep breath, she ripped the envelope open with her finger and pulled out a single sheet of thin, brittle paper.

Dearest Shelby, the letter began, the handwriting achingly familiar. *If you are reading this, I am dead.*

A rush of heat charged through her body, her fingers and head and chest tingly in its wake. *Oh my god.* She clapped a hand to her mouth as tears welled up in her eyes. *Mom.* The letter dropped from her hand onto a butcher-block table and Shelby, weak-kneed, lowered herself into a wooden chair. Her mother died 15 years ago. She smiled feebly through her tears—this was the first time Mom had written; that was what Shelby got for going out in the rain without a slicker....

She stared at the letter, a white blur on the table through her watery eyes. How? How does a person send a letter from their grave? And why?

She reached a shaky hand out for the envelope, reexamined it. Plain white, no return address, nothing but her name and Back Bay address typed neatly on the front. Trembling, she picked up the letter, but her eyes refilled before she could read a word. Giving in, she pressed the yellowed paper to her chest and allowed the sobs to rise in her throat and escape....

Enough of that. Her mother had something to say. Something important, apparently. So Shelby sniffled back her tears and spread the letter out on the table in front of her. She ran her fingers over the paper her mother had held, the words she had written, and, blinking, began to read.

How strange it is to think of you reading this, perhaps years after I have died. And I can't even begin to imagine the circumstances under which Abraham would see the need to present it to you.

So. Eccentric old Uncle Abraham. That explained the mysterious little delivery man.

Nonetheless, Abraham has asked me to write this, so it must be important. If you are reading this letter, then he needs your help. And I must ask, my darling, that you do whatever he requests of you.

I have never told you the whole story of our escape from Germany, but suffice it to say that your Uncle Abraham was truly heroic. If you're interested, he can tell you the whole story.

In any event, there are many things about him that you don't know. If you are reading this letter, I can only assume that he has chosen to share some of his secrets with you. For what reason, again I do not know. But I do know this: He is a brilliant man, a righteous man, a powerful man. You should feel privileged to be in his confidence. And proud that he sees you as worthy of aiding him.

Shelby, darling, I do not know what Abraham will ask of you. Truly. But I do know he would not ask if it was not important. Please do what you can to help him.

Don't forget that I will always love you, even more than life itself.

Mom

Shelby closed her eyes, squeezing back the dampness that threatened again. *I love you too, Mom.*

She tried to imagine the circumstances under which her mother wrote the letter: The watchful eye of Uncle Abraham peering down at her, limiting her to a single page, preventing her from turning the missive into a doting mother's Mulligan from the grave. *Don't slouch. Wear sunscreen. Wait for the after-Christmas sales.* Shelby smiled at the memory of her mother's words. *See, Mom? I remember. And you thought I wasn't listening.*

She read through the letter a second time. Uncle Abraham needed her help? Shelby shifted, arched her back. Her uncle founded and chaired an international insurance conglomerate, but his importance seemed to extend even beyond that of a powerful business titan. She worked one summer on a Congressional reelection campaign for Geraldine Ferraro, who later ran for Vice President, and had observed the seemingly endless rings of concentric circles that emanated outward from the candidate. Uncle Abraham seemed to have that same type of gravitational pull whenever he entered a room. She had attended a fundraiser once with her mother and father in New York City; they ran into Abraham, watched in astonishment as Mayor Koch broke away from a crowd and practically ran across the room to greet him. What kind of help could her uncle possibly need from her?

And what about Abraham telling her a story about escaping Germany? The thought of her detached, unapproachable uncle recounting a story of any kind struck Shelby as even more peculiar than him asking her for help. She could not think of a single significant conversation she ever had with him. Sure, he scrupulously sent gifts, or at least his secretary did—she still used the Italian leather briefcase he sent when she graduated from law school. And he generously insisted on paying for her law school education, the only caveat being that she maintain at least a 'B' average. But even when her parents and brother died, he remained stoic and distant. He immediately flew into town, made all the necessary arrangements, even delivered an appropriate eulogy. But he did not cry for his sister, did not whisper words of comfort for his sister's daughter.

She shifted again as her muscles began to tighten from her workout and her back began to itch from the dried sweat. Many questions, not many answers. And no way to get them, short of seeking an explanation from her uncle.

She stood, smiled down at the letter, listened for her mother's voice. She longed for a shower. A long, hot one. Before she caught her death from cold.

*   *   *

The two messages flashing on her answering machine when she stepped out of the shower surprised Shelby. The law firm used her cell phone if they needed her, as did most of her friends.

She played the first, a message from Bruce. "Hey, Shelbs, couldn't get you on your cell. I've left L.A., but now I'm stuck in Chicago on my layover." She swallowed her disappointment—she was looking forward to seeing him after three days apart. And telling him about her mother's letter. "My flight is delayed, big storms out here." He worked as a consultant to art museums; they hired him to probe for weaknesses in their security systems. "Grab dinner without me—best guess is I'll be home around nine. Love you."

She smiled. Her *fiancé*. It had been three weeks since she first slipped on the ring, but her tongue still tripped over the word, and the ring on her finger still felt like some foreign appendage to her body, like when braces invaded her mouth as a teenager. She looked down at the diamond, watched the light reflect off it and refract through it, marveled again at how amazing and unlikely it was that she and Bruce managed to reach this point....

The second message straightened her face. She recognized the German accent immediately, the Kissinger-like inflections. "Shelby, this is your mother's brother, Abraham Gottlieb." So formal, so cold. "I will be dining tonight at 7:30 at the Grill 23 steakhouse. I would appreciate it if you would be so kind as to join me."

Like he needed to leave his last name. And no number to call back, no way to reach him, not even a consideration that she might have other plans or not be in the mood for a steak. Just an expectation that she would show. She was tempted to blow him off, but she knew herself better than that. He was her uncle, and her mother's letter requested she help him. Plus she was dying to know what he wanted.

*   *   *

Madame Radminikov stood behind the counter of her kosher butchery. Mrs. Melnick pushed open the heavy door, waddled toward her. The butchery was one in a series of narrow stores that lined Harvard Street, a busy through-street that linked Brookline with its poorer cousin, Brighton. The stores—a bagel shop, a tailor, a Jewish book store, a bakery—serviced the predominantly Jewish neighborhoods around it. The wealthier, established Jews lived here in Brookline; the new immigrants, many from the old Eastern Bloc countries, settled in Brighton until they could afford to move the few blocks south.

Madame Radminikov greeted her sour-faced customer with a smile. "What will it be today, Mrs. Melnick?"

"Corned beef. One-half pound. Sliced thin." In her mind, thin slices meant extra slices. For the same price.

Madame Radminikov sliced the meat and weighed it, her brawny arms and calloused hands hoisting and handling the watermelon-sized slab as if it were no heavier than a hamburger patty. As always, she threw an extra couple of scraps on top before wrapping it in wax paper. As always, Mrs. Melnick complained about the price. And as always, the old woman dug around in her purse for coins, hoping in vain that the butcher would tire of waiting and simply send her on her way.

As her customer fumbled in her purse, Madame Radminikov recalled an incident years earlier—could it be close to 30 years now?—before Mrs. Melnick's husband died. They owned the dry cleaner on the corner. Some Irish kids from the projects over on Commonwealth Avenue were harassing them, breaking windows and painting swastikas on the walls. The police did nothing, so Madame Radminikov contacted an old family friend in New York, Abraham Gottlieb. Abraham had established a network of men and women to defend against this type of harassment. Some of Abraham's men staked out the store one night and ambushed the gang. The men responded in a measured manner—these were just kids, so a few kicks in the butt and slaps to the face did the trick. The boys never returned. But Abraham, and his group, became a permanent, central part of her life.

Mrs. Melnick paid, shuffled away. A short, barrel-chested man entered the shop and held the door for her. "Myron," the old woman wheezed. "I would like to double my bet."

Myron Kline, who owned the insurance agency next door, served also as the local bookie. Local businessmen, and also health professionals who worked nearby at the Longwood Medical area or St. Elizabeth's Hospital, swung by at lunch or on their way home to place a wager on the Patriots or against the Celtics, as did many of the cash-flushed young men attending neighboring Boston University and Boston College. The old woman reached down the front of her dress, pulled out a crinkled $100 bill, thrust it into Myron's fist. "Is it still 8-to-1?"

"No," he stammered. "It is now 6-to-1."

She glared at him, began to reach for the bill, then retreated. "All right, fine. But my first $100 is still 8-to-1. Red Sox to win the World Series."

Myron would take a bet on just about anything—all he asked is that you come by and make your bet in person. He took less action that way, but by not taking phone calls he reduced the chance of being nabbed by the police. He also picked up stray bits of information from these in-person visits—the doctor placing a bet against the Celtics because a colleague just treated their top scorer for back spasms, for example. Madame Radminikov knew all this because she had known Myron all his life. But he looked unhappy taking the old woman's money.

"What's wrong, Myron, you getting a conscience in your old age? Feeling guilty taking money from the weak and elderly?" she teased. What she really wanted to know was why in the world miserly old Mrs. Melnick was making hundred-dollar bets on the Red Sox.

He grinned at her. "Hello, Leah." He was a handsome man—tanned, with even, white teeth and a full head of dark, wavy hair. But Madame Radminikov could not help but think of him as the runny-nosed toddler whom she had baby-sat as a teenager. He still called her Leah, one of the few who did, and hearing it saddened her in a way—she had somehow gone from teen-aged Leah, to young-lady Miss

Bernstein, to newly-married Mrs. Radminikov, to middle-aged widow Madame Radminikov. She was never quite sure when—or for what reason—she evolved from Mrs. to Madame.

Her sadness quickly faded as he bounded toward her, a red knit shirt stretched over a healthy paunch. Just as she saw him as the toddler with a full diaper rather than the handsome, vibrant man he was, he viewed her as the fun-loving, playful teenager of her youth. Nobody had ever called her a beauty, but men a generation ago did not mind big-boned women. Unfortunately, men today liked their women thin and made-up, not broad-shouldered and adept with a carving knife; she had not had a single date since Samuel died 16 years ago, leaving her to run the shop alone. Myron did not exactly flirt with her, but at least he looked at her the way a woman liked to be looked at. "How's my pretty flower today? Any table scraps for me?"

"Sorry, Myron. I couldn't live with myself if I contributed to you losing that manly figure. Already I see your chest starting to drop to your belly—"

He recoiled in mock horror. "Not so, not so." He dropped to the linoleum floor, pounded out 20 push-ups, sprung back to his feet. Always the show-off, always the flirt. He grinned. "See, still a rock."

"Yes, I know. A nice, round rock."

He smiled again, trying to control his heavy breathing. "I will put up with your insults only because I need your advice. I have come to you because I know you are a woman of the world—"

"Uh oh."

"No," he chuckled, "I am not here to ask advice about my love life. It is fine, thank you very much."

"Continue." She smiled, despite herself.

"You just saw what happened with Mrs. Melnick." He shook his head in bemusement. "Well, all week I have had a parade—no exaggeration, a parade!—of people coming in and placing bets on the Red Sox to win the World Series." He began marching around the shop, his arms swinging in exaggeration of a marching band.

She laughed, tossed a hand towel at him. "Stop that. You'll scare away the customers."

He returned to the counter. "Here's the thing: These are not my regular customers. Most have never placed a bet before; Mrs. Melnick wouldn't know a point spread from a bedspread. But they march in with their money, and it's always the same bet: Red Sox to win the World Series. I was paying ten-to-one, then eight-to-one, and now I'm at six-to-one." He held up ten fingers, then eight, then six as he spoke. "And still they come—college kids, professionals, little old ladies with walkers, all of them *meshugana*. I've never seen anything like it."

Madame Radminikov shrugged. "So they're crazy, what's the problem? Take their money. You don't really think the Red Sox will make you pay, do you? They won in 2004, they can't possibly win again. I mean, they're still the Red Sox—"

"That's just it," he declared, slapping his hands together. "Nobody seems to care about their pitching or their injuries or the Yankees. Shit, nobody even cares about *baseball*. All anyone cares about is some bible code or bible prophecy that predicted the Red Sox would win in 2004, and now is saying they're going to win again this year. So people are acting as if they're betting on a sure thing, like it's already been decided by some higher authority. Probably the devil, if you ask me." He sighed. "Do you know anything about this bible code stuff?"

"I've read a little about it." She leaned against the counter, shrinking herself a tad to look him in the eye, edging closer to breathe in his warmth, to smell his cologne and his sweat and his breath. Not intimacy, but better than carving up cold slabs of meat. She inhaled, then tried to gather her thoughts.

"Some scholars claim that, imbedded in the Hebrew text of the Old Testament ... sort of like words in a crossword puzzle ... there are historic facts grouped together which tell the story of history. In the last few years, with computers, scholars have been trying to decode these prophecies. For example, they claim that these codes predicted the assassination of Yitzhak Rabin."

Myron waved his hand in the air, as if swatting a fly. "Sounds like bunk to me."

Madame Radminikov shrugged. "Some mathematicians have done studies, and the odds of some of the things they have uncovered occurring randomly are very slim. Many people—including some rabbis—believe in these codes."

"And these codes can tell the future?"

"Supposedly, in a way. But you have to know what you're looking for. For example, Rabin's name was found in the Torah near the words 'assassin will assassinate.' Pretty interesting, after the fact. But if you looked for 'Rabin' near the word 'terrorist' or 'murdered,' you probably wouldn't have found anything."

Myron rubbed his chin, a dime-sized sapphire ring framed by his tanned skin. "So if you looked for the Hebrew words for 'red' and 'socks' and 'champion,' you might find one year that appears on the page together with all those words?"

She shrugged. "Maybe. But here's the thing: The year might be written in Roman numerals, or be written as 5-7-something-something, the year in the Jewish calendar. And it might say 'winner' instead of 'champion.' And, who knows, next to all these words, you might also find the word 'almost,' which would negate the whole prophecy. If you look hard enough, you could probably find almost anything."

"So I shouldn't worry?"

She arched an eyebrow at him. "I didn't say that, Myron. I mean, whether the Bible Code predicted it or not, the Red Sox did finally win the World Series. That should make us all worry."

*   *   *

Abraham stood on a cement road barrier under a small black umbrella, watched as a group of two dozen white supremacists marched past him down Congress Street in the spring drizzle. He had sent the limo away. And his bodyguard as well. Despite his wealth and his power, he was anonymous here. Just another old man in the city.

The marchers ambled, two-by-two, between parallel rows of hulking gray office towers, toward the black-clad crowd of religious leaders and politicians gathered in front of Faneuil Hall for the Saturday afternoon Holocaust Remembrance Day ceremonies. The ceremony was designed to remind the world of the atrocities of World War II. But the people who had forgotten the Holocaust did not concern Abraham. He was fixated instead on those who remembered it. Fondly.

The marchers wore the same light brown shirts favored by German storm-troopers, adorned with thin black ties and red, swastika arm-bands. Many also wore black knit ski hats. The front two marchers, one a young woman, held a banner in front of them with the words "National Socialist Movement" printed in black alongside a garbage can-sized black and red swastika. The group's website address ran across the bottom of the banner. Other marchers held neatly-drawn signs with messages such as "Holocaust a Myth" and "White People Unite." Those not holding signs simply shuffled along, chins up, unsmiling, their hands clasped behind their backs. They looked busi-nesslike and serious, though perhaps a bit bored.

A protective ring of helmeted police, many wielding plastic shields, escorted the neo-Nazis. A group of counter-protestors, a mix of most-ly elderly World War II survivors and young college students, jeered the marchers, pressing against the police lines in an effort to confront the supremacists. The marchers ignored them, eyes forward, feet moving in unison.

Abraham withdrew the black-and-white photo of his family. Even as the Nazis had begun their reign of terror, his parents believed that the good, peace-loving people of Germany would stop Hitler and his madness. Had he been a little older, perhaps he could have saved them. He caressed the photo gently before returning it to his pocket, then raised a camera, snapped a picture, and spoke into a small recording device. "Photograph number one. White supremacist rally in Boston. Add faces to database." Normally his underlings handled this type of mundane surveillance work. But the best generals regu-larly returned to the battlefield to look into the eyes of the enemy.

The march continued slowly, the crowd surging against the police lines like a storm-driven tide. A thin young man wearing a dark suit and skull cap rushed at the marchers, his fist shaking. A police baton stopped him in his tracks.

Abraham snapped another picture, spoke again into the recorder. "Photograph number two. Jewish protestor. Careless, but brave.

Possible recruit."

The marchers passed only a few feet from Abraham's position. A tall, slouching, young man caught Abraham's eye, scowled. Abraham aimed, snapped the shutter. "Photograph number three," Abraham hissed. "Gregory Neary." Neary was barely old enough to drink legally, but already hatred burned in his eyes enough to last a lifetime. Worse, he was also highly intelligent—over 1400 on his SATs, according the high school records Abraham obtained. And he seemed to have recruited quite a few other young men and women for today's march. Abraham sighed. Hatred, charisma, intelligence. A potentially lethal combination. A potentially lethal adversary.

But perhaps a bit too arrogant—he was mistaken if he believed it safe to come out of hiding. Abraham pulled out a cell phone, dialed. "I have located Gregory Neary. Have him followed. Priority is high." He glared at the young man. If someone had put a bullet into Hitler's head while he was spewing his venom in the beer halls of Munich as a young man, well, it is likely that the world would now be a vastly different place.

Abraham hopped off the barrier, pushed his way forward. The procession stopped. A television reporter interviewed the group leader, a thirty-something man with a neat haircut, straight teeth and a tailored blue suit. Wool, no doubt. Sheep's clothing.

He spoke slowly in a low, firm voice. Neary stood by his side, apparently the second in command. Even Abraham's non-native ear noticed the Southern drawl. But the man was polished, articulate. Abraham snapped his picture. "Our government already knows who sent those anthrax letters through the mail." He pronounced it 'anth-a-rax.' "It was some Jew scientist by the name of Zack. That's right. We know who did it. So why don't we arrest him? Because our government *protects* the Jews." As if it was spelled 'Joooos.' "Our government is *afraid* of the Jews."

Abraham had read the rumors of a Jewish scientist sending the anthrax letters; many websites were reporting it as fact. The accusation was false, of course, spread by Arab hate groups and neo-Nazis. Both of these groups claimed the anthrax attack was a Zionist ploy to trick the U.S. into attacking Arab countries suspected of having ties to terrorism.

The supremacist with the southern drawl turned, put his arm around Neary's shoulder. "Now, I know you all don't like to hear people with my kind of accent"—ac-a-cent—"telling you what to think. So maybe my young friend here can give it to you in a language you can understand."

The reporter put the microphone in front of Neary. He spoke forcefully, passionately, not nervous in the spotlight. "We just want to know: How much American blood is going to be spilled to help the Jews? We've told you about the anthrax. Well, we also know that the cause of September 11th was our support of Israel. That's right—the Arabs attacked us because this country supports the Jews." He jabbed a finger at the camera. "Now, thousands of Americans—young men and women, just like me—are dying in Iraq. I, for one, am not willing to die just to save the Jews."

The older man smiled, nodded, leaned into the microphone. "The Arabs"—Ay-rabs—"are animals. But like all animals they reckon to leave you alone if you just stay out of their business. So, fellow Americans, ask yourselves this: Are you willing to let your sons and daughters continue to die, just to benefit the Jews?"

Abraham shook his head. This was a dangerous message, this blaming of September 11 and terrorism on Israel and the Jews. Dangerous, but effective: *If you don't want to die at the hands of fanatical, towel-headed marauders, stop supporting the Jews.*

It was a message that must not be allowed to spread. There were two ways to accomplish this. The first was to silence the messengers, men like Neary and his Southern mentor. The second, and more difficult, task was to ensure that terrorists like Gabriella Garcia-Ring did not succeed.

*   *   *

The rain had stopped, but the early summer humidity still hung in the evening air. Shelby wore a simple khaki skirt and a white blouse, accented by a strand of pearls she inherited from her mother. A couple of college guys approached as she stood on the corner trying to flag a taxi, the blouse sticking to her back as she raised her arm.

"Hey, we'll give you a ride. We're parked right over there." They pointed up Commonwealth Avenue, toward Kenmore Square.

Shelby smiled. They were drunk, or at least well on their way, probably celebrating the end of finals. "Sorry, guys, got a date with a rich uncle." A taxi pulled up. She started to climb in, then turned back. The boys were staring, trying to peer up her skirt. She rolled her eyes, offered a wry smile. "Easy, boys. I'm old enough to be your … big sister." She paused while they laughed, waiting for them to look her in the eye. Theirs were bloodshot, but alert. "Guys, seriously, don't drive tonight. Take a cab, walk, whatever. It's not worth it, okay?" The boys shrugged, nodded, walked away unsteadily. Away from their car. Maybe tonight at least some family would not get torn apart, as hers had been, by a drunk driver....

The taxi inched its way along Boylston Street, the streets filled with vibrant, energized people not going to dinner with their bizarre uncle. Fifteen minutes later they arrived at the restaurant. It reminded her of the places the law firms used to bring her for job interviews—heavy, dark, wooden, leathery. But maybe not so … patriarchal. The haze of cigar smoke was absent, for one thing, and a number of women, some even without chaperones, occupied seats both in the restaurant and at the bar. In many ways Boston in the past decade had turned into some kind of monster that its Brahmin creators could no longer control—a smoking ban, a female governor, gay marriage. Somebody had made some kind of deal with the devil, and Old Boston had been dealt out. Maybe someday they would even take down the statue next to the State House of General Hooker, infamous for inviting women to pay nighttime visits to his troops.

A maitre d' intercepted her before she could reach the crowded hostess station, guided her to a large round table in the corner.

She recognized her uncle, his back straight against his chair, his gray eyes darting and alert. His face was long and thin and Semitic, a beardless, business-suited version of his biblical namesake. He stood as she approached, his hands behind his back. His eyes may have softened a bit as they found her face, or maybe it was just the light reflecting off his gray irises. He proffered the same kind of half bow that the little delivery man had exhibited earlier. Shelby pictured them practicing their bows together in the mirror, like two little girls working on their ballet twirls....

A sweep of his arm directed her attention toward their table; she was surprised to see a group of other diners. The note was so mysterious, and her uncle so secretive, that she assumed they would be eating alone. She did get the secretive part right—though the restaurant was full, the maitre d' kept the three nearby tables empty.

His words silenced his dinner companions as he motioned toward her. "This is Shelby Baskin, the daughter of my sister."

She smiled at the men, the professional smile she used when meeting clients or other attorneys or public officials. Just an upturn of the lips, then a nod as her uncle made the introductions.

"This is Mr. Clevinsky, whom you have already met." He gestured toward the small, mottled-faced man with the kind eyes who had delivered the letter to her apartment. He smiled up at her, his lips pursed together in a deep 'U' that further wrinkled his face. "Mr. Clevinsky is unable to speak."

Shelby waited for some further elaboration, but her uncle instead continued in his matter-of-fact tone. "Next is Dr. Walters." A thin man wearing a white button-down shirt and a yarmulke on his head turned shyly in his seat, his hand on his chin, heavy glasses slipping down his nose. "Young Dr. Walters is performing his residency in anesthesiology at Beth Israel Hospital." Young was right. He looked about 12, a row of pimples lining his forehead where his bangs hit. Nice Jewish doctor or not, even her mother would have thought him too drab to be husband material.

"Adjacent to Dr. Walters is Reb Meyer." 'Reb' denoted a term of respect, roughly equivalent to 'Sir.' "Reb Meyer is the descendant of a great family of rabbis and scholars from Warsaw." A jowled, pink face glanced sideways at her, then refocused a pair of tiny eyes on a buttered roll clasped beneath four fat fingers and a bulbous thumb. He licked some butter off his pinky, then stuffed the roll in his mouth and washed it down with a gulp of red wine. Hostility bubbled over in the middle-aged man. Whether directed at her, or more generally at the world around him, she did not know....

Her uncle continued in his formal tone, his sentence structure and syntax that of a man who had learned English later in life. "Finally, here is Madame Radminikov." A middle-aged woman stood and nodded at her. Dark suit, short hair, broad shoulders—at first glance, the figure of a man. But upon closer inspection, Shelby saw a softness in the woman's eyes and the absence of any facial hair on her cheeks and chin. "Madame Radminikov owns a butcher shop just a few miles from here, in Brookline." That explained the short hair and broad shoulders. The woman extended her hand to Shelby, a meaty, calloused paw that grasped hers gently.

The gathering reminded Shelby of the Island of Misfit Toys. What could possibly have brought this group together? A tiny old man unable to speak. A shy, pasty anesthesiologist. A fat, hostile, middle-aged scholar with poor table manners. An androgynous butcher. And her stiff, old uncle with the wolf-like eyes.

She sat at the round table's one empty seat, her uncle on her right and Madame Radminikov on her left. A waiter appeared and filled her wine glass. She took a small sip, settled into her chair and prepared for the inevitable round of small talk.

Her uncle spoke. "You are an attorney."

Was this a question? Shelby set down the wine glass. "Yes," she stammered.

"We would like to hire you, retain your services."

So much for the small talk. "All right...." She looked around the table. "When you say 'we,' what do you mean? And hire me for what?"

Madame Radminikov responded. "We are a Jewish ... fraternal organization, sort of like the Knights of Columbus. We can tell you more about our specific activities later, but essentially we are dedicated to preventing the spread of anti-Semitism." She swept her beefy arm around the table. "We are all descendants—either directly or through our parents—of the Holocaust. It is a horror that must never be allowed to happen again." She paused for a few seconds and lowered her head, then turned and smiled sadly at Shelby. "You are familiar with the practice of placing canaries in the coal mines, yes? The birds are extra-sensitive to dangerous gases; their distress would alert the miners to unsafe conditions. Well, we are like the canaries, and anti-Semitism is like a poisonous gas. We are extra-sensitive to it."

Reb Meyer chortled from across the table, waved a hand dismissively at the butcher. "That is a stupid analogy. If Jews were so sensitive to poisonous gas, we never would have entered Hitler's gas chambers."

Madame Radminikov raised her chin, lowered her voice. "The canary is a metaphor, Reb Meyer. Nothing more, nothing less."

"And all I'm saying is that it's a poor one—"

"Enough," Abraham barked. The table fell silent. Even Mr. Clevinsky's smile faded. "Continue, Madame."

The butcher took a deep breath. "In any event, we have many activities in the Boston area. And, as your uncle said, we often find ourselves in need of legal representation."

"I still don't understand. What kind of legal representation?"

Again, Madame Radminikov responded. Clearly her uncle was the group's leader, but he preferred to allow the butcher to speak for him. "Well, for example, we have some real estate interests, and may need legal counsel related to purchases and sales and leases. And we often make financial donations to various entities, which we sometimes choose to make anonymously through our attorney. Sometimes we are involved in demonstrations and there are freedom of speech issues involved. And sometimes even small criminal matters arise."

This made no sense. Surely her uncle had a team of lawyers at his disposal….

Abraham seemed to read her thoughts, offered a quick response before she could voice the question. "I prefer not to use our company's attorneys for these matters."

Shelby nodded. It made sense to keep business matters separate. "I specialize in First Amendment law, so I guess I could help out on the free speech stuff. But I don't do real estate law or criminal work—"

Abraham cut her off. "You work at a large firm, correct?"

"Medium-sized. About 75 lawyers."

"Fine, then. I am sure you have associates who can assist you when necessary."

She nodded again. He seemed intent on retaining her. Which may not be such a bad thing. The senior partners expected her to generate a certain amount of new business every year. Doing so gave her the leverage she needed when she wanted to take on an interesting first amendment case pro bono. Still, something about this group just seemed … off. "You mentioned criminal cases. What kind of stuff are you talking about?"

"Dr. Walter, please describe your recent incident," her uncle directed.

The young doctor fidgeted in his seat, twisted the napkin in his hand. "I have a young child, a girl, in first grade in the town of Arlington. This past December, the teacher required the children to sing *Silent Night*. I made a bit of a stink in the principal's office, and the police came and arrested me."

Reb Meyer chortled again. "Stupid country. They arrest the victim. Next time they will arrest the good doctor's daughter for singing off-key."

"In any event," Madame Radminikov interjected, "we need an attorney in cases like this."

Shelby nodded. "All right." Her uncle was reaching out to her, the first real contact since her parents' and brother's funeral two decades ago. Hardly a Hallmark moment, but better than nothing. She was feeling especially … orphaned … lately. She and Bruce were planning a wedding, and she had come to the sad realization that, other than a few cousins, she would have no family in attendance. Abraham was odd, and he was distant, but he was still family. And her mother asked, in a letter from the grave, that she help him….

"Good, then, it is done." Abraham removed an envelope from his pocket, handed it to Shelby. "It is a retainer. A check for $10,000, payable to your firm."

The waiter arrived, and Madame Radminikov ordered a set of appetizers for the table. Unlike her uncle, the butcher seemed to have command of informal, colloquial English. Abraham watched Shelby tuck the envelope into her pocketbook before continuing. "You should also know that many of our group members are *sayanim*." Shelby had read about these people: A sayan was a civilian helper who assisted Mossad agents when they needed things like safe houses or travel documents or medical care. "As a result, we sometimes get involved with counter-terrorism."

Shelby angled her head. "How involved?"

Abraham related how, a few months earlier, Dr. Walters administered a general anesthesia to a woman having shoulder surgery to repair a tennis injury. As she lost consciousness, she mumbled the words 'LNG tanker' and 'rocket launcher.' "Perhaps this was nonsensical babbling," Abraham said. "Or perhaps she has knowledge of a terrorist attack."

Shelby eyed her uncle. Something in his face, perhaps the way his pupils narrowed and his nostrils flared, told her he was convinced it was the latter.

"As Jews," he continued, "we need to be especially vigilant when it comes to terrorism. When al-Qaeda strikes again, and it will, they will be sure to target an area with a large Jewish population."

Shelby nodded. It never made sense that, in the immediate aftermath of the Oklahoma City bombing, people suspected Arab terrorists. Why target Christian Americans when you can just as easily target Jewish Americans?

A cell phone chimed. Reb Meyer bent his arm around his girth, reached inside his blazer pocket, grunted a greeting. He listened for a few seconds before grunting again, then addressed Abraham. "Change of plans. Our target's departure has been advanced by two hours. We go now, or else we abort."

Uncle Abraham glanced at Madame Radminikov, then at Mr. Clevinsky. They both nodded. "Very well." He turned to Shelby. "I would like to explain our activities to you in more detail. We will talk in the van—"

"Wait, Abraham," Madame Radminikov interrupted. "We discussed this. You cannot come. What if we are detained? Or if the mission fails? It is too dangerous."

Abraham cut her off with a chopping motion of his hand. "My decision is final, Madame."

"Well," Reb Meyer growled, "either way, we cannot bring the girl."

Abraham stood, looked down at Reb Meyer. "She comes. She needs to see for herself."

The fat man flushed, hoisted himself from his chair. "You are asking for trouble. She might overreact—"

"Excuse me, but can *the girl* ask where we're going?"

The men ignored her, began walking toward the exit, continued their debate. Madame Radminikov grabbed a few rolls from the basket and stuffed them into her jacket pocket, then locked her eyes onto Shelby's and answered her question. "To collect an eye, and perhaps also a tooth."

*   *   *

Shelby had no interest in collecting eyes or teeth, but, after a few seconds hesitation, she climbed into the van alongside Madame Radminikov. She did so partly because of her mother's letter, partly because it did not seem all that dangerous, and partly because she had just read one of those pithy quotes about it being better to be boldly decisive and risk being wrong than to agonize at length and be right too late. And also because she was just plain curious. These were people who should be playing bridge at a senior center someplace. Instead they were leaving dinner uneaten to go on some secretive, urgent mission....

The van looked more like a delivery truck than a van, with a hospital bed bolted to the floor in the back and a couple of rows of seats in the front and middle. Nobody offered an explanation for the hospital bed. In fact, nobody said much of anything.

Mr. Clevinsky drove, his little head barely able to peer over the dashboard. But he adeptly maneuvered the vehicle through the labyrinth of Boston's streets, and he seemed to know exactly where they were going. Unlike Shelby.

Reb Meyer rode in the front with Mr. Clevinsky. Shelby sat in the back seat, behind Reb Meyer. She half expected someone to hand her a lollipop to keep her quiet....

Madame Radminikov was squished up next to her, with her uncle on the far side behind the driver. The scent of freshly-applied perfume wafted from the butcher; maybe she was not so androgynous after all. The young doctor sat on a bench in the back. Mr. Clevinsky accelerated up an onramp, headed north on the expressway.

After a few minutes of riding in silence, during which her mother's voice reminded her to mind her manners, she glanced at her watch and cleared her throat. "Uncle Abraham. At dinner you said we'd talk in the car." Reb Meyer half-turned, snorted derisively.

Her uncle responded by handing her a newspaper article and a small flashlight. She sighed—he could not have given her the article a few minutes ago?

She quickly scanned the short article, cut from a suburban newspaper. Someone had assaulted an elderly woman at a Jewish cemetery in Peabody, a suburb north of Boston. The police were working with the community to try to catch the culprits. That was it.

"Okay. I've read it. I dealt with similar cases when I worked as an Assistant District Attorney. Usually it was just local kids, drunk and bored." Often responding to the subtle signals sent by society—the penny left on the Jewish kid's desk at school, the princess moniker assigned to the Jewish girl down the street, the Christ-killer comments whispered outside churches during Easter. Anti-Semitism, like racism and homophobia, were weak spots in the fabric of American society. When that fabric tore—whether from boredom or drunkenness or resentment or fear—it usually did so along these thread-bare fault lines.

Madame Radminikov turned toward her, speaking for her uncle, the red wine from dinner mixing on her breath with the dour words. "The problem is, these kids, these little monsters, can grow up to become big monsters." The butcher pointed her chin at the newspaper article. "Anyway, we know who did it. There's a small group of skinheads active on the North Shore. They've been getting more brazen, growing into bigger monsters." Madame Radminikov took a deep breath. "The article doesn't give all the details of the assault. The woman was 82, visiting her husband's grave. It was his birthday, and she was bringing him some kugel she baked. They attacked her just before dusk, when the cemetery was empty. Broke her ribs, smashed her nose. Then one of them defecated on her."

Shelby shuddered. Who could do such a thing? How could the fabric of society be put under such pressure that it ripped apart so violently? But nobody would have believed the Abu Ghraib prison abuses or the black man in Texas dragged to his death behind a pick-up truck, either, and those crimes were even more grotesque....

Shelby could not think of an appropriate way to respond. She lowered her eyes, waited for Madame Radminikov to continue. "This wasn't just some drunk kids out for a good time who happened to stumble upon an old woman in a cemetery. They were waiting, looking for someone to attack, someone to spew their hatred upon. In fact, we believe this was a calculated attack, meant to spur copycat incidents."

Shelby sighed. "Have the police done anything?" she asked.

Madame Radminikov began to respond, but Abraham silenced her with a bony hand on her knee. He took a deep breath, turned to Shelby and locked his gray eyes onto hers. For the first time tonight he looked directly at her. She searched for some of her mother in him, but found no resemblance. In fact, she found little that was human at all—his face was like one of those wax figures at a museum, the features both lifelike and lifeless at the same time.

"Listen to me carefully. There are three ways to respond to evil of this kind. The first choice is that we do nothing—we ignore the problem, or we wait for others, such as the police, to act on our behalf. For us," he gestured to the others in the van, "this is not an option. All of us, we lost family members in the Holocaust. Many of us lived through it ourselves. We saw our people being herded like sheep to the slaughter. And did we fight back?" He slapped his thigh with an open hand. "No. We did nothing." Abraham swept his arm in a gesture that, again, included everyone in the van. "We reject inaction. We choose to fight back."

He turned to her, lowered his voice. "Did your mother ever tell you how your grandmother died?"

She shook her head. "No, just that she died during the war. Her letter actually said I should ask you for the details if I was curious—"

"Your curiosity is irrelevant. You should know the story. This was 1937, before the war began. But already Hitler had enacted the Nuremberg laws and began attacking the Jews. My mother was walking to the market one day, and a group of four or five *Hitlerjugend*, the Hitler Youth group, surrounded her and began taunting her. She was in the Jewish section of town, and there were plenty of Jewish shopkeepers around, but none of them did anything to help her. One of the boys reached out and squeezed her breast, so she slapped the boy across the face."

Abraham withdrew a laminated photo from his pocket, held it cupped in his hand the way Shelby, as a child, once watched her mother cradle a baby bird dislodged from its nest. "The next day, I walked with my mother back to the market. Your mother was with us as well. I was only six years old, and your mother just a baby in a stroller. The *Hitlerjugend* were there again, all wearing their uniforms. The boy she had slapped spotted us—he was perhaps 15 years old, a bit younger than the other boys. The others snickered and elbowed him, pointed at my mother. 'There she is, Heinrich. Watch out she doesn't hit you again.' His face turned red, and he walked over to us, spat at my mother. I could smell the beer on him. She went to slap him again, but he was ready this time and blocked her hand. With his other hand he punched her in the stomach, and she fell to the ground. Then he began kicking her, with his big black boots. 'No Jew is going to hit me,' he yelled down at her. Again, the shopkeepers were watching, and other shoppers also, Jews, but they all just looked away. He kept kicking her, her face, her head, her torso. I ran over and grabbed his leg, but he just kicked me aside. Then the other boys started stomping on her. I heard her moan, saw the blood start to pour out of her ear, saw her eyes close. I was still trying to help her, but one of the shopkeepers held me back. 'You must go,' he said. 'Run home with your sister and get your father. Run, before they come after you also.' So I ran home, pushing the stroller, faster than I ever ran before, and found my father. When we came back my mother's body was wrapped in an old blanket. One of the shopkeepers was washing the blood off the street."

Abraham's gray eyes were now fiery in the darkness of the car, his enlarged pupils somehow reflecting and magnifying the random headlights of passing cars. His voice dropped to a hiss-like whisper; the words came out slowly between clenched yellow teeth. "Those men—Jewish men—did nothing to help my mother. Doing nothing now is not an option. Not. An. Option."

Shelby crossed her legs, edged away from her mother's brother. Or, more accurately, from the story he recounted. Of all the details, she could not shake the vision of the young boy clutching the leg of a black-booted thug, trying to protect his mother. How powerless he must have felt. And how much rage he must still feel now....

Abraham took a deep breath and continued, seemingly under control again. "The second possible response, if we reject doing nothing," he stuck up two fingers, as if in a peace sign, "is that we can try to educate people against anti-Semitism. This sometimes works—it is the rare person who willingly allows hatred to live in his heart. There are people who do this work, who visit schools and hold interfaith prayer services and invite their neighbors to Passover seder. To them, I say thank you. Many times they are successful. Their work is important. But it is not our work."

Abraham added a third finger to the peace sign. "For people who do allow hatred to live in their hearts, for these people who cannot be taught and must not be ignored, there is a third response. This is our work."

They exited the highway, stopped in front of a Tudor-style brick house on a quiet, leafy street in Medford. A towering bearded man, closer to seven feet tall than to six, wearing a long black coat and rimmed hat, climbed in and plopped onto the bench next to the doctor. His beard and attire, along with his uncut sideburns, called *payos*, were customary for a Hasidic Jew, an observant sect of Judaism that lived according to centuries-old Jewish laws and customs. The stale odor of dried sweat wafted off his heavy clothes.

"Barnabus, this is my sister's daughter, Shelby Baskin. She is an attorney. She will be joining us tonight." Shelby turned to study the giant. She read once that custom forbade Hasidic men from looking directly at a woman, but Barnabus' cold black eyes leered at her. *Rasputin,* she almost gasped, a long-forgotten monster from an Anastasia-loving teenager's nightmare, returning to haunt her. He held her gaze, then seemed to remember she was Abraham's niece. He offered her a wet, yellow-toothed grin from behind a graying black beard and turned quickly away.

She, too, turned away, stared out the window for a few minutes, tried to find something familiar. These people should be stealing sugar packets from an early bird special someplace. Instead they were like the old Japanese soldiers lost in the jungles of the Philippines, still fighting a 60-year-old war. She reflected on her uncle's words, turned back toward him. "So, that's what tonight is? A demonstration of this third response you were talking about?"

Madame Radminikov began to answer, but Abraham silenced her again, this time with a quick chopping motion of his hand. "Later," he ordered. Apparently they were approaching their destination, and this conversation was over. Abraham leaned forward to better hear what Reb Meyer was saying to Mr. Clevinsky.

The Reb spoke in a thick European accent, but with the clipped staccato of a man used to giving orders. "There is the Burger King. Turn in and proceed to the back of the parking lot. Avoid the security camera near the drive-through window."

Madame Radminikov leaned toward her and whispered, "We can talk more later. Reb Meyer is in charge—he used to be a Mossad agent, one of the best. He was involved in the Entebbe raid to free the hostages."

Entebbe? That was a military operation. Were they planning a raid on the Burger King?

Madame Radminikov continued, smiled at Shelby. "Of course, he was in better shape back then...."

Shelby peered out. A small group of college-aged kids laughed and rough-housed at a couple of tables near the window. Reb Meyer grabbed a pair of binoculars, wrapped a fat hand around them. "That is him, at the table in the corner. Gregory Neary." He turned his gaze to the parking lot, settled on an older red sports car. "And that is his automobile." He handed the binoculars and a photograph to Mr. Clevinsky. "Do you confirm?"

Mr. Clevinsky studied the men at the table. His smile faded, and he nodded slowly.

Madame Radminikov stood, began to climb over Shelby toward the van's sliding door. "Not that I don't trust you boys, but I'm going in. We need to be sure."

Reb Meyer sighed, then nodded. "Agreed. But go quickly. His friend's shift ends at 10:00, and it is now already 9:13."

Madame Radminikov returned in less than five minutes. She dropped a bag of food on the front seat next to Reb Meyer. "I agree, that is Neary. As you said, his friend's shift ends at 10:00. I heard them talking—their plan is for the friend to go home and shower, then meet up with Neary at a party later."

From the back, Barnabus guffawed, then switched to a sing-song voice. "Neary thinks he's so smarty, but he's not going to any party…."

Reb Meyer, peering through his binoculars, ignored the giant. "Neary is now leaving the restaurant. Clevinsky, prepare to follow. Everyone else, be ready."

Shelby stood. "You know what, maybe I should just get out now—"

Madame Radminikov gently pushed her back to her seat. "Stay, dear. This is important."

Shelby studied the butcher's face. Hard and strong, but kind. Resolve, but not hatred or anger. Again, Shelby's curiosity overcame her trepidation. "Only if you tell me what's going on."

"Fair enough. You probably figured out that Neary is the guy who assaulted the old woman in the cemetery. He's been laying low for the past few weeks. Abraham spotted him today at a white supremacist parade, an event organized by a Nazi group based in Minnesota. Apparently Neary is looking to ally himself with the national neo-Nazi movement, to become more organized and establish himself as the regional leader of their hate group."

Abraham continued. "We cannot allow this. We need to stop him before he becomes more powerful." He was describing Neary, but Shelby guessed Abraham was thinking about Hitler. "Our men followed him here. We are going to teach him a lesson."

A lesson? Was that the eye and the tooth reference? She looked around the van, at her uncle, at Mr. Clevinsky, at Madame Radminikov, at Reb Meyer. Elderly, infirm, weak. Yet strangely confident, strangely vibrant. She recalled a book she read a few years ago. A young Jewish woman, posing as a journalist, traveled to Israel to try to avenge an assassination attempt on her father years earlier. Shelby, still raw from the loss of her parents to the drunk driver, identified with the woman's rage and felt disdain for the apathetic brother who urged her to let the matter go. But now, riding in the van with an angry, ugly posse, she thought perhaps the brother had the wiser approach....

A lanky young man with baggy pants and a baseball cap sauntered toward his car. He walked with the kind of slouching, shuffling stride that suburban boys adopted to make them look like tough city kids. He tossed a plastic soda cup into a bush, climbed into his car. Immediately the sound of heavy metal music filled the parking lot, quickly joined by squealing tires as Neary screeched out.

"Stay with him, Clevinsky," Reb Meyer barked. Mr. Clevinsky had positioned the van near the exit and now quickly tucked in behind the Firebird.

Reb Meyer slipped on a fishing hat and some tinted eye-glasses as he continued to give orders. "Continue with him. At the second light, he will turn left. We will engage him in front of the office park."

Mr. Clevinsky followed for another minute or two, then abruptly accelerated and pulled alongside the Firebird. Madame Radminikov squeezed Shelby's knee, leaned toward her. "Hold on." The van shook; Shelby leaned to her left, peered at the speedometer. Seventy-five. On a winding suburban road. Mr. Clevinsky's smile was, if anything, more pronounced....

Reb Meyer rolled down his window, yelled to the startled young driver. "Pull over. You have a flat tire." Reb Meyer gestured first to the tire, then to the side of the road, then to the tire again. He cupped his hands around his mouth. "Flat tire! Pull over!"

Madame Radminikov provided commentary. "Look, Neary sees a fat, middle-aged guy in a van. He knows we might be after him, but he expects we'll come after him with soldiers—you know, young guys in black clothes, driving some muscle car. But he won't feel threatened by Reb Meyer. So of course he'll pull over."

Mr. Clevinsky timed it perfectly; a small office park appeared just ahead. The Firebird pulled in to the parking lot and stopped. The van followed, braked alongside the Firebird's passenger door. Reb Meyer stepped out, waddled toward Neary crouched next to the rear tire on the driver's side. He looked up angrily at the fat man in the fishing hat.

"Look, dude, my tire's fine. What're you talking about?"

Reb Meyer smiled, waved a flashlight. "Not that tire, young man. The one on the other side."

Neary shuffled around the car, kneeled down and inspected the tire. As he did so, Barnabus slipped soundlessly out of the van. The giant took two quick strides, grabbed Neary from behind in a choke hold and yanked his head back. "What the fu—"

Reb Meyer shoved the flashlight into Neary's side. "Shut up." Neary screamed out in pain, convulsed. Shelby knew from her experience in the District Attorney's office that stun guns could be disguised as everyday objects, but it surprised her to see Reb Meyer's action jolt the young man into the air much like a defibrillator bounced a heart attack victim off the ground.

Neary spat at Reb Meyer. "I'll kill you, asshole…." He struggled against the giant's grip, thrashing about, then tried to free himself by biting Barnabus' wrist.

Reb Meyer gave him a second shock, this time holding the stun gun against Neary's side for an extra few seconds. Another spasm, then Neary slumped back against the giant, dangling by his neck like a vagrant asleep in the stockade. His blue eyes were wide with fear, even as his body trembled and drooped.

Reb Meyer slipped a blindfold over Neary's eyes, then Barnabus dragged him to the back of the van and tossed him onto the hospital bed. Madame Radminikov joined the young doctor in the back of the van, and together they strapped Neary down while the giant stood watch. Meanwhile, Reb Meyer drove the Firebird around to the loading docks behind the buildings.

Through it all, Abraham sat impassively, his gray eyes darting from scene to scene, his right hand rubbing the concentration camp tattoo on his left forearm….

They picked up Reb Meyer, who hopped into the van with surprising agility. "Drive. Avoid the busy streets. And obey the traffic laws."

Abraham left his seat and stood, hunched over in the back of the van, watching the doctor and Madame Radminikov. The doctor spoke for the first time. "I'm going to administer a sedative."

Abraham nodded. "Yes, fine. But only so much so he doesn't move about. I want him conscious. I want him to know what is occurring. And why."

He turned to Shelby. "Come, I want to show you something in the back."

She remained in her seat. "You know what, I've seen enough. You people are over the edge. I'd like to get out."

Abraham set his gray eyes on her. "Unfortunately, the world does not always give us what we want."

"What the hell does that mean? Are you saying I can't leave?"

Madame Radminikov touched her arm, a light touch with calloused fingers. "What we're saying is that now is not a good time to leave. It is important that you understand—that you see—exactly what it is that we do. Afterwards, you can choose to leave or to stay, as you wish."

Shelby shook her head. Somehow dinner with her uncle had spiraled into a witch hunt with a bunch of vigilantes. She had no interest in witnessing the events in the back of the van. But these people were not going to spare Neary just because she did not have the stomach to watch. She shook Madame Radminikov's hand off her arm and marched to the back of the van, followed closely by Abraham.

Leaning against a wall, Shelby gritted her teeth. "What are you going to do to him?"

Abraham responded by nodding at Madame Radminikov. Wearing surgical gloves, the butcher unbuttoned Neary's cargo pants. Despite the sedative, he began to squirm and writhe, his muscular body pulling at the restraints. Unable to free himself, he spat at Madame Radminikov, splattering her face. She calmly took a towel from under the table and wiped herself clean, then addressed her patient. "Spit on me again, and I'll cover your mouth with duct tape."

He tried to muster saliva for another salvo, but, like a child with a mouthful of beach sand, this second discharge was dry. Madame Radminikov shrugged sadly, pressed gray adhesive strips over his lips. She put her finger under his nose to make sure she could feel his breath, then returned to his pants. She slid them down to his knees. Then she cut off his briefs. They were wet and yellowed with urine. She dropped them into a plastic garbage bag.

The doctor spoke. "I am ready, sir."

Abraham raised an open palm to the young doctor. "One minute, if you please." He addressed Shelby in a matter-of-fact tone, as if it had not occurred to him that his audience found him repulsive. "Members of our group visited Mr. Neary twice before. The first time we warned him, explained to him that there would be repercussions—severe repercussions—the next time he and his friends behaved like animals. The second time, after he ignored our warning, we left him with a reminder of our visit."

He nodded to Madame Radminikov, who grabbed Neary's penis in her gloved hand and stretched it away from the curly blond hairs that surrounded it. Neary tried to turn away from her, but she shoved his pelvis back to the table. With her free hand, she shined a flashlight on the shaft of his member. Shelby gasped—midway up the shaft, a dime-sized Jewish star had been branded onto his skin.

Madame Radminikov seemed to read Shelby's thoughts. "Yes, the branding was quite painful."

Barnabus guffawed again, again adopted a melodic tone: "Mr. Tough Guy cried like a baby, now he's going to be a lady...."

Madame Radminikov shot the giant a look, then dropped Neary's penis back onto his pelvis. It shrunk to the size of an airless balloon. She spoke. "The star is a reminder that we will punish those that attack us. So not only does he see the brand every time he urinates, but the scab pulls apart every time he gets an erection. A rather painful reminder, I'd imagine." Unlike the giant, there was sadness in her words. Like a mother resigned to having to punish a naughty child.

Shelby pulled her cell phone out of her pocket. "This is sick." She dialed 9-1-1, pressed the send button.

Abraham's hand shot out like a viper, snatched the phone away, terminated the call. "You may wonder how we can be certain Neary is the same man who attacked the woman in the cemetery." It was as if her attempt to phone the police never occurred.

"The answer is DNA. We took a sample from him when we did the branding. It matches the feces on the woman's chest."

Abraham continued. "Remember, this is his third offense. The first time, we warned him. The second time, we branded him. This time we will take a more drastic measure." He turned back toward their hostage. "Doctor, you may proceed."

"This is barbaric," Shelby hissed. "Since when do we torture and mutilate our enemies?"

"The girl is right," said Reb Meyer. "We should just kill him, be done with it."

"No, that will only make him a martyr," Abraham responded. "This will be a more effective deterrent." He turned to Shelby. "Yes, it is barbaric. Purposely so. We could teach our lesson, exact our revenge, in a less ... brutal ... fashion, but we find that symbolic measures such as these, brutal as they are, have a way deterring others who might be inclined to follow Mr. Neary's lead."

The pasty-faced doctor reached up and turned on a bright light. Barnabus yanked a curtain closed, separating the windowless rear of the van from the passenger area. They were now cocooned in the rear of the vehicle—Shelby, her uncle, the doctor, Madame Radminikov and the giant. And, of course, Neary. Only the single overhead light erased the darkness of the night.

Neary began to thrash on the table, arching his back and biting blindly at the shadows moving in front of his blindfolded eyes. The doctor motioned to Barnabus, who jolted the patient again with the stun gun. Neary's body went limp, and the doctor, his hand steady, quickly inserted a large needle in the pelvis area near the shaft of the penis. Neary cried out, the sound muffled by the duct tape, but quieted to a whimper as the anesthesia entered his bloodstream. He breathed in short, rapid intakes through his nose, clearly laboring for breath; the doctor motioned to Madame Radminikov, who removed the duct tape from his mouth.

The doctor checked his pulse and blood pressure, waited a few seconds, then reinserted the needle directly into the bottom of Neary's scrotum. Neary howled, a high-pitched wail that came more from his gut than from his mouth. Shelby had only heard such a cry of pain once before—as a hospital volunteer one summer in high school, she had watched a small-boned woman almost die while delivering a 10-pound baby. Like the woman, Neary begged for relief. "Stop, please stop. I'll do anything. Please, please…."

The smell of feces filled the van, and Madame Radminikov quickly wiped the table clean with a wet towel, then sprayed a disinfectant. She slid a thick green cloth that looked like a diaper under Neary's body, turned to Shelby. "I know this seems extreme to you—"

"Actually, the word 'barbaric' doesn't do it justice. By doing this, you're no better than he is—"

"Fine, I agree then, this is barbaric. This boy is someone's son, someone's brother. A human being. But we did not choose him; he chose us. He chose to attack our people. What choice do we have?"

She clenched her fists. "Your choice is to let him go, report him to the authorities. Your choice is to act like members of a civilized society."

Madame Radminikov sighed but did not respond. Moisture again formed in the large woman's eyes as she turned back to her patient/victim and wiped the sweat from Neary's face. She spoke in a soft, soothing voice. For whose benefit, Shelby was not sure. "The injection will actually lessen the pain. And the doctor is well-trained—he used to work on a kibbutz, neutering the farm animals. He will make sure that the wound heals and there is no infection." As she spoke, she taped the shaft of Neary's penis to his pelvis area with some medical tape, then spread a red liquid over the entire area.

Ten minutes after the injections, the doctor pulled out a surgical knife. He looked at Abraham, who nodded and barked a command at Mr. Clevinsky. "Stop the van. The doctor is ready."

The van slowed, then stopped. The doctor took a deep breath, and with a quick, sure, vertical cut, sliced open Neary's scrotum. Blood poured out, soaking the cloth. Shelby turned away.

Her uncle's dead gray eyes were watching her. Probably had been for the last few minutes. He spoke in the same matter-of-fact tone, continuing his discussion of the three ways to deal with anti-Semitism as if he had not been interrupted by the kidnapping and mutilation of the screaming man strapped to the table next to her. "As

I was saying earlier, if the police cannot or will not help, and if these
… animals … will not listen to reason, the third option is that we
fight back."

"Speaking of animals…" she muttered.

Her uncle ignored the jab. "As I am sure you have deduced, the
doctor is going to castrate Mr. Neary. We do not do this lightly. We
realize it is a grave act, a drastic step. The enormity of it is the reason
I have flown in from New York, the reason I have insisted on being
in the van tonight. *I alone* have authorized the procedure, *I alone* gave
the order to proceed, *I alone* will take full responsibility for the events
of this evening."

Shelby remembered reading about firing squads and how the
custom was that the gun of one of the shooters, randomly, be
loaded with blanks instead of bullets. That way, each squad member could put his head on his pillow at night and delude himself
into believing the victim's blood did not stain his hands. Her
uncle, in his own perversely noble way, was trying to absolve his
cohorts of any responsibility for the barbarism about to take place.
Not that it did Neary any good.

Abraham continued. "Some people think castration means to
actually cut off the male member, but in reality it is the removal of
the testicles only. This is meant as a punishment to Mr. Neary and,
as I said earlier, also a deterrent to others who may follow him. But
the beauty of this punishment is that it serves also another purpose:
Removal of the testicles will eliminate much of the testosterone from
Mr. Neary's body. In addition to taking away his sex drive, the procedure will take away much of his aggressive nature. He will become
more docile, and he will lose much of his muscle mass. In short, he
will become far less of a threat to us." He paused, look back at Neary,
then continued. "This is why, through history, men inside palace
walls were castrated; eunuchs were not only less of a sexual threat,
they became less of a physical threat to the royal family."

"Fascinating," Shelby retorted. "If the castration doesn't work,
perhaps you can feed him to the lions."

Neary strained against the straps as the doctor leaned over him, but
the sedative and the stun gun and the shock of the injections had

sapped his strength. His straining turned into a moan, then a whimper. The doctor opened the sack, then removed one of the grape-sized, bloody testicles. He tossed it into the same plastic bag that Madame Radminikov tossed the soiled cloth and urine-soaked underpants. "Swish," Barnabus sang out. "Throw it in the bag and make a wish." Neary continued to alternately moan and whimper. Blood continued to gush onto the quilted pad. The van resumed its journey through the darkened suburban roads.

The smells of feces and antiseptic and blood and body odor assaulted Shelby's nostrils. Her stomach, already queasy from standing in the rear of the lurching, windowless van, began to heave. She took a deep breath, staggered through the curtain and dropped into her seat. It seemed like years had passed since Mr. Clevinsky had met her outside her apartment building and handed her the letter from her mother. Is this what her mother envisioned when she asked Shelby to help her uncle?

In the distance, ahead, she spotted the neon lights of a convenience store. She waited until they passed the store, then reached forward and squeezed Mr. Clevinsky's shoulder, her other hand over her mouth. "Stop the van. I'm going to be sick."

His eyes searched for her uncle in the rear-view mirror. She could not take the chance that Mr. Clevinsky would see a shaking head in the glass. "I said to stop the van! Now!"

Mr. Clevinsky slowly eased his way onto the shoulder of the road. Shelby slid the door open even as the van rolled to a stop. She jumped out, ran into the brush.

She knew she had a few seconds head-start before they would come after her. They would either have to back up along the highway, drawing unwanted attention to themselves, or chase her by foot. The elderly and the over-sized filled the van; the only one who might conceivably catch her was the thin doctor, though she doubted he could outrun her.

She fought her way through the underbrush, turned to her right and ran back toward the neon lights of the convenience store. A few seconds passed, then Reb Meyer's angry voice called out. "She's running back to the 7-Eleven! Barnabus, go after her." But she was now approaching the parking lot of the store, and she knew they would not pursue her here, in public. But she also knew her uncle would not give up that easily.

*   *   *

Abraham placed a bony hand on Reb Meyer's shoulder, pushed him back into his seat. "Call Barnabus back. Allow her to run."

Reb Meyer began to argue, then obeyed. But not without the final word. "It was a mistake to bring the girl. She is weak."

"Strength of character is not a weakness," Abraham responded.

"Well, I don't see how it helps us to bring her along, only to find out she has no stomach for assisting us."

Abraham smiled sagely, a professor tutoring a dim-witted student. "There is a rule in negotiation: Always ask for more than you expect. In my niece's case, we have asked her to participate in something she, apparently, finds completely repugnant. I wish it were otherwise, but that is how she feels. However, going forward, when I ask for something less repugnant, though still considerable, she will be more likely to abide us. It is human nature."

"I, too, think it was good that we brought her tonight," Madame Radminikov stated. "It is as I hoped. She is pure of heart. By rejecting us, she has proven her worthiness." She looked from Abraham to Mr. Clevinsky to Reb Meyer. "We, we are all old and angry and filled with hatred. We may not like what we do, but we accept it as necessary. We sleep at night, we look into the mirror and do not turn away. But Shelby is still pure."

Abraham nodded. "Which is what makes her such an ideal weapon."

*   *   *

Shelby slowed to a walk, took a last look behind her to make sure nobody followed, then brushed the wet leaves off her clothes and hair. She entered the brightly-lit convenience store, spotted a pay phone, and asked the clerk for the number of a local taxi company. It

was a busy Saturday night, but for a fare to Boston—$40, plus tip—
they agreed to pick her up in five minutes.

She dug more change from her purse and called home. Bruce
answered on the first ring.

"Hey, Shelbs. I've been worried—"

"Long story." She gave him a quick summary, leaving out the more
gory details. "So I jumped out of the van, and now I'm at a 7-Eleven
in Stoneham. I just called a taxi—"

"No way. I'll come get you."

She sighed. "No, Bruce. Stay there. With the cab, I can be out of
here in five minutes. But if I have to wait for you, I'll just be sitting
here for at least twenty. I don't think they'll come back for me, but
I'm really not enjoying Stoneham very much." Her eyes scanned the
front of the store, settled on a couple of teenagers sucking on a frozen
Slurpie drink. Just another night in suburbia. Unless you happened
to be fleeing a crazy uncle, or strapped to an operating table in a van.

"All right. But stay on the line with me until the cab comes, just in
case. I'd like to hear more about this uncle of yours." He paused, then
continued. "Maybe you should call the police."

She shook her head. "I didn't even think to get a license plate—"

Bruce cut her off. "I don't mean call the police to stop your uncle,
I mean call them to protect you."

"Oh." She still had not gotten used to having somebody home
worrying about her. She had lived alone for practically her entire
adult life. No family, no serious boyfriends, no roommates. Not even
a cat. Most of her friends had moved to the suburbs and started families; they were now acquaintances more than true friends. She had
her work, and she had a rewarding series of relationships formed
through the Big Sister program. But nobody who would notice if she
did not make it home one night. Until Bruce. She found his concern
comforting and yet mildly uncomfortable, like a new down com-
forter with a few prickly feather quills poking through. Once in a
while, a quill poked her and reminded her how much her life had
changed.

She refocused on Bruce's comment. "Don't worry. Even if they
come back, they don't want to hurt me. They want my help."

"What kind of help?"

"My uncle wants me to be their lawyer. I think he even wanted me to help them with this vigilante stuff. It didn't occur to them that I might think they're crazy."

*   *   *

Bruce stayed on the phone with Shelby until she got into the cab, then began to pace restlessly around the living room. No way Shelby's uncle would just let this go. Abraham had a favor to ask of Shelby, had gone so far as to produce a note from the grave to enlist her aid. Yet the favor remained un-asked. For now.

His heart thumping, Bruce threw on a dark sweatshirt, changed his white tennis sneakers for some dark hiking boots. Shelby had been in danger. Perhaps still was. The thought sickened him, turned his stomach into a knotted, convulsing spasm. Tears of anger welled, blurred his vision—if anyone laid a hand on her....

He took a deep breath, unclenched his fists, forced himself to push the fear and anger and tumult aside. He remembered his grandfather's words: *Emotions can empower you, as long as you don't let them overpower you. Harness them like you would harness the wind.*

From what Shelby said, her uncle and his crew still had to make sure that the skinhead was stable before they could dump him off, so the earliest they could be in Boston was a half hour or so. He slipped an army knife into his jeans pocket, then splashed cold water onto his face. He eyed his reflection in the mirror, glad to see resolve in the brown eyes—life had turned cushy over the past year. He hoped he had not turned soft along with it.

In fact, as the adrenaline begin to surge through his body, it occurred to him that maybe life had gotten a bit too comfortable. Sure, he remained physically active—he ran five miles every day, lifted weights, and regularly battled Shelby on the racquetball court. Sometimes he even won a game from her, his size and tenacity overcoming her strategic mastery and pinpoint control. But physical activity and exertion were more of an addiction than a hardship for him. He taught sailing to kids on the Charles River in his free time, and a fellow sailing instructor, a retiree, commented that Bruce seemed to have the same boundless energy, the same need to constantly move and run and exert himself as Red Sox great Ted Williams. When Bruce mentioned it to Shelby, she—a big baseball fan anyway—went out and bought the Williams biography.

"You know what else?" she had said. "You look a lot like him during his playing days. Actually, you guys have a lot in common. Did you know he was estranged from his parents?"

Bruce read the biography as well, intrigued by Williams' insatiable need to feel challenged, even threatened. Bruce understood that need. He used to share it, in fact. It began as a little boy's desire to prove himself worthy to parents who did not care. And evolved into an adult's constant and fruitless quest to establish his own self-worth.

It took Bruce seven years, alone in a boat, to figure it all out. To understand why he had always lived on the edge, one mistake away from jail. Or from death. Copping trading cards from the local convenience store as a young teenager. Masterminding a series of art thefts while in college. Scamming his law firm's banking clients out of a small fortune as a young lawyer. Sailing the oceans, alone, for seven years as a man in exile. Then one day, in a sleepy port town in the Caribbean, he watched a young peasant woman pull a small girl, perhaps three or four years old, in a rickety wagon. The girl had no legs, only a pair of stumps where her knees should have been. The mother and the girl sang some nonsensical song as they rolled through the village, giggling and laughing together. At one point the woman turned and smiled at her crippled daughter. Bruce stared: The mother's eyes filled with love and adoration. No resentment or anger or sense of burden. At that point Bruce finally understood: His parents had been unable to love him because they were flawed, not him.

So here he was, content and happy for the first time in his life. He earned a comfortable living as a consultant to insurance companies—they paid him well to probe for weaknesses in the security systems of museums and private collections they insured, the new Bruce providing a detailed plan of how the old Bruce would have robbed them blind. And, most importantly, he had Shelby. They would soon marry, start a family, allow him the chance to love a child the way the peasant woman had taught him a parent should love....

He peeked out the front window. No one on the street below. He went down the back stairs to the alley behind the building. Garbage and rats and a couple of homeless men pawing through dumpsters— a typical alley but for the gleaming luxury cars packed fender to bumper on every square foot of pot-holed pavement.

He crossed the alley, slipped behind a dumpster. From there he could see the rear door of their building, and also see if Shelby returned and put a light on in their apartment. He tried to picture the scene unfolding—an old man in a suit and a giant Hasidic Jew, fresh from a castration, casing a Back Bay condominium, lying in wait for a beautiful Boston attorney. Too silly even for Hollywood, yet Bruce's gut told him that this was how it would go down.

Ten minutes passed, then a dark sedan—what else?—cruised slowly down the alley, the outline of a large man, bearded and hatted, visible in the driver's seat. A second man sat rigid in the passenger seat; the back seat looked empty. The car stopped, turned around, passed a second time, then sped up and left the alley. They would park and return by foot. Bruce bounded across the alley, unlocked the back door to the building, crouched in the darkness of the vestibule. A shuffling in the alley, followed by muffled voices. He slowly pulled the door closed. Shelby had not yet returned.

Bruce climbed the narrow stairs to the landing on the fourth floor, unscrewed the light bulb in the hallway light. A key—or, more likely, a lock-picking device—scratched around inside the door lock for a few seconds, then the door creaked open. Bruce clenched his fists— were they here to abduct Shelby? To coerce her? To scare her?

Heavy feet moved slowly from stair to stair, the men too large and the stairs too old to muffle their progress. The staircase was an old servants' entrance, turning on itself every six steps or so. Bruce stood outside the door to their apartment on a landing no more than the size of a coat closet. He could hear the intruders breathing, the heavy gasping of the giant seemingly the closer of the two.

Bruce pulled out his flashlight, pressed his back tight against the stairwell's inner wall, took a deep breath. His eyes had begun to adjust to the darkness. He shook his head—a brawl was not the way he had intended to introduce himself to Shelby's family....

The giant's blackened form appeared first, turning toward Bruce as he reached the top stair and continued in the spiraling pattern. Bruce aimed the flashlight at his face, clicked on the powerful light. The Hasid raised his hands to shield his eyes, and Bruce windmilled the flashlight in an underhand throwing motion, burying the butt deep into the giant's mid-section. "Oof," bellowed the man, spittle showering Bruce. The giant doubled-over, reflexively covered his midsection with his arms, his hat tumbling to the ground. Bruce remembered the fear in Shelby's voice when she called earlier; he could not risk leaving the giant standing like he might a normal-sized man. He stepped toward his folded-up adversary and thrust his knee up into the giant's nose, crushing it. The Hasid dropped to his knees, moaning, then rolled onto his side like a lilting ship. Blood squirted from his face, pooling on the wooden landing.

An angular, elderly man emerged from the shadows of the stair well. "Mr. Arrujo, I presume." The man spoke impassively, as if he had just witnessed Bruce stepping on an ant. He waved a gun at Bruce, motioned him away from the giant. The motion was casual, the hand steady. Bruce did not doubt he had used the gun before, and would use it again if necessary. "I am Abraham Gottlieb, Shelby's uncle. I see you have been expecting us."

Bruce straightened himself, met Abraham's gaze, glanced down at Abraham's fallen soldier. "Maybe next time you should just ring the buzzer."

*   *   *

Twenty-four hours ago, walking into her apartment and seeing a giant Hasid sprawled on her couch with a bloody towel held over his nose would have stunned Shelby. But tonight, after everything else, it was not totally unexpected.

"What are you doing here?" she challenged, stepping into the living room....

Then she saw Uncle Abraham, seated in a flowered armchair.

Bruce sat on the hardwood floor in front of him. Her uncle casually held a gun, its muzzle pointed at the back of Bruce's head.

Her cheeks burned. For almost two decades, since the death of her parents and brother, she had been totally alone. She had finally found someone to build a new family with, and her deranged uncle—her mother's own brother—was an ounce of finger pressure away from snuffing out both Bruce's life and any chance she had for happiness. She glared at Abraham. "Put that gun down. Now."

Her uncle blinked, surprised at her tone. He nodded. "Very well." He lowered the gun, rested it in his lap.

She continued to glare at him as she reached down, took Bruce by the hand, and pulled him to his feet. He smiled at her, his eyes twinkling, and kissed her gently on the lips. "My hero."

She allowed herself a moment to linger against him, then straightened herself and turned back to her uncle. "Perhaps it didn't occur to you, but the reason I jumped out of the van is because I want nothing to do with you. Now get out of my apartment."

It was if she had not spoken. Her uncle stared straight ahead, focused on some spot outside her window. He addressed her in that same, infuriating, matter-of-fact tone. "I brought you with us tonight because I wanted you to see what we do. We were even hoping you would join our group. However, I can understand that you find our methodology distasteful." He shifted his gaze toward her momentarily, then shrugged. "I cannot afford to indulge in questions of taste, or even propriety."

He paused. He was not exactly seeking her approval, but he at least was acknowledging she might not give it. She waited for him to continue, resigned to the fact that he would stay until he completed his business.

"After you left the van," he said, "the doctor completed his work and bandaged the patient. He will be in pain for a number of days, but as long as he takes antibiotics and keeps the area of the wound clean, he will recover within a few weeks."

Barnabus removed the ice pack from his nose, broke into a weak, nasally verse: "In the Nazi choir he'll have a place, but he won't be the one that's singing bass." Abraham ignored the giant. In fact, his face did not even register a reaction to the comment.

"What if he goes to the police?" she asked.

"It is a small risk. Reb Meyer is a professional, adept at planning these types of operations. The license plate on our van is untraceable, and, in any event, it will soon be nothing more than spare parts and scrap metal. Mr. Neary was blindfolded during the abduction, so he did not see our faces. Nor did we use our names within his earshot." He checked his watch. "The Burger King is now closed; soon one of Reb Meyer's men will be removing the video tape from the surveillance camera." He raised a finger. "Most importantly, we are confident Mr. Neary will not report the incident to the police. It is too much of a humiliation to him, especially in a small town."

"And if you're wrong?" She tried to picture Neary, baggy pants and baseball cap, strutting—well, maybe not such a strut anymore—into the police station to report a pair of missing testes. Not likely, but still possible.

"It would not matter. The chief of police already has been informed that Mr. Neary might have an ... accident ... tonight. If Mr. Neary demands, the police will do a brief investigation, which will yield nothing. You must understand, we are not just a fraternal organization as Madame Radminikov said. We are part of a vast network around the country, a network that I have built over the past 60 years." His voice contained no conceit, nor even any pride. He was simply stating a fact. "The name of our group is *Kidon,* the Hebrew word for sword. In the bible, it is a kidon that David uses to slay Goliath. *Kidon* happens also to be the name of the Mossad's death squad, though that is not our primary function. I believe you are aware that I founded and continue to chair Continental Casualty, now one of the largest insurance conglomerates in the world. What you do not know is that the profits from this endeavor are used exclusively to fund *Kidon,* the function of which is to protect and defend the Jewish people. And when I say profits, I am speaking of tens or even hundreds of millions of dollars. Such a sum of money can buy many friends, and many favors."

Shelby shook her head. She remained standing in the middle of the living room, though Bruce had dragged a pair of oak kitchen chairs in and dropped into one between her and the giant on the couch.

"All right then, how do you know I won't report you to the District Attorney?" Abraham blinked twice, the equivalent of an emotional outburst. Her words must have sounded blasphemous—the act of reporting him to the authorities would be, in his mind, the moral equivalent of the shopkeepers doing nothing to save his mother. In the perverse, delusional world in which he lived, the Nazi evil was a constant, a given, something he learned to accept and deal with. But he found truly incomprehensible the evil of those who did nothing to oppose the evildoers. She took a deep breath. "What you did was illegal, not to mention barbaric. As a lawyer, I'm sworn to uphold the law." Whether he found it comprehensible or not, she knew what she had to do—she could not let the crime go unreported.

"Yes, I am aware of your duties and responsibilities as a lawyer." Abraham held her eyes. This time he did not blink. "And I believe one of those duties is to respect and observe the attorney-client privilege."

The words slapped against her ears like the wings of a swooping bat on a moonless night. *Attorney-client privilege.* She shook the words away with a toss of her head, challenged him. "There are exceptions to the rule."

He nodded. "Yes. You may violate the confidentiality in order to prevent a serious crime. But it is too late for that. The crime has been committed; there is nothing to prevent."

He had set her up. By retaining her as their attorney during dinner, anything she learned later became confidential. Unless Abraham and his gang gave their permission, she was bound to respect that confidentiality. *What an asshole.*

Her hands shaking in anger, Shelby reached into her purse and pulled out the retainer check. With a violent snap, she ripped the check in half and let the two pieces flutter to the floor. "You can consider our attorney-client relationship terminated. I am formally advising you that I will not hold any further communications in confidence."

He steadied his eyelids, then responded. "Yes, I used the attorney-client privilege as an insurance policy in case you did not condone our actions. But I had hoped that you would see ... if not the wisdom, at least the necessity ... of our actions."

"Wrong on both counts. Not wise. Not necessary."

"Then you are blind." For the first time tonight, a touch of humanity shone in her uncle's eyes as he spoke. It might even have been sadness. "A Jew is a Jew—European or American or Middle-Eastern, Orthodox or Conservative or Reform, it does not matter. If we are attacked again, the attack will be against us all. You are one of us, united by faith and by family. It is all we have. We must remain united."

Faith and family. How poetic. Since her family's death, she had had precious little of either. But the memories of her childhood that still tugged at her were of family dinners and Purim carnivals and ski vacations. Not stun-guns and kidnappings and castrations. "Listen to yourself. Castrating your enemies, paying off police chiefs, this whole thing about being part of a big family. Well, that's not the family I remember. The family you're talking about—this *Kidon*—sounds more like the Mafia—"

Her uncle shook his head. "On the contrary, it is exactly the opposite. We are the hens, not the foxes; we buy protection, we do not sell it. We know we cannot always rely on our Christian neighbors. The bible tells us to love our neighbors and also to love our enemies; I read once that is probably because they are generally the same people. Inquisitions, pogroms, holocausts—history teaches us that our countrymen can at any time betray us."

He closed his eyes, seemingly trying to blind himself to what the future would certainly display. "We must protect ourselves. *Kidon* is a sword used only in defense of our people."

Shelby turned to Bruce. She expected a roll of the eyes, or a sardonic smile, or some other indication that he viewed her uncle—and his words—as absurdly misguided. But he offered only a half shrug. Apparently Bruce did not find Abraham's explanation as irrational as she did. Was it possible that her uncle made sense, that she rejected the message because she found the messenger so abhorrent?

She sighed. Her uncle was approaching 80. He spent his childhood watching the Nazis murder his family and his neighbors. Something she heard recently: *Each of us is the accumulation of our memories.* It was no surprise that he viewed the world—and reacted to it—through the prism of that nightmare. No argument she mustered would make him see grays and tans after 70 years of blacks and whites. And yet her mother had turned out so different. Perhaps she had always worshipped Abraham because she understood that, in her childhood, he served as her human shield, deflecting the world's ugliness so that she could grow up unscarred.

Which brought Shelby back to her mother's letter, and the request that she assist her uncle. "So what is it you really want from me? The whole story about needing a lawyer was obviously a ruse."

"Again, I hoped you would agree to join *Kidon*, assist Madame Radminikov here in Boston. But, failing that, I do have one other specific request. It is a request you will find less objectionable." He locked his eyes on hers. "It is a request that will honor your mother."

Shelby took a deep breath, sighed, dropped into the chair next to Bruce. "Fine. I'm listening."

Her uncle turned to the giant. "Barnabus, you may leave now." Barnabus rolled himself off the couch, keeping the towel tight against his nose. He glared at Bruce, bumped against Bruce's knee as he walked past. Bruce kept his head turned away, ignored the affront as the giant plodded out the door and down the stairs.

Abraham reached into his jacket pocket, pulled out a color picture torn from a magazine and handed it to Shelby. "Do you recognize this woman?"

Shelby glanced at the picture; the back of her neck tingled. "You know I do." Monique Goulston, her old law school roommate. Coincidentally, or perhaps not, Monique had phoned Shelby just last week. "Are you tapping my phone?"

Her uncle shook his head. "Not yours. Hers."

After everything that happened tonight, she could not get too worked up over phone taps. "Why? Is she another one of those enemies of our people?"

"No. But she is a concern to us."

Shelby looked back at the picture. Monique glared at the camera, striking as always in a dark, wild-haired way. People dismissed her as some kind of fringe, counter-culture type at their peril—the black clothes and body piercings and wild lifestyle masked a fiery intensity and a sharp legal mind.

"Why should she be?" Monique worked for one of those public interest law groups in Washington. Sort of like Common Cause.

"Do you know what it is exactly that she does?"

"No. We had a falling out during law school, so I haven't talked to her in a couple of years. Until she called last week—" She stopped. Her uncle already knew why Monique called—he had been listening in. She turned to Bruce, continued for his benefit. "She asked if I was still doing First Amendment law, said she might need my help on a free speech case in Boston—"

Abraham spoke over her, signaled her to stop talking with a single chopping motion of his hand. "A falling out? This means a fight, yes?"

Again, the rude chop of the hand seemed trivial in the context of the night's other events. Welcome to her uncle's world. "Yeah, something stupid. I called her a hypocrite."

Bruce chuckled. "You told me about her. Isn't she also the one who organized a hunger strike to get free meals for the homeless and then, when they won, she broke the fast at some fancy restaurant instead of celebrating with the other protestors?"

"Yeah, that was the contradiction of Monique. It's one thing to starve yourself nearly to death. It's another to actually share a meal with the Great Unwashed. That was Monique. She came from an old WASP family in Cleveland—railroads and banking, I think—and she lived like a classic trust-fund rich kid, always going to boutiques and salons and exotic places. But she was way left politically. She never really figured out how to make all the pieces fit together. Maybe by now she has." Her uncle listened intently. "I tried to rekindle the friendship. We had lunch a couple of times after that, just acting like nothing ever happened, but we were never really close again."

"She was at your mother's funeral," Abraham said matter-of-factly.

Shelby shrugged. "Was she?" That would have been about a year after their fight. It did not really surprise her. Monique could be petty and bitchy and selfish, but underneath it all she had a good heart. "How do you know?"

The question seemed to baffle Abraham, as if she had asked how he knew the earth was round. "I saw her there," he declared.

Right. She had forgotten her uncle had a photographic memory. "Well, whatever. So, what about her?"

"She is doing more than just lobbying work in Washington. Do you remember the demonstrations and riots in Seattle in 1999 during the world economic conference? Young people roaming the streets, throwing Molotov cocktails, overturning cars? Miss Goulston is the one who organized those demonstrations."

"Do you mean she organized the riots, or the demonstrations? Not everyone participated in the riots, if I remember correctly," Shelby stated.

"Suffice it to say that Miss Goulston gathered the twigs and kindling and matches together. Whether she actually struck the match is not important." Abraham explained how Monique united the labor groups, the socialists, the environmentalists, the anarchists, the dispossessed—anyone opposed to the status quo. After Seattle, the fringe members of these groups rioted in Quebec and Genoa as well. "Your friend has become one of the most powerful people in the world, yet few people have ever heard of her."

"Monique? Why would all these people follow her?"

Abraham raised a forefinger. "They follow her because she has identified for them a common enemy—globalism and the multinational corporations. More importantly, she has given them a forum to fight that enemy. Every time there is a global economic conference, Miss Goulston's group organizes the protest. This is a huge task, and she is an expert at performing it. She arranges the logistics, manages the publicity, provides housing and food and medical care and communication. The Seattle demonstrations gave her credibility with all these radical groups; she did a good job, so now they listen to her. She tells them when and where to arrive, and everything else is taken care of for them—"

Bruce interjected. "I read about this. It's like spring break for these people—all they have to do is show up with their bandanas and backpacks. A weekend of rioting, maybe a night in jail, then off they go until they get an email that rallies them again a year later."

Shelby was unwilling to trivialize the demonstrations as Bruce did; some of the causes were legitimate, and most of the demonstrators were peaceful. Even the rioters were passionate about righting the injustices of the world. Just as Monique had always been. But that was a discussion for later. "But Seattle and Quebec were before September 11. I haven't heard about any rioting since then."

"Actually, there were some violent protests recently in Edinburgh. But for the most part, you are correct." He explained that host governments had been able to restrict travel and limit demonstrations in the name of post-9/11 security. And organizers had been holding the conferences on remote islands and cruise ships to keep activists away.

"Miss Goulston's army is still out there; they are just waiting for the proper battlefield," he declared. "And now they have found it, their new battleground. There will be a world economic conference at Harvard University next October. It is not as large as the yearly G-8 economic summits, but the industrialized nations will all send representatives. According to our sources, as soon as the announcement was made Miss Goulston's group reserved thousands of hotel rooms around Boston, no doubt to house protestors. In Seattle there were 40,000 demonstrators—it could easily be twice that number in Boston."

Shelby asked the obvious question. "If they're worried about demonstrations, why would they be stupid enough to host a conference at Harvard?"

"That is a good question. From a political perspective, Miss Goulston's group has been dormant for some years, so perhaps an assumption exists that they have been disabled. In addition, the Harvard event is technically an academic conference, rather than an economic summit, so the organizers may feel it will not be a target for demonstrations."

Shelby shook her head. "So my old friend Monique gets to come back to her alma matter and lead a crusade against the evil multinationals. It's really perfect for her. She never would have been happy— or successful—practicing law in some law firm somewhere. Her ego needs to be fed; she needs to be the center of attention. And she needs to believe she is fulfilling her destiny, changing the world." She turned to Bruce. "I just wonder where she'll shop if she takes down Prada along with the other evil multinationals…."

Bruce laughed, but her uncle stared quizzically back at her. Shelby looked at her watch. "Look, this is very interesting. But what does all this have to do with me?"

Abraham's eyes moved from Shelby to Bruce and back to Shelby. "We believe that terrorists are preparing to infiltrate these demonstrations and use the chaos of the events to unleash a massive attack on Boston. I have personal knowledge of a cell planning to ignite a tanker filled with liquefied natural gas in Boston Harbor." Right. The woman muttering under anesthesia. "In addition, there are other groups who may be planning to target a specific Jewish site—perhaps the Holocaust Memorial in downtown Boston, perhaps Brandeis University."

Shelby did not carry the paranoia that Abraham did, but she understood one of the reasons the terrorists targeted the Twin Towers was that many Jews worked there. The buildings symbolized not only New York and free trade, but also Jewish commerce.

Abraham continued. "If they can attack a site within the United States that also is viewed in the Arab world as an attack on Jewish interests, that is a double victory. And, in their minds, even more rewarded in paradise."

More rewarded? What was a double victory, 144 virgins instead of 72? How many virgins did one terrorist need?

Bruce challenged Abraham. "You're not just concerned about preventing injuries and death, right? You have another agenda." A statement, not a question.

Abraham turned his gray eyes to Bruce without blinking. "Not just one other agenda, but two. First, like so many host nations before it, the United States eventually might conclude that its alliance with the Jewish people is more trouble than it is worth. Already the white supremacist groups are blaming the Jews for both September 11 and the problems in the Middle East. This message is as dangerous to us as the physical attacks on our people. While a hate crime is isolated, a hate message can resonate throughout society."

"That's ridiculous," Shelby countered. "Nobody's going to blame the Jews for another terrorist attack."

Abraham shook his head. "Wrong. People already are. You must remember, alliances can change quickly. In the 1980s, the U.S. supported Saddam Hussein; in the 1990s, it supported the Taliban."

Shelby sighed. There was a difference between the U.S. supporting the Taliban in its war against the Soviet Union on the one hand and blaming American Jews for a terrorist attack on the other. But she was tired of banging her head against the wall that was her uncle. "You mentioned you had two reasons for wanting to stop an attack."

"Correct. The second is the one Bruce was hinting at. *Kidon's* ability to function effectively is directly dependent on our insurance business remaining profitable. We paid hundreds of millions of dollars in damage claims after the September 11 attacks. Then we paid almost as much again from the Florida hurricanes, then another sizable amount after the tsunami, and finally a massive amount resulting from Hurricane Katrina. We cannot afford another major terrorist attack. It would bankrupt our operation."

Shelby shook her head—this conversation had gotten ahead of itself. "Wait, back up a second. Are you saying that you think Monique Goulston would willingly allow terrorists to attack a site in Boston?"

"No," Abraham answered. "But she will have no way of controlling things once she unleashes her mob. The terrorists will simply blend into the crowd and take advantage of the chaos. If we know exactly when and where her group is planning the demonstrations, we might be able to stop the terrorists."

"You say 'we.' Are you planning on stopping them yourselves?"

"Of course not. We have been sharing our information with the proper authorities, working together with Homeland Security officials. But we are in need of more specific information, information that only Monique Goulston can give us."

Shelby sighed. She saw where this was going. "So, you want me to spy on Monique."

"Correct. She trusts you, and as her lawyer you will be privy to information that nobody else will have."

Shelby shook her head again. "I'm just helping her on the legal stuff, making sure the city doesn't prevent them from demonstrating. It's not like I'll be down in Washington with her planning the whole event."

"No, but you will be in Boston, which is where Miss Goulston will eventually have to come. And if she wants you to go to court to make sure the police do not interfere with her demonstration, she is going to have to give you details about that demonstration. Shelby, she is very private, and we have nobody else who can get close to her. And since it was she that contacted you, it is unlikely she will suspect that you have any ulterior motive."

Abraham stood up abruptly. "I will leave you now. Perhaps I made a mistake bringing you tonight. Perhaps you were not ready to witness the … ugliness … of the Neary operation. But remember this: I am not asking you to assist *Kidon* in punishing our enemies. I am instead asking you to help prevent a massive terrorist attack." He proffered a half-bow. "You may let me know your decision in a few days. But ask yourself this: What would your mother have done?" He spun on a heel and strode out the door.

Bruce waited until the door closed behind Abraham. "Wow. You have any more relatives I should meet?"

Shelby allowed a quick laugh to escape. "Wow is right. What a night."

Bruce embraced her. "You okay?"

"Yeah." She rested her head on his shoulder.

"Listen, I think you should think about it. You're always talking about wanting to use your law degree to do something good, to have a cause to fight for—"

She pulled back. "But I didn't mean using it to spy on my client—"

"No, but if you have a chance to prevent a major terrorist attack, isn't that a small price to pay? Remember how you told me you sat there at work, watching the Twin Towers burn and crumble, how powerless you felt? Well, here's your chance to do something. You may not agree with your uncle's tactics, or this whole Jews versus the world thing, but it's pretty hard to be opposed to stopping the terrorists."

She shook her head. "Pretty simple, huh? Black and white, good versus evil, either with us or against us. Sometimes the world's more complicated than that, Bruce."

Bruce nodded. "Yes it is. But sometimes it really is that simple."

*   *   *

Bruce cleaned up the blood in the stairwell, while Shelby did her best to fumigate the couch. They climbed the ship's ladder through a hatch to the roof deck above their unit. It was well past midnight; the clouds had thinned to allow a few stars to peek through, and a cool breeze rustled the still-wet leaves of the majestic elms and maples lining Commonwealth Avenue. Shelby carried the ice bucket, Bruce the spiced rum and a couple of glasses.

Shelby leaned on the wrought iron railing, looked out over the city still very much alive with lights and laughter and an occasional tire screech. The merriment of the Saturday night below seemed misplaced, like the sound of a television blaring from an adjoining hospital room while a terminal patient struggled for life. Like the television watcher, the people on the streets below had no idea that death loomed just around the corner.

Bruce brought her a drink, stood next to her. "Any chance we can get your uncle to give a toast at the wedding?" He would, as always, try to keep things light. It was one of the things she liked best about him—since her parents' death, she had the tendency to slip into periods of self-pity and moroseness. Being around Bruce made her more carefree. Even, at times, irreverent.

"I was thinking of having Barnabus do it. Did you notice he always speaks in rhyme? Might be a nice touch."

"All I got out of him were some growls and grunts and moans. I don't think they rhymed."

She sipped at her rum. It bit, soothed, warmed. Her mind drifted back to the teenagers sipping Slurpies at the 7-Eleven. Did they have any idea how simple their lives were? She took a deep breath. "So. You really think I should help?" She tried to ask the question without an edge.

"I don't know. Isn't Abraham the guy in the bible who made everyone get circumcised, even the adults? I'm not sure he's the best guy to listen to."

"Come on, seriously."

He turned, looked hard into her eyes. "Yeah, I do. I think you'd never be able to live with yourself if you had the chance to stop a terrorist attack and you didn't. There's an old Bulgarian proverb my Grandpa used to quote: *In time of great danger you are permitted to walk with the devil until you have crossed the bridge.*"

Shelby looked up, wished the city lights would disappear so she could see the stars. "*Walk with the devil.* That's what it feels like with my uncle. But you're assuming we can believe what he says. I don't trust him."

"I don't trust him either. It's like a holy war for him and his gang, anything goes. Just ask that guy Neary."

"Well, which is it, Bruce?" She was tired and stressed, and he was not making sense. "First you say I should help him, then you say not to trust him."

"It's both." He smiled. "If he's trying to stop a terrorist attack, it doesn't really matter what his motivation is, it doesn't matter why the devil is helping you across the bridge. But helping him is one thing. Trusting him is another."

*   *   *

Gabriella Garcia-Ring swatted at a mosquito, wiped the bloodied sweat from the back of her neck. It was a couple hours past dawn, and they were deep in the woods of northern New Hampshire. The mosquitoes in this area of the state likely had not feasted on human blood since the loggers left a few years ago. "Ahmad, give me that bug spray again."

Ahmad flashed his Omar Sharif smile. "You should have eaten the humus I made for dinner last night." He set down his backpack, pulled a can of spray from a side pocket and tossed it to her. "I put in extra garlic—the bugs don't come near me."

"Yeah, and neither will the girls." It was a lie. Despite his paunch, women flocked to Ahmad—as much for his BMW convertible and thick wad of cash as for his sad, brown eyes and wet, playful smile. Gabriella knew better than to get involved with one of her young operatives, but she knew men found her attractive, and she knew how to flirt. At a different time in her life, she might have allowed Ahmad to seduce her. That he reeked was probably a blessing.

She closed her eyes, doused herself with bug spray for the third time today. When she opened them, she spotted the brothers, Hosni and Mushin, sauntering up the old, dirt logging road in the streaks of morning sunlight. Unlike Ahmad, who was soft and fleshy but could seemingly hike all day, Hosni and Mushin appeared fit but had the energy of a pair of house cats. They weren't twins, but they were almost impossible to tell apart with their matching long faces, full beards and coal-black eyes. And, again unlike Ahmad, the brothers were silent and sullen. It did not help their mood that they were taking orders from a woman. And a Christian one at that.

"Come on men, let's get going." She was careful not to call them 'boys,' though that's what they were. "We're almost there." The brothers would not necessarily have been her first choices, but it wasn't like she could just take an ad out in the *Globe* seeking volunteers for a terrorist mission. At least she knew she could trust them—their father fought with her brother in Afghanistan, and this mission constituted a right of passage for them as similar missions did for many young men in their Iranian village.

The four of them had left Boston in the middle of the night, breakfasting in the car during the four-hour drive after stopping at the self-storage facility to retrieve the weapons. At first light, two hours ago, they began their hike into the woods. Gabriella now pulled out a hand-sketched map, studied the steep ravine falling to their right. "The clearing should be just ahead, maybe another fifteen minutes. We'll have a snack when we get there."

Hosni grunted in response, while Mushin merely stared at his feet and shuffled along. Ahmad turned to her. "You want to trade packs? You've been carrying the heavy one all morning." Classic Ahmad—a selfish playboy, condescending and haughty. But also a gentleman. At least to the women he wanted to sleep with.

She wanted to say yes—her muscles ached, the straps dug into her surgically-repaired shoulder, and the day, which had started out cool and dry, had turned warm and humid as the sun penetrated the forest. But a woman commanding Arab men must not show weakness. "I'm fine, thanks. It's not too heavy."

Ten minutes later they reached the end of the logging road. A lunar landscape, ashy and pitted and undulating, opened in front of them. A clear-cut. Acre after acre of nothing but a grayish ash, with only a few hearty weeds pushing through the crust. The loggers extracted every ounce of wood from the site, then burned what remained to prevent the debris from fueling a fire that would consume other trees before they could harvest them. The scene captured perfectly the obscenity of capitalism—a pristine forest gashed and scarred, an entire ecosystem decimated in the process, all so a few rich gringos could afford to costume their mistresses in jewels and fur.

They sat on a couple of large rocks at the edge of the clearing. Gabriella handed out protein bars, apples and some bottled water, then looked at her watch. "We have another ten hours of daylight left, so let's make the most of it." She commanded as if it had not occurred to her she might be ignored.

She took a can of red spray paint and a small tent-pack from her backpack, walked about fifty yards along the edge of the clearing and marked a large X on the trunks of a dozen trees. She yelled to the men. "You guys need to be able to hit a target at 300 meters. That's how far away the LNG tanker will be." She pulled out a pedometer and began walking toward the middle of the clearing. She looked over her shoulder. "Mushin and Hosni, see if you can figure out how to put the grenade launchers together. They're in my pack."

She resisted the urge to turn around and check on her troops. Mushin and Hosni were typical soldiers, the kind that every army needed—not overly bright, and not overly motivated, but devoted and competent. More than capable of setting up the weapon and firing it accurately. Just do not expect them to strategize. That was Ahmad's job.

During their morning hike, she learned a lot about her young comrade. He fancied himself the John F. Kennedy of the Arab world—born to politics, intent on parlaying wartime heroics into a political career. Like Kennedy, his patrician upbringing and advanced education would endear him to his country's ruling elite, while this mission—if successful—would win the respect and loyalty of the religious hard-liners and nationalists. He hoped to return to Saudi Arabia with both a Western diploma to hang on his wall and a number of Western scalps to hang off his ever-expanding belt.

She reached the 300 meter mark, spray-painted a red line on the ashy soil. The trees she marked were easily visible across the open expanse. Just like a tanker across the water. She knelt down and quickly erected the pup tent.

She returned to the three men. "Any luck with the launchers?" They were RPG-7s, Russian-built, with standard PG-7 85-mm anti-tank grenades. Light, effective and reliable, they were deployed all over the world, the weapon of choice for guerrillas targeting tanks and helicopters. And, now, LNG tankers. She knew better than to ask the old man how he had smuggled them into the country.

Hosni offered a slight nod, his eyes averting her face. Both brothers understood English, largely because they had spent the past six months watching television in a small, basement apartment in East Boston, biding their time until the mission began. Ironically, the brothers and Ahmad communicated with each other in English rather than Arabic because Ahmad barely understood the Iranian boys' peasant dialect. Unlike Ahmad, who attended Boston University and had a valid student visa, Hosni and Mushin had snuck across the border from Canada. The threat of arrest and the frigid winter—not to mention the temptations of Western society—kept them in the apartment most of the time. While in Boston, they were under orders not to contact Ahmad. She guessed Ahmad preferred it that way—his cosmopolitan image would suffer if seen with these bumpkins.

"Good. Hosni, Mushin, take the launchers apart and put them back in my pack. Ahmad, that small pack is full of grenades. Bring the launchers and the grenades, and put the rest of our gear behind those rocks. Then follow me."

They gathered in the clearing. She took the packs containing the launchers and grenades and tossed them into the tent. "Okay, here's the plan. I haven't picked the day yet, but at some point we're going to mix in with a crowd gathered along the Boston waterfront. You three are going to blend in, and you're going to have a tent to stay dry or keep out of the sun or smoke dope or whatever. You'll assemble the rocket launchers in the tent, and when the tanker goes by you'll fire on it. That's what we're here to practice."

Ahmad smiled at her. "And how do you propose that we escape after firing?" No martyrdom for this future politician. Which was fine with her also.

"We'll get to that later. But first we need to make sure you guys can shoot these things. Mushin and Hosni, get in the tent. You will load the weapons and wait in there until Ahmad gives the word. Ahmad, your job will be to stand watch and make sure nobody interferes. You'll have a gun, of course.

"Now let's see how well you can shoot. Remember, the gas is in holding tanks that are like giant camel-humps rising above the hull of the ship, maybe ten or fifteen meters in the air. So aim for the tops of the trees marked in red. Fire when ready."

She stepped back as Mushin and Hosni unzipped the duffel bag and began to fit the two tubes of the launchers back together again. They then stuck a grenade on the end—it looked like an ear of corn, still in its husk, impaled on the end of an assault rifle. "Ahmad, you should be standing in front of the tent, making sure nobody can see what they are doing."

He nodded, sauntered over to the block the entranceway. There was something regal about Ahmad, unlike the smarmy Americans who comprised the ruling elite. Societies would always differentiate between classes of citizens—even as a socialist, she knew this to be true. But U.S. culture glorified cable-TV preachers over inner-city teachers, taught children to aspire to be Irish step-dancers rather than curers of breast cancer. U.S. society needed—even demanded—to be jolted back into some semblance of a moral equilibrium. In the meantime, it exported its depravity by installing puppet dictators around the world....

About 30 seconds passed, then Hosni appeared, kneeling on his right knee in the mouth of the tent. He balanced the launcher on his right shoulder, angled the nozzle into the air, sighted with his right eye. "Remember, you want to hit the tanks, not the tanker itself. So aim at a point on the trees 15 or 20 meters into the air." Simple, really—one of the articles she read referred to the RPG-7 as the point-and-shoot camera of the weapon world. He took a deep breath, released it slowly, then squeezed the trigger. The missile hissed toward the target in a flat trajectory, broke through the top leaves and branches of an evergreen, and disappeared from sight. A second or two later they heard a muffled explosion from deep in the woods. Hopefully the recent rain would prevent the trees from igniting.

She turned toward Hosni, now shrouded in a blue-gray haze of smoke. "Too high."

He scowled. "I think missile go like this." He made an arcing motion with his hand.

She shook her head. "For the first 500 meters, the rocket will keep the trajectory flat, so there's no need to account for gravity. Just aim where you want it to go. Mushin, you try."

The missile whizzed out, struck a thick branch high in one of the targeted trees, exploded on impact. They waited a few seconds for the smoke to clear. The missile obliterated the entire top portion of the tree. Ahmad nodded, patted Mushin on the back. "With shots like that, we will all be heroes, cousin."

They spent the morning practicing. Gabriella moved them back to 400, and then 500, meters, and also narrowed the cluster of targeted trees. The launcher, light and accurate, enabled the boys to succeed even from the extended distance. Even Ahmad hit on a few shots, though he flinched every time he pulled the trigger.

Gabriella nodded. "You guys are doing great." After lunch, they would hike deeper into the woods, toward the Canadian border. Old logging trails crossed into Canada; she wanted the boys familiar with the route in case she could not lead them on a post-attack escape. Once in Canada, her troops would go underground for a few months in Montreal, then return to Saudi Arabia on a commercial flight.

Canadian officials had tightened airport security for travelers coming into Canada, but nobody screened passengers as they left....

But none of it mattered if they could not hit the tanker. She pulled out a photo, showed them a bright red tanker with holding tanks rising above the deck of the vessel like giant breasts. "There are five tanks. We'll only have two launchers, so you're each going to get just one shot. Our goal is to have a cascade-like effect, where the gas leaking from the first tank will be ignited by the explosion caused by the grenade hitting the next tank over."

The three boys nodded, grim-faced. Gabriella liked the fact that none of them, even the brothers, took joy from the prospect of thousands being incinerated. Theirs was a necessary operation, though not a pleasurable one, much like amputating the limb of a sick patient. They were removing a cancer from the body of mankind, not in punishment but in salvation. The patient was the world; the cancer the depraved wickedness that had become the United States.

Ahmad brought her back to the present. "So you don't want us to reload, even if we miss our shots?"

"No, there will be no time for that." She turned to Mushin and Hosni. "You should be able to aim and shoot in less than ten seconds each—Ahmad can keep the crowd away from you for that long. But beyond that, the police will have time to get to you."

"What do we do once we've fired the two shots?" Ahmad asked. Mushin and Hosni edged closer.

"You run. Fast. I'll be waiting for you in a car nearby."

He looked at her skeptically. "How fast?"

She waited until all three boys focused on her. "Understand this. All of you. I have no more intention of being burned alive than you do. It will take a couple of minutes for the wall of fire to reach land. If you fire your shots, then get back to the car quickly, I will get us out of there." She smiled at Ahmad, young and nervous. "You'll be fine as long as you don't stop and flirt with any girls on the way."

*   *   *

By the time Shelby joined him at the small oak table in the kitchen, Bruce had been awake for a couple of hours, trying to learn all he could about her crazy old uncle. If they were going to get involved with him, best to do it with their eyes wide open.

Shelby shuffled over and hugged him from behind, letting her chin rest on his head. He breathed in the musky sweetness of her skin, her hair, her breath, then reached up and stroked her cheek with the back of his hand. "Good morning, love," she murmured into the back of his neck. "The printer woke me. What're you doing up so early?"

"Sorry." He stood, guided her into his seat. "I was doing a Google search on Abraham. Here, take a look. Pretty interesting stuff." He handed her a stack of papers.

She yawned. "What happened to sleeping in on Sundays? My eyes can't focus this early. And my brain needs some coffee first." She handed the papers back to him. "Maybe just summarize for me?"

"Sure." He was accustomed to sleeping in two or three hour shifts. If you overslept while sailing in the waters along the Atlantic coastline, you would likely find yourself bobbing in them. Plus, the encounter with Abraham and Barnabus the night before kept his mind racing all night.

He poured Shelby a cup, added some cream. "Here's the deal with your uncle. You know when he talked about having this whole network of powerful people he knew? Well, he wasn't exaggerating. Have you ever heard of the Bilderberg Conference?"

She sipped at her coffee, stifled another yawn. "No."

He dropped into the chair next to her. "It's a group of world leaders, organized after World War II by the European royal families. They meet secretly every year and basically decide how to run the world."

"Sounds like some cheap spy novel."

"Yeah, it really does," he said, smiling. "But it's real. They invite about 120 people to the conference every year, two-thirds from Europe and one-third from the U.S. and Canada—"

"That's it? Nobody from Japan or India or Brazil?"

"Remember, this was all set up by the European royalty. Can't have the Asians or South Americans or Africans setting world policy—"

"Or eating their salad with the wrong fork—"

Bruce sat back. "Exactly. So, in addition to the royals, they have politicians and bankers and industrialists and media people—basically, everyone who runs the Western world. The list is supposed to be secret, but it gets leaked almost every year. Some of the right-wing whackos are convinced it's a plot by the Jewish bankers to control the world's money supply."

"That's nothing new," she sniffed. "Shakespeare wrote about Jewish bankers four hundred years ago." She paused. "But are there lots of Jews involved in this Bilderberg thing?"

He could not resist. "Sure. Didn't you know all the European royal families are secretly Jewish?"

She looked up quickly from her coffee, then smiled. "Don't do that to me. It's too early."

"Anyway, the group changes every year, but some of the core members are Jewish. Guys like Kissinger, Alan Greenspan, one of the Rothschilds. Anyway, your uncle is not a core guy, but he's been invited two or three times."

Shelby took a deep breath, sighed. "I guess I shouldn't be surprised. Old Uncle Abe sure seems to get around. Though I do have trouble picturing him sipping tea with the queen...."

"Here's the thing: When he said he had a network of contacts, he was being modest. He could probably reach senators and governors and federal judges if he wanted. Maybe even the White House. When you've got billions of dollars at your disposal, and when you spend your summer vacation with the Rockefellers and the Rothschilds and the royals discussing how to run the world, people tend to take your calls."

"You say 'run the world' like they just push a button or something and it happens. Last I checked, the world didn't work that way." Shelby chewed her bottom lip, tilted her head to the side the way she did while she worked through a problem. He was tempted to lean over and kiss her, but who knew where that would lead, and they really did need to figure out what to do about her uncle....

"No, you're right, they don't just push a button. For one thing, I imagine they don't even agree on very much themselves. But what they have in common is that they depend on the current political and economic systems for their power. That's really the whole gist of what Monique and her friends are saying, that the current world order exists just to benefit the ruling elite, at the expense of the people—"

"She's probably not far off—"

"Probably not. Anyway, the Bilderbergers, as they're called, need the so-called Western way of life to continue. They need stable democracies, a healthy global economy, stuff like that. Without that, none of them stays in power, and none of them stays rich. So that's what they concentrate on, big picture stuff."

Shelby sipped again at her coffee, looked out the window. "So if my uncle is that powerful, and he has such powerful friends, why does he need me?"

"Good question." He put down the printouts detailing the Bilderberg Conference, reached for another stack of papers. "I've also been doing some research on these anarchist groups."

She raised an eyebrow at him. "My, you've been busy...."

Not exactly a 'come hither' look, but it still caused a stirring in his groin. He got up, poured himself a large glass of orange juice. "I always thought the anarchists went out of style after World War I. But it turns out there's an active group here in Boston. Most other big cities also. Basically they believe that all the Western governments are evil. They're also against capitalism and organized religion, which they say are rigged to keep the ruling class in power. Oh, and they want to get rid of all laws and all prisons."

"So what are they *for?*"

"Lots of them actually call themselves libertarian socialists, sort of like socialism without the Soviet-style centralized authority. They believe that, once government is brought down, people will join together to form some egalitarian society. You know, everyone holding hands and singing and stuff."

"Have they ever seen how a mob behaves? It's not like human nature is always so benevolent...."

Bruce shrugged. "Again, it's like being the minority party in politics—you don't have to actually propose solutions, you just take shots at the status quo." He thumbed through his stack of documents. "I have to hand it to them, though. For people who are fighting for chaos, they're pretty organized. They have a bunch of links on their website, lots of interesting stuff. Check this out." He handed Shelby a piece of paper. "It's a list of 'helpful hints' for demonstrators—did you know that breathing through a vinegar-soaked rag neutralizes the effects of tear gas? They also have a team of medical professionals who treat injured demonstrators. They even have daycare—drop your kid off, go demonstrate for a few hours, be back by nap time. And here's another funny thing—they went Christmas caroling this year to the shopping malls and changed all the words. My favorite was, *Jingle bells, Nike smells.*"

Shelby smiled, leaned into him, glanced at the page in front of him. He smelled her hair, felt himself stirring again as she spoke. "At least they have a sense of humor," she said.

"I'm not sure I always get the joke. They made up a flyer opposing the war in Iraq. It says, 'Surgical bombing is a lie. But we can be far more precise.' Then they give a list of local companies and their addresses and say, 'Attack the real enemy.'"

"Nice."

"Anyway, Abraham is right—the anarchists are going to be all over this Harvard summit. Your uncle can reach judges and politicians and bankers, but he knows he can't get to these people on the fringes of society. Monique can, but he needs a way to get to Monique. You're it. Lucky you."

Still an hour before he had to be at work. He took her hand, caressed her wrist. She narrowed her eyes and smiled at him, then set down her coffee cup and pulled him to his feet. Her voice turned throaty. "Speaking of getting lucky...."

CHAPTER 3

It was one of those rare spring days in Boston. Many years it seemed like New England went straight from nineteen degrees to ninety degrees with nothing but a couple of weeks of rain in between. But today offered a blue sky and dry air. And a wind whipping down the Charles River.

Bruce's hair whipped around with it. He did not need the money he earned teaching sailing part-time—the insurance companies paid him plenty to make sure other people like him did not steal their treasures. But teaching kids to sail brought him back to his childhood, Grandpa and he on the harbor on a windy day....

He turned to the pale, serious boy seated next to him. Anthony Donato was his name, and his father, a lieutenant in the Boston police department, drove Anthony in twice a week from Medford, where he lived with his mother, for sailing lessons after school. "All he's interested in is science fiction stuff; that and some dragon game he and his friends play," the father confided to Bruce. "I've given up trying to get him to play sports, but I thought sailing might interest him. You know, the science of the wind and the angles and all that. At least he'll be outside."

Something about the father's earnestness appealed to Bruce. A divorced dad trying to connect with his teenage son, but unable to use the football or baseball or hockey crutch that so many fathers relied on. Especially tough for a cop. Hard to imagine dad down at the station bragging about Junior's Dungeons and Dragons exploits. Yet instead of trying to force the boy onto the football field, Anthony's dad sought a middle ground, some way to accommodate the kid's interests and personality. A hell of a lot more effort than Bruce's father had ever made.

They were midway through their third lesson. "Okay, buddy, helm is yours." Time to throw caution to the wind. Literally. They were in a Mercury, a stable, 15-foot centerboard sloop. The worst that could happen would be they would capsize, swallow some water and, depending on whether the storm drains up-river had overflowed after the recent rain, maybe have to go for a tetanus shot.

Anthony's acne lit up like Rudolph's nose as what little color there was in his face drained. "But—"

Bruce tied off the main sheet and stood, keeping one hand on the tiller, then stepped past Anthony toward the front of the boat. He pushed the tiller into the boy's hand, released it before the youth could argue. The kid was 13—by 13 Bruce had been sailing alone for 4 years, the last two on the ocean. "Nothing to it, Anthony. You can handle it. There you go…."

The boy's knuckles whitened as they gripped the tiller, but he kept the boat on a good heading, and even came up again after a sudden gust caused him to fall off. After a few minutes, he seemed to relax, and Bruce patted him on the back, careful not to give too hearty a shove. "You're a sailor now, Anthony. Not many kids can say that any-more. But you are a sailor." The boy flashed his braces at Bruce, even took one hand off the tiller to push his glasses back up his nose.

They approached the shore and, with prodding from Bruce, Anthony brought them about. It was a tentative effort, which made the sail flap and the boat stall mid-turn, but eventually the bow rounded and the sail refilled, and they skimmed across the water on a near reach toward the opposite shore. They sailed in silence for a few minutes, the boy now grinning widely and occasionally even breathing. He surprised Bruce with a question. "Do you have any, like, souvenirs or anything?"

"What do you mean by souvenirs?"

"Well, my dad was in the war in Vietnam, and he has all this old stuff he brought back, like an old hand grenade and a machete and even a compass he took off a dead Charlie." The boy seemed more excited by the compass than by the weapons, but at least he was talking about something his dad had shared with him. Again, finding some middle ground.

Bruce's grandfather, who fought in World War II, kept some dog tags he took off a dead German officer. But Bruce had nothing like that. "You know, Anthony, that's an interesting question. Your father has souvenirs because he fought in a war. It wasn't a very popular war, but he served his country just the same. Same as my grandfather, who fought in World War II."

Bruce looked east to the granite obelisk—the Bunker Hill Monument—that rose in the distance. "My generation has never had to fight in any wars. In a way, that's good—only a few of us have had to go off and get killed, mostly the ones who signed up for Kuwait or Iraq or Afghanistan. But for the most part we've had it pretty easy." He smiled, shrugged. "I guess you could say my generation is the sports memorabilia generation—we collect autographed baseballs."

The boy listened, processed this for a few seconds. "I don't mean anything bad by it, but, I mean, it doesn't sound very ... I guess ... impressive."

Bruce nodded. For some reason, he thought about the steely resolve in Abraham's wolf-gray eyes. Something he once heard the comedian Lily Tomlin say: *I've always wanted to be somebody, but I see now I should have been more specific.* He envied the old man's fervor.

"You're right, Anthony. We've never really had to fight for anything. We're not a particularly impressive generation."

*   *   *

Monique Goulston sipped on her martini, then took a long drag on her cigarette, slowly letting the smoke escape between her lips. Haze filled the corner booth of the Chinese restaurant, wafted out over the high, red-cushioned seat backs and enveloped the nearby tables. The other diners might complain, but the hostess would simply 'yes' them and allow Monique to finish her smoke. The arrangement worked for both of them: Monique got the private, secluded booth she needed, and the underpaid hostess got a $50 bill for holding it for her.

Speaking of arrangements that worked for both of them, Russell—Senator Erickson to the rest of the free world, excepting his wife waiting for him someplace in the Virginia suburbs—slipped through the side door adjacent to the booth and slid onto the bench opposite her. He smiled at her, more of a leer really. She smiled back, rubbed his ankle with her foot, wondered why he risked so much to have an affair with her....

Power, for one thing. Just as New York loved sophistication, and Los Angeles fame, and Las Vegas money, Washington got off on power. And she had it. Hers was not the normal, the-Senator-will-see-you-now power. Hers was scary, intimidating, rally-the-anarchists-and-riot-in-the-streets kind of power. Dangerous power, to match her appearance. Which was the other reason the Senator lusted for her. A lover once confided that her darkened eyes and untamed hair made her look almost theatrical, like an actress portraying some jungle animal in a Broadway production. The Senator enjoyed taking a walk on the wild side....

He slipped a gift box across the table to her. A small piece of jewelry. No doubt something his secretary picked out at a department store during her lunch break. She ran her foot higher up his leg. "I'll take the gift receipt, too—sometimes your secretary's taste isn't exactly my style." If he insisted on treating this like a business transaction, so would she. He nodded, dug the receipt out of his wallet, dropped it on the table in front of her.

He smiled at her, winked, arched his eyes toward the door. *Don't write when you can talk; don't talk when you can wink.* She called the waitress over. "We'll take our meal to go."

His driver waited in front of the restaurant, double-parked on the narrow side street near Capital Hill that hosted a small cluster of Chinese restaurants. Monique waited in the restaurant a few seconds, left another $50 bill as a tip for the waitress, then walked to her black Ford Mustang parked around the corner on Massachusetts Avenue.

The car offered something to all the special-interest groups that comprised Monique's network of allies—for the Greenies, it offered fuel efficiency; for the unions, a 'Made in the U.S.A.' stamp; for the Vegans, upholstered seats rather than leather. She freely lent it to her staff members, pleasing the Socialists. And a series of speeding tickets kept her popular with the anarchists....

She took a shortcut to her apartment on Capitol Hill, cutting through one of the city's dilapidated neighborhoods in the Northeast section of the city. Shattered windows, drug-dealers, gangs of kids—how could this country purport to lead the world when it could not even care for its citizens living in the shadow of the Capitol building? That's what happened when you allowed Capitol Hill to become Capitalism Hill. Everything was for sale, even the people.

At a corner, a young black woman—probably still a teenager, in fact—pushed a baby carriage. Monique pulled over, rolled down her window. "Here, honey, take this." She held the gift box out the window. "It's okay, take it. And here's the receipt. If you don't like it, you can change it for something you like better."

She and the Senator met ten minutes later at her apartment. She could easily have afforded someplace glitzier, and in fact did own a beach house on the Maryland shore, but she wanted to maintain her image as being a champion of the working class. Just as importantly, the apartment, comprising the first floor of a brick row house, had a private entrance shielded by shrubs and a fence where her lovers could enter and leave without being seen.

"Can I pour you a drink?"

"Yes. Scotch on the rocks."

She poured the drink, led him by the hand to a bedroom. She used a second, adjoining bedroom for her clothes and personal belongings, and also for when she just wanted to sleep. In this room, she entertained men. And occasionally women. He pulled aside the beads hanging from the ceiling, sat on the bed, removed his shoes. She lit a couple of incense candles and put on a classical CD; she also considered getting some lotions and rubbing him down, but she did not want to work that hard, and she did not want to have to change the sheets. He would be satisfied with a quick screw, and then she could get to work.

She knelt on the floor in front of him, removed his pants and boxers, caressed his member until it firmed up. He sucked loudly on his drink, cuing her, then clinked the ice cubes around the glass. With her free hand, she removed her panties and her shoes. As his breathing quickened, she pushed him back on the bed and mounted him from above, then reached for his free hand and guided it up under her shirt. He groped aimlessly for a few seconds, then the arm flopped to his side.

She let her eyelids half-close and peered at him through her lashes. Blurred, he was as handsome as he appeared on television— tanned, square-jawed, blue-eyed. But she knew better. The drinking and carousing had taken its toll: The blue eyes were often blood-shot, the classic nose often red-veined, the tanned skin often sprayed-on. Even the erection itself was often Viagra-ed. The years never seemed to wear well on the frat boys.

She moved with him for a few more minutes until he thrust into her, panting. He would, as always, go straight for the shower to wash her smell off him before returning to his wife. And she would, as always, go straight for his laptop.

She rolled off him, feigned exhausted satisfaction. He cleared his throat, patted her on the head and swung his legs onto the floor. He gathered his clothes and shuffled into the bathroom.

Monique threw on a bathrobe, listened at the door for the sound of him stepping into the shower. Then she grabbed his laptop from his briefcase, flipped it open on the bed. While it booted-up, she pulled a compact disc from her purse. The Senator—or, more likely, his staff—knew enough to restrict access to the computer by requiring a password. Unfortunately for him, he had not known enough to hide the password from Monique. She typed 'Senator007,' smiled at the irony of her underwhelming lover associating himself with the fictional ladies' man.

She opened his desktop, found the email folders, slipped the disk in. The hard drive whirred and hummed for a few seconds. It coughed when it was finished, and then the screen went blank. Just like the Senator.

*   *   *

The Senator had been gone for almost an hour. During that time Monique read through half the emails she had taken from his laptop—nothing particularly interesting so far, just the normal ugliness of large corporations buying votes and dictating law and policy at the expense of the people. Churchill said that democracy was a terrible form of government, except when compared to all the others. In the unlikely event her anarchist friends succeeded in bringing down the government, she would find out if Churchill was correct.

She picked at the Chinese food while she read. She did not mind eating alone, and in fact enjoyed the solitude at the end of a frenzied week. She continued scrolling, stopped when she read the same message for the third time. What was bothering her? She rummaged around her subconscious, searching for the burr on her brain. Russell, she decided. More to the point, the way he just flopped there and did nothing, treating her like some office floozy who was just happy to soil her panties with his sperm so she could sell them on eBay. A few years ago a book came out saying that JFK, because of his bad back, always stayed still and flat on the floor while his mistresses mounted him. Now every elected official in Washington believed it his Constitutional right to be serviced from above. She had come to expect mediocrity from Russell in bed. But he no longer even made an effort. Yet, for the near future, she would continue to service Senator Sedentary. She needed access to his laptop, and the only way to get it was through his, well, lap top.

She grabbed a Diet Pepsi from the fridge, returned to the Senator's emails. Halfway through a yawn, she hit gold: A message from a senior staffer, summarizing a recent security briefing: "Decision final. Harvard summit in October not designated NSSE." NSSE—in Monique's world, a four-letter compilation worse than any curse or vulgarity: National Special Security Event. The feds gave an NSSE designation to any event worth protesting, which meant that hundreds of Gestapo-like Secret Service agents, thousands of local police, and millions of federal dollars were allocated to the task of stifling free speech in the name of providing security. If a member of her group so much as double-parked, the police clubbed him over the head and dragged him off to jail.

But even Washington could not print money indefinitely. It was becoming too expensive to use the NSSE designation liberally, and the Harvard trade summit—though likely to attract foreign dignitaries and a sizable number of attendees—had, she now knew, just missed the cut. Which meant Monique finally could unleash her dogs. And when they bit, the world would be watching.

CHAPTER 4

[July]

Shelby stepped out of the lobby of her office tower, spotted Bruce leaning against a bike rack, stretching his quads. She admired him for a few seconds. He looked like one of those guys you saw in the old cigarette ads—tall, rugged, chiseled. No surprise all the secretaries on their lunch breaks were staring at him. And now glaring at her as she pinched his buttocks to announce her arrival. *Shelby,* her mother's voice chastised her, *that is not very lady-like!* She raised herself to kiss him as he turned toward her, lingered against him for an extra second, flicked her tongue against his teeth playfully. *That any better, Mom?*

Their summer lunchtime routine was that they would run a few miles—snaking their way through the Financial District and Boston Common—and then grab a pretzel and some lemonade for a quick lunch on the Swan Boats in the Public Garden. She would shower in her office, pull her hair into a bun, and be back at her desk within an hour. He would continue home for a shower, then return to his duties either protecting museums from thieves or teaching kids to steal wind.

At least that was the plan. Today might take a bit longer.

She stretched, then they broke into a jog. After a mile of small-talk, she took a deep breath. "So, I've made a decision," she announced. The castration debacle took place almost a week ago; she had been dodging her uncle's daily calls since Tuesday.

"We get to have those little hot dogs for an appetizer?"

Funny how the issues that seemed important only a week ago no longer mattered. "It does sort of involve wieners, but that's not it. I'm not going to help my uncle."

Bruce was silent for a few strides. "Really?"

"Really. What he's doing is wrong. It's immoral, and it's misguided."

"I'm listening." His tone told her he was trying to stay calm, trying to hear her out. And also that he disagreed with her decision.

"I just can't accept vigilante justice." There were times in history, when government was inept or corrupt, when citizens had the right to take the law into their own hands. But this was not happening here. "They should have reported Neary to the authorities." They ran along the red-bricked Freedom Trail, past the Granary Burial Ground where Paul Revere and Samuel Adams were buried. She could use their help. Then again, maybe they would not agree with her—they were not averse to taking justice into their own hands themselves. "That's how this country works. We have laws, and everyone is subject to them." It was not perfect, but for the most part it worked.

"Okay, I hear where you're coming from when you say it's immoral. So tell me why it's misguided."

She wiped the sweat off her forehead. "Because this whole Jewish paranoia thing has got to end. Pretty much everyone responsible for the Holocaust is already dead. It's time to stop reliving it."

"You know, I've been reading up on Jewish history—"

"No, I didn't know." Her mother's voice again: *What a nice boy.* Mom seemed to be a constant ever since the letter from the grave, almost as if the missive had opened a previously-clogged channel.

He turned to her, smiled. "I figure that my children are going to be Jewish, so it might be a good idea if I wasn't so ignorant."

She squeezed his hand as they ran. "Thanks. That's sweet."

"Well, I may be sweet, but I still disagree with you. Your uncle isn't just reliving the Holocaust, he's reliving hundreds of years of Jewish history. He's connecting the dots of modern history, from the

Crusades to the Spanish Inquisition to the Russian pogroms to the Holocaust and a bunch more in between. He wants to make sure there's not another dot."

Their course took them through the inner parts of the large park, away from the bustle and traffic of the street. A few homeless men gathered around a bench were sharing the contents of a brown paper bag. Bruce continued. "It's like when the Europeans came here. If the Native American tribes united and defended themselves when they had the chance, they might never have been decimated."

So that was it—Bruce drew a parallel between Jewish and Native American persecution by the Europeans. Ever since he discovered he was one-eighth Wampanoag, he had become particularly sensitive to the treatment of minority groups. Shelby rubbed the sweat off her forehead with the sleeve of her t-shirt. She would have to be careful here. "But nobody's killing the Jews in America now. Nobody ever has. So Abraham and his gang running around castrating everyone they don't like is exactly the wrong approach. They're starting a war that otherwise wouldn't exist."

"You're right, nobody's killing Jews in America. Yet. But his point is that there's a lot of anti-Semitism in this country. It's the same here as it was in Germany in the early 1930s—the Jews were part of society, part of government, even part of the ruling elite. Nobody in Germany in 1930 would have thought someone like Hitler could come along and march the Jews off to the gas chambers. Discrimination, yes. Persecution, maybe. But not genocide."

"Come on, Bruce. That's not going to happen here. I mean, we have the Constitution, the Bill of Rights—"

He picked up the pace. She had to practically sprint to keep up. He continued, his breathing heavier but not strained. "Tell that to the Japanese-Americans who got stuck in internment camps in World War II. Or the Arabs being held at Guantanamo now. All of a sudden it became really convenient to just set the Constitution aside for a little while. Look, I'm not saying there's going to be another Holocaust, but you can't ignore the reality that minority groups in this country—in every country—sometimes get screwed. All these laws are great, until some politician or judge decides to ignore them. That's why I like the idea of people like your uncle watching my back."

"Well, I don't want my kids growing up in a world like that."

"And I don't want mine dying in it," he snapped.

This was getting more heated than she had expected. "Look, Bruce, you're overstating your case." She gasped out the words. "I'm not going to try to defend it, but there's a big difference between holding a few thousand Japanese-Americans in internment camps and murdering six million Jews."

"Only in degree. We had no right to separate the Japanese-Americans from their families, to take their homes and their businesses. I wouldn't have blamed the Japanese at all if they fought back. Just like the Jews and the Native Americans and the African slaves should have fought back. And just like your uncle is doing now."

Shelby sprinted a few strides, reached ahead, grabbed Bruce's elbow. He took a few steps before turning toward her; she shook her head slowly without breaking stride. "No, Bruce. Abraham's wrong. Without our laws, we're no better than animals."

Bruce refused to bend. "Speaking of animals, maybe someday Neary would have taken a baseball bat to the head of my kid, *our kid*, and I'm thinking thank God your uncle got to him first."

Shelby began to respond, but she could not fill her lungs with enough oxygen to continue the conversation. She stopped mid-stride, waited for him to do the same and then come back a few steps to face her. It gave her a second to gather her thoughts. And for her frustration to rise. "And I'm thinking maybe Neary was just some stupid, misguided kid going through a phase. Until my uncle turned him into an angry punk hell-bent on taking revenge on every Jew he can find."

*   *   *

Monique Goulston strolled east down Pennsylvania Avenue, away from the white dome of the Capitol building, past the shops and restaurants and taverns that fringed Capitol Hill. The July sun beat down on her black blouse; sweat droplets ran down her back, pooled along the waistband of her skirt. A couple of generations ago, before the advent of air conditioning, foreign governments designated the city—built on a swamp—as a hardship post for the diplomatic corps because of the oppressive humidity. Managua, Calcutta, Washington, D.C. Good company.

"Fuck, it's hot," she said. Sometimes this whole dressing in black thing was a drag....

She looked at her watch. Twenty past noon. Already 20 minutes late. She slowed her pace, tried to walk in the splotches of shade produced by the occasional sidewalk tree or shop awning. Maybe her cousin Burt would decide not to wait for her. Not likely—how else could Burt the Nerd possibly keep himself busy in Washington?

Actually, he probably had plenty of business in D.C. Somehow the little runt that nobody would play with, the teenager who could not get a date for his prom, ended up owning a whole strip of hot night clubs in Boston. And he published a weekly newspaper focused on arts and entertainment news, which meant that the dweeb who did not know the first thing about style or cool or trendy ended up pretty much deciding which restaurant or gallery or theater production would be hot and which would flop.

But he was still a nerd.

And he would wait for her, no matter what. As much as she had tried to avoid him in high school, he followed her around their Cleveland suburb, a barnacle on her otherwise fashion-plated hull. It was the one thing, the only thing, he had going for him as a kid— Burt Ring was Monique Goulston's cousin.

"Hey, Cuz!" The schmuck waited out in front of the restaurant, waving two stumpy arms at her in the summer heat, showing the world his sweaty armpits. And announcing that they were related.

She raised a hand to acknowledge him, waited until she stood under the restaurant awning before responding. "Easy, boy. Calm down. No need to hump me here on the sidewalk." She guided him into the diner, waved her hand in front of her face in a failed attempt to disperse the greasy air that hung like a fog in the low-ceilinged room. Her hair would smell like onion rings all day.

She spent her life fighting for workers' rights; she sometimes liked to drink in smoky dive bars; she even liked a good, rough fuck once in a while from a hard-bodied construction worker or fireman. But she made it a rule not to share meals with the proletariat. Too much grease, too many burps. Yet she insisted on meeting at the diner because it ensured she would not be spotted by anyone she knew.

She found a booth in the back. A couple of flies buzzed around some ketchup splattered on the off-white tabletop; Monique waved them away and wiped down the table with a wad of thin paper napkins. The back of her knees stuck to the cushioned vinyl seat as she shifted her body. The fan above them blew hot, hazy air around the room. Despite her mood, she remembered an old Woody Allen joke, figured it was better than chatting with Burt about the weather. "I wonder if, when they open the freezer, the two fronts will meet and it'll start raining in the kitchen."

Burt grinned at her, that same crooked, brown-toothed grin that he had as a kid. His parents spent a ton of money on braces, but they could not change the fact that only half his mouth moved when he smiled. And years of pipe smoking and coffee drinking turned his teeth the color of, well, coffee and tobacco. "Hey, Burt, you really should get your teeth whitened. You look like something out of a Stephen King movie."

He shrugged. "Who's got the time? I had them done before the wedding, but that was three years ago."

Ah, yes, the wedding. All of Boston's cultural elite were in attendance. "And how is the beautiful Gabriella Garcia-Ring?" She rolled her r's as she spoke the name.

"She's great, really great." He sighed. "Here's a picture of her." He pulled out his cell phone, pushed a button, displayed his wife for her to see.

"Nice, Burt. Are you also wearing a locket with a strand of her hair?"

He ignored the jab. "You know she's running for State Senate, right? The incumbent just dropped out, so she jumped in."

"Yeah, I got your email. She going to win?"

"It looks pretty good. She should get the Hispanic vote, of

course, and I have a lot of favors I can call in. And she's sharp and polished and—"

"And way too hot for you."

He grinned again. "Yeah, there's that too."

Somehow it did not seem fair that Burt, who looked like a bruised, blotchy, over-sized pear, was married and she was not. "So, when she wins are you guys going to help me bring down the government from within?"

He sat back, offered another crooked, colored smirk. "Bring it down? No. But you know we wouldn't mind seeing it veer to the left. In Gabriella's case, way to the left."

She nodded. Nerd or not, he was an influential publisher, possibly a useful tool in her own crusade. "To the left, to the right, what difference does it make? You think Kerry or Gore would have been any different than Bush? There is no real left in this country—both parties are controlled by big business. Shit, Clinton signed NAFTA. People were upset he fucked Monica, but he really was screwing the workers. With Democrats like that, who needs Republicans...."

"Yeah, the NAFTA thing wasn't his best moment."

"Please—it wasn't just that. The bottom line is that the Democrats are no better than the Republicans when it comes to workers' rights, or the environment, or human rights, or any of the other issues they are supposed to be championing. In the end they won't do anything because they can't risk losing support from the multinationals. It's the only way they can afford to compete at election time."

"So your solution is to riot in the streets—"

"No, Burt, that is not my solution." The little shit was toying with her. "My solution is to stop letting big business make law and policy for this country. There's a lot of groups who happen to agree with me, including the anarchists. But that doesn't make me one, any more than it makes you a Communist just because some of your readers are."

He shrugged. "My relationship with my readers is a passive one. You actively ally yourself with the anarchists every time you organize one of those demonstrations of yours. They turn over a car, or torch a building, or beat up a cop, you have to take some responsibility for it."

"Bullshit I do. These people have been disenfranchised—they have just as much right to civil disobedience as the Colonists who fought the British. What they're doing is no different than the Boston Tea Party."

"Interesting analogy. So are you saying you want to overthrow the government?"

"No, Burt. What I'm really hoping for is that somebody cloned Nixon so we can put him back in power. Stop asking stupid questions. You're supposed to be a journalist."

He let the attack sail by. Years of being teased and mocked had, apparently, hardened him. The waitress came, took their orders. Burt leaned forward in his seat, rested his elbows on the table. "Anyway, one of the reasons I came down here is that I wanted to make a proposition."

He eyed her expectantly, waiting for her to respond. She stared back at him, disinterested, sipped Diet Coke from a straw as if his last sentence had never been spoken. Finally, realizing she had refused his bait, he continued. "Okay. Here it is: We have good relations with the Hispanic community, of course. And I have good connections with a lot of the suburban liberal voters—"

She interrupted. "We call them Volvo Democrats. They think just because they recycle and watch public television they're doing their part to change society."

He shrugged, continued. "But we don't really have any connections to the far left groups, the people at UMass-Boston and in Cambridge. If we could get them to support Gabriella, that would ensure the election."

She slurped soda through her straw. Nobody glared—at least that was one good thing about diners. "And you want me to put out the word."

"I do."

She doubted it would do any good—radical groups showed up at demonstrations she organized because it was in their best interests to do so. She had very little control of them beyond that. Not that Burt needed to know that; the more valuable he thought the favor she did for him, the higher the price he would pay for it. "I know a bunch of activists up in Boston I could contact. What's in it for me?"

"You could use my help in October."

Nobody was supposed to know about that. Yet. "October?"

He winked, an infuriatingly exaggerated gesture in which he held his eye closed an extra beat. Monique resisted reaching across the table and yanking his eyelid open by the lashes. He leaned toward her and spoke in a conspiratorial voice. "Oh, nothing. Just a world economic summit up at Harvard that doesn't have a top security designation."

She tried to remain impassive. "So?"

"Look, Monique, I may not be as plugged-in as you are, but I run with a pretty liberal crowd. I hear things—at the clubs, from my reporters, whatever. And what I'm hearing is that the next big happening is up in Boston in October."

The good news was that the event already had a buzz. The bad news was that the buzz arrived three months early—early buzzes often got so loud they turned into alarms. Hopefully things would quiet down now that the college kids had dispersed for the summer. Whatever the case, she would not deny it to Burt. If she pissed him off by lying to him, he might blow the whistle and ruin the whole event. "You're hearing correctly."

He grinned. This time with French fry debris in his teeth. "I didn't think it would be so easy to break you."

"Maybe you should go work for the CIA. You said you could help. How?"

"Well, first of all, I can promise not to let the cat out of the bag."

"And I can promise not to put the word out that Gabriella put her way through college giving blowjobs at the Park Plaza Hotel." She had learned that juicy—but until now, useless—tidbit from a drunk friend of Gabriella's at the after-hours party at Burt and Gabriella's wedding. The bartender was a hot Aussie, and Monique bedded him after drinking the other lonely hearts under the table. Unfortunately, it had not been worth the effort, or the hangover—the stud from Down Under had been under-endowed. Now, at last, she had a pay-off for the next morning's hangover. "Your suburban housewife friends will have a ball with that one."

"Mutually Assured Destruction—I drop a nuke on you, you return the favor. How very Cold War-ish of you."

Burt surprised Monique by being so matter-of-fact. Either he thought she was making it up, or he heard the story of Gabriella's entrepreneurial exploits himself and somehow came to grips with it. Maybe in a perverse way he even liked the idea of getting for free what other men had paid for. She put her sandwich down, leaned forward. "Look, Burt, don't fuck with me. You're out of your league. Way out. You asked for my help, and you promised something in return. Now what is it."

He folded his arms in front of his body, turned sideways in his chair. Monique had studied body-language, knew the movements were a sign of Burt's discomfort. He had lost. "Actually, speaking of Gabriella, this was all her idea. There's a bit of revolutionary in her— she admires what you're doing."

Monique snorted. "Great. Another chicken-shit radical, just what we need. Tell her to get off her ass and come march with us."

Burt shrugged. "She thought you might want to use *The Alternative* as a way to communicate with the demonstrators. I imagine you use email, or post messages on a website. Some of the demonstrators will have laptops, but not all. But *The Alternative* is available all across the city. You could encode messages in it, then tell people what to look for when they got to Boston."

She sat back. Not a bad proposal. Communication was usually a logistical nightmare. "And why should I trust you?"

That crooked, ugly, half-grin again. "Well, I pretty much support what you're doing. But more importantly, I know you'd kick my ass if I screwed you."

*   *   *

Shelby pulled Bruce along, past the peanut vendors and sausage stands and ticket scalpers. "Come *on*. I don't want to miss the first pitch."

He laughed. "No, can't have that."

She yanked him. "Come *on*." Three days had passed since their argument in the park about helping her uncle. They had not talked about it since, but the shadow of the disagreement still hung over them. Some light-hearted fun might help reconnect them.

They fought through the crowd on Brookline Avenue, turned left onto Lansdowne Street and approached a group of people lined up along the backside of the Green Monster, the famous Fenway Park left field wall.

"What are we doing here?" Bruce asked. "This is the bleachers entrance."

"I know. Please don't be upset. Do you mind if we sit in the bleachers today?"

"Whatever," he shrugged.

She kissed him quickly, turned to a young boy and his father standing near the back of the line. "Excuse me. I have a strange request. We have two tickets for those luxury seats behind home plate—but I really don't want to be in the shade today. Do you have any interest in trading your tickets for ours?"

The father eyed her suspiciously; luxury box seats were nearly impossible to get, short of buying a share of the team. Shelby nodded in understanding, pulled out her wallet. "Look, here are the tickets. See, they're legit. And here's my business card; I'm a lawyer, for what that's worth. And here's my driver's license—see, today's my birthday, which is why we're here."

The father looked at his son, shrugged. "All right, lady. We'll trade. I guess if you were going to scam somebody, you wouldn't pick a little kid going to his first game, right?"

Shelby did a little hop in celebration, then pulled Bruce through the gate. "I'm sorry, I know you worked hard to get those tickets. But I don't want to spend the afternoon with a bunch of suits. I spend all week with those people. I want to sit in the bleachers, in the sun, eating cold hot dogs and drinking warm soda."

Actually, she really wanted a beer, even a watered-down one. But she was a week late on her period. The news did not surprise her—at 41, she did not want to wait much longer to have children, so they stopped using birth control right after their engagement. So no beer.

Maybe she should skip the hot dog also—who knew how many body parts had been deformed by those things....

Bruce shook his head. "Great. Sounds like fun. Maybe we can ask someone to spill something on us."

They grabbed some popcorn and bottled water. Normally, she would have told Bruce about her late period. Or at least she imagined she would have, had the possibility of him fathering her child ever come up before. But they needed to resolve this rift on their own, not simply eclipse it by the news of a baby. They found their seats, deep in right-center field behind the Red Sox bullpen, and settled in. Shelby took Bruce's hand, pulled it onto her lap and held it in both of hers. Her ring glistened in the afternoon sunlight. "Made it. Just in time for the National Anthem."

Bruce rolled his eyes. "That's always fun. Half the time the celebrity they parade out to sing can't remember the words. Or can't hit the notes."

The words poured out of her before she could stop them. "My father could. He used to stand, his hand on his heart, and belt it out. Every time I hear it I think of him."

The moisture pooled in her eyes; she tried to sniffle it away. Could be melancholy, could be residual sadness from their fight, could even be hormones. Bruce gently turned her chin toward him and kissed a tear from her eye. The gesture only served to sadden her further—nobody had ever cherished her the way Bruce did. Her previous boyfriends had admired her, swooned for her, doted on her, lusted after her. But cherish was different—it was about her, not him; about her worth, not his needs. She leaned her head against his shoulder, remembered a time when, as a girl, her father brought her to Fenway for her first Red Sox game and she leaned against his shoulder in much the same way. Maybe somebody *had* cherished her in that way before, so many years ago. But those people were now gone. Could she bear the loss again?

She tried to lighten the mood. "Of course, my father also was the one who used to ask why people sang *Take Me Out to the Ballgame* when they were already there. Every game, seventh inning, he'd ask the same question. Without fail."

They stood for the National Anthem, then sat for the first inning, but her thoughts were on her family—her parents now gone, her baby perhaps to come. Action on the field jarred her from her introspection. But not baseball action. Some drunk had jumped the fence and was running naked through the outfield, a team of security guards in pursuit. He zigged and zagged, his privates flopping back and forth, then reversed course as the crowd cheered him on, and finally ran out of gas. Six guys in blue uniforms lifted him by his arms and legs, their hands careful to avoid touching anything else, and hauled him away.

She sighed. Time to approach the third rail. "Every time I see something like that now, I think of what my uncle said about a terrorist attack. There's 35,000 people here—what if that guy had a vial of nerve gas or anthrax or something?"

Bruce smiled. "Where would he be hiding it?"

She could not help but laugh. "All right, so he's a bad example." Bruce would not engage this topic until he knew she wanted to go there herself, especially on her birthday. "But it would not be that tough to come into the park with some kind of weapon; all they really care about is that you don't bring in any beer. Somebody could take out half the Red Sox team with a bomb or something. Can you imagine the effect it would have around New England? Talk about attacking a shrine—"

Bruce kept things light. "Wow, that's some curse you've got here. Buckner muffs the grounder, Grady Little leaves Pedro in the game, the security guard confiscates the beer bottle but misses the plastic explosives…."

She smiled again. "The curse is gone. Kaput. See that banner out there? The one that says World Champions? That proves it."

"Just one?" Bruce raised an index finger to make his point. "Even a broken clock is right twice a day." She elbowed him in the ribs. "Anyway," he continued, "you're right—if a terrorist wants to come into Fenway Park and wipe out a few hundred, or even a few thousand, people, he could. That's what makes your uncle's concerns so … concerning. I mean, there are hundreds of targets just here in Boston, and they'd all be easy to hit."

He began to list them. "Think about it—500,000 people packed onto the Esplanade for the July 4th fireworks, or thousands of people lining the streets for the Boston Marathon, or all those Ivy Leaguers picnicking on *fois gras* at the Head of the Charles Regatta—"

"Sitting ducks eating duck, huh?"

Smiling, he continued. "Not to mention the every-day targets like bridges and tunnels." Her mind raced: And subways and hospitals and beaches and universities and chemical factories and nuclear power plants.... "It's impossible to protect them all, or even any one of them. If a terrorist wants to get us, the only way to stop him is to keep him out of the country or else stop him before he gets started. There's just no way to defend every target."

"That's a depressing analysis."

Bruce shrugged. "I'm just being realistic."

"If you're right, it means that if the terrorists infiltrate Monique's group, there'd be no way to stop them."

"Exactly." He took her hand, looked into her eyes. "Look. We clearly disagree on how your uncle should deal with the Nearys of the world. That may just have to be one of those issues where we agree to disagree." As she suspected, he had been thinking a lot about this as well. "But I think we were missing the point the other day during our run. This isn't about Neary. This is about stopping terrorists. Your uncle may have ulterior motives, and you may not agree with his tactics, but the cause itself is just. That's why I think you should help him, why we should help him. Together."

On the one hand, she recognized Bruce's argument for what it was—he took the disagreement between them and marginalized it by pointing out the many things, the many important things, they agreed on. The dispute between them remained, but now a larger accord dwarfed it. It was a classic negotiation ploy, and it usually worked because common sense and common ground tended to carry the day. On a less cynical level, she also recognized it as Bruce's attempt to bridge the gulf between them. Essentially he was saying that, despite their disagreement on her uncle's vigilantism, he was committed to their relationship, was committed to respecting her values and beliefs without trying to alter them.

In the end, what more could she really ask from her spouse? "And you think we can help him on just this one thing, and not get caught up in all his other sick stuff?"

"Yeah, I do. You spy on Monique, and that's it. No castrations. I promise. You don't even have to clip your toe-nails if you don't want to."

She tried to keep from smiling, but failed. Maybe this is what it meant to be partnered for life: Sometimes you backed down even when you knew you were right.

That was it, then. "All right, I'll help my psycho uncle."

Bruce smiled. "Great. I'll go tell him—he's down there in the runway with a scalpel, helping the police deal with the naked guy."

She elbowed him again, then nestled against him. In the morning she would tell him about her late period, then go buy a pregnancy test kit.

"Before we get off the subject, have you heard from Monique?"

Shelby started to answer, then hesitated. Monique was her client, and the rules were clear: Conversations between an attorney and her client were confidential, same as those with a doctor or clergyman. A strange world it must have been, generations ago, when priests and lawyers were so revered and trusted that whole areas of the law were carved out in recognition of their elevated standing in society....

She sighed. "Yeah, she called." If she was going to spy on Monique, and try to stop a terrorist attack, she needed Bruce's help. Which illustrated the problem with breaking the rules: It quickly became a slippery slope. And the irony of it all was that she was violating the privilege with Monique, who had done nothing wrong, and yet had honored it with Abraham, who had castrated a man in a cargo van. "She's flying up here next week to scout things out."

"What kinds of things?"

"I really don't know. I didn't want to seem too pushy—I'm just supposed to be her lawyer. But she probably wants to see where the conference events are going to be held, where the delegates are staying, that kind of stuff. Then she can plan the demonstrations."

"You should invite her to stay with us."

"Seriously, do you really want her staying with us?"

"No," he exhaled, "not at all. I don't think we'd get along all that well, from what you've told me about her. And she probably doesn't really want to stay with us either, especially when she can afford to stay in some fancy hotel. But if she really is part of the anarchy movement, she must know she's probably being watched, and she's less likely to draw attention to herself if she makes the whole visit look like a trip to see an old friend rather than a trip to plan a street riot."

"Sounds like a fun time. She doesn't want to stay with us, and we don't want to have her."

He took a sip from his beer, his eyes smiling at her over the rim of the cup. "Did I mention I have to work late that whole week?"

*   *   *

They made love after the Red Sox game—the kind of desperate, frantic coupling that always seemed to follow rough patches in a relationship. She had a friend once—Monique, in fact—who used to pick fights with boyfriends just so she could have "make-up sex" afterwards.

Bruce's lovemaking had been, as always, passionate and intense. He seemed to want to soak her up with all his senses, as if the mere tactile coupling of their bodies was insufficient. He needed to see her, taste her, smell her, hear her. When she asked once about this desire for multi-sensory stimulation, he responded that it had nothing to do with stimulation. His words, in a moment as intimate as anything she had ever experienced, still echoed in her ears. "It's just that I need to be sure it's really you, that you're really here with me. I missed you for so long, and I dreamed of you so often, that I still have trouble believing we're together."

It was classic Bruce—incredible intensity and passion and energy and fire wrapped around a scared, lonely boy. He was raised by a disinterested father and a hostile stepmother, with only a grandfather to bond with. The resulting adult was a loner, trusting little and relying on even less. But those things he did trust, those things he did rely on, he clung to with a desperate intensity. Such as Shelby. And those things he did not trust, those things that had let him down in the past, he rejected completely. Such as the rule of law.

Which is why she woke up this morning with the acute, and not particularly welcome, realization that her plan for the day—first, tell Bruce about her late period; second, buy a pregnancy test kit; third, pee onto a plastic strip with a stopwatch at the ready—would have to wait.

Yesterday's conversation had resolved how to deal with the Abraham dilemma—she would help him by spying on Monique. But it only served to mask the fundamental conflict in the Shelby/Bruce relationship: She devoted her professional life to upholding the law, while he disdained it. Maybe it was because the law had killed his grandfather—a silly, warped Cambridge rent control ordinance, perverted by activists, had forced his grandfather first into bankruptcy and then to his grave. Or maybe it was because, as a lawyer, he knew how laws were crafted—like sausage, someone once said, full of all sorts of things you would not want your family exposed to. Or perhaps it was because he saw how unevenly the law was applied. "Laws are like cobwebs," he once observed. "Strong enough to catch the weak, but too weak to catch the strong." He returned from his seven years at sea a changed person, finally at peace with himself. But his disdain for the rule of law remained. With her uncle's prodding, he might cross the line into lawlessness again—not for selfish reasons, but because he refused to let the law stop him from doing what he believed to be right. This bomb had exploded in his life many times before, and it was ticking again. It was bad enough that she was at ground zero, but now that there might be a baby to consider, the equation had totally changed....

It was the one flaw, perhaps the fatal flaw, in the Bruce package— the brilliant, strong, handsome, generous, loving man who had appeared in her life straight out of a Hollywood movie. As an action hero, he would have been ideal. As a boyfriend, he was intoxicating. But as a husband, and more importantly as a father, he just might be fatal. She needed to figure this whole thing out before complicating things with talk of a baby.

CHAPTER 5

Shelby resisted taking the pregnancy test for two days, alternately thrilled by the prospect of starting a family with Bruce and haunted by the thought of bringing a baby into a world in which danger attracted its father with an almost gravitational pull. Not that she really even needed to pee on the strip—she knew her body, and her cycle, and she had little doubt what the test would reveal.

She returned home from work to find a message on her machine from Madame Radminikov. A person hearing the gentle voice for the first time would assume it belonged to a demure woman planning tea or bridge with her friends. "I was hoping we could sit and have a dinner together. I know you are busy, but there are some things I want to discuss with you. I am free any night this week"—she paused here, then filled the silence with a short, ironic laugh—"and any night next week as well."

They met the next evening, a Tuesday, at the Fireplace, a restaurant in Brookline. Madame Radminikov suggested it, surprising Shelby; it was a trendy spot, and best of all, nothing like the men's club masquerading as a steak house where they had eaten, or not eaten, two weeks earlier.

She greeted Shelby by grasping both of Shelby's hands and squeezing them to her chest. Something about the gesture touched Shelby, and she resisted the impulse to pull away. For the second time this week somebody gazed at Shelby with a look of adoration. Bruce's adoration she had grown to accept, though she still wondered at it. But Madame Radminikov had only just met her, and under perverse circumstances at that. Could her affection for Abraham be so strong that it extended to his entire family as well? If so, Madame Radminikov—and, come to think of it, her mother as well—saw something in Abraham that Shelby just plain missed.

They took a table by a large window looking out over Beacon Street. Madame Radminikov wore a black blazer over a red silk blouse. Not overly stylish, but at least feminine, unlike the business suit she wore last time they met.

"They have a nice wine selection here, Shelby. Do you prefer white or red?"

"I'll probably have fish, so white would … actually, I'll just have a seltzer water."

Madame Radminikov raised an eyebrow. "Well, I'll order a carafe of chardonnay in case you change your mind. I'm having the fish, too. I am elbow deep in meat all day—it is a joy to eat fish or pasta. Anything without blood." She ordered the wine, then sat back and studied Shelby. "You know, I met your mother many times over the years. She was a beautiful woman, just as you are. And a kind soul, again just as you are." She sighed. "I know you must miss her. You see, I have the same pain, but the opposite. I lost my daughter when she was eleven. She would be 34 now, almost as old as you."

Shelby did not know how to respond. "How horrible. What happened?"

"We—my husband and Rachel and I—had gone to Israel for a vacation. A bomb went off where we were shopping, in Jerusalem. My husband and Rachel were killed. I walked away. Unharmed, but dead."

Shelby reached across, squeezed the older woman's hand. "I know what you mean, about feeling dead."

Madame Radminikov forced a smile, waved the sadness away. "Nonsense. You are as vibrant, as alive, as anyone I've ever met."

Shelby's face flushed. "You wouldn't have said that if you had met me a couple of years ago."

"Yes, I know, I know. Love is a wonderful thing. Invigorating. And this Bruce of yours, your uncle was very impressed; few men get the better of Barnabus." She lowered her voice, leaned forward. "Also, I saw a picture and he is—what is the expression?—he is a looker." The waiter poured the wine, and Madame Radminikov raised her glass, Shelby her seltzer. "So, *mazel tov!*"

They each drank, then Madame Radminikov continued. "That is one of the reasons I wanted to see you tonight." She held Shelby's eyes. "That, and to personally thank you for agreeing to help us."

Shelby fought back a smile. The butcher—all shoulders and jowls and calluses—was trying to charm her. And succeeding. No doubt Abraham sent her on this mission for that very purpose. Theirs, apparently, was a symbiotic relationship: He was the planner, the intellect who, like some kind of brilliant savant unable to read the simplest human emotion on a face, was unable to navigate his way through the minefield of human relations. She served as his interface with the world.

Shelby shrugged. "Just to be clear, I'm only helping on the terrorist threat. I want nothing to do with the vigilante justice stuff."

Madame Radminikov nodded. "Understood," she smiled. "Anyway, back to Bruce." She folded both hands over her heart. "Your uncle would like to help with your wedding. And since he would not know a soup spoon from a lobster fork, he asked if I would help him to help you." She sat back, her eyes expectant, waiting for Shelby to respond.

"I'll be honest, I'm not sure what to say...." Shelby had always expected to plan her wedding with her mother.

Madame Radminikov seemed to read her thoughts. "Shelby, dear, I don't mean that I want to help you in the way your mother would have helped you. I would never be so presumptuous. But there are things we can help with. For example, have you been able to find a rabbi?"

Shelby used her straw to swirl the ice around her seltzer glass, eyed the carafe of wine. "Actually, no. We were hoping to have a rabbi and priest co-officiate, but the rabbis we talked to won't do it. Apparently they can't do it."

"There, here's an area we can help. Tell me your date, and your uncle will find a rabbi for you."

"What is this, like getting an annulment in the Catholic Church? You have to know the right people?" She tried to smile as she said it, but doubted she succeeded. These kinds of double standards infuriated her. It was like a judge taking a bribe.

Madame Radminikov shrugged, the muscles in her neck visible under her shirt. "I guess it is, sort of. The world being what it is, sometimes practicality takes precedence over piety."

"Practicality over piety," Shelby repeated. "Interesting concept. I was under the impression that one had nothing to do with the other. Perhaps I have been naïve."

"Not naïve as much as idealistic. Sometimes concessions are made to the realities of this world that would not be made in an ideal one."

"Which brings me to my next question: Why would my uncle want to help me marry Bruce? He's not Jewish."

"No, but he doesn't actually practice any other religion—"

Shelby sat up. "How do you know that?"

Madame Radminikov nodded in response to Shelby's unspoken accusation. "Yes, we have been watching him." Which explained how she knew what Bruce looked like. "Despite the admonitions in the Book of Ezra, your uncle feels, and I agree, that it is acceptable for Jews to intermarry, so long as the children are raised Jewish. One of the vulnerabilities of the Jewish people over the centuries has been our isolation from the rest of society—we built no alliances, forged no inter-family bonds. It's no wonder we were so often the target of persecution."

Shelby was still bothered by the thought of her uncle spying on Bruce. "So you guys see me marrying Bruce as just a way to build alliances with mainstream America? Like medieval kings marrying their children off…."

Madame Radminikov, her face reddening, swatted the words back at her. "Let's be clear, Shelby. You chose Bruce; we did not. So don't throw it back at us like we somehow orchestrated your decision…."

Shelby leaned forward, help up her hand in a gesture intended to slow the conversation. "No, of course you didn't. It's just that, I resent the fact that you guys are out there in the shadows, watching me, judging me, spying on me. If my uncle was so concerned about me, who I married and what religion my children would be raised, why didn't he just pick up the phone and call?"

Madame Radminikov sighed, then refilled her wine glass and took a sip. "In some ways your uncle is a very complex person. I have known him practically my whole life, and even I don't really know what he's thinking, what he's feeling. But in other ways he is very simple—his entire life, his every waking moment, is devoted to *Kidon,* which of course includes ensuring the profitability of Continental Casualty. He is like a general preparing for battle. Did you know he has no house, not even an apartment? He just sleeps at the office when he's not on the road." She shook her head. "You sometimes read about these football coaches who do nothing all week except prepare their team to play—they don't see their families, they don't eat right, they sleep at the stadium—"

"I know some lawyers like that, especially when there's a trial they're preparing for. It's like the rest of the world doesn't exist. Total tunnel vision."

"Yes, exactly. That is what your uncle is like, except for him the day of the war or day of the game or day of the trial never comes. I have never seen him rest, or take a vacation, or watch a movie, or even take a leisurely walk. In his free time, when he has any, he studies weather patterns or actuarial tables or seismic activity reports."

Shelby thought about the owner of the Red Sox, an obsessive, reclusive sort who parlayed his childhood fascination with baseball statistics into a wildly successful computer trading program that allowed him to dominate the commodities market. Like her uncle, the man had limited people skills. But, again like her uncle, this afforded him plenty of time to build a multi-billion-dollar company.

Madame Radminikov continued. "Once you understand this about him, the answer to your question becomes simple: Picking up the phone and calling you does nothing to promote his cause. But spying on Bruce to make sure he would not object to you raising your children Jewish directly impacts on the thing he cares most about— the survival of the Jewish people."

"Sounds like he cares about me the way Darwin cared about his finches."

The lady butcher surprised Shelby. "Hmm. The birds that survived were the ones whose beaks evolved to accommodate the kinds of foods they ate. Survival of the fittest. Interesting analogy." Madame Radminikov shrugged. "I'm not going to lie to you. In a sad sort of way, that's true. He sees you as a link to future generations— in fact, he may even want you to take over *Kidon* someday. And he sees Bruce as a good mate for you because he adds fresh, strong, intelligent genes to our gene pool."

"No offense, but I'm thinking Hitler and his whole Superior Race thing."

"Again, in a way you're right. For humans, like for animals, it all always seems to go back to our instinctive need to make sure our genetic line continues." Madame Radminikov clapped her hands together. "Now, enough of that. Your uncle is what he is, and neither of us is going to change him."

They studied their menus for a minute, then placed their orders. The owner strolled over and greeted Madame Radminikov with a hug.

"Jimmy's a nice man," she commented, tilting her head at the owner as he left, "but the real cutie is his friend standing over there at the bar." Shelby followed Madame Radminikov's eyes to a dark-haired man in an Italian-cut suit. "What do you young people call it when a man is handsome—eye sugar?"

Shelby smiled. "Eye candy."

"Well, I'd say he's worth a few visits to the dentist...." They laughed, and Madame Radminikov raised her glass in the direction of the bar. Something about the gesture saddened Shelby—it was one thing to be old and unattractive and lonely. It was another to be all that and still feel your heart race at the sight of a handsome man. It was almost better to be all dried up. At least then you could sleep at night....

"Jimmy's a local kid," Madame Radminikov was saying. "I've known him since he was a boy—I remember his parents dragging him into the butcher shop. I used to give him a knish to keep him quiet. Now he gives me the best table when I come in." She grinned. Shelby wondered how many things there were to grin about in Madame Radminikov's life.

Shelby wanted to shift the conversation back to her uncle. "You mentioned you've known my uncle almost all your life…."

"Since I was a baby. Abraham and my father were in the concentration camp together. I'm sure you've heard the story of how they escaped—"

"Actually, no."

"Oh. I have heard the story so many times I feel I actually lived it. Well, your uncle was only a boy at the time, probably 14 or so. My father was in his early 20s, but already he and the other prisoners looked to Abraham as their leader. They called him The Wolf. There was a ferocity in him that even life in the camps could not tame; some dogs are like that—they could live in your house for years without incident, then you leave the room for a minute and they attack the baby. Even the guards seemed to treat him a bit differently—they weren't exactly afraid of him, but they were careful not to turn their back on him.

"They were in the Dachau concentration camp, and the end of the war was growing near. The Allied troops were approaching. Hitler didn't want the prisoners to be liberated by the Allies, so he gave the order to kill the prisoners before they could be freed. Abraham's plan was to approach the nastiest guard in the whole prison, Holtzman. In fact, this Holtzman is the one who stuffed a hot coal in poor Mr. Clevinsky's mouth…."

The two woman sat in silence for a few seconds, then Madame Radminikov shook her head as if to clear the image from her mind and continued. "Anyway, the other prisoners argued with Abraham, tried to get him to approach one of the less brutal guards. But Abraham refused. 'Listen,' he said. 'Holtzman is cruel because all he cares about is Holtzman. His selfishness is the one thing we can rely on. These other guards are scared and desperate, which makes them irrational. But Holtzman's greed is constant. We can use it against him.'"

"So what happened?"

"Well, he approached Holtzman: 'I have a business proposition for you.' The other prisoners thought that this was where Holtzman would laugh at him, maybe even shoot him. After all, he was a 14-year-old boy who had spent the war in a concentration camp, so what could he possibly have to offer? But Holtzman agreed to listen. 'Before the war, my father, who was a wealthy businessman, was able to fill a safe deposit box in Zurich with gold and jewels. To get into the box, you need the account number, a key, and a signature that matches the signature card.' Abraham pulled out a key ... he had been able to hide it from the Nazis by swallowing it and then defecating it out later ... and a scrap of paper. 'Here is the key and the account number. Meet me at the Union Bank of Switzerland, in Zurich, in exactly one year, at noon. You cannot access the account without my signature, and I cannot access it without the key and account number. If we both survive the war, we can split the treasure equally. If we do not, the treasure will be lost to both of us.' The guard examined the key carefully—it was clearly authentic. And it seemed plausible that the poised and crafty boy standing in front of him came from a wealthy family. Since there was no way to steal Abraham's signature, he agreed, probably figuring he could steal your uncle's half from him at a later time.

"Now, here is where Abraham became truly heroic. 'There is one more condition to our deal,' he announced. 'I will not abandon the other prisoners here. The war is over; the Allied troops are near; there is no reason for more to die. You must agree to let us all escape. When you are on duty tonight, let us run to the woods. The Americans are only a few miles away.' And that's what happened. A few of the prisoners were recaptured, but most made it safely to where the American troops were camped. Your uncle saved close to 40 lives that night. Including my father, and Mr. Clevinsky, and Reb Meyer's father. It is these people, and their descendents, who make up the core of *Kidon*."

Shelby tried to blink away the images of concentration camp life that the story conjured for her. She had seen enough pictures and read enough books to have an appreciation for the horrors faced by the prisoners. To survive was miracle enough. But for a 14-year-old to act with the courage and steeliness that her uncle exhibited ... well, she understood why people like Madame Radminikov practically worshiped him. "Was my mother at the camp with him?"

"No, that is another story entirely. She was only a baby when the war began. Your grandparents arranged for her to be placed with a German family, to be raised as their own daughter. After the war, Abraham retrieved her."

"A German family?"

"Yes. The family maid, in fact. You see, not all the Germans were animals. Some did what they could."

Shelby remembered, as a young girl, a visit from an elderly German couple. She wished she would have talked more about this with her mother. She always meant to. Then it was too late....

"So, what happened to the safe deposit box?" Shelby asked.

"As they agreed, your uncle met Holtzman at the bank one year later. And, just as Abraham expected, Holtzman insisted that Abraham wait in the lobby while he, Holtzman, retrieved the gold and jewels from the box."

Madame Radminikov paused now, so Shelby asked the obvious. "Did Holtzman try to take the entire fortune?"

"Oh, Holtzman got everything that was in the box, all right. Abraham had emptied the box out months before. But he also booby-trapped it with explosives. When Holtzman opened it, it blew up in his face."

Shelby shook her head. Wasn't that what the Nuremberg trials were for? Holtzman should have been tried by an international tribunal. Not executed by Uncle Abraham.

Madame Radminikov sensed Shelby's disapproval. "Remember, this Holtzman had murdered hundreds of prisoners, many of them children. And he had brutalized hundreds of others, like Mr. Clevinsky." She jabbed her fork deep into her salmon, watched the juice squirt out and pool on her plate. "Believe me, dying instantly from a bomb blast was a better fate than he deserved. Abraham sold the jewels, used the money to launch Continental Casualty. Now, if I haven't ruined your appetite, let's eat."

Shelby pushed her food around her plate. There was an old expression in legal circles: *Hard cases make bad law.* That was the problem with cases like Holtzman's—many people would agree with what Abraham did. But that did not mean it made for good law.

Madame Radminikov interrupted Shelby's debate with herself, one in which she was not sure she was winning. "So, when is the baby due?"

*   *   *

Madame Radminikov's words bounced around inside Shelby's head. She did not even know if she was having a baby, so how could she know when it was due?

She stammered a response. "I don't know. I don't even know if I'm pregnant."

"Oh, you're pregnant all right. I noticed the change in you as soon as you walked in. When you didn't take any wine, I knew I was right."

These people knew too much. "I'm sorry, but what change in me?"

"Just a little puffiness in the face. You wouldn't notice it day-to-day, but it's been a few weeks since I've seen you. Your mother looked the same way when she was pregnant with you." With that comment, Madame Radminikov sat back and took another sip of wine, as if she had just checkmated her opponent.

Shelby sighed. She might as well try to keep secrets from her subconscious. "Well, if I am, it's not a very convenient time—" She stopped herself. She could not really complain about her uncle and his gang knowing too much when she sat here ready to spill her guts. On the other hand, Madame Radminikov might be the ideal sounding board. "Things are a little … unsettled … right now with Bruce and me."

Madame Radminikov studied her for a few seconds, then reached across and took her hand and folded it into her own. "From what I know about this Bruce of yours, he is a good man. But I sense you are worried that he is too independent, too uncontrollable." She paused. "Too much like your uncle."

The comment slapped Shelby like an icy wind. "Like my uncle? In … in what sense?"

"In the sense that he thinks he's smarter than everyone else. In the sense that he does what he thinks needs to be done, and doesn't give a damn about what anyone else thinks. In the sense that you fear that even your love for him is not enough to convince him to back off sometimes…."

Shelby stared back at the burly woman across from her. Suddenly it was Shelby who knew too much. "Oh my God. You're in love with my uncle, aren't you?"

Madame Radminikov shrugged, turned and blew her nose into her napkin. "Love, who knows? It is such a complicated thing. Maybe I am just lonely and want someone to call me Darling or Sweetheart or even Leah instead of Madame. Or maybe it's just admiration for him." She sipped at her wine. "But it does not matter; he and I are old and used-up. I will leave the love to the young and beautiful, like you."

"Gee, thanks."

Madame Radminikov looked out the window, spoke in a sad, soft voice. "If youth only knew; if age only could."

"What?"

"Oh, nothing, just something I read once." She sat up. "Anyway, sometimes your generation can be a bit melodramatic when it comes to love. You should realize that no relationship is perfect—there are going to be things you disagree on, things you have to fight through. You know the old expression, that opposites attract. You and Bruce each brings unique things to the marriage. Your goodness tempers his aggression. And his passion empowers and energizes you. This makes for a wonderful, complete union. But you can't then complain when you disagree on something."

The lawyer in Shelby quickly honed in on the argument's weak spot. "I see your point, but we're not talking about a disagreement over what to put on our pizza. We're talking about a pattern of behavior—illegal, reckless behavior—that could put our family in jeopardy. Or at least put Bruce in jail."

"Shelby, listen to me. This Bruce of yours is a man of a different

time. Centuries ago he would have been one of Cleopatra's generals,
or one of King Arthur's knights, or one of France's musketeers. He is
an alpha male, a man of action, a warrior. For him everything is sec-
ondary to his duty to protect and to serve."

"But that doesn't make it right. Or make him any more qualified
to be a good husband and father."

"Maybe it does. Maybe it doesn't. Like I said, Bruce is like your
uncle in many ways. And it was men like your uncle who survived
the Holocaust." She sipped from her wine. "You are right to challenge
him, right to make him defend his actions. That is your job as a
spouse, just as it is his job to challenge you. And you are right to wrestle with these issues now, before you get married. But remember:
Society is not always right, not always just. Sometimes today's laws
legitimize tomorrow's gas chambers. A healthy skepticism about the
sanctity of the rule of law may not be such a bad thing."

*   *   *

Monique exhaled some smoke, winked at the young African-
American intern watching wide-eyed from across the office.
Handsome kid, looked a bit like Denzel Washington. Quite a step up
from Senator Sedentary. She spoke into the phone. "If you'd just listen, you dumb asshole, you'd hear my reason…." The leader of a
Colorado anti-war group had wanted to disrupt the G-8 Summit in
Savannah, Georgia back in 2004, but Monique refused to commit
her resources to it. Now the whiny little prick was giving her a hard
time about coming to Boston. "Wait, I'm going to put you on speaker so everyone in my office can hear what a schmuck you are."

She placed the receiver in the cradle, spoke into the speaker. "For
the last time, Savannah was horseshit. There was a wall around the
whole resort, so you couldn't get near the delegates, and Savannah
itself was crawling with cops and soldiers and marshals—most of
them good old boys who went home at night and changed into white
sheets and hoods. So why the fuck would I want to go down there?"

No response. "Now," she continued, "on the other hand, we can
go up to Boston and get close enough to the delegates to put our

tongues down their throats and play tonsil-hockey if we want—"

A shrill male voice on the other line finally cut in. "All right, all right, Monique, I understand your point. All I'm saying is that we can't let them scare us away like that. Savannah was a G-8 summit, and we should have been there. If you had just given the word, we could have had 20,000 people on the streets—"

She rolled her eyes at the intern, blew out some more smoke. "That's exactly what they wanted—they wanted us to go down there so they could beat the shit out of us and throw us in jail, all in the name of national security. Listen, General Custer: This is a war, and in war you have to pick your battles. The Harvard conference is our home turf, with hundreds of thousands of students and a state full of people who voted for George Fucking McGovern, for Christ's sake." She softened her tone. In the end, she needed the little prick. "Also, by not going to Savannah, we lulled them into a false sense of security. They probably think we all died of AIDS or fell out of old-growth trees or got squished by whales. Trust me: Boston's going to be big. And I need your help."

He sighed. "All right, you know you can count on me. I just really think we should have been in Savannah...."

She hit a button, and the line went dead. She turned to the intern, smiled. "That guy is such an idiot he should have been a Republican." She focused on a bicep fighting to escape from beneath his shirt sleeve. "It's lunchtime. You as hungry as I am?"

*   *   *

Shelby threw a few files into her briefcase, prepared to leave work early. For most people, 5:15 was not that early, but most big-city lawyers considered it midday.

Unfortunately, she was no closer to resolving the issue of Bruce's fitness for family life than she had been when she first noticed her period was late. But the calendar was indifferent to her inner doubts, and at some point she needed to confirm the pregnancy. And inform Bruce....

She walked down the mahogany-paneled hallway. Nobody asked

if she was working a half-day, but a number of the senior partners glanced at their watches and scowled as she passed. Maybe she should have left her briefcase in her office and her suit jacket on her chair, or made a point of announcing she had a client meeting. But she was getting too old for these games—she was a partner now, albeit only a junior one, and the days of coming in on a Sunday morning to read the newspaper, just for 'face time' in the office, should have been long behind her.

She had worked at the firm for six years now, after a stint at the District Attorney's office, and she still had not fully adjusted to the mercenary culture of the private law firm. Essentially, private practice reduced the world to the following equation: The firm paid its associates a fixed wage, but billed their time out to clients at $300 per hour. So every extra hour the associates spent in the office, all fixed costs and overhead having already been covered, resulted in $300 profit to the firm. Therefore the firm did things like offer free bagels and muffins in the morning, but purposefully under-purchased to reward, and induce, early arrivals. The economics were brilliant—a $1.39 investment in pastries in exchange for $300 of billable time. Of course, the partners were expected to lead by example. And to buy their own breakfasts.

In the end, the clients paid for everything, even the muffins. Lawyers billed on an hourly basis, regardless of the quality of service. In effect, there was a built-in disincentive for efficiency: A bumbling lawyer who took ten hours to complete a task generated twice the revenue of a skilled one who completed the work in five hours. The system baffled Shelby—if you asked a house-painter for an estimate, he quoted you a price for the job. If he underestimated how long the job would take, he ate the loss. But lawyers simply shrugged, as if matters of the law were too esoteric to reduce to a firm estimate, and clients paid whatever the final bill totaled. The system begged for reform—a senior partner once called her into his office and explained that a legal brief she researched and drafted in eight hours should have taken twelve, and altered the bill accordingly.

She had no time for these games today. Bruce usually spent Wednesday afternoons at the sailing club, but she asked him to try to be home tonight. She entered the apartment. Footsteps above indicated he was up on the roof deck, no doubt grilling dinner. She called up through the hole in the roof at the top of the ship's ladder. "I'm home, Bruce. Can you come down for a minute?"

His face appeared, framed by the gray, dusky sky. "Sure. Let me just turn this chicken...."

She stood at the bottom, watched his muscular legs carry him toward her. He jumped down from the third step, leaned in to kiss her. She breathed him in, a hint of mesquite on his face. Her hand reached for his, pulled him along. "Come with me. I want you to watch me pee."

She tried not to look at him, afraid of what she might see. Her stomach churned. It suddenly dawned on her what a man felt when he asked a woman to marry him—in effect, he proclaimed, *Here's my life, I want you to be the one to share it with me.* All would be fine if the woman said yes, but how devastating would it be otherwise? She was about to make herself equally vulnerable: *I have a baby—your baby— growing inside of me. Are you happy about it?*

There really was only one correct answer. And, more importantly, one correct reaction.

Bruce slowly repeated her words back to her. *"Watch you pee?"* Then he leaped into the air. "Oh my God, Shelby, are you pregnant?!? Really, really?"

Correct answer. She stopped, turned, leaned her head into him and whispered a response. "I think so, my love."

*   *   *

"Let me just start this meeting by saying that, officially, it never happened." FBI Agent Grace Ng—"Not my real name," she made clear—rested her walnut-shaped eyes on Shelby, but did not wait for a response. She smiled, revealing a row of small, even, white teeth. "Having said that, we appreciate you coming here today. And we appreciate your help."

In her previous life as a lawyer in the D.A.'s office, Shelby was never invited to these kinds of illicit meetings. She and Abraham sat on one side of a cheap mahogany-colored conference table in a small office on the fringes of Chinatown; he flew in on his private jet especially for the meeting, planned to fly back to New York immediately after. The room's ceiling tiles were yellowed by water damage, and the smell of fried dumplings hung in the air and escaped from the worn beige carpet. Good to see that the government was not wasting money on lavish office space.

Agent Ng sat opposite them, alongside an unsmiling thirty-something man with a long neck and a short haircut. They both had that straight-backed, chin-raised posture that suggested military training. Shelby studied the female agent—late twenties, Eurasian features, quietly confident. "As you may know, the Homeland Security team here in Boston is really a task force made up of federal and state law enforcement personnel. Agent Crawford—not his real name, either—and I work for the FBI. For reasons that do not concern you, we have chosen not to include any state authorities in this investigation at this time."

That explained the run-down digs—they used annex space to avoid the prying eyes and ears of coworkers. "Are you worried about leaks?" Shelby asked. Normally Abraham would ask this type of question, but he remained silent. Apparently he considered this Shelby's meeting, a chance for her to get comfortable with the operation.

Agent Ng shook her head. "No, not leaks. But we do need to make sure our involvement with Mr. Gottlieb and his group remains ... unofficial. Like your uncle, we believe there is a very real possibility of a terrorist cell embedding itself amongst the demonstrators at the October economic summit. And, like your uncle, we intend to stop it."

Shelby nodded. "And I said I'd help. But what does that have to do with keeping things unofficial?"

"Suffice it to say that your uncle's organization, which we have worked with before, is very useful to us because of the fact it is not ... constrained ... in the same way the government is."

"You mean he can break the law," Shelby stated. She waited to see if Abraham would dispute her inference. He did not.

Agent Ng pursed her lips. "Unfortunately, that is the reality of the world today. The Homeland Security Act gives us wide powers. But, as a simple example, it does not authorize us to tap the phones of someone like Monique Goulston, who is not a suspected terrorist." Her unspoken words: "But *Kidon* can do so for us."

Shelby sighed, shook her head. "Why do I get the sense we're not just talking about phone-tapping here...." She thought about what the government was doing to suspected al-Qaeda operatives in secret prisons, all in the name of homeland security.

Agent Ng did not rebut the statement. Shelby took a deep breath. "Look, you should know I'm really not comfortable with all this. I happen to believe in the Fourth Amendment and the First Amendment and client confidentiality and due process and all sorts of things that I know make your job really difficult sometimes. But that's America. So, like I said, I'll help you when I can, but I'm not going to do anything that would keep the protestors from exercising their free speech rights, and I'm not going to help the government perform illegal surveillance on my clients." She hoped she did not sound like that ridiculous library director in Newton, who refused to allow the FBI to search a library computer from which a bomb threat had been sent only hours earlier. At a certain point, common sense took over. But they were not at that point yet.

Agent Ng nodded. "I see." She and Abraham exchanged a quick look, then she continued.

"You are correct. Fighting terrorism is dirty, and it's ugly. Like all wars. Sometimes we are forced to rely on soldiers who are not ... ideally suited ... for the task. You are one such soldier, apparently. But your relationship with Monique Goulston makes you uniquely qualified." She shrugged. "So we'll take whatever help we can get—"

"Look, I think you're overstating my value here. I'm just helping her out with some legal stuff, getting permits to demonstrate and stuff like that...."

Agent Crawford spoke for the first time. "Yes, but those details— the times and places of the demonstrations—will be crucial for us. If we know where the terrorists will be and when they'll be there, we can have teams in place to stop them. Otherwise we're just out there blind." His Adam's apple bobbed as he spoke. "It's the difference between the hunter waiting for the lion outside its den on the one hand, and hoping to stumble upon him in the jungle on the other."

Grace Ng looked at her watch, stood, slid a business card across the table. "In an emergency, you can call my cell. But, again, the less contact between us, the better, so report directly to your uncle." She held Shelby's eyes. "Ms. Baskin, please understand that you may be our best weapon in preventing this terrorist attack."

*   *   *

Abraham sat at a small table in the front part of Madame Radminikov's butcher shop. He looked down at the corned beef sandwich on the plate in front of him. Nobody made a sandwich like Madame Radminikov—the perfect cut of meat, a not-too-thick slice of Swiss cheese, just the right amount of mustard, a lightly toasted pair of rye slices. Still, he forced himself to eat slowly, a full sixty seconds between each bite. No sense consuming food your stomach did not need just because your mouth could not control itself.

"What, you don't like the sandwich? Eat."

He waved his hand at her. "You know I prefer to eat slowly, Madame."

She sighed. "You want me to add more mustard?"

He took a small sip of ginger ale. "Madame, you said you had news for me. What is it?"

She plopped into the seat opposite him. "Shelby is pregnant."

He looked out the window, studied a young mother pushing a stroller along Harvard Street much as his mother had pushed his sister on the way to market the day she had been stomped to death. The mother stopped and waited for the 'Walk' light. Nobody in Boston waited for the 'Walk' light. He turned back to Madame Radminikov. "That is unfortunate."

"I must say, that is a strange reaction."

Abraham shrugged. "The timing is bad. It will make her weak, timid. Pregnant women do not make good soldiers."

"Ever seen a mother bear protect a cub?" Madame Radminikov responded.

"That is my point exactly. The mother will do anything to protect the baby. And nothing to endanger it. Until now, her willingness to help has been limited—she still does not agree with our methods. This will limit it further." He took a bite of his sandwich, chewed slowly. "To ensure her continued help, we need to make this mission personal for her, make her believe she is fighting to make the world a better place for her baby."

*   *   *

Shelby jogged a half-block up Commonwealth Avenue, turned right on Massachusetts Avenue. The Back Bay. One hundred fifty years ago, it had been a putrid bog of trash and raw sewerage, a dumping ground for the growing city's rubbish and a breeding ground for disease. The city fathers filled it in more out of necessity than out of design. Today it constituted some of the most valuable real estate in the world—jail cell-sized condominiums in the brick and brownstone rowhouses sold for hundreds of thousands of dollars. What were the three most important things in real estate? Location, location and luck.

She ran along the sidewalk, hopscotched over a few cracks. *Step on a crack, break your mother's back.* She smiled. *See Mom, I'm still watching out for you.* A short block later, she crossed Marlborough Street; another short block and a sprint to catch the Walk light brought her across Beacon. The Charles River unfolded in front of her; Cambridge loomed in the distance.

Would the terrorists strike in Boston, or in Cambridge?

The terrorists popped into her head without warning, as they had hundreds of times in the past weeks. The looming threat seemed to hang from the clouds, blow in the wind, waft from the open windows....

She shook the thought away, wiped the sweat from her face with the sleeve of her t-shirt. The gesture reminded her of Madame Radminikov wiping Neary's blood off the operating table in the van. She shook that thought away also—she had spent the past month, since the Saturday night follies with her uncle, shaking thoughts away like a swimmer shaking water from her ear.

She forced herself to focus on the running. Her breathing became regular as her body adjusted to the exertion; more people would jog if they could just make it past the tortuous first quarter-mile and allow their bodies to find the natural rhythm of the exercise. After all, anthropologists believed that *homo sapiens* evolved largely because of their ability to outrun other animals over long distances.

She began the long cross over the Charles River on the sidewalk of the Mass. Avenue bridge, a distance of 364.4 smoots plus one ear according to the MIT frat brothers who measured the bridge's distance in units equal to the height of their shortest pledge. This was her regular route, and she once calculated (with all due respect to pledge Smoot) that the bridge's distance approximated the 600-yard run in middle school gym class, where she used to outrace the boys.

The sun was setting over the river to her left. To her right, into the downwind, downstream shadows, she tried to spot Bruce sailing in one of the scores of boats tacking from riverbank to riverbank. He was there, somewhere, the father of her child. She closed her eyes for a few strides, allowed herself to imagine him teaching their baby to sail, to fish, to swim.

She looked down at the line for the 90-smoot mark, prepared for her regular sprint. Ten smoots later, she accelerated, pushed herself to maintain her pace for a full 50 smoots, or about 100 yards. She worked hard, her arms pumping at an angle a bit more oblique to her thickening body than in the past. The sprint took her to the crest of the bridge, where she slowed. To her right Boston unfolded as she pictured it in the postcard of her mind—brownstones rising from the water's edge, the gold dome of the State House rising from behind the brownstones, the office towers rising from behind the State House. The natural, the old, the opulent and the new....

A car horn startled her from her musings. An older-model red muscle car slowed in the right lane just behind her. A couple of guys in the front seat, maybe a couple more in the back. Not college kids, not in that car. Locals, probably, cruising the city for a good time. She waited for the whistles, the invitation to jump in, the beer bottles raised in salute.

But nothing. Just a red car holding up traffic, its window rolled up to the hot July air. A tingle of apprehension ran up her spine; blood rushed to her ears and face and back of her neck. Why would four guys in a sports car putter along quietly at half the speed limit?

Shelby increased her speed again, targeted the far bank of the river. The car sped up to match her pace, kept a steady distance a few yards behind. Fighting back a wave of panic, she resisted the urge to break into a full sprint. She fished the rape whistle from her pocket, clenched it tightly in her fist, forced herself to stay calm. The whistle might help draw attention, but the few cars that had been slowed by the Pontiac swerved around it and were gone, and no pedestrians walked on her side of the bridge. Her heart began to race. She was in the middle of a bustling city, yet somehow suddenly alone on a bridge.

She was about a hundred feet from the end of the bridge. If she could clear the span, she could cut to the right and sprint to the safety of the MIT sailing pavilion. She took a deep breath, sprinted.

Nothing for a few seconds other than the wind in her ears. Then the thud of a car door slamming throbbed through her like a blow to the mid-section. The squeal of tires quickly followed. Her lungs tightened and her vision blurred, yet she forced herself to sprint ahead, even as the red car shot past her and the sound of footsteps echoed from behind. The car skidded to a stop where the traffic barrier ended, angling itself over the curb and onto the sidewalk. Escape path blocked.

A lanky man with a shaved head and a black t-shirt jumped out of the front seat and charged her. She stopped, forced her lungs to fill with air, blew hard into the whistle. A shrill shriek filled the air. The man sneered, reached out and swiped at the whistle with a slapping motion. She tried to turn away, but his hand raked across her face and knocked the whistle out of her mouth. She tasted blood, felt the sting of his blow on her cheek.

Another sneer, another step toward her. Footsteps approached from behind. She spun, lunged, scissored a leg over the traffic barrier. One hand clasped her arm, another grabbed her hair, both pulled her back. A third yanked on her shirt, a fourth grasped her waist. She tried to claw with her free hand, but yet another pair of hands snared her wrist and wrenched it behind her back. They hauled her back over the barrier, pushed her to the pavement.

Help will come. Buy some time. She kicked, landed a solid blow to the side of one of their heads. "Fuck, that hurt!" the man cursed, then grabbed her legs and wrapped a piece of thick rope around her ankles.

The man with the shaved head stuffed a rag into her mouth, yanked her head back by her hair. "Hold still, you bitch." The third man grabbed her under the arms. They hoisted her up, hauled her toward the car.

Not the car. Suspended in the air, she torqued her body, thrashing like a game fish on a line. The man holding her arms began to lose his grip, and she reached up, scratched at his face. He cursed as her fingernails dug into his flesh, but he held strong. The shaved head spat out in anger. "I told you to hold still." He reached into a sheath hanging from his pants, removed a long hunting knife. He held the flat edge against her throat, sneered. "One flick of my wrist, and you bleed like a pig."

Oh my God. What is happening? Cold metal pressed against her skin; strong hands bound her limbs. She looked up, into her assailant's eyes. *Think!*

He was the leader. She nodded to him, relaxed her body in apparent submission. They were now only feet from the car. *Now or never.*

She spun herself like a top, rotated her body so that she faced downward. The man holding her under the arms adjusted, caught her before she fell, continued to hold her aloft. Clasping her hands together, she thrust her fists up toward his groin, as if hitting a volleyball bump shot. She hit hard. An "oomph" sound—his breath leaving him—escaped from his mouth. His grip weakened. As he dropped her to the ground, she kicked out, trying to free herself at the other end as well—

The shaved head cursed, pushed Shelby to the pavement, spun her onto her back. He straddled her, pinned her shoulders to the sidewalk with his knees. She fought, but he was stronger than the other men, stronger than her. "Hold her down," he barked. "I'm going to use the ether." He pulled a moist washcloth from his pocket, yanked the rag from her mouth, covered her face. She smelled a turpentine-like smell, tried to turn her head away, fought to squirm free. But he forced the washcloth over her nose and mouth, held it firm....

Her brain commanded her to continue to fight. She raised a fist into the air, aimed at shaved head's nose ... then watched helplessly as her entire arm flopped to the pavement like a slab of meat. Sounds faded in and out, and the faces of her assailants turned gray and misty and distant. She had no choice but to breathe, but every lungful sent her body further away, like a kite soaring skyward in the wind. Frustration swept over her—she knew what was happening, knew that she needed to fight these men, but there was a total disconnect between what her brain commanded and what her limbs could perform. She was the infant trying to ice skate, the pig trying to fly....

All she could do was hope that someone was witnessing the three men dragging her into a red car.

*   *   *

Shelby was squeezed into the back seat between two of her abductors; another sat in the front seat with the driver. *Who were they?*

She tried to stop herself from shivering, but her arms and legs and teeth were refusing all commands from her brain. Whether from fear or from the ether, she did not know....

The one with the shaved head, the leader, was on her right. He leered at her. "Remember me?" His breath smelled of cigarettes; fire smoldered in his eyes.

She forced herself to study his features. Someone she had prosecuted while in the D.A.'s office? No, too young. Maybe the son of somebody she had helped send away? She could not place him....

He spat in her face. "Cunt! You cut off my balls, and you don't even recognize me?"

Her heart raced. *You cut off my balls.* A red Firebird. *Gregory Neary.*

She commanded her arm to rise, clumsily wiped the spit off her face with her sleeve, forced herself to respond. "I, I didn't have anything to do with that. I was in the van, but—"

"Shut up! I don't want to hear any of your fucking lies."

She took a deep breath, tried to keep her voice steady. Her only chance was to somehow reason with him. "They're not lies. I'm not part of that … group."

"Not part of that group? You're a Jew bitch, right? You're totally … polluted … with Jew blood." He spat on her again. A thick wad of saliva slimed her cheek, oozed down along her jaw line.

The scrawny guy on her left guffawed. He was the one who first grabbed her from behind, the one she scratched in the face and hit in the groin. "You know, other than the clam on her face, she's not half-bad looking…."

She ignored him, addressed Neary. "Where are you taking me?"

"Hey, guys, she wants to know where we're going." He forced out a short laugh. "Someplace where my boys here are going to have some fun with you, teach you some fucking respect." He pulled a large black dildo out of his fatigue pants, waved it in her face, laughed again. "Then it'll be my turn. I can't fuck you myself, thanks to your friends, but this salami will rip you up enough. Teach you a fucking lesson about who your master is." He grabbed the back of her head, shoved the dildo in her mouth, held it there as she gagged. "When we're done tearing you up, maybe we'll poke out your eyes and skull-fuck you."

The others in the car howled. "Good one Greg, skull-fucking. Never heard that before." The driver banged the steering wheel in amusement. Neary removed the phallus, glistening with her saliva, and used it to caress her breasts. She felt a distant, wet sensation—the ether was starting to wear off, her body starting to return to her.

She allowed him to caress her, hoping he might tire of the sport if she did not squirm. He hissed at her. "Your friends hadn't planned on me taking testosterone pills. I'm more pissed off than ever." *Testosterone.* That explained the heightened aggression.

She scanned the car's interior, searched for some kind of weapon. *There.* A cigarette lighter protruded from the back of the armrest between the two front seats. Her abductors were strong, but they were not exactly experienced in this type of thing. And they would underestimate her because she was a woman.

She allowed her eyes to fill with tears. The weaker they thought she was, the more they would let down their guard. She sobbed. "How did you find me?"

Neary lowered the dildo, turned to face her. "What, you think you Jews are so much fucking smarter than everybody else?"

She edged away from him, turned her body and pushed her right knee against the lighter as she did so.

"No, no I don't. I really don't...." Another sob, then she buried her face in her hands. As she did so, she tested her muscles, ordered them to flex. They seemed to be listening....

"I heard you get out of the van, heard them say you were going back to the 7-Eleven. I found the dude who was working that night, then found the taxi that picked you up. Wasn't too fucking hard to get your address after that."

She was dimly aware of them driving along Memorial Drive, the river on their right. The road cantilevered out over the water's edge—if she looked, she would probably be able to spot Bruce's outline in one of the sailboats. Instead, she focused on the traffic light ahead, just in front of the Royal Sonesta Hotel. It was green now; if it turned red, that might be her chance....

She needed a few more seconds. She lifted her face from her hands. "You know, my friends have lots of money. If you let me go, I'll make sure you're well-rewarded—"

"We don't need your Jew pennies," Neary chortled. The others joined in. "But there is one thing I need from you—the names of those other assholes in the van."

Shelby nodded. They were slowing now, approaching the red light. "All right, I'll give them to you. Just please don't hurt me." She had a sudden thought. "The leader's name is Lejbka Gerszkiewicz." She raised her eyes to Neary. "I can spell it for you if you want...."

Neary leaned forward, smacked the shoulder of the man in the passenger seat. "Give me a pen and some fucking paper. Goddamn Jew names...."

The light turned green. The Firebird accelerated, Neary still leaning into the front seat. *Now.*

In a single motion, Shelby grabbed the glowing lighter with her right hand and swung her left elbow backward, crunching it into the scrawny man's nose. As he yelped in pain, she shoved the lighter into the driver's neck. He screamed in agony, lurched forward. The car swerved to the right, into a lane of parallel traffic. A horn blared; she dove across the scrawny man's lap, braced for impact.

It was more of a thump than a crash—the light had just turned, and the cars had yet to gain much speed. But the collision jolted the car and sent Neary flopping to the floor of the backseat. Shelby pulled the door latch, pushed the door open, fought to free herself from the grip of the scrawny man she had elbowed. He grabbed a handful of her hair, tried to yank her away from the door. She reached behind her, pressed the lighter into his hand. It burned into his skin. "Aaah," he bellowed, releasing her. *Now.* Pushing with her feet and pulling with her hands, she swam across the body of her assailant, then tumbled to the street and crawled onto the median.

She grabbed a signpost, clawed it like she would a life line. "Help!" she bellowed. "Help me!" She prepared to scream and run and claw, waited to see if they would pursue her again. Doors opened, bodies emerged from cars. A wave of relief spread over her. *I'm safe. Thank God.*

Neary's voice bellowed. "Fucking bitch!" Then again, lower. "Let's get the fuck out of here." The Firebird's engine roared to life, the screech of its tires announcing its escape. Neary stuck his head out the window. "We know where you live!"

She watched the car disappear into traffic. A sense of numbing relief spread through her body. It was quickly replaced by a prickly feeling of apprehension.

They would return.

*   *   *

It was the same conversation, only different. Bruce paced the apartment, his fists and teeth clenched, his nostrils flaring, his eyes aflame with anger.

"Please, Bruce, sit down, relax. The doctor said I'm fine, the baby's fine."

"Relax? No way, Shelby. I'm going after him. I'm gonna kill that punk—"

She tried to keep her voice steady, hoped her serenity would act as a counterbalance to his rage. "No, no you're not, Bruce."

"Are you kidding me? Who knows what they would have done to you if you hadn't escaped?"

In recounting the episode, she had left out the sexual threats and the dildo shoved down her throat. But Bruce knew men like Neary, knew that sexual humiliation would have been at the core of his concept of a proper revenge. More to the point, Bruce had sensed her cold terror in the hospital. His mind, like hers, would insist on envisioning a series of ugly possible scenarios. It was a nightmare they both would have to deal with.

"I'm the one they attacked, so it's my decision. And I'm not going to get caught up in this eye-for-an-eye thing. That's my uncle's game, not mine."

He kept his voice steady. "You said to me recently that part of being married is understanding that what happens to one of us, happens to both of us, right?" She nodded, sensing where this was going. "Well then, I'm a victim of this attack also. He attacked my fiancé, my baby, my family...."

She took his hand, pulled him down the to couch next to her. "You're right, you are a victim. But where does this all end? I saw it in the D.A.'s office, these gang wars where they just kept taking turns shooting each other, one dead body after another. Neary attacks an old woman, so Abraham castrates Neary, so Neary abducts me, so you go after Neary. Enough already." She lifted his chin, forced him to look into her eyes. "There was so much anger, so much hatred in him. I can't imagine what it's like to live that way, to be so consumed by dark thoughts and feelings. I almost feel sorry for him. I mean, what kind of life will he have?"

He shook his head. "Who cares? This guy attacked you, and all you feel is sympathy for him?"

She released his hand. "No, Bruce, that's not all I feel! I'm scared to death of him. But I just think that, if someone could sit down and talk to him, some professional, he might let go of some of his hatred. Remember we saw that Skinhead on the news, talking about how he was reformed, telling kids not to get caught up in the whole neo-Nazi thing? That could be Neary."

Bruce shook his head. "So that's it? We do nothing?"

"What else can we do? I gave the police Neary's name, told them where he lived, gave them the license place off the Firebird." She had skirted the whole castration issue by telling the police Neary was feuding with one of her clients. "But I'm sure the plate was stolen, and I doubt he's still living with his mother, just waiting for the police or my uncle to come knocking on his door."

"Speaking of your uncle, what about telling him? He'll find the little piece of shit."

"No. That'll just escalate things again, and I'm more convinced than ever that my uncle's vigilante justice just makes things worse. In some ways I'm more angry at Abraham than Neary—he's the one who put me in the middle of all this, he's the one who made the brilliant decision to castrate the guy." She sighed. "I think all we can do is be careful, and hope Neary crawls back under his rock...."

"Shelby, there is no way that's going to happen. He came after you once, he'll do it again. I mean, what else does he have in his life?"

She offered a brave smile. "Like I said. I'll have to be careful."

*   *   *

Shelby sat in the law library, her eyes on a stack of court cases discussing the rights of protestors and demonstrators, her mind someplace else entirely.

She rested her hand on her belly, watched the summer sun begin to set over the river—normally by this time of night she was playing racquetball, or rollerblading, or reading at home on the roof deck waiting for Bruce to finish up at the sailing center. But in the week since the Neary attack, she had changed her routine. Now she waited at her office until Bruce swung by to walk her home. Not the most fun she ever had. But preferable to another ride in the Firebird.

The library phone extension rang. Probably Bruce calling to say he was on his way. "Hello."

"Shelby Baskin?" A poor connection, a man's voice.

"Yes. Who is this?"

"We're coming after you again, bitch. You can't hide forever."

Cold spread through her. It was bad enough he knew where she lived and, now, where she worked. But how did he know to call the library extension? She forced herself to stay calm—the only way she could get answers was to continue the conversation. "I'm not hiding, Gregory." He had such a boy-next-door name—when his parents named him, did they expect him to grow up to be such a monster? For that matter, Adolf probably seemed like a perfectly nice name until the 1930s. "I'm living my life, same as always. But if you want to talk, let's set up a place to meet—"

"Shut the fuck up and listen. I'm coming after you, and then I'm coming after your Jew-scum friends."

The line went dead.

*　　*　　*

Shelby was back in the law library. Bruce suggested that Neary resorting to contacting her by telephone was a sign he could not reach her any other way. Neither of them believed it for a second—the fact that the lion roared did not mean it would not also attack.

There was not much she could do about it. Bruce was willing to go after Neary, but she forbade it: She had no interest in being a single mother while her baby's father sat in some jail cell. Likewise, her uncle was capable of eliminating Neary from her life, but enlisting his aid would be a tacit endorsement of his vigilantism. The police were the best possibility, but it wasn't exactly their top priority.

She took a deep breath, let it out slowly. Down the road, perhaps, a solution would present itself. But for now there was nothing to do but re-check that the door was locked and get back to work on Monique's permit....

The line of court decisions basically held that protestors had the Constitutional right to be close enough to be seen and heard by their target audience. That was the law. The reality was that local governments, in the name of public safety, imposed a whole menu of restrictions on demonstrators, from the mundane (requiring a separate permit for demonstrations using a bullhorn) to the ridiculous (mandating that demonstrators provide toilet facilities at the demonstration site). She shook her head: Did Sam Adams and his gang bring in sky-blue Port-A-Potties for the Boston Tea Party?

Since the September 11 attacks, the restrictions had become even more, well, restrictive. At the 2004 Democratic Convention in Boston, protestors were confined to a protest zone around the convention site that was really nothing more than a chain-linked, barbed-wired holding cell. And even more stifling than the holding pen itself was the reality that all groups, no matter what their politics, were supposed to peacefully coexist within it. Shelby pictured the possibilities: marijuana legalization advocates toking alongside Bible-spewing anti-abortionists; gay rights advocates tongue-kissing next to Christian fundamentalists; bullhorn-led soldiers of labor chanting on cue beside urine-throwing anarchists. The idea was to keep the protestors confined to a single area so they could not run wild. The reality was that the groups, wildly divergent in both method and message, chose simply to ignore the regulations.

She jotted down some notes, then sat back and looked at the stacks of yellowed case books surrounding her. There were thousands of books, and each book contained written opinions for maybe a hundred cases. The amazing thing was that, despite all these cases, there was rarely one having the same facts as the case at hand. As a lawyer, it was incredibly frustrating to have to explain to a client there were no court decisions 'on point,' that you did not know which way a court would rule. As a client it must have been infuriating. *And how much do I owe you for telling me the court could go either way on this?*

In some ways the city would be better off granting the permit. That way, the demonstrators would be centralized, contained. She had read about the Seattle demonstrations—one of the problems was that the police had no idea where the next gathering would be. Most of the demonstrators in Seattle were peaceful, but a small, violent percentage garnered the headlines—overturned cars, looting, fires. It was the anarchists who sparked the rioting, joined by the drunk and the young and the angry. Monique bore some responsibility—she gathered the dry tinder, then waited for someone to light the match. The fire spread where it spread. From a law enforcement perspective, it would be preferable to keep the tinder stacked in a single pile.

By Monique's calculations, the chaos was a necessary evil, a way to ensure the anti-globalism message would be the lead story on the evening news. There had been violence in Seattle, in Quebec, in Genoa, in Edinburgh. There would be violence in Boston as well. And, just as Abraham did not need a permit to castrate Neary, and Neary did not need a permit to abduct Shelby, the anarchists would riot whether they had a permit or not. The question was, would that riot be the cover for a terrorist attack?

*   *   *

Short, plump and bald was bad enough. But short, plump and bald with a beautiful wife was in some ways even worse.

His sophistication first attracted Gabriella, and their involvement in the city's arts and cultural activities kept her stimulated, but Burt Ring knew he had better continue to provide some excitement in their lives if he wanted to keep her. Monique's words, hissed into his ear only moments before he was to exchange wedding vows, haunted him: "You know, Cuz, Danny DeVito at least had the common sense to marry Rhea Perlman instead of some runway model."

He sighed, watched Gabriella work the crowd, her smile and poise and Latin charm winning over the would-be check-writers gathered at the home of one of his Princeton friends. She had honed her skills as a restaurant hostess, a job where survival depended on knowing how to usher parties a half-hour late to a table by the kitchen and still make them feel like they had just cut to the front of the line.

Not that this charm made her any more qualified to serve in the State Senate than half the people in Massachusetts. Or did it? Ronald Reagan had not much more going for him than a folksy decency and an innate ability to communicate a simple, straightforward message. Gabriella, like Reagan, coupled her people skills with a simple message, albeit not one Reagan would have endorsed: *It was time for Massachusetts to elect representatives who were neither Anglo nor male.*

Burt glanced at the television set in the living room. It was an oversized plasma screen, surely left on just so the guests could ogle it. It used to be that people bought art work or oriental rugs to impress their friends. Now these wide screens had become the centerpiece of multi-million-dollar homes. He pulled out an electronic organizer, made a note to write an editorial panning the trend. His readers spent their evenings at poetry readings or art exhibits or political lectures. They did not watch *American Idol.* On any size TV.

Nor did his readers, for the most part, watch the damned Red Sox. Not that they could avoid news of the Old Towne Team; the box in the corner of the plasma set that displayed the score was as large as the television Burt had in his college dorm room. What a nightmare when they won the World Series—millions of teary-eyed New Englanders, among the most educated people in the world, worshiping a bunch of unshaven knuckle-draggers. How could a group of sweaty ballplayers evoke such passion when an exhibit featuring history's greatest Impressionist paintings barely registered on the area's radar?

Gabriella glided into the room, took his arm, leaned into his ear. "I think I've talked to just about everyone here. You want to head home?" He could smell the wine on her breath; the chardonnay mixed with her musky perfume, arousing him. He glanced down the front of her dress, caught the shadow of a dark nipple peeking out at him. It had been almost a week since they had made love....

No. He needed to avoid this type of temptation. The formula for keeping Gabriella from leaving him involved entangling their lives to such a degree that it would be impossible for her to untangle them. Many couples employed children to this end, but starting a family was not compatible with a political career. For now the best he could do was continue to promote and cultivate their image as Boston's newest power couple—he, the cutting-edge newspaper publisher and trendy nightclub owner, and she, a rising star of the Democratic Party whom some people were already talking about as a possible future candidate for Lieutenant Governor.

"If you're not too tired, Hon, I think we should stay for a while longer. The men all love you—they always do." In fact, some stood a bit too close, held her hand a bit too long. "But maybe you should spend a little more time with the wives." He had overheard a remark from one of the wives earlier: *My husband could afford to buy me a State Senate seat also, but then who would take care of the kids?* Burt shuddered at what they would say if they knew she worked as a professional escort in college.

She strolled over to a cluster of women, a confident smile on her face. A few seconds passed, then her voice rose among the others. "Oh, you went to Colgate? Burt was just mentioning that *The Alternative* is excerpting a novel written by one of their graduates...." And off they went, comparing notes on famous authors and artists and musicians they had met during their lives, Gabriella nodding and smiling in admiration.

*   *   *

Gabriella waded into the crowd of smiling mannequins, pasted on a plastic smile of her own. She preferred another weekend in the woods fighting off the mosquitoes and Ahmad, each relentless in their attempt to ravage her body, as opposed to an hour of listening to these women complain about their domestic help. If only there was a way to ensure that this entire gathering of horrid little people could be sitting on the shores of Boston Harbor when the tanker blew....

The sliver of her brain that was paying attention to the conversation alerted her that a response was due. "You can't be serious!" she gushed, her eyebrows rising in concert with the words.

"Isn't it horrible?" came the response. "I mean, I understand that her kid was sick, but she knew I was hosting book group that night. What was I supposed to do, just serve crackers out of a box?"

Gabriella excused herself, found a bottle of water and filled a wine glass. The opportunity to win a seat in the State Senate was simply too good to pass up, even if it meant spending night after night making small talk with tiny people. The seat would not only be the ideal cover for her activities, it would give her access to the kind of critical security information that could mean the difference between a successful operation and a failed one. She just needed to get through the election process.

Burt's eyes focused on her from across the room; she smiled at him and raised her glass. Prince Charming he was not. But she did not need a prince, she needed a cover for her extra-curricular activities. And Burt was not a bad guy, not a bad companion—intelligent, open-minded, sensitive, cultured. In other words, all the things his country was not.

*   *   *

An hour later, they finally made it out to the car, a Mazda Miata Burt bought when he first started dating Gabriella. He purchased it to show his young, fun side. He kept it for the same reason. He put his hand on Gabriella's knee, gave a quick squeeze to her shapely thigh before taking it off to shift the car into gear. "Great job with the wives."

She shrugged. "I really do abhor these women, with their manicures and country clubs and personal shoppers. They do nothing with their lives, then they look at me like I'm just some wetback who stole one of their men while I was supposed to be cleaning his house."

He laughed, appreciating the fact that, in her mind, *she* had stolen *him.* "They might think that at first, but once they meet you they seem to like you. But maybe you should have stayed and helped with the dishes—"

She cuffed him playfully. "Pig. You're sleeping on the couch tonight."

They rode in silence for a few seconds, his hand back on her warm, naked thigh. She put a jazz CD into the player. He did his best to sit tall in the seat. "I was talking to a couple of the guys from the state Democratic Party. They did some polling, and you're very popular with the urban voters, and not just the Hispanics. The radical groups are behind you, thanks to Monique. And, in the suburbs, you're doing well with the liberals and with women." Their district had been gerrymandered years ago and ran haphazardly from Boston's North End to Revere on the north shore. "The only weak area is the moderate male voters, but that's not surprising." That had always been the plan—combine her natural appeal to the minority voters with his connections and influence among the liberal suburbanites. "Things are going great. Except the damn Red Sox won again."

She laughed. "Don't worry. They'll find a way to blow it."

He was not so sure anymore, now that they had broken the curse. Unfortunately, and absurdly, Boston's baseball team was the single biggest threat to the life he had built. He had never really explained it all to Gabriella. "I'm not sure you understand why it's so important the Red Sox don't win the World Series again." He powered the Miata through a curve on Storrow Drive, the moonlight gleaming off the Charles River to his left and the lights of the city sparkling to his right. "Everything we have feeds off itself—*The Alternative*, the nightclubs, your political career." He had not planned it this way, but an efficient synergy had developed. All the young, trendy people hung out at his clubs, and they helped his staff break stories and get interviews for *The Alternative*, stuff readers could not get in the mainstream press. "*The Alternative* gives us the influence to determine which gallery is hot and which restaurant is not. That gives us a lot of power in this city, which helps your campaign."

She reached over, touched his knee. "I know all this already, Burt. It's why all the women at the clubs flock to you." He pressured the accelerator; the car jumped ahead. "Power is sexy."

He nodded, tried to act nonchalant. *Of course* women liked him. "Anyway, there are thousands of people in town with more money than us, but they'll never be part of the power elite."

She teased him. "Elite, huh? The geek from Cleveland and the Spic from Chelsea." At least she used the word 'geek' rather than 'nerd'; somehow geek seemed like a transitory stage in life, while nerd was more permanent. She continued. "But what does this have to do with the Red Sox?"

"The Red Sox are trying to turn the whole Fenway Park area into a giant tourist destination, like Faneuil Hall. They want outdoor cafes, a Red Sox museum, statues of players, tours of the park. They're even renting the place out for weddings and Bar Mitzvahs. Basically they want that whole area to be a giant Red Sox theme park, like something out of Disney World."

She snorted. "Yuk."

"The problem is that the kids that go to our clubs don't want to party at a theme park. They don't like sterile. They want gritty warehouses, dark alleys, places they know they won't bump into Uncle Mort and Aunt Sally visiting from New Jersey."

Gabriella nodded. "And you think that if the Red Sox win the World Series again, the politicians will let them keep expanding around the ballpark."

"Bingo. I think we're at the tipping point. If they win again, the city will let them do what they want."

"And if they don't win?"

"Then I think we'll be okay. They've got the same problem the Patriots used to have—their owners are not particularly well-connected politically. They're not from the area, and a lot of people are still pissed-off that a local businessman, an Irish guy, didn't get the team."

They winded their way through the North End, toward their condo in an old warehouse. Burt had bought it cheap in the early 1990s, when the real estate market crashed and the developer went bankrupt. A similar unit recently sold for over a million dollars, four times what Burt paid for his. The unit sported a private roof deck with an oversized hammock that looked out over the city. He hoped to get Gabriella into the hammock before she ran out of gas. Gabriella never had much of a sex drive, which, as Monique had so delicately pointed out the day of their wedding, was probably not such a bad thing—"If she was a nymph she would have married some macho Latin guy, not you." But she understood his needs. And satisfied them.

"Well, even if the Red Sox did change the neighborhood, couldn't we just sell the buildings?" she asked.

"We could, but the land itself isn't all that valuable." Just a bunch of old warehouses bordering the Mass Pike. He pulled into the garage under their building. The real problem was that the clubs generated a ton of income, much of it cash, which was the only way he could afford to keep publishing *The Alternative*. Even if he sold the buildings, it would not leave enough to subsidize the newspaper for more than a few years.

As they entered the elevator, Burt tried to imagine his life without the clubs and the newspaper. He packed his days now with meetings and phone calls, challenges and strategies. He anchored the center of his own little universe, with hundreds of employees orbiting around him and thousands of others within his gravitational pull.

If the Red Sox succeeded in transforming the Fenway Park area, his clubs would fail. He would have to sell the warehouses, trading them for a couple of million in cash—enough for a home in the suburbs, a summer place at the Cape, and a day full of nothing to do. Just like thousands of other wealthy, middle-aged men.

It would be bad enough, away from the action and energy of the city's power center. It would be even worse when Gabriella bored of it all and left him.

*   *   *

Shelby kept her back to the graffiti-covered wall of the Back Bay train station, her eyes on the crowd, her hand on a can of mace. She was venturing alone in public for the first time since Neary and his gang dragged her off the bridge. Bruce had put her safely in a cab, watched to make sure nobody followed. Logic told her Neary had not tracked her. Still, she edged closer to a security guard standing further down the platform.

She had pictured the months before her wedding differently. For one thing, she did not plan on being a pregnant bride. Not that it bothered her—at 41, she and Bruce wanted to start a family quickly anyway. But the whole stop-the-terrorists-while-dodging-the-stalker thing had not been on her radar. And her friend should have been coming to town to help pick out bridesmaid dresses, not make plans to bring anarchy to the city. Ironically, her years at the D.A.'s office—as edgy a job as a lawyer could have—were pretty mundane. But now that she practiced in an office tower, the fringe members of society seemed to orbit her world like so many dusty, gaseous moons. She was now inviting one of those moons to leave orbit and settle into her home.

The train pulled in and Monique stepped off, a shadow of black amid the whites and tans and yellows of the other summer passengers. She spotted Shelby, waved, smiled. Even her teeth seemed gray.

Shelby waded over, reached out to grab one of Monique's bags. Monique mistook the gesture, perhaps purposefully so, and folded herself into Shelby's arm and offered a half-hug of her own. "Hey, Roomie." Monique pulled back, surveyed Shelby. "Wow. You still look great. Still fighting off the men?"

"As a matter of fact…." Shelby held up her hand, showed the ring. "Just don't try to steal him."

"Yeah, like I have a chance." She linked her arm into Shelby's as they walked toward the exit, turned to look Shelby in the eye. "I've missed you, Shelby. I really have. I'm sorry I screwed things up between us back in law school…."

Shelby had forgotten how charming Monique could be—sweet, fun, vulnerable. But she had not forgotten how ephemeral Monique's attentions were. She was like the frat-boy who dumped his girlfriend because she was frigid and would not put out, and then dumped the next one because she did and so must be a slut. Shelby's challenge would be to stay close enough to the spider to keep her salivating, but not so close that she ended up as lunch.

CHAPTER 6

[August]

An August day, thick and stifling, half of Boston on vacation at the Cape or the Islands. The other half wanted to be. Shelby composed a legal brief on her office computer, concentrating on the words on the screen in front of her.

Something pulled her eyes away, redirected her attention to the doorway. A body loomed, framed in the opening, a pair of eyes locked on her. The scream escaped from her, involuntarily, much as a finger recoiled from a burning stove even before the brain registered the pain impulse.

Gray eyes. Angular face. *Abraham.* By the time her eyes communicated with her brain, and her brain gave instructions to her mouth, there was little of the scream left to swallow.

She closed her eyes, tried to settle her breathing. "You startled me."

He offered a quick nod in greeting. "Have you won Monique Goulston's confidence yet?"

I'm well, thanks. And it's nice to see you, too. In a perverse way, it was nice to see him—she had feared the figure in her doorway was Neary's. She collected herself. At least his terse manner kept their encounters short. "Not really. She was up here a few weeks ago—"

"Yes, I know."

Of course he did. "I would have called you, but there was nothing to report. We didn't really get into anything substantive."

"But she stayed in your apartment."

Yeah, and she flirted with my fiancé. And she snores. "We went over some legal strategies, talked about the permitting process in Boston and Cambridge, had a few laughs about the old times. But she went off on her own lots of times. I couldn't exactly tag along...."

"Very well." He paused, seemed to weigh something in his mind. "Madame Radminikov fears that you think we are nothing more than a ... I believe she used the phrase ... 'cold-hearted, zealous group of vigilantes.' She suggested that I show you some of the ... non-violent ... things we do to protect the Jewish people."

"Ah, the kinder, gentler vigilante. Sort of like the first President Bush before he cut the food stamps budget."

Abraham stared back at her with a quizzical look. Kinder and gentler or not, her uncle still had no sense of humor. "Please follow me."

He half-turned, began to move away from the door. She looked at the cursor on her monitor, blinking at her, beckoning her to return to her work. Or perhaps warning her of impending danger. She rested her hand on her stomach. "Now is not a good time."

Abraham retreated a half-step, studied her. She looked for irritation in his face, saw only surprise. Irritation she could have met with anger of her own. But surprise was tougher to respond to. He continued to look at her, waiting. She sighed. "I can be ready in an hour."

"I will be in front of the building at noon."

An hour later she pushed through the revolving doors, slammed flush into a wall of thick, humid air. Mr. Clevinsky stood in front of a dark sedan, his hands folded behind his back, his lips turned up in the same kind of exaggerated, closed-lip smile that appeared on those yellow, smiley-face bumper stickers plastered around town. She waved to him and strolled over, surprised not to see any sweat on his face despite his heavy gray suit.

He bowed in greeting, opened the back door for her.

"I'm glad we're not taking the van again," she said, smiling at Mr. Clevinsky.

He smiled in return, and she slid in next to her uncle. Mr. Clevinsky, his chin raised and his back straight as he peered over the top of the steering wheel, snaked his way through the Financial District as her uncle addressed her. "You are familiar with the Underground Railroad?"

"Of course."

"Boston, specifically the Beacon Hill neighborhood, comprised a crucial part of this network. Many of the citizens of Beacon Hill modified their homes with fake walls and trap doors to provide hiding places for slaves using the Underground Railroad to escape. I became interested in this history because it so closely mirrored the experiences of many Jews who were given shelter by their friends and neighbors in attics and hidden rooms during the Holocaust." He paused. "Including your mother."

They broke free of the traffic in the Financial District and skirted past City Hall. Shelby had no idea where this conversation was going. But she could see that their car was now climbing the steep north face of Beacon Hill, past red-brick rowhouses and narrow, wrought-iron-gated alleys fronted by cobblestone sidewalks and gas streetlamps. The noise and bustle of the city faded. Her uncle continued. "Many years ago I came to Boston, to Beacon Hill, to inspect these properties. Very few of the old hiding places remain, but the neighborhood itself had hardly changed—with narrow alleys and maze-like streets, it must have been an ideal spot for slaves to hide from the authorities." A hint of a smile played on her uncle's face, the old, sullen man now a kid again, playing hide-and-seek in the centuries-old streets and alleys of Beacon Hill.

A wave of sadness passed through Shelby. Her uncle never really had a childhood. He was only six or seven when his mother died, his childhood a daily battle against starvation and street gangs and black-booted storm-troopers kicking in doors in the dark of night. The thought of maze-like alleys and trap doors and hidden rooms—all things that would have aided a young boy in surviving the Nazis—probably came as close to the concept of an idyllic childhood as a war-scarred old man could imagine. She wanted to reach over and take his hand in hers, to wrap her arms around his bony shoulders and comfort the sad, scared little boy living inside. But Abraham seemed to sense her pity, turned himself away from her and stared out the window....

They pulled into an empty parking space—another testament to
the August exodus from the city—under street signs that indicated
they were on the corner of Grove and Revere. Abraham opened the
door, continued. "I began to think that every city in America should
have a neighborhood where Jews could retreat in the event of an anti-
Jewish uprising—"

"An uprising?" She tried to keep the incredulity out of her voice as
she stepped out of the car. "Uncle, that's crazy. This is America, not
Eastern Europe. Who's going to rise up?"

He turned on her, almost viciously. "No, Shelby!" he roared.
Spittle showered her face; she stepped back against the car. "Crazy is
when you have *no* plan, crazy is when you assume it can never happen *again*, crazy is when you assume it can never happen *here*." He
took a breath, stepped back, lowered his voice. "What, exactly, is
America? It is not the Blacks, it is not the Hispanics, it is not the
Asians—none of these groups is part of the mainstream. America is a
melting pot of Europeans—English, Irish, French, Italian, Polish,
and, yes, German. What makes you so certain these people, these
European Americans, do not have the same hatred in their blood for
Jews as their ancestors?" He did not wait for her response. "For centuries the Europeans have persecuted us. Why should it be any different because we happen to be on the other side of the Atlantic?"

Mr. Clevinsky took her arm, gently guided her away from the car.
She stared at her uncle, suddenly afraid. Not afraid of what he might
do out of hatred. But afraid of what he might do out of fear. He was
like a trapped, injured animal, ready to lash out at anything—friend
or foe—that approached.

Abraham fell into step behind them, continued his soliloquy as if
the outburst had not occurred. "So we began to buy properties on
Beacon Hill, just to have in case our people were ever threatened
again. And we made certain ... shall we say ... modifications. Mr.
Clevinsky, please lead the way."

Shelby did not want to blindly follow her uncle, but Mister
Clevinsky caught her eye, nodded kindly. Apparently this version of
show-and-tell would be less offensive than the episode in the van....

Mr. Clevinsky ushered her to a brick rowhouse a few doorways down the slope of the hill on Revere Street and opened the front door. He led them through the foyer to a door marked "1." He jiggled the lock, and they entered the apartment.

The furnishings were sparse: a futon and a cheap coffee table in the living area, an army cot in the bedroom, a single bar stool in the galley kitchen. Only the curtains, plush and pulled tight over the windows, hinted at the wealth of their owner.

Mr. Clevinsky unlocked a door recessed into the back wall of the living area, pulled it open to reveal a narrow stairwell. Mr. Clevinsky used a flashlight to brush aside some cobwebs, and Shelby followed the men down the staircase and into a rectangular underground room about the size of a toilet stall. An indoor-outdoor carpet covered the floor; the air smelled musty and rubbery, like wet boat-cushions. Abraham spoke. "We are, obviously, in the basement of the building. But if you went down to the basement from the main part of the building, you would never notice this room was here." He knocked on the wall; dust particles danced in the beam of Mr. Clevinsky's flashlight. "The back side of this wall is bricked, to match the rest of the basement."

He nodded to Mr. Clevinsky, who pulled a brick out of the side wall, unlatched a hidden lock, and pushed. A small rectangle of bricks, four feet high by two feet wide, swung open on a hidden hinge. They slipped through the passage, stepped down into an adjoining basement. They were in a similar cobwebbed, hidden room, with a similar wet-rubber smell and a similar narrow staircase.

"From here, we go up." Even in the dim light, there was a flush in his cheeks, a glisten in his eye. A little boy, playing hide-and-seek with the Nazis. And winning.

They climbed a tight spiral staircase up two flights, stopped on a narrow landing. Unlike the basement rooms, the tightly enclosed space was stiflingly hot. Shelby was surprised that neither of the men, both elderly and both wearing wool suits, seemed taxed by the climb; she tried to control her breathing as well. Abraham turned to Mr. Clevinsky. "You are certain the tenant is out?" Mr. Clevinsky nodded, and Abraham unbolted and eased open a narrow door. He moved aside to allow Shelby to peer into the bedroom of an apartment on the second floor. A burst of air-conditioned air cooled her; she kept her face in the room while her uncle spoke. "In most cases, we own the entire buildings. But in some, such as this one, we own only one of the condominium units, so we cannot use the basement as a passageway. We inform the tenant that this closet is for the owner's use, and lock it from the inside."

"Why bother renting them out? Wouldn't it be easier to just leave them vacant?"

Abraham shook his head. "The properties are too valuable to be left vacant. Furthermore, to leave so many apartments unoccupied on Beacon Hill would cause neighbors to ask questions. We leave the first-floor unit in the first building vacant because we need it as our entry point. The other units we rent to sons and daughters of trusted associates. They pay a reduced rent and, in exchange, they go away for a few weeks if we need them to."

"For what?"

Abraham shrugged. "There are times when it is to our advantage to offer anonymous lodging to our associates."

Right, the *sayanim*. She remembered their conversation in the restaurant.

They continued from building to building, sometimes through hidden basement corridors, sometimes simply through passageways cut into the brick walls separating adjacent buildings.

"How far does this all go?"

"This chain has about two dozen buildings; it is our largest. Up ahead, there are a couple of narrow alleyways that branch off of Revere Street. The buildings there are very private and very secluded, and we now own many of them. That is where we will gather if we need refuge. Of course, we would sneak in using the entrance further up the hill."

Again with the refuge. Not a bad plan if you bought into the whole paranoia that the Jews were about to be chased from their homes by black-booted marauders....

Abraham lifted an arm to tug a light chain. The movement pulled back the sleeve of his suit coat, revealing a series of five dark gray numbers tattooed along his inner forearm. Shelby choked down a gasp: concentration camp identification numbers, permanently branded into his skin. It was as if the numbers had revealed themselves in stark rebuttal to her skepticism. She viewed Abraham's crusade as quixotic, a fight against enemies that existed only in the damaged psyche of a paranoid mind. She suddenly regretted her impudence. Abraham's enemies had been real. And far more lethal than windmills.

*　　*　　*

Shelby leaned back, played with the straw in her fruit shake. She and Bruce were sitting in the food court of the Galleria mall in East Cambridge, taking their first tentative step into the world of infant clothes and baby furniture and safety latches. It was a Friday night, and the mall was swarming with packs of tweeners (Shelby now thought of them as almost-grown-up babies), flitting around like dogs nosing each other in the park. They wanted to get close and intimate—to sniff, to fight, to breed—but the virtual parental leashes, now just beginning to fray, kept yanking them back to a safe distance. Ten years ago, Neary had probably been in a similar group. Maybe somebody should have yanked his leash a little tighter. Or maybe all he needed was a kind hand to scratch under his chin. What he got was her uncle....

"You know," she said, "it's hard to buy infant clothes when you don't know the baby's sex...."

"You think we should find out?"

"I didn't think I'd want to, but now I do—"

"Fine with me."

"Actually, I'm pretty sure it's going to be a girl."

"How can you tell?"

She smiled, shrugged. "Just a mother's intuition, I guess." She reached out, took his hand. "I have another favor. If it is a girl, I'd like to name her after my mother."

"Sure." He furrowed his brow. "I don't think you ever told me her name."

She tried to keep her expression impassive. This was going to be fun. "Her name was Beulah."

"B-Beulah?"

"Yes, Beulah. Isn't it perfect?" She clasped both hands over her heart. "Our little Beulah. Oh, thank you, Bruce, thank you!" She leaned over, kissed him to hide her grin. "Baby Beulah."

Then her mother's voice: *That is mean, Shelby. Now you tell him the truth.* Shelby offered an exaggerated sigh of contentment, eyed Bruce out of the corner of her eye, ignored her mother.

He shifted, cleared his throat. "Nothing against B-Beulah—it really is a nice name—just that it might be a bit old-fashioned—can it just be a name that begins with 'B'?"

"You—you—don't like ... Beulah?" she moped.

"Well ... I do ... it's just...."

Shelby tried to pout, to paint a hurt look on her face. But one look at Bruce's consternation and a burst of laughter erupted from deep inside her throat, interrupting his stammered response. Her eyes began to water; she reached out and squeezed his hand, spoke between the waves of laughter. "My Mom's name wasn't Beulah, it was Sarah. But you should have seen the look on your face!"

He laughed along with her. "Very funny. But I owe you one. And, yes, Sarah is much better."

They sat quietly for a few seconds, hand-in-hand, each quietly trying the new name on for size....

Bruce brought them back to the real world. "So, Abraham thinks that showing you that he's built secret passageways all over Beacon Hill, like some kind of ant digging tunnels through the sand, will make you think he's *more* rational?"

She sighed. "I'm not really sure what Abraham is thinking. To him, these passageways are a big secret. Maybe he's trying to get me to be more forthcoming about Monique, sort of like, 'I'll tell you my secret if you tell me yours.'"

Bruce nodded. "Could be. Who knows with him?"

She eyed the bookstore bag on the floor, the corner of *What to Expect When You're Expecting* peeking out at her. It was hard to think about Abraham and terrorism and Monique when all she really wanted to do was go home and get the condo ready for her baby. "Mostly

I think he's still trying to get me to see the world the same way he does, as some ongoing fight for the survival of the Jewish people."

"That makes sense. He knows that you don't buy it, and until you do you're not really going to be 100 percent behind him."

"And I pretty much told him again that I thought what he was doing was misguided, that vigilante justice was the wrong way to go. I wanted to tell him it almost got me … hurt, but I bit my tongue."

"What did he say?"

"He didn't really respond. He just looked off into space with those gray eyes of his, acted like he didn't hear me."

Bruce smiled. "Sounds like some good quality family time…."

"Actually, in a sad sort of way, it was. I really do think he was just trying to … reach out to me, I guess. Trying to share something about himself, like sharing his secret was the closest he could come to intimacy. I guess I should be flattered." Shelby straightened herself in her chair and kicked off her sandal, then lifted her foot and rested it on Bruce's thigh. There were no virtual leashes holding her back. In fact, the *What to Expect* book said many woman experience an increased sex drive during pregnancy. "But it's not really the kind of intimacy I'm interested in right now." She wiggled her toes into Bruce's crotch; he stirred against the ball of her foot.

"All right, then," he announced as he stood. "Time to leave the mall."

*   *   *

They were sitting in a dimly lit Lear jet on an empty runway at the Hanscom Field airport northwest of Boston. Abraham sat across from Madame Radminikov in a leather swivel-chair, a half-eaten corned beef sandwich and a can of ginger ale on the mahogany table between them. He had phoned her before he left New York, directed that she meet him at the airport.

Abraham conferred with the captain, then returned to his seat opposite Madame Radminikov and picked at his sandwich while he read the *Wall Street Journal*. Every time he turned the page, the scent of menthol wafted over her. It was his only real concession to his years in the concentration camp—he allowed himself a hot shower and a fresh shave daily, sometimes twice.

Knowing better than to interrupt him, she used her cell phone to call Myron, her bookie neighbor. She asked him to put a note on the door of the butchery telling customers it would be closed for the rest of the afternoon.

"Sure," he responded, "if you do me a favor."

"Uh-oh. What is it?"

"Ask your rich insurance friend if he's interested in buying part of my book. I'm way over-exposed on this Red Sox stuff—this Bible Code prophecy thing is crazy, everyone betting on them no matter how much I cut the odds. It reminds me of the whole Y2K thing when a bunch of crazies were convinced Armageddon was coming." He snorted. "I'm waiting for people to sell their houses and use the money to buy canned vegetables and duct tape."

She grunted an affirmation, remembered how Abraham made a killing in the stock market predicting that the risk of Y2K chaos was drastically overstated. Myron continued. "In their mind, God has already decided this year's World Series, so who are they to argue?" He sighed, lowered his voice. "I've got a huge imbalance on my books." He admitted it the way she imagined other men conceded incontinence.

She smiled to herself. Myron liked the income from being a bookie, and he liked the women its mystique attracted, but he was still an insurance agent at heart. He was risk-averse; he did not sleep well knowing he had exposure that he could not cover. "Can't you just lay some of it off with your friends in the North End or Providence?" She had been around him enough to know that when a small-time bookie took a large bet, he would often get other bookies to share it with him to minimize the risk. It was much the same in the insurance industry—when a company wrote a particularly large policy, or had too many policies insuring a particular risk, they sold participation in these policies to other companies to spread the risk. Likewise, a bookie would try to sell participation if he had too much action on one side of a bet and not enough on the other; bookies made money by being right in the middle, not on either extreme. For example, Myron might give 5-to-1 odds if you were betting on the Red Sox to win the World Series, but only 1-to-6 if you were betting on them to lose. As long as the action on each side was even, Myron would win either way, collecting six for every five he paid.

"I tried that, but they're all having the same problem. This could be even worse than when the Patriots won back in 2002." The Patriots Super Bowl victory had almost sent Myron over the edge, both financially and psychologically. The Patriots were 14-point underdogs to the high-powered St. Louis Rams, and paid 5-to-1 to win outright. As game-time approached, a bunch of local wise-guys, not to mention thousands of rabid Pats fans looking to support their team, swamped the local bookies with bets on the Pats. The bookies were heavily exposed, with no time to lay much of it off. Myron lost $80,000 on the game, and had to pay another $55,000 in interest to the Chicago mob just to keep his head above water for a couple of weeks until he could raise cash by selling his vacation condo on Cape Cod. He even had to go into hiding—Madame Radminikov had prevailed upon Abraham to allow him to stay in the Beacon Hill properties for a week while he dodged angry gamblers. He still spat every time someone walked by him on the street with a Tom Brady jersey.

She sighed. "Myron, it's like I always say: Just don't take the bets."

"You know I can't do that. I don't take the bet, they find another bookie. And then I've lost their business forever. I tell you, it's almost enough to make a man a Yankees fan."

She laughed. "Wow, this is serious."

"So you'll ask your rich friend if he wants a piece of my action?"

"No, Myron. But I'll make you a nice sandwich when I come back. Now please don't forget to put that sign up for me...."

Ten minutes later they taxied down the runway. Abraham lowered his paper once they were airborne. "We are flying northwest, toward the Adirondack Mountains in upstate New York. We will land at a small airport near Lake Placid. From there, an automobile will bring us to an institution for the ... what is the term? ... mentally unstable. We will be meeting a gentleman by the name of Rex Griffin."

"He is a patient there?"

"Yes, though he claims he should not be."

"Why do I get the feeling that's a common complaint?"

"Undoubtedly. But in the case of Mr. Griffin, he is correct. He was put there against his will, and without good cause. By Bruce Arrujo. With the acquiescence of my niece."

Madame Radminikov leaned forward; the seat belt tightened around her waist. "By Shelby and Bruce?"

Abraham stared back at her, his eyes fixed on hers. He would ignore her question—they both knew she heard him the first time, which meant that her query was purely rhetorical. He would wait a few seconds for a more productive conversation and, failing that, would return to his newspaper. She regrouped, tried to keep the irritation out of her voice. "Why don't you tell me the whole story."

He nodded, pushed a button on the side of his armrest.

A woman's voice—crisp and clipped, with a slight New York accent—responded. "Yes, Mr. Gottlieb."

"Tell Mr. Kasten that we are ready. Put him on the screen."

Abraham pushed another button, and a video screen descended from the ceiling. A younger man, perhaps in his late thirties, filled the rectangle. He was wearing a dark suit with a white shirt and red tie. Standard lawyer costume. Sitting in what looked like a standard conference room in some big city office tower.

Abraham spoke into a small microphone on the opposite arm of his chair. "Mr. Kasten, I am with a trusted associate, whose name does not concern you." He turned to her, away from the microphone. "We can see him, but he cannot see us. He can only hear us." He returned to the mike. "If you will, the story of Rex Griffin."

The man cleared his throat, looked down at some notes. "This all took place on Cape Cod, in the town of Mashpee. A few years ago, Mr. Griffin found the body of an ancient Indian chief buried on his property. I will not go into all the details now—I have a full memo on it if you are interested—but this discovery, if shared, would have enabled a local Native American tribe to bring a lawsuit against the town, claiming land worth hundreds of millions of dollars. Mr. Griffin was willing to share his discovery with the tribe only in exchange for a sizable share of the proceeds from the lawsuit. To ensure he would not be cheated by the tribe he committed some unsavory acts."

The lawyer paused. Madame Radminikov guessed he was not sure if Abraham wanted him to go into specifics or not.

"Continue, Mr. Kasten."

"Here are the highlights: First Mr. Griffin drugged his mentally retarded sister and arranged for a teenage boy from the tribe to impregnate her. Then he murdered his brother."

"*Unsavory?*" Madame Radminikov exclaimed. Neither man responded. She continued. "How does this involve Shelby?"

"Shelby Baskin had a long-term relationship—both personal and professional—with one of Mr. Griffin's neighbors. These neighbors were involved in a totally unrelated lawsuit against Mr. Griffin, and Ms. Baskin was acting as their attorney. At some point Mr. Arrujo also became involved, assisting Ms. Baskin and the neighbors. Eventually, Mr. Arrujo figured out what Mr. Griffin had done to his brother and sister."

"So why is Griffin in a mental hospital instead of a jail?"

"Again, it is complicated, but Mr. Arrujo chose not to report Griffin's crimes to the police. The tribe and the town were on the verge of settling the lawsuit, and the arrest of Mr. Griffin would have derailed the settlement and caused considerable hardship in the town. Instead, Mr. Arrujo figured out a way to get Mr. Griffin committed to this mental hospital. The money Mr. Griffin scammed is being used to pay for his stay."

"Why does Griffin go along with it?" Madame Radminikov challenged. "Can't he convince them he's not crazy or unstable or retarded or whatever it is they think he is?"

Abraham took another sip of ginger ale, which signaled to Madame Radminikov that the next piece of information would be particularly interesting. The lawyer continued. "Mr. Griffin believes that the only reason he has not been charged with the murder is because everyone believes he is unfit mentally to stand trial. He is under the impression that, were he to be found to be 'normal,' he would then stand trial for murder."

"And that's not the case?"

"No. He could leave there today and the authorities would take no notice of him. But, again, Mr. Griffin does not know that; he believes he would be arrested immediately. That is the beauty of the plan Mr. Arrujo crafted—Mr. Griffin believes that he must remain in the hospital or else face a life in prison. The hospital is, essentially, a virtual prison."

"Thank you, Mr. Kasten." Abraham pushed a button, and the lawyer disappeared.

Madame Radminikov stared at the blank screen for a few seconds. "Are you planning to use this information to blackmail your niece into helping us?"

"Originally, that was my plan. What is your opinion?"

"It would fail. Shelby is an idealist—she will always try to do what is right, not what is expedient. She responds to persuasion, not coercion. The best way to get your niece to help is by convincing her it is the right thing to do. Not by threatening her."

He nodded. "That is my conclusion as well. But I believe Mr. Griffin can be of assistance to us in other ways."

Something the lawyer said echoed. "Kasten said Griffin is in a *virtual* prison. Let me guess: We're going up there to explain to him how he can escape."

"I like to think of it instead as explaining to him the terms of his parole."

A knot formed in her stomach. Abraham was planning to unleash Griffin on Shelby and Bruce in some convoluted strategy designed to induce Shelby's cooperation. "As I've said before, Abraham, you must not harm her."

He arched an eyebrow at her. Then he reached over and patted her on the hand, a gesture about as intimate as he was capable of. "You have grown fond of her, I see. But not to worry, Madame. No physical harm will befall her."

He did not emphasize the word 'physical,' nor did he need to. She understood the implication. "They will not be easy to manipulate," she observed.

"Agreed. But Mr. Griffin himself is a formidable adversary. And, apparently, a highly-motivated one."

*   *   *

Madame Radminikov peered through the car window at the dark, hulking, granite building. Towers and turrets and iron bars on the windows. The type of structure that vodka- and garlic-emboldened villagers of Eastern Europe might have stormed with pitchforks and torches, searching for the vampire within. She and Abraham were here to meet a different kind of monster, one that Abraham seemed intent on unleashing.

Abraham had made a few phone calls during their 90-minute drive from the airport, while she read the lawyer's full report on how Bruce caused Griffin to be committed to the mental hospital. She half-listened: Reb Meyer and Barnabus were meeting them at the hospital; a judge had signed a court order releasing Rex Griffin; hospital administrators had received funds to suitably compensate the institution for its cooperation. Arrangements had been made. But that was not a plan.

She turned to him as the car pulled to a stop in the circular driveway fronting the hospital. "So, what is our plan?"

"Much of it will depend on Mr. Griffin. He has been in this institution for more than two years, a sane man living among the insane, a healthy man being treated for a mental illness. It may be that he is not capable of assisting us. That will be for you to judge."

"Abraham, you know I am not a psychiatrist—"

He cut her off with a chop of his hand. "I am fully aware of that. But you are an astute judge of human nature. You see things—sense things—that others do not. The question is this: If we liberate Mr. Griffin from this hospital, will he do our bidding? Or will he simply disappear, worthless to us?"

Not much pressure. All she had to do was look into the soul of a man who thought nothing of breeding his sister like a farm animal, thought nothing of killing his brother. Did he even have a soul? And, if so, did she really want to look into it? These were concerns she could not raise with Abraham—he had seen things, lived through things during the Holocaust far worse than anything Rex Griffin could ever conceive of doing. And what good would it do if she did raise them? He would dismiss them with a wave or chop of his hand

and, in the end, she would do what Abraham asked anyway. His cause was noble and just. And she could deny him nothing.

They entered the building through an oversized wooden door recessed into the granite façade. The air was stale and thick and earthy, like a cave or a dirt-floored basement. Madame Radminikov shivered, crossed her bare arms in front of her chest and rubbed them with her palms. She glanced over at Abraham; his eyes were fixed on a row of monitors illuminating a small security room near the entrance. These types of institutions were prevalent decades ago, during the era of forced lobotomies and electro-shock treatments. But not all the dinosaurs had succumbed to the advances in mental health—there were a handful of private facilities, like this, tucked away in the mountains and the woods of America. Ideal spots for people with an abundance of money and a paucity of remorse to stash the black sheep of their family….

A thin, middle-aged woman in a white lab coat met them at the door. She lifted her head, peered at them through tinted eyeglasses, her eyes hidden by the lenses. "Follow me," she sighed.

Abraham addressed her in a clipped tone. "You have taken him off his medications?" She nodded, her lips pursed.

"We are expecting two more associates. Bring them to us when they arrive."

They followed the woman down a hallway and through a swinging door, the musty air suddenly replaced by the twin smells of disinfectant and sour vomit. The melodramatic voices of a daytime soap opera from an unseen television filled the hallway, the humming of florescent lights overhead and the squeaking of the escort's rubber-soled shoes on the linoleum floor below serving as musical accompaniment to the histrionic dialogue.

They stopped abruptly in front of a closed metal door. The guide removed a chain of keys from her lab-coat pocket, spun a few keys around before settling on one. She peered through a small glass window before inserting the key, then pushed open the door and entered. Abraham followed close behind; Madame Radminikov lingered by the doorway.

The woman pointed to a small man with stringy hair seated at one end of a rectangular cafeteria-style table, his face turned away from them. She took a deep breath, as if speaking required her full energies. "You have visitors." She turned and left the room.

The figure turned slowly toward them, close-set eyes peering at them from above an angular nose and a recessed chin. Madame Radminikov involuntarily took a step back, just as she did whenever she encountered a rat in an alley. Something about the rat's willingness to go places and eat things that repulsed her gave the animal a strange advantage over her. He lifted a bony finger, picked at a scab on his cheek. "Since I have no friends, I can only assume you are here because you need something from me." He flashed a yellow smile, scratched at his scalp as a bit of thick drool congealed on his lower lip.

Abraham moved into the room, lowered himself into the seat opposite Griffin at the far end of the table. "You are correct." Madame Radminikov walked around the table, sat with her back to the window. She watched as Abraham's gray eyes studied Griffin. Griffin leered back at him, his eyes shifty and impatient. Occasionally he twitched, but mostly he just scratched at the sores on his cheeks and on his scalp and on his ear.

Abraham's strategy in these situations was to elicit information before offering any. 'A man has two ears and one mouth; he should use them proportionately,' he was fond of saying. He addressed Griffin. "Tell me about Bruce Arrujo."

Griffin continued to leer. "What's to tell? Sometimes you get the bear, sometimes the bear gets you, sometimes the bear shits in the woods, sometimes a tree falls in the woods and nobody hears it." He shrugged, plucked a hair from what was left of his eyebrow.

"You will have to do better than that, Mr. Griffin. There is a possibility that we may be able to help you. But first you must answer our questions."

Madame Radminikov studied Griffin, tried to get inside his head. It was likely he sensed his sanity slipping away, realized that their sudden and unexpected arrival might be his only chance at escape. But he had no idea what they wanted, no idea what answers to provide to their questions, no idea what truths to hide or what lies to tell.

And he also probably sensed that Abraham was not likely to make things any easier for him by tipping his hand.

He probed Madame Radminikov instead, leaning toward her and breathing deeply. "Ah, you smell good. The women here all smell stale and medicinal, like rubbing alcohol." He offered an exaggerated sigh, his sour breath wafting over her. She turned away, looked to Abraham, fought to keep an old memory of two rats mating in an alleyway from crystallizing in her mind.

Abraham drummed his fingers on the table, made no attempt to hide his irritation. "Your thoughts on Mr. Arrujo, Mr. Griffin. Or we leave."

Griffin stared out the thin, barred window, sensing that the correct answer to Abraham's question might win his release. "What is there to say? He is the reason I am here. Wherever he is, I would happily trade places with him." His words were now measured, rational. "He cost me millions of dollars. And my freedom."

"In the end, he defeated you, outsmarted you, correct?"

"Wrong!" Griffin erupted from his seat, pounded his fist on the table. Madame Radminikov edged away. "It was never a fair fight. He was unknown to me, a complete stranger. He was plotting against me, moving in the shadows—I never had a chance to defend myself. He sucker-punched me...." Griffin dropped back into his seat, the tirade over as quickly as it had started, a pair of clenched fists and a spray of spittle on the table its only remnants.

Abraham continued to prod, to probe. "Are you saying you would have defeated him in a fair fight?"

Griffin unclenched his fists, rubbed his hands together as he leaned forward in his seat. "Yes, yes, I would have defeated him. Most assuredly. Yes, yes. It was an unfair fight." He stood, began pacing, stopped suddenly and eyed his visitors. "That's why you're here, isn't it? Arrujo is your enemy also."

Abraham simply stared at him, his face a mask, the wolf studying the fox. But the fox could sense that the hen house door was ajar....

Griffin bobbed his head in a fast nod, like one of those children's toys they give out at baseball games. "Given another chance, I would defeat him. Yes. I would find him, destroy him." In Griffin's mind, the theoretical question asked by Abraham about what would have happened in the past had turned into what might happen in the future.

Abraham stood abruptly. "Rubbish. You are no match for him. Come, Madame, we are leaving."

Griffin's eyes filled with alarm. "No, wait! Don't leave. I would defeat him, I would! Just give me the chance, I swear it, I would defeat him." He was shouting at their backs now. "I must defeat him!"

Abraham ushered Madame Radminikov from the room, closed the door behind him. She peered through a small window as Griffin dropped his head onto the table. "Your impressions, Madame."

She sighed. "In his mind our leaving indicated that we would not be helping him get out of here. His reaction was telling—instead of being upset about being stuck here, he seemed upset that he wouldn't have the chance to defeat Bruce. My impression of the man is that, as much as he hates being confined here, what he's really fixated on is the fact that Bruce outsmarted and outmaneuvered him. His ego just can't accept losing."

Abraham nodded, which she took as a sign to continue. She took a deep breath of stale, musty air. "Everyone has one thing they value in themselves, one thing they take consolation in no matter how bad things are. For some people, no matter how bad their life is, they find it bearable because they believe they are making things better for their children; they cling to that, and it gives them strength. Others are able to accept their suffering because they believe they will be reward-ed in some afterlife. From what I read about Griffin, what gave him comfort and solace was the belief that nobody could outsmart him— he had no friends, and his neighbors hated him, and he was broke, and he may even have been on his way to jail, but he could always cling to the fact that he was the mastermind surrounded by a world of fools. It made everything else in his life bearable. Well, Bruce took that away from him. Getting it back is even more important to him than getting out of here."

Abraham stared down the hall for what seemed like minutes, his gray eyes fixed on some distant point. He was clearly contemplating her words—her analysis of Griffin and his need to be a mastermind

applied to Abraham as well, and whether he was digesting her message in the context of his own behavior, or that only of Griffin, she
would never know. The longer he stared down the hall, however, the
more she guessed he was looking within himself in a rare moment of
introspection. It was an exercise he normally would have found a
worthless pursuit. But because it might help him understand Griffin,
he might just take a minute or two for reflection....

He spun suddenly, faced her. "Excellent. Excellent analysis. It is
consistent with everything I know of the man."

She found herself blushing, covered it up with a fake cough. "So,
what's next?"

"My concern was that, if we were to arrange for his release from
here, he would simply disappear and be of no use to us. Now, however, based on your analysis, I am confident he will do our bidding
and pursue Mr. Arrujo. But we will need to keep a close watch on
him—"

The thin woman with tinted glasses arrived, the portly Reb Meyer
and the giant Barnabus in tow, and interrupted Abraham. Madame
Radminikov whispered to Abraham. "So, we're going to take Griffin
with us?"

He leaned down to Madame Radminikov, spoke in a low voice. "If
we unleash Mr. Griffin now, he will engage Mr. Arrujo in a battle
within weeks. That is too early for our purposes." He showed her his
yellow teeth, turned to face the arriving group. "Reb Meyer,
Barnabus, thank you for coming so quickly. Alas, it turns out you
have come in vain. We will all return at a later date."

Reb Meyer's face showed his frustration. He would not question
Abraham, at least not openly, but lately he had become increasingly
sullen and belligerent. His background was in the military, his incli-
nation to use force and aggression at every opportunity. An old saying fit him: "To a man with a hammer, the whole world is a nail." For
Reb Meyer, the whole world was a battleground, a gun the proper
tool to control it. He had no use for the political and economic and
social tools Abraham used so effectively to advance *Kidon's* cause.

Barnabus, meanwhile, had crouched down and was peering at
Griffin through the window in the door. Griffin paced around the

room, ranting wildly. The Hasid watched for a few seconds, then straightened himself and backed away. Madame Radminikov half-expected one of his silly, cruel rhymes, something poking fun at the caged patient. Instead, fear filled the giant's eyes.

*   *   *

"We've only got one more lesson after today, then it's back to school for you, Captain." Bruce put his hands behind his head, rested his feet on the fiberglass bench opposite him. The sun broiled his face, and the orange life vest gummed to the sweat on his skin despite the brisk breeze. A hot, humid August day in Boston. Most of the city had left for vacation.

"My dad said he was going to talk to you about more lessons in the fall." Anthony paused, shifted his weight, the back of his thin white thigh sticking to the fiberglass as he moved. "If you want to...."

Bruce furrowed his brow. "I don't know. I feel like I'm taking my life in my hands every time I'm out here with you. Hate to push my luck...."

Anthony flashed his braces. "Oh yeah, right. I'm not the one who forgot to secure the jib."

Bruce had not forgotten, either; he just wanted to see the boy's reaction to the sail flapping angrily in the wind. Anthony reacted well—he pointed the boat into the wind, then ducked forward to quickly re-hoist and tie off the sail. Bruce taught the kid to sail; the sailing taught the kid self-confidence. "Hey, I read something the other day I thought you might be interested in. You watch *Star Trek*, right?"

"Yeah. The old ones especially."

"Any idea where this came from?" Bruce held his hand up, palm facing Anthony, a V-shaped gap between the middle and ring fingers.

Live long and prosper. Anthony smiled. "It came from Vulcan, right?"

Bruce shook his head, pointed toward the State House dome perched above the brick rowhouses on Beacon Hill. "Actually, it came from up there. Leonard Nimoy, the actor who played Mr. Spock, grew up on Beacon Hill. He's Jewish, and that symbol represents the first letter of the word *shalom*, which is Hebrew for peace. So that's a Jewish symbol for peace. He suggested it to the writers, and they liked it. So there you go." Shelby was Jewish, and their baby was going to be Jewish, and there were people like Neary who would hate them for being Jewish, so Bruce had been doing a lot of reading. Maybe too much.

Anthony nodded. "Cool. I have a friend who, like, can't make his fingers do that."

"I had a friend once who couldn't wink. So he used to blink at girls. Didn't seem to work, though one time at a party a girl brought over some Visine for him."

Anthony laughed. "My dad and I are going to the Sox game tonight." Whenever Bruce brought up girls, Anthony changed the subject. The kid just had his 14th birthday, on his way to high school in a couple of weeks. Plenty of time to worry about girls later.

"Yeah? I thought you didn't like baseball?"

"I don't like watching it on TV, but it's, like, okay if you're at Fenway."

"Think they have a chance this year?"

Anthony focused on the approaching shoreline. "Prepare to jibe." The boy pulled the tiller toward him, turning the boat downwind. "Jibing now." The wind caught the back side of the sail, whipping the boom across the boat as Bruce and Anthony ducked under and scampered to the windward side. They headed toward the Cambridge side of the river, pointed at MIT's granite Great Dome. The boy continued the conversation without missing a beat. "I hope not."

"Really? Why?"

"I mean, I like the Red Sox. But my dad's real worried about them winning again. He says every time Boston wins a championship, there's, like, a big riot and someone gets killed. He wants them to lose this time. The guys he works with are always joking about it, saying they should, you know, trade their good players to the Yankees."

Bruce nodded. After both a recent Patriots Super Bowl victory and the Red Sox World Series win, college kids were killed in the ensuing street parties-turned-riots. Innocent bystanders, caught in the crossfire of alcohol and testosterone and police bravado and fan lunacy. Young lives lost. And careers in law enforcement ruined. "Is that part of your dad's job, controlling the riots?"

"Yeah. He's usually in the command center, trying to figure out a way to stop the college kids from getting too rowdy. His boss got demoted when that girl got shot." Police on horseback fired pepper-spray pellets to try to break up a raucous crowd outside Fenway Park after the Sox beat the Yankees to get to the World Series. A pellet struck a girl in the eye, killing her.

"So is your dad now in charge?"

"Him and another guy. I forget what they call it, special operations or something. Whenever there's a big demonstration or parade or celebration, he has to work, like, all night."

Bruce nodded. Maybe Anthony's dad would soon have the pleasure of meeting Monique Goulston.

*   *   *

Shelby scrolled through her emails, waited for her morning cup of Dunkin' Donuts coffee to cool. Her secretary buzzed her. Shelby used to answer her own phone, but Neary's call changed that. Last week her secretary slid a note on her desk while she talked on the other line. It read: "Man on phone won't give name. Wants to know if you want to go for ride in Pontiac Firebird." Shelby smiled bravely, asked her to take a number if she could.

"Shelby, I have Monique Goulston on the line."

Shelby's eyes moved from her monitor to her phone to her coffee. Could she deal with morning sickness *and* Monique at the same time, *before* her coffee? If she took the call, the one cup that the doctor allowed would get cold. But if she waited, the anxiety of knowing she had to call Monique back would ruin the enjoyment of the cup anyway. And sipping it while they talked would be like trying to enjoy a backrub while waxing your bikini line....

"Shelby, are you there?"

"Sorry, yes." She sighed, slurped a quick sip from her Dunkin' Donuts cup, sucked in air to cool her mouth, reached for a pen and legal pad. "Put her through."

"Glad I caught you, Roomie. I'm heading to the beach for the rest of the week, but I need you to get started on something."

Everyone, it seemed, was on their way to the beach. She had foregone time off in order to bank vacation days for the baby's arrival. A good idea in theory, but nobody warned her that being pregnant was like wearing fur on a 90-degree day. "Sure. What's up."

"I need a permit to hold our demonstration at Columbus Park, down by the Aquarium."

Shelby could see the park from her office—a large, clamshell shaped expanse of green fronted by the harbor, just a short walk from Faneuil Hall and the downtown Financial District. She scanned the area, involuntarily seeking hiding spots for terrorists. "Okay. What dates?'

"October 25 and 26, the entire weekend. We're going to hold a demonstration in Christopher Columbus Park, in opposition to the Columbus-like economic imperialism this country is using to subjugate the citizens of the world. Pretty cool, huh?"

Shelby had no interest in a political debate with Monique so early in the day. "So you want the permit for the entire weekend?"

"Yeah, we're going to have a rally, speakers, some music, maybe even burn some McDonald's gift certificates. Maybe you and Bruce can camp out with us."

Shelby glanced at her calendar, ignored the jab. "You know, by the time I get this filed the event will be seven weeks away, and we're supposed to file these applications eight weeks in advance…."

Monique snorted. "Right. Show me where in the Constitution it says I have to give two months notice before exercising my First Amendment rights. Please, Shelby, stop acting like such a friggin' suit."

She ignored this jab as well. "I'll need to specify on the application the number of people attending the event."

"What the fuck, put down 50,000. And make sure you tell them we've got plenty of Port-a-Potties. They like that."

Monique apparently expected Shelby to laugh. Hearing nothing, her tone turned edgy. "Christ, Shelby, you take everything so fucking serious. I mean, don't you see how perverse this is?'

"How perverse what is?"

"This *whole country,* our way of life. We're the fucking Roman Empire, corrupt and immoral and just plain ... putrid. Look at us— we fight wars just so we can drive our fat-ass cars and ... just *freeload* off the rest of the world. Our kids sit around playing video games, and our adults think Paris Hilton is more interesting than Paris, France. Then we have the nerve to tell the rest of the world what a great way of life we have!" She snorted. "I look around this country and all I see are a bunch of Fred Flintstones. Everyone's fat, dumb and happy."

So much for it being too early for a political debate. "I think what's *perverse,* Monique, is that you're so cynical. You think anyone not trying to bring down the government is wasting their life—"

"That's bullshit. I don't give a damn what people do, as long as they do something beside sit on their ass and just *consume.* Just look at our law school classmates—how many of them are doing anything that even remotely impacts or changes or, God forbid, actually improves the world? Maybe one or two are doing something worthwhile, but the rest are all just suits. The best and the fucking brightest, my ass. They're just a bunch of hired guns for the goddamn multinationals."

Monique's words hit home, no doubt as she knew they would. Shelby had been in private practice for six years, and her legal efforts consisted almost entirely of helping her clients grab a bigger piece of the pie. She never made the pie larger, never grew it in any way, never actually created anything. And, to Monique's original point, she did nothing to make sure the pie was divided more equitably—she represented her rich corporate client in a fight against some other lawyer's rich corporate client. The irony, of course, was that Shelby had finally decided to do something worthwhile with her law degree—spying on her client in hope of preventing a terrorist attack.

Not that she could throw that back at Monique. So she settled for: "There are plenty of people from our class that aren't working for a big law firm or some multinational. Some work in government, some teach, some are involved with the United Nations—"

Monique cut her off with a sharp laugh. "You just don't get it, Shelby. All those things you just listed, all those jobs, they're part of maintaining the status quo, part of keeping the Western economic system in place. The scary thing is that you see these jobs as somehow different from working for the multinationals. But they're not, they're all part of the same world order."

Monique took a deep breath, continued in a more conciliatory tone. "You know the people who come to our demonstrations—the greenies and the labor groups and the immigrants and the socialists and, yes, even the anarchists? Everyone always says we have nothing in common. But we do: We see the same thing, we understand that the Western governments and corporations and schools and churches and foundations all have the same vested interest in keeping things just the way there are. That's what we all have in common—we see the truth, we see the unfairness."

She paused, the anger returning to her voice. "We see it all so clearly, and yet this whole country is totally blind. What we see is not that the Emperor has no clothes. We see that the Emperor has *all* the fucking clothes."

Shelby had never been able to win these political debates with Monique. And she had a desk full of work to do. "We're going to have to continue this discussion some other time, Monique. I'm too busy today, helping my rich clients steal from the poor. But I do know this: If you want to demonstrate at Columbus Park, we're going to have to convince one of the Emperor's bureaucrats to give you a permit. And my guess is they might give you an afternoon, but not a whole weekend."

Monique shifted gears from the world of political theory back to the reality of their local permit fight without missing a beat. "Fuck 'em then, we'll go to court." She apparently did not see the irony of using the courts to help bring down the judicial system. "A thing called the Constitution says we have the right to protest, and it does-n't say anything about banker's hours. Shit, the Boston Tea Party was in the middle of the fucking night. You might want to bring a copy of the Constitution with you to court, show it to the judge. Maybe even pass out copies to the press for some publicity."

"All right, I'll file the application. But you might want to have a back-up plan if they say no."

Monique snorted. "Back-up plan? My back-up plan is we hold the rally without the goddamn permit."

*   *   *

Gabriella stared across the harbor, watched the planes ease skyward off the Logan Airport tarmac. An ocean breeze brought the smells of low tide to her nostrils and cooled what was, only a few blocks inland, an already steamy August morning.

Something about the old man with the wolf-like eyes bothered Gabriella. He seemed to have access to *too much* information, to be able to provide *too much* money. But her instructions had been clear: accept any assistance he could give and trust any information he provided.

Which was why her morning walk through Christopher Columbus Park, only a few blocks from her North End condo, was suddenly taking on a new meaning. Today, for the first time, she viewed the park as a battleground rather than a playground.

She studied the expanse: A grassy, open area abutted the water's edge, with benches and walking paths designed to attract picnickers and pedestrians. Further from the ocean the park offered shade trees, fountains and child play areas. A tree-lined trellis bisected the park, highlighted by a dazzlingly white statue of Christopher Columbus presiding from atop a large gray throne of granite.

According to the old man, in late October the park would be packed with demonstrators. An ideal cover. Hopefully the tanker would cooperate and cruise into the harbor during the height of the rally, squeezing its way between the waterfront and Logan Airport, a floating bomb only 300 meters offshore.

Originally, she intended to target the tanker from the balcony of a condo building overlooking the harbor. A fine plan in theory, but the logistics were unworkable. She, unlike the September 11 suicide bombers, did not plan to die in the attack, nor did she intend to spend the rest of her life in jail. Which meant she somehow needed to gain access to a waterfront building without leaving a paper trail and without showing up on a surveillance camera video. After months of trying to arrange an apartment rental anonymously, she concluded that she instead needed to target the tanker from some public locale.

Which was why a dense crowd of demonstrators was such an attractive setting. The question was where to place her operatives. They needed a clear, unobstructed view of the harbor; even small branches would interfere with the flight path of the rocket-propelled grenades. They also needed to be somewhere in the middle of the crowd, blending in, away from perimeter security personnel. Finally, they needed to be close enough to the street to be able to make a quick escape, on foot, during the chaos that would follow.

She started with the escape plan. It would be tight. Based on recent studies of an LNG explosion, the fireball would be fatal in an area radiating approximately two-thirds of a mile from the tanker, and would take three minutes to encompass that area. She needed a plan that would get her operatives at least two-thirds of a mile away in less than three minutes.

She dropped her half-full cup of coffee in a barrel, walked to the middle of the park, and stretched her hamstrings and quads. She set her stop-watch, then began running in a zigzag pattern through the park, mimicking the path the boys would likely take while navigating through a tightly-packed crowd of demonstrators. When she reached Atlantic Avenue, which ringed the inland side of the park, she broke into a sprint, away from the harbor. She bent right around an old warehouse, raced toward the brick warehouses of the North End. Three short blocks later she stopped, at the mouth of the Callahan Tunnel. She checked her watch—52 seconds. They would jump in a waiting car and have a little over two minutes to drive a mile to safety. Thirty miles per hour through the tunnel. Not a problem, even with traffic....

Her plan was to wake early the day of the attack, go to the outdoor lot and find the SUV the old man would be leaving for her. She would then drive to the self-storage facility and retrieve the RPG-7s.

She closed her eyes, tried to picture the rest of the day unfolding: Ahmad phoning her as the tanker appeared in the distance. Putting on a blond wig and thick glasses as she navigated the stolen SUV. Listening to the traffic reports on the radio, confirming that the Callahan tunnel was clear and, if not, phoning Ahmad and notifying him that they must instead run down a highway off-ramp and meet her inside the new underground central artery. Driving toward the tunnel entrance, then pulling over and idling on a side street nearby. The boys launching the grenade attack on the tanker, Ahmad firing shots in the air to panic the crowd and provide cover for their attack and escape. The boys sprinting out of the park, three short blocks to her waiting car. Racing through the Callahan tunnel. Emerging on the far side of the harbor, in East Boston, still within the perimeter of the death zone. Speeding north, finally, to safety.

Safety from the fireball, that is. They would still have to deal with the manhunt that would begin almost instantaneously. But the old man had a plan for that, too.

CHAPTER 7

[September]

College move-in weekend in Boston. The city teemed, as if someone hung a giant "Free Beer Kegs, Boston Exit" sign on the Massachusetts Turnpike.

Hundreds of yellow moving trucks and vans and trailers, crammed with college students and their wares, reduced the city to a harried, honking halt. They double-parked on the streets, live-parked outside dormitories, straddle-parked on the sidewalks. They even wedge-parked, unintentionally, under the low-clearance bridges of Storrow Drive, stuck there until mocking tow truck drivers arrived to deflate their tires and yank them free.

During this annual migration, anyone with half a brain stayed away from the college neighborhoods—the Back Bay, Allston-Brighton, the Fenway. Yet Abraham insisted on meeting for Saturday night dinner at the Pizzeria Uno in Kenmore Square—ground zero of Boston's university universe, where the three college neighborhoods intersected.

He had secured a large table in the corner, where he and Madame Radminikov were waiting for Shelby and Bruce when they arrived. A collage of college students filled the space, an open, high-ceilinged room that used to serve as a ballroom for the once-grand Hotel Buckminster. Anxious freshmen shared a last meal with doubly-anxious parents, sophomore guys checked out the new meat, upper-classmen tested their fake IDs at the bar. The student crowd shared the space with a handful of suburban families fresh from the after-noon Red Sox game. Shelby felt over-dressed in a pair of tan linen pants and a white silk blouse. Bruce had it about right—khaki shorts and a dark blue tennis shirt. She wondered why her uncle chose to meet here....

Abraham stood, offered Shelby one of those half-bows he and Mr. Clevinsky favored, then turned to clench Bruce's hand. The rigidity of the gestures, along with his dark suit in the informal setting, seemed of a different time. She pictured an old man at the beach in one of those full-body bathing suits.

Madame Radminikov, seated to his right, smiled at both of them, motioned for them to sit. Shelby returned her smile; Bruce took the seat against the wall so he could keep an eye on the crowd. "Sorry we're late. We walked—it's only a few blocks, but the sidewalks are packed." And Bruce thought someone was trailing them, so he made them double back.

Abraham turned toward Madame Radminikov, waited for her to make the necessary small talk. "Not at all; you're right on time—"

Abraham cleared his throat. Madame Radminikov's seven words were apparently sufficient chit-chat for the occasion. "Agent Ng is running late. In the meantime, it is crucial that you understand the dangers we are facing." Abraham stared across the table at Bruce and Shelby, gestured toward the crowded bar. Not sure what he was get-ting at, Shelby merely stared back at him.

He continued. "The problem is all these college students." He looked around, the lone adult in a room full of toddlers in need of fresh diapers. "So many of them," he muttered. "Any one of them could be a terrorist, anonymous in the dormitories or apartment buildings of the city. How easy it would be for one of them to join Monique Goulston's demonstration, use it as a cover for setting off a bomb or releasing anthrax or spreading a virus. For example," he low-ered his voice, "one of the young men, sitting at the bar, wearing the yellow golf shirt..." Shelby and Bruce glanced over. She spotted him, drinking a beer, watching a soccer game on the television, laughing with a group of friends. Other than his olive-toned skin, he looked like any other college student in Boston.

"He is the son of a Saudi prince, one of the richest men in the world. This prince, like many Saudis, is also a financial supporter of many Wahhabi *madrassas* and mosques." Wahhabism was a fundamentalist branch of Islam, funded by and closely allied with the Saudi royal family. Many of these mosques and schools existed in the U.S., a dirty little secret that in post-September 11 America had become an awkward situation for the Bush administration. "I brought you here tonight to illustrate a point: Would you have picked him out of the crowd as a potential terrorist?"

"I guess, maybe," Bruce answered. "If I knew about his family, where he was from. He fits the profile. So, yes, I would have."

Abraham nodded. "How about his friend? The tall one with the long blond hair."

Shelby turned again. This little demonstration explained why her uncle had insisted on dinner at Pizzeria Uno. "The one that looks like a surfer, with the cut-off shorts and orange t-shirt?"

"Yes."

"If you're asking if he looks like a terrorist, no."

"The truth is that the blond boy, not the Saudi, is the terrorist. He may look Caucasian, but he grew up in Syria, the son of a Syrian man—a commercial pilot—and a Norwegian woman. He has dual citizenship, and is here on a Norwegian student visa. But he is not 19 or 20 years old, like the other students. He is 26, a trained Syrian intelligence officer. His real purpose is to familiarize himself with American customs, lifestyle, culture. And to put himself in position to orchestrate a terrorist attack. Perhaps soon, perhaps not for ten or twenty years."

Bruce's skepticism showed. "How do you know all this?"

Abraham's eyes flashed. "It is our business to know these things, Mr. Arrujo."

"We have our ears to the ground," Madame Radminikov said. "The Syrian made an offhand remark, questioning whether the Holocaust ever occurred. In the Middle East, these comments are common. But our network is trained to key in on these types of give-away statements. The more we investigated him, the more we found. We have reported our findings to the authorities."

Shelby glanced back at the Syrian, watched him. He could easily take a job here, marry an American woman. A snake in the grass. That her uncle had reported the Syrian to the authorities was comforting. That the authorities had not figured it out themselves was not.

Bruce spread his hands, palms up. "Okay, we get the picture—the terrorists could be anywhere. And none of us wants to see a 9/11 in Boston. That's why Shelby agreed to tell you and Agent Ng what she learns from Monique. But this Syrian guy has nothing to do with Monique, right?"

"As far as we know, that is correct," Abraham said.

Bruce shook his head and sighed. Shelby shared his frustration. "Look," she said. "You still haven't told us what you know. You asked for our help because you had specific information of a specific threat, enough information to get the Homeland Security people all riled up." She leaned forward. "So what is it?"

Abraham looked to Madame Radminikov, who nodded. "Very well," he said. "The intelligence we have points to an attack on a liquefied natural gas tanker as it travels through Boston Harbor. You have read about this danger in the newspapers, yes?"

Shelby nodded; her stomach tightened. Fear? Baby? Hunger? "Yes, I did—it's a nightmare scenario." Boston was one of the few areas in the country, and the only major city, serviced by tankers carrying natural gas in its liquefied form. The newspaper recounted a recent study concluding that a rupture of the tanker's holding tanks could release a vapor cloud that, when ignited, would result in a giant ball of fire that would cause buildings to vaporize and crumble. The fireball would destroy entire city blocks and cause second-degree burns to people as far as a mile away. It had happened once before, in Cleveland in 1944—gas escaped from a holding tank, then ignited. An entire square mile of the city incinerated, turned to ash. Over 100 people perished.

Shelby closed her eyes, pictured the ugly, hellish scene. A whoosh, like the sound of a gas grill being ignited, then a flash of blinding light and heat. Children frolicking with the seals at the Aquarium would be the first victims, their skin blackening and then curling and finally melting away completely, the seals wailing and then dying moments later in their now-boiling tanks of seawater. Tourists, some strolling through Quincy Market, some walking the Freedom Trail, would be next, the wall of fire approaching like a searing tornado spinning across the prairie; they would run inland, away from the hot breath of hell, only to be engulfed and incinerated seconds later. Further inland still, in the steel and glass office towers, workers would see the flash, feel the heat, hear the rumble; they would press their faces to the windows, watching open-mouthed, then begin to feel their buildings sway and crumble beneath them as the steel supports melted and drooped like ice cream cones left in the sun. Beyond the office towers, in the residential neighborhoods of the North End and Beacon Hill, the fire cloud would ignite trees and cars, torch apartment buildings and rowhouses, taking life and leaving ash and char and soot in its place....

Shelby gulped some cold water, shook the visions away. "But they claim they've tightened security, that there's no danger—"

A voice from over Shelby's shoulder responded. Agent Ng, dressed in a white golf shirt and blue shorts. She looked young enough to be a coed, but there was a confident authority in her voice. "If that were true, the mayor wouldn't be fighting so hard to ban the tankers altogether. He's convinced a giant ball of fire is going to roll through Boston. I'm not sure he's wrong." She lowered herself into the chair facing the wall.

As Madame Radminikov introduced Bruce, Shelby reflected on the agent's words. Her hand on her belly, she flashed to the pictures she had seen of the Indonesian tsunami—an enormous wave of water engulfing and destroying slow-moving humans in its path. The ball of fire would be the same, except faster-moving and more lethal. Some people survived the tsunami—outrunning it, floating on its crest, moving to higher ground. Nobody could float atop a ball of fire....

Bruce spoke. "I've been reading about this LNG danger for a few years now, and it hasn't happened. If these tankers are so vulnerable, why hasn't anyone hit them yet?"

Abraham fixed his gray eyes on Bruce. "That there has not been an attack thus far is irrelevant. We know that the absence of a past attack is in no way preclusive of a future one. We learned that on September 11."

Bruce challenged him. "I happen to think it is relevant. If we're going to try to prevent something from happening in the future, it would be helpful to know what worked in the past."

"Maybe I can answer that," Agent Ng interjected. "Here is what we know: An attack on a tanker could come from the air, from the water, or from the land. A water attack—similar to the attack in Yemen on the USS Cole—is considered the most likely by Homeland Security. A small, fast boat, laden with explosives, could ram the tanker, setting off an explosion large enough to penetrate the tanker's hull and breach one of the LNG holding tanks. Of course, we are aware of this risk, so security is extensive while the tankers are in transit—the harbor is closed to other boat traffic, and a number of armed vessels circle the tanker ready to intercept any attack boat."

A panting, bedraggled waitress appeared. Madame Radminikov ordered appetizers for the table.

"Do you think those precautions are sufficient?" Shelby asked.

"My personal opinion is that the Western world's whole methodology for defending terrorism is flawed," the agent answered. "We are *reactive* instead of *proactive*. This is a good example: The terrorists attacked the USS Cole with a boatful of explosives, so we react by concentrating our defenses against another boat attack. But the terrorists are clever, nimble. They alter their tactics in response to where our defenses are weak. You'll never see another suicide airplane hijack again because we've tightened our airport security. So, next time, the attack will be on our water supply or on a nuclear power plant or, perhaps, on an LNG tanker. To answer your question, I think our security is adequate to defend against a Cole-like attack, but that doesn't mean I think our security is adequate."

Shelby nodded. Agent Ng impressed her—confident, articulate, bright. Which made her sober analysis even more sobering. "How about from the air?"

"Same thing. We learned our lesson with air attacks. While the tanker is in transport, Logan Airport is closed and air traffic is restricted, other than an armed helicopter escorting the tanker. If a suicide plane approached, it would be shot down before it reached the tanker."

"So that leaves an attack from the land," Bruce concluded.

"Yes. And that is where anti-globalism demonstration comes into play. If the demonstrations take place anywhere near the Waterfront area, the terrorists could use the crowd as a cover to set up a rocket-propelled grenade launcher. But since the terrorists have never attacked in this method before, my superiors remain focused pre-dominantly on air and water attacks."

"And you disagree with this assessment?" Abraham asked.

"Yes. I think the most likely attack is from the land."

"But I thought that these tankers were double-hulled," Bruce said. "How could a rocket-propelled grenade penetrate?"

"Yes, the tankers are double-hulled with thick steel," Agent Ng con-ceded. "They're designed to protect against running aground, which also makes them well-fortified to withstand an attack from a suicide boat. But the actual tanks are not. They're just a thin membrane."

"So why hasn't anyone taken a shot at a tanker yet?" Bruce asked. "There are hundreds of condos and offices and hotels along the waterfront, and most have balconies. I read that Osama bin Laden's brother owns a condo over in Charlestown, out on one of the piers."

"First of all, everyone who buys or rents a property overlooking the harbor is screened. Second, during tanker transit, we have snipers watching the balconies."

Shelby nodded. "How big are these rocket-propelled grenade things? You said a terrorist could set one up during a rally?"

Agent Ng reached into a briefcase, pulled out a picture of the weapon and explained the basics of firing it. "That thing on the end that looks like a husk of corn is the grenade."

"But how would they set it up without being seen?" Shelby asked.

"I've been to these demonstrations, and it's not unusual for groups to set up little tents to escape from the sun or rain or just for some privacy. So they come in the morning, and they set up a tent, and then they just wait for the tanker to appear in the harbor."

Tents. Bruce had the same thought, turned to Shelby. "I think you should tell them about your conversation with Monique."

Shelby explained Monique's request that she obtain a permit for Christopher Columbus Park for the October 25-26 weekend.

"For the entire weekend?" Abraham asked.

Shelby nodded. "She's planning a big rally, with music and speeches and … well, whatever else they do at these things. Since it's for the whole weekend, we have to assume there'll be tents."

Abraham sat back. "A protest near the harbor, for the entire weekend. The terrorists will see this as an ideal opportunity."

Bruce interjected. "But wait. You're assuming that the tanker will arrive in the harbor on that weekend, at the same time as the rally. These tankers don't come in every day."

"Correct. They come in once a week, more often as the weather turns cold," Agent Ng answered. "The civilian authorities prefer that deliveries occur on the weekend because they have to shut down the Tobin Bridge while the tanker passes underneath and they don't like to disrupt traffic during the week. We also don't want tankers coming in during business hours because we'd just be compounding any tragedy by putting all the workers in the Financial District in danger. But these are just preferences—sometimes the tankers arrive at inconvenient times, and we just have to deal with it."

"The only thing that is certain," Abraham added, "is that the tankers need to move through the harbor during high tide to avoid running aground."

Agent Ng continued. "So, you're correct, Bruce—we don't know for sure that the tanker will arrive during the weekend rally. But there's a good chance that it will, so we'll need to be prepared." She looked around the table, her eyes resting first on Shelby and Bruce, then on Abraham and Madame Radminikov.

"Wait," said Shelby. "What's all this 'we' stuff? This is out of our league."

Abraham sat back, intertwined his fingers on the table. "Agent Ng has been unable to convince her superiors that an attack is imminent."

"What?" Shelby blustered, "You guys are called Homeland Security for a reason, right?"

Agent Ng elaborated. "Look, all we have is a theory—we don't have any hard evidence. The way our intelligence organizations are set up is that we respond to specific intelligence. Intercepted communications, for example. Or movement of suspected terrorists across borders. Or an increase in chatter on certain monitored communication networks. That's just the culture of our intelligence community."

"So?" Shelby blurted.

"So, we're not much good at taking random strands of information from the public domain and drawing conclusions from them. One of the think tanks just did a report criticizing the FBI and CIA for not paying attention to information unless it's marked 'Top Secret.' Well, right now, we don't have anything 'Top Secret.' All we have is common sense."

Shelby leaned forward, tried to keep her voice level. "You mean they're just ignoring this threat?"

The agent shook her head. "Not ignoring, downplaying. They consider it one of many possible attack scenarios. But now that we have a definite date for the demonstrations, I'm going to try to convince my superiors to cancel them—"

Cancel? "No, that's not the way this is supposed to work! Homeland Security is supposed to protect our way of life, not destroy it. You're not supposed to do the terrorists' jobs for them, keeping us scared and cowering under our beds." Shelby took a deep breath. "Look, I think I've made myself clear on this. I'm willing to help you. I want to help you. But not at the expense of just throwing the First Amendment away—"

"Okay, okay," Agent Ng held up her hand. "I hear you. I doubt they would've agreed anyway—they're under orders from Washington not to let it look like we're caving in to the terrorists. But I am going to try to get them to reschedule the tanker delivery. Okay?"

Shelby nodded. Agent Ng looked around the table, continued. "Anyway, when I said we need to be prepared, I was hoping that your group could provide extra eyes and ears on the ground."

Abraham was quick to agree. "Of course. Reb Meyer and his men are very well trained."

"Do you want us there as well?" Shelby asked. She was not sure she could trust the agent not to try to shut down the demonstrations.

Agent Ng nodded, held Shelby's eyes. "Definitely. We would like you ... we *need* you ... to be at Monique Goulston's side at all times, wherever she is. You will be our primary source of information regarding the movement of the demonstrators."

The waitress dropped some potato skins on the table. They sat, untouched. Madame Radminikov turned to Shelby. "Speaking of Monique, how many people does she expect at this rally?"

"She told me 50,000, but it could easily be twice or three times that, especially if the weather is nice. It'll be early enough in the semester that the college kids will still be looking for a party, so you could have lots of kids coming down just to check out the scene, listen to some music."

Bruce shook his head. "If you're a terrorist, you've got to love the symbolism. You've got tens of thousands of people living the American dream, rallying against the government, a big, beautiful display of democracy in action. And they're going to end up as toasted marshmallows. Them, and a bunch of college students, all captured on film for the local news. It's not the World Trade Center, but talk about an attack on our way of life...."

Abraham took a sip of his ginger ale, turned to Shelby. His gray eyes bore into hers. "I cannot stress this enough. This is a crisis situation. Tens of thousands of lives are at stake. At some point, it may become necessary for you to convince Monique Goulston to move this demonstration. You must be prepared to do this."

Shelby sighed. Monique was stubborn and strong-willed, and she loved the symbolism of protesting in Christopher Columbus park. It would be like convincing a lioness to abandon her kill. She raised her chin. "I'll do my best."

Abraham's eyes had not left hers. "No. That is not good enough, Shelby. You will do this if necessary. You *must* do this."

*   *   *

Gregory Neary slipped into the Pizzeria Uno, found an empty stool at the bar. He was pretty sure that Shelby bitch and her boyfriend had come in here....

He kept his head bowed, pulled a baseball cap low over his fore-head. He was even wearing a friggin' Boston University t-shirt. As if he would ever go to a school with so many kikes and so many dikes. Not to mention all the fuckin' Arabs. Not so many Niggers, at least. Drop a bomb on the whole worthless bunch of 'em....

But first things first. Half-hiding behind a pole, he scanned the restaurant, his eyes moving slowly across the room. There. Corner table. Five of them. The old man with the wolf eyes was there. And the Amazon woman who had helped hold him down—she looked like that old bitch of a teacher of his from sixth grade, Mrs. Shapiro. He wrote a whole paper on Israel, really worked hard on it, and she gave him an 'F' just because he spelled it 'Isreal,' like anybody fuck-ing cares. His dad was bullshit, beat him with a belt. Then made him quit the hockey team. Fucking bitch....

He refocused on the table. He didn't recognize the slant-eyed fox with nice legs. Shelby was there. And the boyfriend. He looked like a tough son-of-a-bitch. Best to stay away from him. Or maybe get some buddies to help stomp him. The fat bastard who stuck him with the stun gun was missing. So was the smelly giant with the beard. No doctor, either. But this was a start.

It was the old geezer who said that cutting him would make him more ... docile was the word he used. Yeah, right. If anything, thanks to the testosterone pills he was taking, he was more pissed off at the world than ever. The difference was he smartened up since the cut-ting. The fire still burned inside him, but he was better able to con-trol it, to focus, to plan. He had learned to be cunning and sneaky. Just like the Jews.

He looked around, at the restaurant full of people eating and drinking, talking and laughing. What was wrong with everyone? Why couldn't they see that the dirty Jews and the dumb Niggers and the greasy Mexicans were contaminating America? Well, he was going to do something about it. And he would start by getting revenge on the Hebes who cut him.

He walked over to the hostess station, smiled at the fat pig with a nose ring. "Hey, can you help me out? I think that old guy in the cor-ner over there was my history professor last semester. I didn't turn in my final paper yet, but I need to take a piss, and I don't want to walk right past the dude, you know?"

She smiled. "I hear you."

"Any way you can check your list, see if it's the same guy?"

"No prob." She ran a pencil down a pad of paper. "We were holding a table for him. His name is Abraham Gottlieb." She raised an eyebrow. "You want me to bring you to the employee bathroom?"

He had the name. That was enough for tonight. "No, fuck it. I'll just go piss in the alley."

*   *   *

"Come, Madame, let us walk," Abraham proclaimed.

They had said their goodbyes to Shelby, Bruce and Agent Ng on the sidewalk in front of the pizza restaurant. They then turned to the left, followed Beacon Street west as it crossed up and over the Massachusetts Turnpike and into Brookline. Abraham flipped open his cell phone, turned away from his companion. "Make sure Mr. Neary is followed. And make sure he does not interrupt us." That Neary had not crawled under a rock someplace was fine—Abraham had simply harnessed the young man's hateful rage and was now employing it to his own ends.

The baseball crowd had dispersed. After a few strides, Madame Radminikov reached down and picked up a mustard-stained hot dog wrapper pinned tight against a brick wall by the late-summer breeze; a few feet up the wall, someone had spray-painted the words "YANKEES SUCK" in giant black letters. She dropped the wrapper in an overflowing trash can, walked with him again. "See that girl climbing into the SUV up there, alone?" she asked. "All we need is someone to eat half an apple pie and throw the rest away."

"Pardon me?" What was this drivel about throwing pies? He had important things to discuss with her....

"Oh, nothing, Abraham. Just something Bruce said about the American way of life made me think of an old TV commercial— 'Baseball, hot dogs, apple pie and Chevrolet.'" He had no idea what she was talking about. She continued nonetheless. "It used to be much more simple. When my parents first came to this country, after the war, America was the ideal. America fought against the Russians because ours was the better way of life. Now, nothing is so clear. Look around—we throw trash in the streets, we drive huge cars that waste gas, we're overweight, and we care more about our sports teams than our political leaders. Is that really what we're fighting for, the right to pollute and waste and laze and, just, *consume?* Maybe Monique Goulston is right, maybe we have become the modern-day Rome."

Abraham had no interest in this commentary. It was irrelevant to his mission, and, frankly, beyond the scope of things he had any ability to change. Of more interest was the fact that the corruption of American society seemed to so bother Madame Radminikov. It always surprised him that she thought of herself as an American. A Jewish-American, yes, but an American nonetheless. He was a resident of the United States, but he no more thought of himself as an American than he would think himself Japanese after spending a week in Tokyo. America was where he lived, not who he was. He was a Jew. That was enough. Sometimes, in fact, too much.

He allowed a few seconds to pass. He had known Madame Radminikov for decades: Speaking aloud was her way of organizing her thoughts. She would not expect him to respond, not to a comment so extraneous to their mission. He cleared his throat. "I was pleased that Shelby chose to confide to us Monique Goulston's plans to rally in Columbus Park."

Madame Radminikov shrugged, reached out and took his arm. She must have known it pleased him, though he had never told her so. Never told her that his mother used to take his father's arm in the same fashion. "Why does it matter?" she asked. "We've been listening in on Monique's phone calls; you knew all this already."

"Yes, but I am still not convinced that my niece is completely ... trustworthy." Shelby had hidden the Neary abduction from him, apparently afraid he would seek vengeance. Abraham in turn had concealed the incident from Madame Radminikov, fearing she would blame him for putting his niece in danger. So many lies, so much deceit. Sometimes it was difficult to remember which lies were lies and which lies were half-truths. It was easy to remember that there were no full-truths.

"There are many things I need to tell you tonight, Madame." He began by describing Shelby's abduction, her escape, Neary's continued threats.

"My God, Abraham, who knows what those beasts would have done to her if she hadn't escaped."

"She was never in danger." He faced straight ahead, though he could feel Madame Radminikov's eyes boring into him.

Her voice was firm. "How can you know that for certain?"

"Because we had a man with Neary. One of our operatives infiltrated his group."

She processed this information, came to the inevitable conclusion. "Well, then you must have known of the plan to abduct her."

"Yes, we did."

"Then why did you allow it, Abraham?"

He sighed. "I did not just allow it, I orchestrated it." He had brought Shelby in the van that night, exposed her to Neary, because he anticipated it might become necessary in the future to use Neary against her. Then he made sure Neary was able to track her down through the taxi driver. "My hope was that, by showing her the ugliness of anti-Semitism, by subjecting her to personal attack, it would make her see the merits of our work. She would be forced to see that the only way to fight these monsters was with force. She would realize that sometimes it is acceptable to ignore the legal niceties."

"For this you allowed your niece to be terrorized?" She released his arm.

"Not terrorized, Madame. Frightened, yes, but not terrorized. Terrorized is something quite different." The memories came, without warning, cascading out of the dark recesses of his semi-consciousness. Children machine-gunned. Young girls raped. Infants harpooned. He took a deep breath, willed the visions to recede into the fetid corners of his mind like rats burrowing deeper into an alley dumpster. "As I said, Shelby was never in real danger. The operative was well-trained." In fact, Abraham insisted on using *Kidon's* best man. "His orders were to allow them to frighten her, but to make sure she escaped before she was harmed." His arm tingled in the areas her fingers had rested. "If necessary, he was authorized to ... I believe the term is ... blow his cover. I also had a team of men following in a second car just in case. I must say, however, Shelby escaped far earlier than was planned. She basically overpowered her captors only minutes after her abduction. Quite impressive."

They continued walking, Madame Radminikov silent for almost half a block. Finally, a sigh, followed by yet another inevitable conclusion. "You didn't tell me of this plan because you knew I would disapprove."

"Some decisions are mine alone to make."

"Yes, they are. But this plan did not work."

He nodded. His niece and her idealism were a complete mystery to him. "Perhaps I have erred, perhaps I have misread my niece."

Madame Radminikov offered a wry smile. "Perhaps." She rejoined her arm around his, her touch warming him. "At least you're able to admit when you're wrong."

He raised an eyebrow at her. Why wouldn't he be? "As I read once, *He who never made a mistake never made a discovery.*"

She lifted her chin, shook her head. "Fascinating." He waited for her to continue. "Anyway, if you want to recruit Shelby, you need to appeal to her goodwill, not to her darker emotions. She is a nurturer, a healer, a protector. Not a warrior. You need to convince her she has a chance to help people, to make the world a better place for her baby."

"That is exactly what I am trying to do, to protect the Jewish people. Is that not good for her baby? How can she not see this?"

"She doesn't see the world as we do, Abraham. You see yourself as a Jew who happens to live in America. I see myself as a Jewish-American. Shelby sees herself as an American who also happens to be Jewish." Abraham nodded. It was called assimilation. If not arrested, it would eradicate the Jewish people.

The rumbling and screeching of a Green Line transit train silenced them. It passed, and Madame Radminikov continued. "At first we thought she would help us because she was Jewish, and because her mother asked her to. But we underestimated her disdain for our tactics. Then you thought you could frighten her into aiding us with this abduction escapade, by making the anti-Semitism personal to her.

But that also failed, because she believes, as an American, that problems like anti-Semitism can be dealt with peacefully. You Europeans are cynical, but we Americans are still quite idealistic. We think we can fix the world."

Abraham nodded. "Yes, I've seen the results. Vietnam, Iraq, Afghanistan." He stopped. This observation was irrelevant. "Continue, please."

"Shelby is not just an American, she's a lawyer. She sees her job as defending the Constitution. That's why she's only been lukewarm in support of us. She wants to help prevent the terrorist attack, but she's torn. She doesn't want to do anything that undermines the free speech rights of the protestors."

As usual, Madame Radminikov captured the essence of the emotional and psychological issues at play. He neglected to consult her at his peril. But she was not as adept as he at seeing the big picture, at understanding how all the pieces fit together. "But we need more from her—she is our only access to Monique Goulston. We need a total commitment. We need a way to make this more personal for her, a way to overcome her ambivalence. My Neary abduction strategy failed. But there is another way."

Madame Radminikov weighed his words. "You're referring to Rex Griffin, right? As I've told you, I disapprove of using him in any way."

"I would prefer not to use him myself. But the stakes are higher than even you know. There is much I have not told you, Leah." Her eyes showed surprise at his use of her first name. Fatigue washed over him; he tried to remember the last time he had slept. "Come, let us sit on this bench, under this tree."

*   *   *

Abraham and Madame Radminikov settled onto a wooden bench in a small park in Brookline, just off of Beacon Street. A light wind stirred the leaves in the oak tree over their head, and an occasional acorn fell near them.

Abraham took a deep breath. "I am afraid that we are in a rather desperate situation—Continental Casualty's net asset value is down by almost one-half this year alone. We are getting close to the point where we can no longer use the insurance business to fund *Kidon's* operations."

She turned her bulk toward him. "Down a half? How could that be?"

Her disapproval stung. "We have been paying numerous claims on the Florida hurricanes, the tsunami disaster, Hurricane Katrina. Never have we had so many natural disasters concentrated in such a short period of time." It was not his fault, yet it was. He had ceded control of the insurance business to younger minds; when other companies shied away from the risky Florida and Gulf Coast markets, they made the decision that Continental should fill the void. "Also, many new companies entered the market after September 11, companies that were well-capitalized and saw the opportunity to compete against those of us that were weakened by paying September 11 claims. We raised rates sharply after September 11, but these new companies have driven them back down. So, our revenues are down as well." Again, not his fault. At least not directly. "Our final problem is that the stock market has been stagnant, so our asset values are down." As he had with the insurance business, Abraham had ceded control of investment strategy to the next generation of executives. It was not his fault the strategy failed, but he was to blame for choosing poorly in delegating the task. "Put it all together, and Continental Casualty is a single natural disaster away from insolvency."

Madame Radminikov's eyes searched his face. He looked for disapproval, disappointment. If the company went bankrupt, the entire operation—his life's work, her life's work—would die with it. Yet she looked at him the way he remembered his mother looking at him when he skinned his knee as a boy. "Poor Abraham." She touched his cheek.

He pulled away. "Leah, this is not about me." He tried to control his anger. "We must find a way to keep *Kidon* alive. There are young people, good people, in place to continue long after we are dead. But there is nothing to continue unless we can bring profitability back to the insurance business."

She pulled a tissue from her pocket, wiped her nose. "Abraham, what does any of this have to do with Shelby?"

He took a deep breath. "Nothing, and yet everything." It would be so much more efficient if information simply flowed from his brain to those of his associates, like a computer file copied and shared. But he needed Madame Radminikov's help, and she would not give it blindly. Not on something like this. He would have to explain.

"Come, let us walk again." He would rest later; it would be more efficient to make progress on their journey while they talked. "Of the three variables, the only one I can exert any control over is insurance rates. I cannot prevent natural disasters, and I cannot orchestrate the performance of the stock market. However, I have a plan that will increase insurance rates significantly. Enough, in fact, to put Continental back into a stable financial position." He paused here.

"I'm listening, Abraham. Continue." It was an old trick he had learned years ago from a business psychology book. Her requesting that he continue brought her incrementally closer to accepting his plan. 'Buying-in,' it was called.

"After September 11, rates rose quickly in anticipation of further terrorist attacks. When years passed and no further attacks occurred, rates decreased. What we need is another attack, one that will allow us to raise rates again."

She heard his unspoken words. "That's your plan, to sponsor a terrorist attack? No, Abraham, that's crazy." Her eyes searched his face again, this time without any sympathy. He looked back at her impassively—he knew death, and she knew it did not frighten him. She leveled her voice, tried to reach him with reason. "And it is also self-defeating—if there's another attack, you'd have to pay out huge claims again. Thousands would die, and Continental would still be insolvent."

He allowed her to finish. He had purposely walked her to the edge of the cliff, allowed her to peer over the side and consider the possibility that he was planning to orchestrate a terrorist attack. That way when he pulled her back, when he proposed something risky but not quite as shocking, she would be less steeled against it. "No, Leah, that is not what I am proposing. I agree, a successful terrorist attack would not benefit us. It would cost us huge sums in claims, it would embolden other groups to make further attacks, and the white supremacists would blame it all on the Jews. But, an *unsuccessful* attack would bring many of the benefits and few of the costs."

She took a deep breath, exhaled slowly. Red wine and tomato sauce and a warm, floral perfume wafted, not unpleasantly, over him. "An unsuccessful attack. I see. And how exactly does one orchestrate such a thing?"

She was asking how rather than why—again, she had begun to buy in. "First of all, nothing is exact when it comes to terrorism. And I am not orchestrating anything. But I have recently infiltrated a terrorist cell, one that is targeting an LNG tanker in Boston Harbor. You are the only one who knows this—I have not yet told Mr. Clevinsky, or Reb Meyer, or any of the others."

She raised an eyebrow. "Abraham, that is not how we operate."

He set his jaw. "Not customarily, no." He plowed ahead. "In any event, the demonstrations at Columbus Park are an ideal opportunity for this terrorist cell to strike, and I believe they will do so. I also believe that, with Shelby's assistance, we can stop them. To borrow an old saying, there will be lots of smoke but no fire. If we are successful, the attempt will come close enough to succeeding to cause widespread panic, but will not actually cause significant loss of life or property."

The word 'significant' hung in the air.

Her words came slowly. "I see."

"Leah, this is the reality we live in. You see the threat of a terrorist attack as horrific. I see it as an opportunity. Either way, we must respond to it. Our choices are to try to stop the attack, or to do nothing and allow it to happen. The choice is obvious."

"No, Abraham. There is a third choice as well. You say you have infiltrated this group—you could share what you know with the authorities, let them arrest these animals and stop the attack now."

"Madame, I have worked for months to infiltrate this cell, at substantial cost and grave danger to *Kidon* members." He fought to keep the frustration—and desperation—out of his voice. He was playing with fire here, literally, and there was no guarantee half the city would not be burned. He had infiltrated Gabriella's terrorist cell, but infiltration was not the same as control. It was like feeding an attack dog—it would accept your food, but that did not mean you could stop it from biting your neighbor. "This is an ideal opportunity for *Kidon.*" In fact, this was probably the last chance to save it. "Why would I give it away for nothing?" If he went to the authorities, they would arrest Gabriella and her gang, send them to Guantanamo for questioning. No panic, no terror. And no rate increase.

"I see." She stared at her feet, sighed, finally spoke again in a low voice. "What if you are wrong, what if they do not attack during the demonstrations?"

"I am confident they will attack. The world's eyes will be on Boston, and the chaos of the demonstrations will provide the terrorists an ideal cover."

Madame Radminikov stared at the ground. "There's one other factor you haven't considered: As the schedule now falls, if the Red Sox make it to the World Series, the sixth and seventh games will be played at Fenway Park that weekend."

He nodded. "Even better for the terrorists. More attention on the city, and the possibility of post-game riots and celebrations will further distract law enforcement."

"So, again, back to Shelby, why is she so important to the plan?"

"Yes. Two reasons. First, she is our circuit breaker: If I have miscalculated, if we are unable to intervene and thwart the attack on the tanker at the last minute, we will need a way to quickly disperse the demonstrators. We need Shelby to be in a position to convince Miss Goulston to move the rally at a moment's notice."

Madame Radminikov nodded. "I understand. Monique will listen to Shelby, trust her. More so than she would the authorities. If Shelby says thousands of lives are at stake, Monique will believe her."

"Second, as I said, the LNG tanker is the terrorists' primary target. But there is the possibility that the tanker will not come into the harbor that weekend. So the terrorists will have back-up targets as well, with other cells ready to strike, using the demonstrations as cover. In fact, a batch of anthrax was stolen from the Tulane University medical school in the aftermath of Hurricane Katrina. It was being quietly shopped around; I received an intelligence report indicating it is on its way to Boston."

Madame Radminikov put her hand to her mouth. "Depending on the strain, anthrax could kill thousands."

"Yes." And it would do nothing to raise insurance rates since no property would be damaged. "In order to foil these attacks, we are going to need Shelby to provide specific details of the demonstrations—times, locations, activities, crowd estimates, back-up plans. I do not believe Monique Goulston intends for her troops to sit placidly in one spot for the entire weekend, chanting slogans and drinking iced tea, despite what her permit application may state." It would do him no good to foil the LNG attack, only to have a different cell attack elsewhere. "And, again, we may need Shelby to convince Miss Goulston to change times, to relocate rallies, to tell people to disperse. By controlling the crowd, we can neutralize the terrorists."

"I see. Abraham, are you are certain you can orchestrate all this?"

"Certain? No, I am not."

She spun toward him. "That's not good enough!" He could see the muscles tighten in her neck and jaw. "Listen to me, Abraham. I have always listened to you, always followed you. But this is different. This plan of yours puts tens of thousands of lives in danger. So you better be damned sure it's going to work."

He modulated his voice to counterbalance her timbre. "I am not at all sure, Leah. What I am sure of is that an attack is going to occur. I am also sure that I am going to try to prevent it. Finally, I am sure that in order to succeed we need Shelby's full cooperation and assistance."

Shelby's cooperation and assistance. Of the dozens of variables in his plan, this was not one he expected would be so unmanageable. Or so frustrating. Years ago, he had procured the letter from his sister. His own parents never had a chance to write him a final message. How could Shelby ignore hers? "This battle needs to become personal to her, Leah. She has agreed to help us, but only if it does not require her to do anything unsavory. That is not enough—we need her to be our zealous ally. I failed to coerce that zeal with the Neary abduction, just as the letter from her mother and our appeal to her Jewish heritage failed."

Madame Radminikov would have to understand that the most difficult part of being a leader was sacrificing soldiers to win battles. He continued, his voice firm. "I am left with no choice now but to enlist the services of Rex Griffin."

*   *   *

Business-suited men and women carrying briefcases and chatting on cell-phones packed the sidewalks of the Financial District. Most of the city vacationed in August; all of the city, including students, returned in September. As if on cue, the weather had cooled, and shadows darkened some of the sidewalks even in the early afternoon. Shelby tried not to allow the shadow of a pending attack to darken her mood.

She and Bruce had just spent her lunch hour picking out wedding invitations. Actually, Shelby picked them, and Bruce nodded dutifully. "I'll save myself for an argument over something I really care about," he laughed. It was a bittersweet experience—she envisioned it as one of those mother-daughter milestone moments, not something done while your fiancé slipped next door to grab sandwiches. Her mother's voice inside her head (pushing for *bright white, embossed with silver wedding bells, but only if they throw in the thank you notes for free*) did not really cut it.

Almost two weeks had passed since Shelby filed the application for Monique's demonstration permit. Yesterday afternoon she received a phone call from a friend at City Hall—application denied. She received the actual denial by fax this morning, reciting the usual concerns about security and crowd control and traffic. She was now on her way to the new federal courthouse to file an appeal, one that she had already drafted in anticipation of the city's denial. The appeal sought an injunction preventing the city from interfering with the demonstration.

She and Bruce strolled past office buildings, holding hands, Bruce carrying her briefcase. She flashed forward 40 years, pictured Bruce carrying her pocketbook through the grocery store aisles, like those old couples in Florida....

They followed Congress Street over Fort Point Channel and entered the Seaport District. The press called it Boston's next frontier, but, other than the federal courthouse and a new convention center, it remained largely defined by the same hulking brick warehouses, scattered seafood restaurants and parking lots that had occupied it for the past half-century. At one point a developer proposed building stadiums for both the Red Sox and the Patriots on some of the open acreage, but in Boston projects lived or died based not on their merits but rather on the political clout of their proponents. Or, in this case, their opponents.

They crossed the bridge; to their left, tethered to a pier, bobbed a replica, Colonial-style ship which housed the Tea Party Museum. She should have appreciated the symbolism—she was on her way to court to uphold the right to protest against the government, the very right the Colonists were exercising during the Boston Tea Party. Instead her eyes drifted to a spot beyond the wooden vessel, to the giant white milk bottle rising whimsically in front of the Children's Museum on the far bank of the channel. A part of her wanted to take Bruce by the hand, throw her briefcase in the harbor like a crate of tea, and go watch a bunch of kids crawl and explore and experiment for a few hours. Somebody else could save democracy; she had a wedding to plan and a baby to nurture.

Bruce waited until her eyes flicked away from the milk bottle. "I get the sense your uncle doesn't think you're doing everything you can to help him." He said it casually, bumping her playfully with his hip to try to soften the comment's edge.

Her face flushed. "Why do you say that?"

"Maybe it has something to do with you saying, 'I'm not going to help you if it means canceling the demonstration.'"

She shrugged. "Whatever. He knew that from the beginning."

"You know, here's the perfect opportunity."

"To do what?"

"To help."

It took her a second to get his message. "What are you saying, that I should purposely lose the appeal?"

"Well, if you lose the case, and Monique doesn't get a permit, she'd have to move the rally away from the harbor."

"She might. Or she might just hold the rally anyway—"

"Exactly." He smiled. "Then we both agree the First Amendment isn't being threatened here. Permit or not, they rally." He had cornered her.

She wriggled out. "I'm not so sure that forcing people to face jail time for demonstrating doesn't threaten the First Amendment. But, even if it didn't, I can't just throw a case like that, Bruce. She's my client, and I have a duty to represent her to the best of my ability."

"I think that's your uncle's point: You see this as just another part of your professional life. He sees it as something very personal, and he wants it to be personal for you also."

"It is personal to me. We're talking about my integrity here." Maybe she should have let Bruce win the invitations argument....

"I'm just saying that professional ethics are nice and all, but they're not as important as preventing a terrorist attack."

Here they were again. Bruce viewed laws like some kind of college elective—optional, depending on the other requirements of his day. She sighed. "I don't see why it has to be one or the other. The reason I agreed to help my uncle is so we can help stop the terrorist attack and *still* allow the demonstrators to rally." Her hand moved to her belly. "Isn't that the whole idea? Aren't we trying to stop the terrorists from taking away our freedoms?"

Bruce did not answer. His head was turned to the left, his eyes focused on the hulking brick hotel built on a pier jutting into the harbor. Christopher Columbus Park sat on the far side of that hotel. She followed his eyes, noticed for the first time how drastically the harbor narrowed in that area. A tanker moving past Christopher Columbus Park would pass only a few hundred yards from the shoreline. In other words, the height of the tanker was roughly equal to the span of water separating the ship from the shore.

She concluded her argument, which until seconds ago seemed so persuasive. "Besides, Monique's not stupid. If my uncle really wants me to win her confidence, I don't see how throwing a case is going to help."

*   *   *

The federal court ordered a hearing on 48 hours notice. More than a month remained before the planned late-October demonstrations, but the judge wanted to give both parties plenty of time to appeal her decision prior to the event.

The judge, a heavy-set woman in her early fifties, had a round face and long, gray-brown hair pulled back in a single ponytail. Joanna Bell, appointed to the bench in 1998 by President Clinton. Shelby filled in the blanks: peace activist in the '60s, feminist in the '70s, anti-nuker in the '80s. Likely a woman with a healthy degree of skepticism when it came to government trampling on the Bill of Rights....

Or maybe not. "I've read your brief, Ms. Baskin. Before September 11, I would have shared your concerns. But I must warn you that I lost a cousin in that attack. It's a whole new ballgame now when it comes to security."

Well, at least she knew what she was up against. Shelby and a thin, stoop-shouldered man were standing in front of matching mahogany tables facing the judge, who was peering at them over a pair of reading glasses perched near the end of her nose. The judge turned to her right. "Mr. Difanzo, you are here for the city of Boston, correct?"

He spoke quickly in a high-pitched, nasal voice. "Yes, Your Honor. The city has serious concerns, very serious concerns, regarding the scope of the applicant's application. The city has concerns regarding security, concerns regarding traffic, concerns regarding crowd control. The city has very serious concerns, Your Honor, concerns that I believe—"

The judge stopped him with a raised hand. "I got it. Serious concerns. Thank you, counselor." Her eyes wandered over to a window. "I have an idea. It's a nice day. Let's take a walk and visit the site. You can brief me on the way. Meet me in front of the building in five minutes." She turned to her clerk. "We are in recess."

*   *   *

Bruce waited for Shelby in the back of the courtroom. She enjoyed the feeling of his hand on her elbow as he guided her through the swinging door. "That judge is going to be tough," he said. "You're going to be talking about Columbus Park, but she's going to be picturing the World Trade Center."

"I know." She looped her arm around his as they walked to the lobby. "That's why I need to win this case." She tried to keep her voice low, but the words poured out of her in a torrent. "Listen. Remember we were talking about whether I should throw the case? And I said I couldn't, because I had a duty to my client? Well, it's more than that." She forced herself to slow down. "If we let the terrorists destroy the First Amendment, they've won, they've beat us, they've taken what is unique about this country and stomped it into the ground. Our right to protest, to vote, to assemble, all these things are at risk. The government is already spying on us, reading our emails, checking on the books we read. Now they're going to tell us we can't protest? The city is just looking for an excuse to keep the protestors away. Even this judge, who should know better, is scared. It's not right, Bruce, it's not America...." She gulped some air. The words had been swimming around in her brain for weeks, but she could never get them to come together to form a coherent thought. Now they had.

"No, but it's the world we live in. So here's a question for you: How can you be saying the city is just looking for an excuse to deny the permit, when you know for a fact that Homeland Security has specific concerns about terrorists infiltrating the rally? You can't have it both ways."

She took a deep breath. It was a good question. One she had been wrestling with for days. "Here's the distinction. The city is trying to shut this down just because it doesn't want the hassle of having to police it, of having 50,000 demonstrators marching in the streets. But the city, as far as I know, doesn't have any real fear of a terrorist attack. If they did, if they had information from Agent Ng or someone else at Homeland Security, they would have presented it to the judge. So what the city is doing is totally unconstitutional. They're just throwing out this 'security concern' stuff to try to intimidate the judge. They're hiding behind September 11, using it as an excuse to keep the riff-raff out of Boston. If Homeland Security wants to come in later on and explain to the judge they've uncovered a terrorist plot and the rally needs to be shut down, well, that's a different story. But that's not where we are right now." She waited for Bruce's reaction, ready to parlay whatever argument he might counter with.

Instead, he looked back at her with a crooked smile. "Hard to argue with that." He winked, grinned, and leaned in and kissed her gently on the mouth. He lingered, then squeezed her hand and pulled away. "Go get 'em, tiger. I'll be waiting here for you when you're done."

"Thanks, Bruce. Thanks for understanding me." They separated, and she walked toward Difanzo, sitting on a bench in the plaza outside the courthouse. The courthouse itself overlooked Boston Harbor. Every LNG tanker that entered Boston chugged past, and was reflected in, the giant glass, sail-like wall that comprised the back portion of the red-brick building.

Difanzo squinted up at her, lowered his eyes from the sun, realized he was now staring at her exposed calves, and then finally stared down at his feet. She swallowed a smile, spoke. "So, a field trip. This is a surprise."

"No, no, actually not. We had a similar site visit with Judge Woodlock for the Democratic Convention protest zone outside the FleetCenter."

Shelby had quoted from the case extensively in her brief. In the Democratic Convention case, the city successfully argued that restricting demonstrators to a protest zone set up outside the FleetCenter—a "holding pen" was how the protestors referred to it— was a reasonable restriction on the protestors' First Amendment rights. But the judge had allowed the restriction only because of the danger of direct physical confrontation between the protestors and convention delegates entering the FleetCenter. That rationale did not apply in this case—the targets of the protestors' wrath would be miles away in Cambridge, not next door.

Judge Bell walked toward them; Shelby almost did not recognize her in a light blue windbreaker, tan slacks and over-sized sunglasses. "Ready to go?"

Shelby and Difanzo stood, fell in on either side of the judge. A federal marshal followed a respectful distance behind. "I keep reading about this Harborwalk," the judge said. "Apparently now you can walk from South Boston all the way to Charlestown, right along the harbor."

They crossed back over Fort Point Channel, then turned right and proceeded along a path behind the hotels, office buildings and condo complexes lining the harbor. Judge Bell questioned them while they walked, accompanied occasionally by a hungry seagull.

"Mr. Difanzo, you say the city has serious concerns. Can you be more specific, please?"

"Well, yes Your Honor. We have serious concerns about security, crowd control and traffic." Shelby's frustration grew. The city had nothing specific. They just did not want the rally. Well, tough luck.

The judge took a deep breath. "Let's take this one at a time. What are your *specific* security concerns?" Good. At least the judge was going to require something substantive.

"Your Honor, anytime you have 50,000 demonstrators loose in a downtown area, there will be security concerns. *Serious* security concerns."

Shelby had learned a valuable lesson as a young litigator: If your opponent was flailing, keep your mouth shut.

Judge Bell pressed him. "So, what you're saying is that the city is within its rights to adopt a policy that, due to *serious security concerns*, all large demonstrations should be banned in Boston?"

The judge pivoted her head to the left and waited for a response from Shelby. She would have to speak after all. "The law is clear on this, Your Honor. The city can impose conditions on demonstrations to ensure public safety, but it cannot ban them altogether. Under the *Forsyth County* line of cases, there is a 'heavy presumption' against the government when it tries to justify a prior restraint on speech. If it does try to restrain speech, it must do so in a 'narrowly-tailored' way. These vague statements about security concerns, absent anything specific, do not overcome this heavy presumption. And even if they did, a total ban is not narrowly-tailored."

Judge Bell turned back to Difanzo. "Ms. Baskin's summary of the law is, I think, a fair one."

"I never said that the city is pushing for a total ban," Difanzo whined. "I didn't. But the size of this demonstration is excessive, especially in the heart of downtown. We would like to see a much smaller demonstration."

Back to Shelby. "With all due respect, Mr. Difanzo, limiting the demonstration would be just as unlawful as prohibiting it. Every citizen has the right to free speech. Not just those who happen to be first in line." Why was it that kids who are taught in grade school to treasure the Bill of Rights grow into adults—lawyers, even—who treat the mandate with no more reverence than an old newspaper?

"Is it your position that the city has no jurisdiction here whatsoever?" the judge asked Shelby.

"No. If the city has specific concerns, it can request that my clients take steps to address these concerns. For example, if the city is worried about safety, it can cordon off an area to allow for access by safety vehicles. If liability is an issue, the city can require liability insurance. Or trash removal. The city can even require Port-a-Potties. In other words, the city can impose *conditions* on the demonstration. But you can't tell people they can't come. If 50,000 people want to rally, they get to rally." Welcome to America.

Difanzo himself tried to rally. "I respectfully disagree, Your Honor. This is similar to the *United for Peace & Justice* case in New York, where the city was allowed to deny a permit for a march on the United Nations because it could not guarantee security. That is the city's position here—we cannot guarantee security. We are concerned about a terrorist attack."

There. He dropped the magic words. *Terrorist attack.* The judge nodded, her face hardening. "I remember the U.N. case. How do you respond, Ms. Baskin?"

They crossed behind the Harbor Towers condominiums, past a piece of modern art that looked like a giant pair of aluminum sun reflectors that women in the 1950s held under their chins at the beach to reflect the sun onto their faces. If the tanker blew, would the sculpture withstand a wall of fire? Or would the metal magnify it? Reflect it?

Shelby shook her musings away, reminded herself that the judge, and apparently the city, knew nothing of any terrorist plot to ignite an LNG tanker. "There are two important distinctions between this demonstration and the United Nations march. First, even in the U.N. case the city did allow a 100,000-person demonstration in a park a few blocks away. It was the *march* that presented the security concerns, because it stretched along such a long route. The *demonstration* was allowed. And second, there were specific security concerns in that case because the protestors wanted to demonstrate right outside U.N. headquarters and the police were not sure they could protect the U.N. and its personnel. In that sense, it was similar to the Democratic Convention case, where the convention delegates were at risk." She took a deep breath. "But there's nobody to protest against in Columbus Park except a statue of Christopher Columbus himself. There can be no overriding security concerns, because there's nobody here that needs to be kept secure."

Difanzo ignored her argument. His approach reminded Shelby of an old saying in the law: If the facts are against you, argue the law. If the law is against you, argue the facts. If they're both against you, just argue. "In light of our serious security concerns, if there are going to be 50,000 demonstrators the city would like a different location, not in downtown. Such as the U-Mass Boston campus." Isolated, inaccessible, far from the city core.

The judge spun her head back to Shelby. "That's an interesting compromise. I'm not sure I like the idea of so many people demonstrating downtown...."

No. The case was slipping away, the judge looking for some middle ground that would give her legal cover for allowing the city to deny the permit. The September 11 attack had paralyzed the judge, as it had other public officials. Nobody would take any action or make any decision that might lead, however indirectly, to another catastrophe. The country's leaders had become like a parent who lost a child to pneumonia and now kept their remaining children locked in the house with the heat turned high. But didn't anyone else realize that the cure was in many ways worse than the disease, that allowing the government to dictate where and when the people could assemble and demonstrate undermined the very foundation upon which America was built?

She took a deep breath, locked her eyes on the judge's. "Your Honor. This is a demonstration, in Christopher Columbus Park, against economic imperialism, while a world economic summit is being held a few miles away. The symbolism of being in Columbus Park is paramount—Christopher Columbus is, in the eyes of the applicant, the very personification of economic imperialism. The Democratic Convention case talks extensively about how the symbolic value of where a demonstration is held can be an essential part of its message. Moving the demonstration would seriously undermine the applicant's message."

Difanzo interrupted the judge before she could question Shelby further. "Again, Your Honor, the court in the U.N. case allowed the demonstration to be moved away from U.N. headquarters, despite the symbolic value of marching right to its doorstep—"

"As I said, Your Honor, that case is easily distinguished on its facts—"

The judge held up her hand. "All right, enough. I assume these arguments are contained in your briefs. What I'd like to do now is view the site." They approached the Long Wharf Marriott, a hulking red-brick structure that stretched over much of the length of the pier. It looked like a giant, red Jersey barrier. They bisected it by passing through the hotel lobby, reemerged on the far side into Christopher Columbus Park. Today, as when Shelby visited a few weeks earlier, the park bustled with activity.

Shelby watched the judge's eyes scan the area, knowing the jurist did not imagine, as she did, a fiery cyclone tumbling in from the ocean like some kind of super-heated funnel cloud....

"Mr. Difanzo, how large is this area?"

"Um, I'd say a couple of acres, Your Honor."

Shelby pulled her eyes from the harbor, took a deep breath. "It is 4.3 acres, Your Honor." She hoped she did not sound smug.

Difanzo tried to recover. "That may be its total size, but I was referring to the areas of the park that would be available for use during a demonstration. The *usable* area of the park is what I meant. And the city has serious concerns about 50,000 people gathering here. Serious concerns."

Shelby waited for the judge to turn to her, then responded. "I'd like to point out that this park is approximately the same size as the area on the Esplanade in front of the Hatch Shell. If you've been to the July 4th celebrations, you know 50,000 people can fit in a site this size."

And you also know they are packed in like rush-hour commuters on the Red Line. In an emergency, there would be no chance of an orderly evacuation. Not that they could hope to outrun a ball of fire anyway....

"I agree," the judge said. "I've spent many a July 4th there myself. As long as you've got rest rooms and a snack bar, everything is fine. What else have you got, Mr. Difanzo?" It was the type of question that signaled to an attorney that he better have an ace up his sleeve.

"Traffic concerns, serious traffic concerns, Your Honor."

Not an ace. Not even a face card. "There's a subway station right across the street," Shelby said. "Most of the demonstrators are going to be college students and people from out of town. They're not coming by car. At worse, the MBTA might need to add some extra trains, and there might be a bunch of bikes piled up by the street."

Difanzo plowed ahead. "But, for a demonstration this size, we'll need security and medical vehicles on the ready. They'll have to park along Atlantic Avenue, which means we'll have to shut down one lane of traffic."

"With all due respect," Shelby said, "Atlantic Avenue has had a lane shut down for most of the past decade because of the Big Dig. And this will be a weekend event, so there will be no commuter traffic."

The judge looked at her watch, took a deep breath. "All right. Here's what I'm going to do. I'm going to grant Ms. Baskin's request." *Yes.* Shelby resisted the urge to hug the jurist. Somebody, at least, understood the importance of the First Amendment. "I'm going to issue an injunction preventing the city from denying a demonstration permit as requested by the applicant. Between now and the date of the event, however, I will allow the city to reappear before me with any new, *specific* security issues it may have identified. Unless and until I see any such evidence, the injunction will stand. I will have a written decision for you by tomorrow."

*   *   *

"You will find we can be very generous, Mr. Ring. But we will also not hesitate to punish our enemies." Abraham sat with Burt Ring at a corner table at the Legal Sea Foods restaurant in the Copley Place mall, surrounded by shoppers, tourists and office workers on their lunch break.

Abraham preferred this type of negotiation—you tell me what you want, I tell you what I want, we agree on terms, and the deal is done. These games he played with Shelby, trying to appeal to her principles rather than her self-interest, exasperated him. Her recent actions— convincing a federal judge to allow Miss Goulston's rally to be held at Columbus park, when she instead could easily have lost the case— indicated she continued to balance the merits of preventing the ter- rorist attack on the one hand against preserving the civil liberties of her client on the other. Like some mythical goddess of justice, she weighed and balanced and parsed. He was right to have recruited Rex Griffin; it would be Griffin's job to tip the scales.

Not that the whole Burt Ring development itself did not exasper- ate him. Abraham had first learned of Ring from *Kidon's* surveillance of his wife, Gabriella. Then Ring's name came up again during the tap on Monique Goulston's phone. That Ring was Monique's cousin was a frightening development—one of those coincidences that no amount of planning could account for. Gabriella and her terrorist cell could now ferret out the details of Monique's plans for the demon- stration weekend through Ring. Whatever advantage Abraham had gained by placing Shelby—still only tepid in her support—in Monique's inner circle had been neutralized, if not trumped. Gabriella no longer needed money from him; the operation was fully funded. If it reached the point where Gabriella no longer depended on Abraham for information as well, he would lose control over her. And over the operation.

At Abraham's behest, an associate of his, who happened to be one of *The Alternative's* largest advertisers, had set up this lunch meeting.

"And who exactly are the 'we' that punish their enemies, Mr. Gottlieb?"

"I have told you all you need to know. You may accept our offer, or you may reject it. But, again, if you accept it you will be expected to abide by our terms."

Ring put down his spoon, wiped some chowder off his chin with a cloth napkin. "So let me get this straight. You're willing to guarantee me one hundred separate $500 contributions to Gabriella's campaign, and all I have to do is introduce some friend of yours to my cousin Monique?"

Abraham considered offering a greater sum, but overpaying engendered suspicion. Ring, though not wealthy, had plenty of wealthy friends, and the offer of $50,000 would probably not normally tempt him. But the Clean Elections law in Massachusetts limited campaign contributions to $500 per contributor. A candidate therefore needed to secure as many $500 contributors as possible. To net a hundred fresh check-writers in exchange for a single favor would be an enormous coup. "Introduce him to her, and convince her that you have known him for a number of years and that he is who he claims to be. Your wife's campaign will receive $25,000 now, and another $25,000 once the introduction has been made."

"I'm sorry, but this still doesn't add up to me. Our mutual friend said you were in the insurance industry. Why do you care about my cousin Monique?"

The best lies always rested on a foundation of truth. "Put the pieces together, Mr. Ring. It seems that wherever your cousin Monique goes, our claims adjusters soon must follow. We would prefer to avoid another Seattle situation. It wasn't a catastrophic loss, but it was an entirely avoidable one."

Ring sat back. "Ah, I see. You want this friend of yours to infiltrate Monique's group so you can get inside information on the demonstrations."

"Exactly. We realize we will not be able to stop the demonstrations, but with enough information we will be able to take the necessary steps to control the damage."

"Okay, you have yourself a deal. So who is this friend of yours?"

"I must emphasize to you, Mr. Ring, the sensitive nature of this ... operation. Your cousin must never sense that our friend is anything other than who he purports to be. If we learn that you have undermined us in any way, the consequences will be sudden and dramatic. Fires can be devastating to a business such as yours, Mr. Ring. Especially when the insurance company refuses to pay."

Abraham fixed his gray eyes on Ring until Ring could hold them no more. Ring turned to reach down for a glass of water, offered a nervous laugh. "Yes, yes, I understand. I can keep a secret."

Intimidating the publisher so easily pleased Abraham. In a few weeks he might need another favor from him, and the fact that Abraham had already established his dominance over the man would make extracting the second favor that much easier. "Very well. You will introduce our friend to Monique Goulston as a casual acquaintance, someone whom you have met at various social functions around town. You will tell her that at a recent event he cornered you and was railing against current U.S. policy in Iraq, against the Patriot Act, against the evils of globalism and multinational corporations. You will tell her that you have also heard a rumor that he was once part of the radical Weatherman group in the late 1960s, but that he changed his name to avoid arrest. Finally, you will tell her that he made his money in software, but now owns a number of apartment buildings on Beacon Hill. You will tell her that this is all you know about him, but that you thought he would be a useful ally to her in Boston. He will take it from there."

Ring nodded. "And this guy's name?"

"Griffin. Rex Griffin."

*   *   *

Madame Radminikov sat in one of the high leather swivel chairs on Abraham's jet, side-by-side with Abraham. She watched the two men study each other across the small table between them.

Abraham addressed his guest. "I will explain things to you once, and once only, Mr. Griffin." Griffin picked at a scab on his cheek, but otherwise seemed less … feral … than during their earlier visit to the mental institution. The staff had cleaned him up and put him in a fresh pair of khakis and a gray-brown golf shirt. And his liberation from the zoo-like conditions apparently soothed him as well.

"We arranged for your release because, as I hinted at during our last visit, we have common enemies: Bruce Arrujo and Shelby Baskin." A knot formed in Madame Radminikov's chest—she still opposed the whole idea of unleashing this monster on Shelby and Bruce.

Abraham explained to Griffin Monique's plan for a massive demonstration in late October. "Here is our arrangement: You will be given information on a 'need-to-know' basis. At this time, it is not important that you know what our group's role in this demonstration is. Nor is it important that you know how Mr. Arrujo and Miss Baskin fit in. You will be given a cover, and with that cover you will win Monique Goulston's confidence. You will then direct her in certain ways as we mandate. If you perform as instructed, we will grant you your freedom. If not, we will lobotomize you and return you to the hospital." With enough money, anything was possible.

Griffin leered at him. "House's money. Freedom or a lobotomy—either way I'll be better off than in that hell-hole."

Abraham looked out the window at the Adirondack mountains in the distance, nodded. "Agreed. Nonetheless, the former is preferable to the latter. There is a new life waiting for you if you succeed—a new identity, the necessary travel papers, enough money to settle comfortably on some tropical island. Most of all, we can arrange it so the authorities do not pursue you." The police did not want Griffin for any crime, but Abraham did not disabuse Griffin of his mistaken belief that he faced a lifetime in jail for murder. Even if Griffin learned the truth, he would probably quickly realize that the same power and influence Abraham used to free him could be used to re-commit him. Abraham paused, waited for Griffin to meet his glance. "And, if you are successful, you will have foiled the plans of Mr. Arrujo and Miss Baskin."

"Foiled their plans? That is not enough! I want to punish them—" Griffin seemed to catch himself, wiped the moisture off his lower lip with the back of his hand and rubbed his saliva-moistened hands together. In a more controlled voice, he continued. "You promised I would have my revenge on them."

Abraham refused to meet Madame Radminikov's glance. "And you shall. But you will do so on our schedule, and under our control. To that end, you will wear an electronic monitoring bracelet on your ankle. The bracelet, through interaction with the perspiration and arterial flow of your lower leg, will monitor your vital signs and transmit them to us via the Global Positioning Satellite system. The bracelet is tamper-sensitive, so we will know immediately if it is removed."

Madame Radminikov hoped that Griffin's mind had lost its sharpness, that he would be unable to fit the pieces together. It took him a second or two longer than it might have, but Griffin asked the relevant question. "Why use a bracelet to monitor my vital signs but not my location?"

"We will also be surgically installing a half-dozen microchips deep into your body. These chips allow us to track you—again, by GPS—at all times. A single microchip is sufficient to track you, but we will install a half-dozen just in case you try to have a doctor remove them. Of course, the removal of even one chip would require a local anesthesia, which would be detected by the ankle bracelet." Abraham sat back, offered a cold smile. "In other words, the only way you can avoid our detection is to convince a doctor to extract a handful of microchips implanted deep within your body, and to do so without anesthesia. You may find a doctor to attempt this, but it would likely kill you. And even if you somehow survived the procedure, the change in your vital signs caused by the trauma would immediately alert us. We would intervene before the procedure could be completed."

Madame Radminikov had insisted they come up with a fool-proof plan to ensure Griffin did not hunt down Shelby and Bruce and then just disappear into the city. According to Reb Meyer, the only way Griffin could escape their surveillance would be to take out the entire GPS system.

Abraham continued. "Of course, just because we know where you are does not mean we can control your actions. We will have to rely on your own sense of self-interest for that. Again, if you do as we say, you will gain your freedom and also have your revenge on Mr. Arrujo and Miss Baskin. Any questions?"

"Just the obvious one. What will be my revenge?"

Abraham locked eyes with Griffin. "You said you wanted to defeat them. Would you feel that dissolving their soon-to-be marriage would qualify as a defeat?"

Madame Radminikov gasped. "Abraham, we never discussed—"

He raised his hand, brought it down in a chopping motion. "Enough, Madame." He turned to Griffin. "So we are clear: Your victory will be in causing the break-up of their relationship. However, they are instrumental to our plan—if you harm them physically, we will return you to the hospital. And make certain that you never leave again."

But Griffin was not looking at Abraham. Instead he was studying the distress on Madame Radminikov's face. She shivered, felt the cold realization that she had just handed the demon the key to the vault. But for her anguish, Griffin never would have realized that breaking up Shelby and Bruce's relationship would constitute such a total victory over them.

Griffin broke into a full, brown-toothed grin. "Yes, I see it now. They ruined my life; I will ruin theirs. Excellent." He leered at her. "Unfortunately, true love is often fleeting, no? A lesson we all must learn, though a painful one." He shifted his eyes back to Abraham, rubbed his hands together again. "I accept your terms. When do we begin?"

"We will be taking off in ten minutes," Abraham answered literally. "When we land in suburban Boston, my associates will be waiting for us. You will go to a medical office, where you will have the microchips implanted and the ankle bracelet fitted. In three days, you will have a meeting with Miss Goulston."

"Sounds like you guys have thought of everything." Griffin sat back. "We'll have to see about that."

CHAPTER 8

[October]

Shelby looked up from her computer monitor to see Bruce standing in her office doorway. For a split second, and for the millionth time, her eyes soaked in the rugged features of the man she loved. But this time there was no color in his face, no teasing in his eyes, no curl on his lips. "What's wrong?"

He closed the door behind him, walked around her desk and leaned over to embrace her. His heart thumped against her. He disengaged, silently handed her a plain, white envelope. "This came in today's mail."

Shelby examined the envelope—simple block lettering addressed to both of them at their Commonwealth Avenue address, no return address, an 'October 2' Boston post-mark disfiguring an American flag stamp. Probably not another letter from her mother. She pulled out a single sheet of white copy paper. It, too, was hand-written, in the same block lettering:

> *Dear Bruce and Shelby:*
> *I just wanted to inform you that I am now in Boston, for a visit of undetermined length. I look forward to renewing our acquaintance; I was disappointed that you never saw fit to pay me a visit at my previous place of residence.*

> *In the interest of fairness, I now extend to you the courtesy*
> *of declaring, "Game on!" You have chosen white in the upcom-*
> *ing battle, so I will play the black pieces. Appropriate, no?*
>   *Regards,*
>   *Rex Griffin*

Her head lightened, her stomach churned, her extremities tingled. The monster was free, and it was stalking them.

She searched Bruce's face for answers. He sighed, swallowed, spoke. "I called the hospital in New York. They weren't very forthcoming, but I was able to confirm that he was discharged last week."

She forced the words out of her mouth. "How is that possible?" Bruce's arrangement with the hospital was that they were not to release Griffin under any circumstances.

"Like I said, they wouldn't tell me anything. I could go up there and try to get some answers in person—"

"Not a chance. No way are you leaving me here alone with that whack-job on the loose." This was a guy who bred his retarded sister like a farm animal, then murdered his twin brother. Not likely he would show much mercy to his enemies. She wrestled with a thought, rejected it. "And even I don't think we can go to the police—by you covering up his crimes and putting him in the hospital, you made us as guilty as he is."

Bruce sighed again. "Would you feel better if we left town?"

Bruce's willingness to flee frightened her almost as much as the letter itself. "And go where? Griffin doesn't seem like the type to just give up. I mean, he came to Boston, obviously, to find us."

Bruce tried to put on a brave face. "Maybe he's just trying to scare us, just mess with our minds."

"Yeah, and maybe you're just dreaming. He's here for revenge, Bruce. We ruined his plans, cost him millions of dollars. Then we locked him in a mental hospital. Can't imagine why he'd be annoyed with us."

Bruce peered out the window, weighing her words. Clearly concerned, frightened even, he kept his emotions in check, coldly analyzed the problem. "The thing that struck me about Griffin, when I was dragging him up to that mental hospital, was that he was so mad about being defeated. It was like he couldn't wrap his brain around the fact that somebody had outsmarted him. He kept complaining that I had cheated, that he didn't know I was out there plotting against him, that it just wasn't a fair fight. He never asked where we were going, or what would happen to him. I think, more than anything, he just wants a chance to avenge his defeat."

"That's what he's saying in his letter. He's in Boston for a rematch, like this is some kind of game."

"Yeah, everything is to him. A game of who's smarter, who's more devious, who's better at manipulating the world. That's the key question—what's the game? I think he's here not to stalk us, but to try to defeat us. All we need to do is figure out when and where the game is."

"No, Bruce, that's not all. Once we figure it out, then we still have to beat him."

*   *   *

Monique stepped closer to the picture window in her suite at the Long Wharf Marriott. The city unfolded in a panorama—the skyline to her left, the harbor and the airport lights to her right. She regularly did battle on behalf of the proletariat and the dispossessed and the downtrodden, but who was to say she could not fight just as well from a Marriott Suite as from a Motel 6? She would check out and move to more modest quarters when the demonstration date approached, but for now she felt like indulging in a bit of, well, self-indulgence.

Only a few weeks until the demonstration weekend. So far, so good. The widespread disdain for President Bush seemed to be mobilizing every activist in North America. She had never witnessed this level of anger toward the White House before—old-timers reported that the loathing of the Administration exceeded even that of the Reagan years, when people like Secretary of the Interior James Watt were arguing that, with Armageddon just around the corner, the government might as well grant permission to strip-mine federal parklands.

She had no way of knowing how many demonstrators would show up in Boston for the weekend—it could be 20,000, it could be 120,000. The key would be the number of hard-core, battle-tested anarchists. The term 'anarchist' usually conjured up visions of a black-coated assassin shooting Archduke Ferdinand to spark World War I. Modern anarchists were more likely to be urban political radicals. She reflected on the ones she knew: A thin, gay, female graphic artist. A twenty-something, lip-ringed web page designer. A bike-repair guy. A college coed studying film. A middle-aged nurse who cut her teeth as a 1960s activist. A song-writer with a gentle voice and angry lyrics. Even a financial analyst intent on steering investment toward socially responsible companies. All of them believed the institutions that comprised the hierarchy of modern society—corporations, government bureaucracies, armies, political parties, religious organizations, universities—were allied against the interests of individuals, culture and the environment. And, unlike other political radicals, they acted to undermine those institutions. But would they show up in Boston? It was an inherent problem when relying on anarchists as your foot-soldiers—they weren't real good at taking direction from a centralized authority.

Early indications were that the anarchists would be coming in full force, largely because she had created a venue they found attractive: The federal government had not designated the conference a National Special Security Event, so security would be limited; Boston's tradition of protest and demonstration helped ensure that the rally at Christopher Columbus Park would not be curtailed; and the hundreds of thousands of college students in the area offered ideal cover, and refuge, for the protesters—soft couches, hot showers, cold anonymity. Most of all, just as bank robbers robbed banks because that was where the money was, the anarchists would come to Boston because that was where the disorder would be.

Monique poured herself a Dewar's on ice, allowed the first sip to bite the back of her throat as the fumes cleared her nostrils. She focused on the skyline. Boston was a world-class city, with a world-class stage. Worthy of a world-class kick in the ass.

*   *   *

The two men waited for Monique, leaning against a brick wall outside a sushi restaurant on Newbury Street. Burt looked ridiculous in his tight black t-shirt, black pants and dark sunglasses—she wore black herself, but his round shape and the sun reflecting off his bald head made him look like a giant piece of glowing charcoal. His friend looked even worse, like something out of 1968 time capsule—a tie-dyed shirt, a pair of cut-off denim shorts with a flower patch over one cheek, leather sandals.

Fearing a hug, she reached out a hand to her cousin and shook his small, clammy paw. "Hello, Burt."

"Monique, I'd like you to meet Rex Griffin."

Griffin squinted at her through beady, blood-shot eyes. "Hey, baby. Peace." In lieu of shaking hands, he held up two fingers. She nodded back, wondering why she had agreed to come. Burt had insisted she meet this Griffin guy, absolutely insisted, so she relented. At least she would be eating outside, enjoying the sun and the sights of leather-clad Euro-males talking on their cell phones as they sauntered from tanning booth to hair stylist to shoe boutique. Maybe she could adopt one for the few weeks she was in town....

"Come on, follow me. I've reserved a table outside for us," Burt announced.

As Monique followed the men through a swinging wrought iron gate and into a patio area, her eyes wandered down to a contraption wrapped around Griffin's right ankle. She peered closer—it looked like a pair of headphones for his ankle bones.

They sat at a table near the sidewalk, the sun filtering through the shade of an overhanging tree. She made sure she grabbed a seat with a clear view of the eye-candy parade. "So, Rex, what's that thing around your ankle?"

He did not seem to take offense. "Pigs busted me for driving under the influence, man. Multiple offender. This thing reads my sweat to make sure there's no booze in me."

"Mind if I have a cocktail?"

"Do it, sister." He had that kind of face that made you think of dumpsters and cheese and hamster wheels. It always amazed her that Disney had turned a rodent into a national icon.

Burt seemed anxious to move beyond the chit-chat. "Monique, I thought you might want to meet Rex because he owns a bunch of property on Beacon Hill that might be helpful to you."

She stated the obvious. "You don't seem like the real estate mogul type."

"You got that right. I bought 'em back in the early '80s from this old dame who used to let artists and poets and musicians flop there for free. Lady liked to think of herself as a modern-day Isabella Stewart Gardner—you know, patron of the arts type, nurturing all these young talents. Anyway, I got to know her, and that was about the same time my software company went public, and she was getting old and wanted to sell the buildings, and so I bought them. Had to promise her I'd keep the rents low and not let the Yuppies move in." Griffin leered at her, showed his pointy, brown teeth. He and Burt must share the same dentist. "I think old Constance had some boyfriends tucked away in a few of the buildings."

Burt interjected. "Don't forget, back in the early '80s, the north slope of Beacon Hill was pretty rough. It's gentrified now, but back then it was a pretty transient neighborhood."

Her glass of wine, Burt's root beer and Griffin's cup of tea arrived. She took a sip, turned to Burt. "And why did you think this would interest me?"

He shifted in his seat. "It's just that, Rex says a bunch of these apartments are vacant now. I thought you might use them as sort of a home base for the next few weeks."

She turned to Griffin. "Why are they vacant?"

"Hey, sister, they're not *all* vacant. A man's gotta eat, y'know? But I keep a bunch of 'em empty, just in case my crowd needs a place to chill." He paused. "Or to lay low."

She would never admit it, but Burt's instincts were dead-on. A group of apartments, centrally located, would make an ideal base of operations. She could house her core group of lieutenants in them and they would be able to operate in virtual anonymity right up until the day of the demonstration. Nothing but a bunch of young professionals moving into some Beacon Hill apartments. "So, you offering these apartments to me?"

"I'm offering 'em to your cause, sister."

*   *   *

Summer had held on through September, and even popped in for a visit in early October, but a mid-month front brought a cold, driving rain that littered the sidewalks and gutters and car windshields with yellow and orange leaves. Would a rain like this extinguish an LNG fire? Or would the fire burn despite the water, like an oil fire did? Shelby did not know the answer. Did not want to know.

Far below, the beginnings of the Thursday evening rush hour inched its way out of the city. This kind of heavy rain made driving tough, and walking tougher. Perfect weather for a taxi. Not that she needed an excuse with Neary, and now Griffin, on the loose.

She grabbed an umbrella, took the elevator down to the lobby. Being pregnant was sometimes like being in somebody else's body—the elevator drop never used to bother her, but this time she felt a wave of roller-coaster nausea. Did that mean the baby would not like carnival rides?

Hopefully her meeting with Monique would only take an hour or two. The city of Boston had just submitted new evidence to the court, along with a motion to reconsider its earlier ruling. Shelby needed to go over the newly-raised security issues with Monique. Bruce would wait for dinner, if for no other reason than to make sure she ate all the foods the books and magazines and doctors told her to eat. It all made perfect sense on paper—three servings of dairy, three servings of protein, plenty of foods with whole grains and folic acid and calcium. And, oh, by the way, don't gain more than 25 pounds. It did not leave much room for chocolate bars or cinnamon buns. And it did not leave room for a late-afternoon snack, even though she was beginning to feel like she needed one.

The taxi dropped her in front of a red-brick rowhouse on Beacon Hill. She splashed through the rain to the covered entryway of the building, found the buzzer next to a fresh label marked simply "M.G." As she waited to be buzzed-in, she noticed a man huddled in a doorway opposite, eyeing her from the shadows. A sharp crash of thunder—not the kind that rumbled in from a distant horizon, but the kind that sounded like a door slamming in your ear—made her gasp. Maybe the baby would not like loud noises either....

A metallic version of Monique's voice materialized. "Come on in. I'm the first door on the left." Shelby glanced back to check on the man lurking in the doorway, but he was gone. Neary would not lurk, he would attack. But Griffin was a definite lurker. In her mind, Griffin was everywhere, and yet he was nowhere. Almost a week had passed—he intruded on her thoughts on an almost constant basis, but had yet to actually reappear in her life. She began to consider the possibility that he sent the letter as nothing more than a postal 'fuck you.'

She entered the building quickly, pushed the door tightly shut behind her. For some reason the mild exertion fatigued her; she closed her eyes, held the doorframe for a moment while her lightheadedness passed, then found Monique sitting in a rolling office chair in front of a folding table. A computer, printer and fax machine sat on the table, and a few file cabinets and a large copy machine lined the walls, but otherwise the apartment-turned-office was empty. Monique smiled. "Here we are. Command central."

The room seemed unusually warm. Shelby looked around as she removed her coat. "No phone?"

Monique rolled her eyes. "No telegraph machine, either. Come on, Shelby, this is the 21st century. I've got three cell phones—one for work, one for friends, one for enemies."

"What, none for lovers?" Shelby knew better than to get into this kind of exchange with Monique, especially when she was feeling so crappy, but she could not let the condescending eye roll just pass. Maybe the baby would be a fighter.

Monique shrugged, apparently missing the sarcasm in the question. "Some use the work line, some the enemy."

Shelby blinked. Not much to say to *that*. "All right, then." The heat added to her fatigue. She looked around for a chair, settled for leaning against the folding table. Monique scribbled out the three phone numbers, handed them over. Shelby spoke. "We need to talk about these new security concerns the city has raised." What she really wanted was a hamburger and a nap.

"Whatever."

"Look, Monique, I'm trying to help you out here. You could at least act like you're interested."

She sighed. "Okay, Shelby. But you know we're just using Columbus Park as our base. At some point we're going to leave, track down the summit delegates, get in their face. That's the whole idea of this—make them sweat, see our rage, you know, smell our working-class breath. So unless they put the delegates on a bus and bring 'em down to the Waterfront for us, we're going to have to go to them."

"And where will that be?"

She shrugged again. "Depends on where they are."

Sorry, Uncle, but I tried. "Well, should I even bother fighting the city on this Columbus Park permit?" Her face flushed; she pulled up her sleeves.

"Don't be stupid. Just because I don't see this little court case of yours as the most important thing of the entire weekend doesn't mean I don't want the permit. We'll demonstrate either way, but I'd rather have the permit than not."

Shelby took a deep breath, forced herself not to respond to the 'little court case' comment. "All right then. Here's the latest from the city: They claim that having a weekend-long event will encourage people to camp out in the park, which is against city ordinances."

Monique offered a sharp cackle. "What about all the people sleeping in Boston Common every night? If the city was really concerned about people sleeping in the park, they'd build more homeless shelters." Shelby could not help but nod in agreement. Monique had built a career fighting governmental agencies, and it had honed in her an adept ability to point out the hypocrisy and absurdity in much of what they did. "You can tell the judge that we promise not to snore so we don't wake up the Yuppies living in the condos."

The door buzzer interrupted them. Monique walked across the room, spoke briefly into the intercom, buzzed the visitor in. She turned to Shelby, offered an explanation. "One of our volunteers, helping with logistics. An older guy, maybe did a little too much acid in the 60s. But I never turn down free help. Anyway, what else does the city have for us?"

Shelby nodded, looked down at her notes, took a deep breath to try to clear her fatigue. "The next two seem pretty easy to deal with." The door opened; she ignored it, continued reading. "First, they say we still haven't shown them evidence of liability insurance. And they also want to make sure you stay out of the Marriott—apparently there's a wedding going on that day, and the hotel is worried about disruptions."

A syrupy voice oozed its way across the room, clung to her ears, leaked into her soul. A numbing cold spread from her core to her trunk to her limbs. The room darkened, and then the floor lifted and lurched and listed. She had a vague sense of the cloying words, though they arrived from far away and settled into her brain only after echoing a few times off the walls. She felt herself falling....

"I, for one," the voice mocked, "would like nothing better than to disrupt an autumn wedding."

*   *   *

Shelby awoke in a hospital bed, opened her eyes to see Bruce peering down at her, his hand gently stroking her hair. She blinked a few times, tried to rewind her memory: She remembered feeling weak, then hearing Griffin's voice, then falling, then waking up in an ambulance. Then doctors and nurses and tubes and wires....

Her mouth felt thick, cottony. "The baby?"

Bruce brushed the back of his hand across her cheek. "Don't worry. Everything's fine."

She licked her lips, tried to force a sentence out. She finally settled for, "Water, please."

He held a paper cup to her lips. The nerves in her mouth told her the liquid was room temperature, but the water chilled her as she swallowed. She shivered, tried to pull the blanket over her. "So cold."

He nodded casually, though his eyes betrayed him. "Probably from the trauma. I guess you banged your head pretty good when you fainted. Monique says you were leaning against a table, then just dropped to the floor for no reason. She called an ambulance, and then she called me."

She took a deep breath, forced her lips and tongue and teeth to form the words. "Griffin was in the room. I fainted because of him." She sounded like someone with a tongue full of Novocain.

Bruce's eyes widened. "Griffin was with you and Monique? That's why you fainted?"

"Also hungry and hot." She had no energy for a nuanced explanation. But she felt like a wimp, fainting at the sight of her adversary. "He's working for her."

"Working for Monique? You mean, helping with the demonstration?"

She nodded again. "Not a coincidence."

Bruce's fist clenched at his side. "I agree, no way it's a coincidence. He's not helping Monique because he cares about workers' rights. He's with Monique because you're with Monique." Bruce paused, then continued. "And I think we also have to assume he knows we're trying to help Abraham."

Another wave of cold washed painfully through her, like an ice cream headache spreading through her entire body. She took a deep breath, waited for it to pass. "That's what he meant when he said we chose the white pieces, so he would play black. We're trying to stop the terrorist attack, so he's plotting to make sure the terrorist attack succeeds. We're white, he's black. That's how he plans on getting even."

"You're right. We're fighting the terrorists, so he's going to help them. It's like that old Middle-Eastern saying. The enemy of my enemy is my friend." Bruce stared out the window. "So the terrorists are now Griffin's friends."

*　　*　　*

Abraham watched the financial news cycle end, stared at the digital clock next to his hotel room bed until it clicked over to 12:00 midnight. He dialed the number of the cell phone he had provided Griffin. Griffin answered on the first ring.

"Greetings, Gepetto. Pinnochio here. Tell me no secrets and I'll tell you no lies."

Abraham knew to be careful—Griffin's flippancy and impertinence and madness camouflaged the demon lurking beneath. Even a wild animal was somewhat predictable, its behavior aimed at protecting itself, finding food, locating a mate. But a monster like Griffin, his sanity eroded by his hospital stay, lashed out irrationally, oftentimes in ways that were self-defeating. Abraham had assured Madame Radminikov he could control Griffin. They both knew he was lying. "Mr. Griffin, do you have anything to report?"

"First I have a question. When you said I'm not to harm Shelby Baskin, what, *exactly*, did you mean by that?" He cackled.

A dull ache throbbed in Abraham's chest, close to where the old black-and-white photo of his family nested. *What was this?* He pictured his sister, perhaps 40 years ago, holding the baby Shelby, poking her playfully with her finger as the baby cooed and kicked. That baby was now in his care. Rough care, perhaps, but care nonetheless. He had assigned his very best operative to infiltrate Neary's group and serve as Shelby's bodyguard when Neary abducted her; he employed the latest in monitoring technology to keep Griffin from stalking her. Madame Radminikov had commented that his protecting her, while at the same time using her as his pawn, was like the fisherman professing concern that the worm not drown while dangling on the hook.

He closed his eyes. Had Griffin really harmed her? He took a deep breath, tried to keep his voice flat. "Explain yourself."

"Well, apparently the sight of me gave her a bit of a start. She fainted, banged her head. I tried to kiss it and make it better. Then an ambulance came, took her away."

Banged her head. Probably fine, then. And her reaction indicated his plan was working: Abraham had sent the 'game on' letter in hopes that Griffin's involvement would personalize the terrorist attack for Shelby, would give the terrorists a face in her mind's eye. Seeing Griffin at Miss Goulston's office—there, presumably, to gather information relevant to an attack—only reinforced that association for Shelby. And, based on her reaction to seeing Griffin tonight, she found that association terrifying. Going forward, she should be a much more enthusiastic ally.

It was time to move away from this conversation—Griffin would smell his concern for Shelby, home in on the weakness. Apparently Griffin did not know Shelby was his niece....

"Listen carefully," Abraham said. "Here are your instructions. I have arranged for the *Boston Herald* to write a story on Shelby Baskin and how her legal efforts have resulted in the anarchists coming to Boston. No doubt the *Herald* will find some catchy headline to splash across the front page—"

"How about: 'Shelby Baskin: 31 Flavors of Sleazy Lawyer'?" Griffin offered a little giggle.

Abraham ignored him. "The *Herald* reporter will be calling your cell phone tomorrow, at 11:00 o'clock in the morning. You will be the anonymous source for this story. You will identify yourself as a volunteer for Miss Goulston's group, and provide whatever corroborating proof the reporter requests. You will then describe how Miss Baskin has successfully championed the legal fight to overturn Boston's denial of the Columbus Park demonstration permit. Finally, you will confirm that hundreds, perhaps thousands, of anarchists are planning to attend the October 25-26 demonstrations, and that they have told you that their intention is to do twice the damage to Boston that they did to Seattle."

"Sounds easy enough. Now why am I doing this again?"

"Mr. Griffin, you are doing this because our arrangement is that you do as I say. But, if you must know, this is part of our campaign to discredit Miss Baskin. Obviously, there are other aspects to this plan that are being hidden from you." Griffin did not know, for example, about the 'game-on' letter sent over his name, or that Shelby and Bruce believed he had allied himself with the terrorists in an effort to even the score. The more Griffin knew, the more difficult he would be to control.

Back to Shelby's safety. "One other item: I see you have been spending time outside Miss Baskin's apartment." Madame Radminikov had been livid when she learned of this.

"Our deal is I agreed not to harm them physically, and in exchange you would give me the opportunity to ruin their lives. You have given me nothing so far. So I am merely doing some reconnaissance work. Some might call it stalking. I call it research."

"Call it what you may, but I am now ordering you to stay away from them. I have seen what Mr. Arrujo can do to a man twice your size. You are of no use to me in a hospital bed."

Griffin's voice rose in excitement. "Beautiful, beautiful words! I am of no use to you in the hospital, eh? Well, do you know what that means, dear Gepetto? It means I *am* of use to you out of the hospital." He cackled, continued in a high-pitch torrent of words. "And that means I have leverage over you! If not me, who will be your mole to the press, who will be your spy, who will kick up his feet at the tug of a string?"

Abraham kept his voice flat. "We are both aware, Mr. Griffin, that I can at any time return you to the institution."

"But you need me, so you can't!" Griffin swallowed the saliva that had gathered in his mouth. His voice was now a low purr. "So, now that we are *equals*, it is time for you to tell me how I can break up the happy couple. It is, after all, our arrangement."

Abraham shook his head. Griffin was at times barely lucid, yet he quickly understood the changing dynamic of their relationship. It was a common hazard when employing an operative: At a certain point the relationship turned symbiotic, with the handler and the operative becoming co-dependent. Abraham could not pull Griffin out now, and Griffin knew it. And that made him dangerous. To the mission, and to Shelby.

Griffin wanted his pound of flesh. Best to throw him a bone lest he stake a claim to the entire carcass. "Very well. Miss Baskin's one concern about Mr. Arrujo is his penchant for resorting to violence or lawlessness or whatever else he feels is justified. This behavior is abhorrent to her morally and, practically, she is frightened that his recklessness will someday put them at risk or him in jail." If the marriage failed, so be it.

"Ah," Griffin hissed, "I understand. Jane falls in love with Tarzan, but then wants him to stop swinging from trees. Perhaps Jane doesn't realize how dangerous the jungle really is."

*   *   *

Shelby's head had cleared, and her tongue had begun to listen to her brain. Still, the doctor wanted her to stay in the hospital overnight. She reached for the phone. Bruce looked at his watch. "It's past midnight. Who you calling?"

"Monique."

"Now?"

"I need to tell her about Griffin." She asked Bruce to retrieve her briefcase, found the list of Monique's three cell numbers. "She has a friend line, an enemy line, and a work line. Which do you think she'll answer?"

"Knowing Monique, probably enemy."

"I agree." She dialed. Monique answered on the fourth ring.

"This better be important," she barked.

"It's Shelby."

Monique's voice softened. "Oh. You okay, Roomie?"

"Yeah, fine. But listen, I need to talk to you about something. That guy who came into your office right before I fainted, what's his name?"

"Rex ... Gifford or something. Why?"

Arrogant S.O.B. did not even bother to change his name. "He's not who he says he is. He's just using you."

"Hey, you just described ninety percent of my world. And those are the people I consider friends."

Shelby needed to convey to Monique why Griffin would view a successful terrorist attack on Boston as a victory over Shelby and Bruce, and to do so without revealing their role in assisting Abraham. "What I mean is he's using your demonstration as a cover for an attack on the city."

"Now you've narrowed it to fifty percent of my world."

"I mean a *terrorist* attack, a major one."

Monique paused. "I see. And how, exactly, is he planning on doing that?"

This was not going well. Maybe her head was not as clear as she thought it was. "I don't now how. But the guy is a con artist, not to mention a world-class scumbag. Trust me—he doesn't care about your demonstration, or about globalism, or about any of the things you're fighting for."

"Yeah, and?"

"And what?"

"And exactly how does that make him a terrorist?"

It was time to start making things up. "The details aren't important, but we know him because he tried to pull a real estate scam on some friends of ours down on Cape Cod. I think what he's trying to do now is unleash a terrorist attack as part of some elaborate real estate rip-off he has planned."

"Look, I know you just banged your head and all, but what makes you think I care? If this guy wants to burn down half the city so he can collect on the insurance proceeds or whatever other scam he's cooked up, I don't really give a shit. In case you haven't noticed, I sort of like it when things get a little wild during our rallies. Now go get some sleep." There was a pause. "Oh, and stick to the lawyer stuff, all right?"

The line went dead. Bruce shook his head. "Not buying it, huh?"

"Not even a sniff. In fact, based on what I told her about Griffin, she'll probably make him her top lieutenant."

*   *   *

Thursday's rain had yielded to a bright, blustery October Friday. The doctor discharged Shelby, and she and Bruce walked home along the grassy, tree-shaded park area that separated the east- and west-bound lanes of Commonwealth Avenue. Summer was now officially behind them—the next time they wore shorts and spread sunscreen and sweated behind their knees, it would be as parents. Terrorists, Neary, Griffin—none of it, today, could dampen Shelby's spirit.

She turned a bit to her right, tried to position herself so she could see the slight bulge of her midsection in her shadow.

Bruce looked at her, bemused. "What are you doing?"

"Trying to see Sarah's shadow." While in the hospital, an ultrasound had confirmed that the baby was a girl.

He laughed. "Any luck?"

"Not yet. Maybe if I take off my coat...." She removed her wind-breaker, flipped it over Bruce's arm, then stretched her shirt tight over her midsection. "There, see it now? See the bulge in my tummy?'

"You know, men are trained at an early age not to answer 'yes' to questions like that."

"That's silly. It's not fat, it's our baby. Women who say they look fat when they're pregnant are being ridiculous."

"That mean you're going to wear a tight-waisted wedding dress?"

"No. Looking pregnant is fine. Looking pregnant in your wedding dress is not so good." She did some quick math in her head.

Bruce sensed her mood change. "What's wrong?'

Hormones, probably. "I'm not usually superstitious, but our baby is due in six months, our wedding is in six weeks, and the demonstrations start in six days. Six-six-six."

"Ah, our friend Griffin. The devil."

"I'm sorry. I'm trying not to let him get to me, but he's like this shadow that darkens all my thoughts. No matter what happy things I try to think about, like our wedding or our baby, he just ... eclipses ... them."

Bruce sighed. "I've been thinking about this, Shelby. I think we should tell your uncle about him."

Much to her own surprise, Shelby had been weighing this option herself. On the one hand, if they told her uncle, he would probably have Griffin maimed or killed, if for no other reason than Abraham needed Shelby and could not afford to have her chased out of town. A neat, effective solution, so long as you bought into that whole vigilante justice thing. She rejected it as a solution to the Neary problem, but something about Griffin forced her to reconsider her core beliefs and values. He was the exception to the rule, the asterisk next to the home run record, the overriding circumstance used to justify things like atomic bombs dropped on Japan. "I don't know, Bruce."

He took a deep breath. "You're not going to like this, Shelby. But if we don't let your uncle handle this problem, I'll handle it myself."

"What do you mean by that?"

"I mean I'll find Griffin. I'll tell him that the game's over, that if he doesn't leave Boston, I'll kill him."

Her body went cold again; she managed to shuffle over and drop onto a bench. Here they were once more, Bruce intent on living their life as if it were some clichéd Western movie. *The bad guys are coming, Little Woman. You just sit right there and churn some butter while I go out and shoot 'em dead.* Well, even in the cheap Westerns, sometimes the good guys got killed, too. And in the real world, murderers went to jail. As they should.

"Damn it, Bruce, no!" The timber in her voice surprised her; a few nearby birds flew from a tree, a dog barked a warning in her direction. "You can't keep doing this to me. You can't just keep running off like a Hollywood action hero. You have a responsibility now, to me, to our baby. You're no use to us dead, and you're no use to us in jail. Not to mention the fact that you have no right to just go off and kill somebody like you'd swat a fly on the wall. That's what being part of a family means—you don't get to take these risks anymore, you don't get to make these decisions alone...."

He settled in on the bench next to her, put his arm around her shoulder. He pulled her into his chest, his warm breath on the top of her head. But his closeness did not comfort her. Instead, despair washed over her, despair at the realization that her words would never get through to him, that Bruce—never having truly been part of a family—never would be able to comprehend the necessity of subordinating his sense of self to the needs of the family as a whole....

And then his words, careful and tentative, pulled her back. "Shelby, listen. I understand what you're saying. And I agree—this is something we need to decide together. I mean, the fact that I didn't go after Neary, that I haven't gone after Griffin already, is proof of that, right?"

She nodded, fought to keep her emotions in check. First despair, then joy. Damn hormones made her want to cry all the time.

He continued. "Okay, so let's go back to my original suggestion of telling your uncle. I think he has a right to know—I mean, we've become a liability to him. Griffin said he's going to oppose us, now he's working with Monique. He might be helping the terrorists...."

She took a deep breath. "We both know what my uncle will do. I just can't have that on my head, Bruce. Griffin is a monster, but that doesn't mean we have the right to just have him ... eliminated."

"All right. But if you don't want me to go after him, and you don't want your uncle to do anything, we're back to square one. We're just going to have to deal with him out there, lurking and skulking and plotting. If we're right, and he's here because he wants to defeat us, he probably won't resort to violence—"

She interrupted. "Unless he loses."

"Right, I agree. But, for now, I think he's just going to concentrate on winning the chess match. So, for now, I promise not to go after him, though we both agree that might change, right?"

Shelby looked down at her belly, nodded.

"So. In the meantime, we know the game he wants to play—we're trying to stop the terrorists, so he'll do what he can to help them. We don't really know the rules, but at least we know who we're playing against. I don't know about you, but I plan on winning."

Bruce's optimism was contagious. Shelby could not help but feel herself pulled along. "If winning means stopping the terrorist attack," she said, "I plan on crushing the bastard."

*　　*　　*

Bruce did not usually read the *Boston Herald*. Today he made an exception.

He had gone out for an early-morning Saturday run. A half-block later, Shelby's picture jumped out at him from behind the caged window of the bright yellow newspaper box. Beneath her picture, the tabloid headline: "Anarchist-at-Law."

He had bummed fifty cents from a homeless man huddled under a blanket on a park bench, quickly scanned the text of the story, then sprinted back to the apartment. He dropped the tabloid next to Shelby's bowl of Corn Flakes. "At least it's a good picture of you."

Her eyes focused on the newsprint, then widened in astonishment. "Oh my God." Bruce watched her hands shake as she flipped open the paper, her pupils dart as she scanned the article, her eyes water as the words registered in her brain, her jaw quiver as she looked up at him. "This is total bullshit. They're claiming I've been *recruiting* anarchists to come to Boston, practically inviting them to destroy the city, just so I can make a name for myself."

Bruce had solved the puzzle on his run back to the apartment. Shelby soon would as well. "Who, exactly, is claiming that?" he asked.

Her eyes returned to the story. "They quote some unnamed staff-member working for Monique. Here's a good one: 'Many of us are concerned that Attorney Baskin's legal maneuverings have paved the way for the anarchists to come to Boston. She says the anarchists have as much right to be here as we do, and that if we're worried about it we should make sure our insurance is paid and just go away for the weekend.' Shit, Bruce, who would make up crap like that?"

He sighed, offered a wry smile as the realization clouded her face.

"Griffin," she breathed. "Of course." Her shoulders sagged, her head bowed. "What's he hoping to gain by this?"

"It could be that this was just a chance to damage your career...."

"No, with Griffin, nothing is 'just a chance'—everything is calculated."

"I agree. And, on the surface, the publicity behind the story is actually going to make it harder for the terrorists...." Bruce's voice trailed off as his line of logic hit a dead-end.

"But that's what *we're* trying to do. So why would he be helping us, if he's trying to defeat us?"

"Maybe it's worth the trade-off for him. Maybe the damage done to your credibility and reputation is worth having the spotlight shine on the anarchists. Maybe he doesn't need the anarchists and doesn't care if they're under extra surveillance...."

Shelby sighed. "And maybe he knows we'll never figure out what he's doing, and he's just trying to keep us off-balance."

He nodded, stumped. "I guess that makes as much sense as anything else."

CHAPTER 9

"So, what have we learned?" Abraham sat at the head of a long, mahogany conference table, his back rigid-straight and his fingers spread in front of him like a concert pianist preparing to play. Illuminated by a single light, eyes on him, his minions awaiting direction, this was Abraham's stage. Shelby promised herself she would not stand and clap, no matter how gripping the performance.

It was a Wednesday night, five days since she had left the hospital, two days until the demonstrators descended upon Boston for the weekend rally. Abraham had taken a suite at the Hotel Commonwealth, a new hotel in Kenmore Square. Critics derided its exterior as a cheap Hollywood-set imitation of a Parisian grand hotel, but its luxurious interior offered state-of-the-art technological amenities. Perfect for a war room.

He had called a 9:00 meeting. He and his key posse—Madame Radminikov, Reb Meyer, Mr. Clevinsky—were joined by Bruce and Shelby. A platter of cold cuts, a few loaves of bread and an assortment of soda cans littered the table, contrasting with both the formality of Abraham's posture and the opulence of the room's decor. The setting called for white-gloved waiters, not Reb Meyer licking potato chip crumbs from his stubby fingers.

Abraham looked to his left, repeated the question. "Reb Meyer, your report."

Reb Meyer reluctantly set down the chips, then brushed his hand on his pant leg and flipped the page on a yellow legal pad. He took a deep, wheezing breath and spoke in a toneless, rapid-fire manner. "First, the LNG tanker. The last tanker arrived Sunday. For the past month, they've been coming in every six or seven days. My sources say no reason not to expect another tanker this weekend—"

Bruce interrupted. "Can you tell us which day?"

Reb Meyer slowly lifted his eyes from his legal pad, glowered at Bruce. Apparently Meyer had not forgiven Bruce for besting *Kidon's* man, Barnabus. Bruce looked back at him, feigning ignorance of the breach of protocol occasioned by his interruption of the briefing.

They held each other's stare for four or five seconds. Madame Radminikov finally interceded. "If you want to stare into each other's eyes all night, *boys*, please get a room. Otherwise let's get on with it."

Reb Meyer's eyes dropped back to his pad, Bruce faked a cough. Madame Radminikov shot Shelby a conspiring look—men were easy. Reb Meyer spoke. "As I was saying, my sources tell me that Coast Guard staffing levels are high for both this Saturday and Sunday. High tides this weekend are at about eleven o'clock, morning and night, of course. Given the choice, they prefer to come in under the light of day, so my guess is late morning. They have to start letting the fire departments and tourist boats and other harbor users know in advance, so we'll have 24 hours notice."

Abraham nodded. "My information is consistent with yours, Reb Meyer. Natural gas levels are low, due to the recent cold. A new shipment is needed. We will proceed under the assumption that a tanker will arrive over the weekend. Agent Ng is also checking on this for us. Continue."

"The delegates for the economic conference will arrive tomorrow; most of the advance teams are here already," Reb Meyer said. "All the countries are sending their Finance Ministers. Also teams of senior diplomats and trade ministers. The U.S. Secretary of the Treasury will be here. Secretary of State also. Definitely the Massachusetts Governor, and both Senators. Maybe the Vice President, but I can't get confirmation on that yet. It's not as big as the actual G-8 summits, but it's not far behind."

"My information is that the Vice President will be attending," Abraham said. Apparently Abraham and Reb Meyer possessed different intelligence sources, which made sense from an operational standpoint; one could serve as a check on the other. He leaned forward, looked around the room. "I am concerned about this report we have of anthrax being shipped to Boston. Nobody seems to know anything about it—it is a complete unknown variable. Reb Meyer, do you have anything?"

The fat man played with his cookie crumbs, shook his head. "No, nothing."

Abraham sighed. "Very well. What have you learned about the summit schedule?"

Reb Meyer straightened himself in his chair. "Conferences scattered around Harvard tomorrow and Friday, then most of the top delegates will be attending the Boston Symphony Orchestra on Friday night. More conferences Saturday. Saturday night is some reception at Harvard. Sunday morning is a working brunch. Most people will be departing Sunday afternoon."

"I'm hearing from my sources that many of the delegates are trying to get tickets to the World Series game Saturday night," Madame Radminikov offered. It had never occurred to Shelby that Madame Radminikov had sources of her own. "That is, of course, if the Series goes to a seventh game—"

Abraham interrupted. "What is the likelihood of that happening?"

There were four men and two women at the table, and Shelby guessed that the only two people who knew the answer to that question were the women. Madame Radminikov responded. "Game 6 would be at Fenway Park Friday night and Game 7, if necessary, on Saturday night."

"And will it be necessary?" Abraham asked.

Madame Radminikov shrugged, then offered: "I have a friend who is a bookie. He's had a steady stream of gamblers placing large bets on the Red Sox. They all claim that a Red Sox championship has been preordained by some bible prophecy—"

Reb Meyer interrupted. "Are you speaking of these bible codes? This is all bunk." He slapped the air with his hand, turned away in disgust.

"It may very well be," Madame Radminikov responded. "But he's a nervous wreck. If you believe the bible prophecy, and if the Red Sox go on to lose tonight—they were behind last I checked—then you must conclude that the Red Sox will win Game 6 on Friday and then play—and win—a Game 7 on Saturday night."

Reb Meyer interjected again. "Meanwhile, back in the real world…."

Abraham turned his gray eyes on Reb Meyer, who shook his head and looked away. "Continue, Madame," Abraham said.

"Yes, back in the real world, I am hearing that the corporations and banks and law firms around town are being pressured to give up their tickets for Game 7 so the delegates can go."

"I'm sure that's going over well," Shelby said.

Abraham responded. "Actually, these companies would be wise to give up their tickets. The IRS has been cracking down on firms claiming these tickets as a business expense when they are mostly used by senior management. A few tickets given as a favor to the White House would likely result in a more-forgiving IRS." Shelby suppressed a smile—Abraham knew a lot about business, and a lot about world affairs, but absolutely nothing about Red Sox fans. Not even the threat of an IRS audit would pry the tickets from their tax-cheating hands.

Madame Radminikov shrugged. "You may be right, Abraham, but locating tickets has been like finding pearls in oysters. Finally, the Red Sox ownership had to step in—they promised that companies that gave up their seats could bring the World Series trophy to their offices for a day if the Red Sox won—"

Reb Meyer interrupted, perturbed that they were wasting time on talk of baseball and tax audits. "Moving along. My intelligence tells me that Monique Goulston has been successful in summoning the Great Unwashed to Boston. Many of the hard-core anarchists arrested in Seattle and Quebec have been spotted on trains and on buses and in airports heading toward Boston. Likewise most of the liberal groups from the local colleges are planning to attend the rally. And the labor groups and environmental groups and human rights groups will also be there."

"Numbers?" Abraham asked.

"Fifty thousand, minimum," Reb Meyer offered. "The weather is supposed to be nice, so perhaps twice that."

"That's consistent with what I've learned," Shelby said. "I've been spending most of my time in Monique's office the last few days, so I'm hearing a lot of the calls coming in. They're expecting close to a hundred thousand."

Madame Radminikov smiled at Shelby. "They've been getting some good publicity, yes?"

Shelby blushed, nodded. Monique, surprisingly, was pleased with the *Herald* article—in fact, she emailed it around the country to her network of would-be demonstrators. A story like that, on the front page of a major newspaper, legitimized the event, gave it a buzz. As for Griffin, he made a point of never being in the office with her. It was almost like he sensed that the thought of him out there, lurking, was more frightening to her than any reality....

Shelby continued. "I'm surprised the city hasn't gone back to court to try to get the permit rescinded. Hasn't Agent Ng been sharing her concerns with the mayor's office?"

Abraham answered her question with a question. "If the permit were to be rescinded, would Ms. Goulston cancel the rally? Or even move it?"

"Probably not."

"Well, then, I believe you have your answer."

She glared at her uncle. He could be such a jerk. And she did not really have her answer—it made no sense that the city would attempt to stop the rally even though it had no knowledge of a terrorist threat, while the feds, with specific knowledge, would make no such attempt....

Abraham continued, oblivious to her vexation. "What else have you heard?"

She exhaled. "The plan is for the demonstration to begin at Columbus Park on Saturday morning, but at some time over the weekend they will move to confront the summit delegates. Nobody knows where or when this will be yet, partly because Monique wants to keep it secret for security concerns, and partly because nobody's quite sure where the delegates will be. My guess is that the anarchists won't even bother joining the other demonstrators at Columbus Park; they're going to save themselves for the second rally." She sipped her water. "Anyway, apparently Monique has a cousin who publishes *The Alternative* newspaper. He's going to put out a special edition on Saturday morning, and on the bottom right corner of page 7 there will be a small personal ad addressed to 'Shrub Cutters,' 'Shrub' being a reference to President Bush. The ad will have the location and the time of the second rally. Monique also has an email tree of about 10,000 people—she'll send a message out on Saturday morning and it will get forwarded to computers and laptops all around Boston."

Reb Meyer nodded, apparently impressed by Monique's planning. "Any way we can intercept the location before Saturday?"

"Wait," Bruce challenged, "I thought you were convinced the terrorist attack was going to occur at the Waterfront, on an LNG tanker. Why are you concerned now about where the rally goes? Does it really matter to us?"

Abraham responded. "Yes, Mr. Arrujo, you are correct. All signs still point to an attack in the harbor, but there is also the possibility that Monique and her mob will leave the Waterfront before the tanker arrives. The terrorists have surely anticipated this possibility as well; the question is, what is their provisional target if the LNG tanker is not available to them, or if their attack on it fails?" He turned to Shelby. "Reb Meyer asked if it was possible to intercept this information before Saturday."

Shelby shook her head. "I don't see how. She's kept it totally secret—she'll have to tell her cousin late Friday night so he can get it into the paper Saturday, but even then she's not planning on calling him until after midnight. I've been trying to listen in on her conversations to see if I can figure anything out, but it's almost like she enjoys having the power of being the only one who knows."

Abraham nodded, as if Monique's secretive approach were perfectly understandable. "Anything else, Shelby?"

"Well, it looks like the court is not going to restrict the rally in any way. Normally I would think this is a big deal, but I don't think Monique really cares one way or another. It's actually a weird situation—I'm working hard to get her a permit I know she doesn't really care about, and she's trying to act like it's important to her."

Madame Radminikov smiled. "Sort of like the old Soviet Union— the workers had an expression: 'We'll pretend we're working if you'll pretend you're paying us.'"

Shelby found the comment amusing, and Bruce chuckled as well. Mr. Clevinsky smiled, though that was a fairly constant condition for him. It was not clear whether Abraham understood the irony, while Reb Meyer took the opportunity to grab an oatmeal raisin cookie and stuff a crumbly chunk into his mouth.

Abraham moved on to other considerations. "The fact that Monique is not overly concerned with the permit for the Columbus Park rally is further evidence that the demonstration will at some point move away from the Waterfront. So, we are back to the one thing we do not know: The rally will start at Columbus Park, but at some point it will move to confront the delegates. We need to spend the next few days trying to figure out where that will be, because that may end up being where the terrorists attack. As Agent Ng stated, this country's intelligence organizations respond best to specific information. I would like to be able to provide that to them."

He turned to Bruce. "Do you have anything to add, Mr. Arrujo?"

Bruce sat forward in his chair. "One thing that may be interesting. I teach sailing to a kid whose father is one of the heads of the Boston police department's special operations squad. Morale there is pretty low—they feel like they were scapegoated for the death of the girl after the Red Sox World Series victory. They also got blamed for the kid who got run down after the Patriots Super Bowl victory. Both times, they think they weren't given enough support by the mayor's office."

"What kind of support?" Reb Meyer asked.

"The typical: They want more money to buy state-of-the-art equipment, and they want more men on duty. And now they're being told they can't use even semi-lethal force to control the crowds. Basically they think they're being asked to do the impossible, and when they fail, they get demoted or fired."

Abraham nodded. "And how do you think this impacts on the demonstrations?"

"Hard to say. All I can say for sure is that the police are complaining a lot. They're really getting sick of these large-scale events like the Democratic Convention and the championship parades. They'd much prefer that the G-8 delegates stay in Europe. Some are even wishing the Red Sox and Patriots would stop winning championships."

"This hardly qualifies as useful intelligence," Reb Meyer sneered.

Bruce turned on him. "You're the security expert. You draw some conclusions."

Reb Meyer cleared his throat. "Well, assuming this information is reliable," he said, raising an eye toward Bruce, "it is safe to say that the officers on the street are going to be hesitant about using lethal force during crowd control. None of them is going to want to be the one who kills the next college student. That's just human nature. Second, studies have shown that, in situations like this, the police may become willfully ignorant of certain activity. In other words, they may ignore things like looting and other mayhem. They've been saying all along they need more funding and manpower, and a wild October weekend may be just what they need to prove their point."

"Are the police really that ... petty?" Shelby asked.

Reb Meyer shrugged his shoulders. "Some are, some are not. But we know for certain that law enforcement will be over-extended that weekend, just with the Columbus Park demonstrations and the G-8 conference. Even the most well-trained and well-disciplined force would have a hard time maintaining the peace if you add a Red Sox World Series celebration to the mix."

Abraham contemplated Reb Meyer's words for a few seconds. "I think you are missing the larger point, Reb Meyer. I am not worried about a little looting or a few overturned cars. I am concerned that the police force will be so over-extended that it will be unable to respond to a terrorist attack."

A thin smile formed on Reb Meyer's mouth. "On the contrary, Abraham. I understand your point exactly."

*   *   *

Rex Griffin hid in the shadows, watched Reb Meyer waddle out of the Hotel Commonwealth. Griffin needed to be careful here—he wanted to follow the fat man, but the fat man's agents were monitoring Griffin's movements via the ankle bracelet. Griffin was banking on Reb Meyer being so secretive that his own men did not even know where he was, and therefore would have no way of knowing Griffin was on his tail. So far it had worked out; he had tracked his rotund quarry for three days, seemingly without raising suspicion.

Reb Meyer took a right turn out of the hotel, looked at his watch, then put his head down and marched up Commonwealth Avenue toward the Back Bay. For a fat bastard, he moved pretty quickly. Griffin pulled his trench coat collar up to shield his face, fell in behind. The streets were fairly busy—it was still well before midnight, and even though it was midweek and the Red Sox were playing in the World Series, a decent number of students and other young club-goers filled the Kenmore Square area. Griffin stopped occasionally and, keeping his mark in sight, peered around to make sure the fat man did not have an agent watching his back. Not that he should—Reb Meyer had no reason to suspect anyone was tracking him.

After a couple of long blocks, the fat man turned right onto Massachusetts Avenue. Griffin scampered to reach the corner before he lost his quarry. Just as Griffin made the turn, Reb Meyer stopped next to a late-model red pick-up truck with Louisiana plates parked at a meter, its engine running. He rapped his knuckles on the glass, then opened the passenger side door and slid in. Griffin froze, edged behind a telephone pole, careful that he was not visible in the truck's sideview mirror. He waited, watched the men talk. Less than a minute passed, then Reb Meyer opened the door and left the truck. He was carrying a small, rectangular cooler by its handle.

The truck put on its blinker, pulled out of its spot, drove half a block up Massachusetts Avenue, then turned right onto the Massachusetts Turnpike. Perhaps heading back to Louisiana, perhaps just back to the Western suburbs.

Griffin ducked into an ice cream shop, focused on the cooler as Reb Meyer walked past the window. Whatever was in that cooler, it was important. So important that there was no chance the fat man would stop for a late night ice cream snack.

CHAPTER 10

Myron Kline cursed, heaved an empty soda can at the 60-inch projection TV anchored in his living room. "Goddamn Red Sox." They were up 8-1 in Game 6, on their way to Game 7.

He flipped open his laptop, opened an Excel file, entered a command to aggregate the running totals in the document entitled "Red Sox—World Series." The numbers had not changed, and they did not lie: He had action going both ways, but wagers on the Red Sox far exceeded those against them. And many of them were at long odds, given at the beginning of the season when a championship was anything but a certainty. A Red Sox win in Game 7 would cost him close to $200,000.

He had about $65,000 in CDs and stocks. Plus $10,000 in emergency cash tucked inside a heating vent in Madame Radminikov's butcher shop. He could pawn some jewelry and his watch for a few grand more. Maybe even hit up family and friends for another twenty or thirty grand, best case. That still left him more than $75,000 short. He broke into a cold sweat, remembering the desperate days following the first Patriots Super Bowl victory—skulking around, dodging bettors and then loan-sharks until he was able to dump his Cape Cod condo at a fire sale. But this time he had nothing left to sell....

He thought about getting up early in the morning, going to the Saturday service at the synagogue, praying for a Red Sox loss. But he quickly rejected the thought—apparently the bible had already ordained a Boston victory, so God would be of no use to him. Perhaps he could make a deal with the devil instead.

*   *   *

Burt Ring peered out the window of the upstairs office of one of his warehouse properties, only yards from the outer walls of Fenway Park. Thousands of screaming fans poured out of the garage door-like passageways carved into the stadium's brick façade, like rats scampering from a burning dumpster. But these rodents were happy, boisterous, giddy. So joyful, in fact, that they might decide to overturn cars and break windows. Maybe even grope a few women on the sidewalk.

The thumping bass of music from his nightclub below concussed through the old warehouse walls, vibrated along the floor, caused Burt's chair and desk and file cabinet to hum in concert with the music. Sure, his clubs catered to the young, many of them self-absorbed and shallow and hedonistic. But the club-goers were also creative and original and energized. Not like the meatheads who obsessed over the local sports teams and thought that the pinnacle of architectural achievement in Boston was Fenway Park's 37-foot high left field wall.

One more victory, tomorrow night, and they would turn the entire Fenway Park area into some kind of shrine to the baseball gods: Come! Drink watered-down beer! Throw up on your neighbors! Shoot your body full of steroids and watch your forehead grow ridges! And don't forget to drop your donations in the collection basket on the way out.

He wished Gabriella was here. At a time like this, with his empire at risk of being swept away in a tide of Red Sox euphoria, he needed her. He needed her reassurance—would she stay with him even after the newspaper and the clubs were gone?

He looked in the small mirror on his wall. A balding, double-chinned, pear-shaped man stared back at him. *Yeah, right.*

If only there was a way he could ensure there would be no joy in Mudville.

* * *

It was well past two in the morning when Monique finally cleared the foot soldiers out of her office. They, of course, did not think of themselves as foot soldiers, or even as lieutenants. They thought of themselves as co-equals in orchestrating the weekend's events. They were, in one sense—they were co-equals in the same way all worker bees are equal with each other. But there was only one queen, and she was dressed all in black.

Adrenaline coursed through her body, intoxicating her. She would not sleep tonight. It had been a pattern in her life, this late-night frenetic activity. In college it was the weekly all-nighters to put the school newspaper to bed. In law school it was the midnight-until-whenever study-group sessions, fueled by caffeine and pizza and the nervous paranoia of her hyper-competitive classmates. Now it was the chaos of last-minute strategic and logistical planning necessary to make a huge mob behave the way you wanted it to. Just in the past few hours: the labor groups, in solidarity with their union brothers in blue, threatened to back out if the anarchists unfurled their 'Make the Pigs Squeal' banners; the company that owned the Port-a-Potties insisted not only on payment up front, but also—apparently fearing that the upright, plastic coffins would make attractive souvenirs—a large security deposit as well; and the deputy chief of police phoned to warn that, permit or not, the police would step in and haul people off to jail at the first sign of lawlessness.

Tens of thousands of people. Thousands of bitter stories. Hundreds of agendas. Scores of special interest groups. Utter chaos. All of it under her control.

Too many years had passed since she felt the power, since she saw her face on CNN or read her name in the *Washington Post* or heard her voice on NPR. At the pinnacle of her power, in the wake of orchestrating the Seattle and Quebec City demonstrations and not long before September 11, a preeminent foreign affairs magazine named her one of the ten most powerful people in the world. Her name in bold-face type, just above Donald Trump and just below

Nelson Mandela. Not bad for a smart-ass kid from Cleveland who could not get a college recommendation from her guidance counselor because she got caught giving her boyfriend head under the bleachers at a football game.

She sighed. When Gore lost to Bush, her name was removed from the party circuit's A-list, Republicans being far less enamored than Democrats with both her anarchist ties and vampish lifestyle. Then, after September 11, it became contra-chic to be an advocate for world chaos, and she had to hook up with Senator Sedentary just to stay in the game.

But that would soon change. In fact, she had already picked out a puppy-dog-eyed graduate student with a wet smile and a hard, long body for tomorrow night's celebratory screw. He was, she knew, too young for her. But he would be older tomorrow....

Tomorrow. Things were lining up nicely. She had worked hard, called in favors, spent money when necessary. And she had been lucky. Her call to rally resonated—the nation's progressive wing had been dormant for too long, overwhelmed by the events of September 11, then defanged by the Patriot Act, and finally numbed by Bush's victory over Kerry. Now, finally, they were ready to emerge as a force again, and Monique's rally provided the ideal forum.

Monique had scheduled the demonstration for 9:00 in the morning, and early estimates indicated that close to 100,000 people would be descending on Columbus Park. The numbers would have been high no matter what, but rumors (spread by Monique, and totally baseless) that Bob Dylan and Bruce Springsteen would be holding an impromptu concert did not hurt. Nor did the forecast for a warm, sunny day.

She planned to let the crowd chill at the park for four or five hours, alternately listening to music and hearing speeches denouncing imperialism and globalism and multi-nationalism and all the other –isms associated with the polo and paté crowd. By mid-afternoon they would be ready for action, and Monique would unleash them.

But where would she attack? She kept her plans secret, but the police were not stupid—they figured she did not plan to spend the entire weekend in Columbus Park, and they knew she wanted to get in the face of the delegates, to rage and snarl and spit at them. So the police kept the ring tight around the summit activities, shielding the elected officials from those that had elected them. It was an effective tactic—instead of trying to contain the demonstrators, they isolated the demonstrators' targets. Sort of a circle-the-wagons strategy.

So Monique had come up with a different approach entirely: A group of exclusive Newbury Street merchants were providing the wives and families of the summit delegates private access to their boutiques and salons during the 4:00 to 5:00 hour on Saturday. The merchants expected scores of limo-driven, deep-pocketed fashionistas. But with so many other security requirements for the weekend, the police would not rank a shopping spree as a high priority.

She typed out a quick note to her cousin Burt: "Page 7 ad to read as follows: 'Shrub Cutters: Meet at 3:30 on Saturday in Public Garden, near Swan Boats. From there we will head up Newbury St. for shopping fun. Cocktails all along the route.'" The last five words served two purposes: She inserted them in case the message otherwise seemed suspicious, and also as a signal to the anarchists that they should bring Molotov cocktails.

That was it then. The second-to-last item on her thousand-item checklist. She opened her laptop, signed-on to her email account. One more task—a simple email. Between the personal ad in *The Alternative* and the email chain, anyone interested in taking a more active role in defeating the forces of evil would know where to re-congregate later on Saturday. She might not get the full crowd of 100,000. Nor did she need it.

She pictured the events unfolding: She would gather the masses at the Public Garden, point them up Newbury Street. The anarchists would emerge from alleys and subway stations and parked cars and blend in just as they had in Seattle and Quebec and Genoa. They would slip vinegar-soaked bandanas over their faces, wait until the crowd had packed the first few blocks of the 8-block street, signal each other via cell phone, then pull out their Molotov cocktails and go to work.

Some of the demonstrators would join them, some would run for safety. Either way, it would make for quite a show—thousands of people breaking windows, overturning cars, starting fires, looting stores. And the wives and children of the delegates would have front-row seats. Many would get caught in the cross-fire of tear gas and billy clubs and pepper spray as the police moved in to disperse the mob. The delegates—cocooned within a protective ring of Secret Service agents—would themselves be witnessing neither the wrath of the dispossessed nor the brutality of the police. But enraged spouses and traumatized children would ensure they heard plenty about both.

She began to type the message....

A floor board creaked. There were volunteers sleeping on stairwell landings and under desks and curled up in office chairs, but this sound was closer, in the room with her. Yet she was certain she had closed the door to her office....

She began to turn, smelled the presence of another being. A quick scurrying, then a gloved hand clasped her mouth closed. *Somebody joking around?* The weight of a body pushed down on her suddenly, forcing her deep into her chair. The chair tilted back on its hinge, bounced. Her feet flew into the air....

Not a joke. She opened her mouth to bite, but the gloved hand jerked her head back and her jaw snapped shut before her teeth could find flesh. Something cold and sharp ripped into her neck. She gagged, gasped, fought for air. The heavy breathing of her assailant filled the room, the wasteful use of oxygen mocking her. She tasted blood deep in her throat, then a dark cloud floated up and enveloped her eyes. A dull thumping filled her ears, then it slowed and faded, replaced by the sound of a distant gurgle. Her brain informed her it was the sound of life escaping from her body, and tears of frustration and anger and sadness and anguish pooled in the blackness of her eyes.

Not like this. Not so alone.

A final, fierce spark of rage filled her, and she thrashed and clawed and scratched in an effort to free herself from the life-sucking strangulation. Then even that spark, like life itself, flickered and faded, snuffed out by the lack of oxygen. There was a brief moment, as her body shut down, when she accepted that the garrote had defeated her. Her assailant, sensing her capitulation, eased the chair off its recline and lowered her, gently, to the floor. She was floating now, no longer afraid, accepting of death. But still she held on, clutching life for a precious few more milliseconds, refusing to let go until her mind could answer the one question that made no sense at all. *Why?*

*   *   *

The call from Abraham came even before their alarm clock had taken the deep breath it needed to shriek the nighttime into morning. His words were flat, succinct. "Shelby. Monique Goulston has been found dead in her office."

Shelby's heart pounded, either from being startled awake or from the bomb dropped on her bed. Bruce was awake, alert, his eyes questioning. She repeated the message. Her thoughts turned to Monique's mother; her hand moved to her belly. Who would make the call, telling the mother that the child was dead?

"That's all he said?" Bruce asked. "Just that Monique is dead?"

"Yes."

"Are you thinking what I'm thinking?"

"Griffin?"

"Yup." He glanced at the digital clock. "It's not even five o'clock yet—you saw her last night at, what, ten?"

"Yeah, a few minutes after. I left after the fifth inning, after the Sox went ahead 9-2." Shelby had insisted on watching the game on the small television as they discussed last-minute legal issues.

"So she must have died late at night or early this morning. How would Abraham know already?"

Shelby shrugged. "He knows everything." She sat up, swung her feet to the floor.

"No, he knows things people tell him. If she got hit by a car or had a heart attack, it would just fly under the radar. But a murder would attract attention, would attract a lot of people to the scene, would be something Abraham would learn about quickly."

Shelby nodded. "Agreed. I think we should go to her office. I'll make some calls on the way, see what I can find out."

They dressed and washed-up quickly, grabbed a couple of energy bars for the short cab ride to Beacon Hill. Shelby phoned an old friend from the D.A.'s office. "Looks like she was strangled," she reported to Bruce. It was an ominous beginning to a day in which death loomed, like a medieval, fire-breathing sea monster, just off-shore in the harbor.

"Any suspects?"

"Don't know. My friend's getting this second- and third-hand."

"What time did they find her?"

"Some college kid found her in the middle of the night—three o'clock or so. She was wandering around, looking for a bathroom, stumbled over Monique's body."

Bruce stared out the window for a few seconds. "I'm still thinking Griffin."

"That was my first thought, but now I'm not so sure. What would his motive be?"

"I don't know." He took a deep breath. "All right, put Griffin aside for now. Who else would want her dead?"

"Who wouldn't?" She shivered. "Start with every industrialized nation and half the Fortune 500 companies, and work your way down from there."

"Yeah, but if they wanted to kill her, they would have done it months ago. Now it's too late—the demonstrations and rallies and anything else planned for today are pretty much on automatic pilot. They're going to happen with or without Monique."

Bruce pursed his lips, corrected himself. "It's actually worse than automatic pilot—automatic pilot can be turned off. This is a plane without a flight crew. With Monique alive, you were in the middle of things, in the command center, in a position to influence her decisions. Even if you couldn't change her mind, at least you could report what she was doing to Abraham. That was the whole idea—stay close to her and hopefully get the chance to do something to prevent the terrorist attack. Now that she's dead, this whole day is just hurtling through time and space without any controls at all. I feel bad for Monique, but if we don't figure out what's going on, she's not going to be the only dead body in Boston today."

*   *   *

The police roped-off Phillips Street, so the cabbie dropped Shelby and Bruce on the corner and they walked to the red-brick rowhouse that Monique had commandeered. It was a cool fall morning with a brisk wind; the sky was already shading from gray to blue. Shelby tried to pull herself out of her melancholy and focus—there would be plenty of time later to mourn Monique.

She stuffed her hands in the pockets of her khakis. Her new khakis, with the elastic waist to accommodate the now-visible bulge in her abdomen. "Just our luck," she commented. "Looks like a nice day. I was hoping for heavy rain." They would have had an easier time finding the terrorists if most of the demonstrators stayed home.

Bruce smiled, nudged her. "Isn't that God of yours supposed to bring plagues and stuff when you need them?"

The biblical reference was not directly on point, but Shelby, her mood already darkened by Monique's death, was struck by it nonetheless. "Well, maybe God thinks we're following the wrong Abraham."

"The wrong Abraham. Interesting thought...."

Her friend from the D.A.'s office had called ahead. The detective greeted her—they had worked together a couple of times in the past. Shelby explained that she was in the office with Monique the night before, asked if she could take a look around to see if she noticed anything amiss.

The police had removed Monique's body, left a white-chalk outline in its place. Shelby stared at the outline for a moment, tried to imagine the black-clad body of her ex-roommate lifeless on the floor. She could accept the idea of Monique being dead. But lifeless, that was different; that was a description that was totally at odds with everything Monique.

She moved around the office, careful not to disturb anything, tried to picture it as it had existed eight hours earlier. Her eye settled on a stray piece of paper, alone in the green, plastic recycle bin, a bin Shelby had emptied the night before on her way out the door. She looked at the detective for permission; he nodded and she lifted it by the edges, turned it over, read through it. A fax cover sheet, with instructions sent by Monique to her cousin Burt for the ad in today's edition of *The Alternative*, notifying the demonstrators to meet in the Public Garden for an evening rally on Newbury Street. No doubt the identical message had been sent to Monique's email chain.

It made sense. Monique had mentioned the delegates' wives' shopping spree, mocking them for their unwillingness to rub elbows not just with the common folk, but even with the local shopping elite. Monique had chosen her target well—Newbury Street was high profile, there were plenty of multinational stores like Nike Town and The Gap to demonize, and the abundance of alleys and subway stations surrounding the street would make it difficult for the police to box-in the demonstrators. She handed the paper to the detective. "This wasn't here when I left last night."

"Notice anything else?" the detective asked. Porras was his name. His face hid behind an over-sized walrus mustache and thick, bushy eyebrows—a face veiled in the high grass, sleuthing for clues. When she first met him, the eyebrows and mustache were jet black; now his head sported more salt than pepper. But he was still thin, still tightly coiled, still seemingly smoldering from some long-ago slight.

"No, nothing. Her laptop is still here, so they didn't take that. It looks pretty much the way it did last night. Did anybody hear anything, a struggle or anything?"

He shook his head, his mustache brushing the air. "No. We're checking out everyone who slept here last night—there must have been 30 people in the building."

"Any sexual assault?" A bunch of twenty-somethings crashed together for the weekend. It would have been Porras' first thought as well.

"No, nothing like that. Best we can tell, someone snuck in, grabbed her from behind, strangled her with some kind of wire, then left pretty quickly after that. Do you know if she carried a purse or wallet or anything?"

"Yeah, she had a big, black leather bag she kept stuff in. Is it missing?"

Porras shrugged. "Yeah, but the killer might have just taken it to make it look like a robbery gone bad. I'm not buying it—doesn't smell like a robbery to me." His eyes moved slowly around the room, his nose sniffing the air like an animal sensing a predator. "Excuse my French, but what the fuck was going on here?" He had always been humorless, cynical. One of the few single cops she worked with who never hit on her. No fun at a dinner party, but well-suited to the ugliness of homicide.

Shelby summarized Monique's activities, told him about the demonstrations and rally planned for the weekend. Bruce's words echoed in her brain: With Monique dead, there was no way to call off the demonstrators, terrorist threat or not.

The detective snorted. "What a fucking country. Daddy makes enough money to send Princess to law school, and she spends her life trying to ruin the country that made him rich to begin with. I guess I don't need to ask if she had any enemies."

"Lots of 'em, probably. I mean, she was a pain in the ass to the big multinationals, but there was nothing personal I know of, no love triangles or anything like that. But there is one other thing...." Shelby briefly summarized their history with Rex Griffin, omitting many of the incriminating details. "He's definitely capable of murder. But he's our enemy, not Monique's, and I can't imagine a motive, so I'm not sure I'd focus on him too much...."

The detective scribbled some notes. Shelby questioned him. "You mentioned she was strangled—does that tell you the person had to be of a certain strength?"

"Well, a kid couldn't do it, but any adult with decent strength could kill her using piano wire, maybe a garrote. You can get 'em on the internet, like anything else. Once you get the wire around her neck and pull it tight, it's pretty debilitating. Especially if she's sitting down and you have leverage over her."

Shelby nodded. "Any fingerprints, hair, stuff like that?"

"Nothing so far. Prints will be tough—there's been dozens of people using this office. Same with hair and fiber." He took Shelby's phone numbers, turned back to his investigation.

She thanked him, left the building to find Bruce sitting on the stoop reading a newspaper. He spotted her, held up *The Alternative.* "Here it is, fresh off the press. Just like you said, bottom of page 7."

He read the personal ad to her: "'Shrub Cutters: Meet at 7:00 on Saturday in Kenmore Square. From there we will head up Brookline Ave. to join the fun around Fenway Park. Cocktails all along the route.'"

Shelby's stomach tightened. "No, Bruce, that's not right. That's not the right message."

She turned around, reentered the building, found Detective Porras. "It makes no sense that the message Monique sent to *The Alternative* by fax would be different than what they printed."

The mustache shrugged. "Maybe she sent the fax and then, after the Red Sox won game 6, she figures it makes more sense to bring all the whackos to Kenmore Square instead of Newbury Street, you know, let 'em blend in with the crowd gathering there for Game 7. So then she calls the newspaper back, tells them to change the ad. Or sends another fax."

Shelby shook her head. "No. That doesn't make sense either. She told me she wasn't going to send the fax to *The Alternative* until the last possible minute because she didn't want word to leak out early. No way she would have sent that fax before one in the morning, midnight at the very earliest. And by then the Sox game was already over."

She paused, tried to put herself in Monique's place. "Wait, I know how we can check this. She was going to send the same message out by email. Have you looked at her computer yet?"

"No. But it's still on. Let's take a look."

The detective stood over the laptop, pulled on some rubber gloves, shook the mouse to disable the screen-saver. Her Outlook Express program appeared. "Lucky for us this is still connected. I don't think she's in a position to give us her password." He clicked on her "Sent" folder, displayed the last message. "There it is, sent at 2:32 a.m." He read aloud the same message Bruce had read from *The Alternative*, instructing the demonstrators to meet at Kenmore Square at 7:00. He turned to Shelby. "Nice try, but it looks like she just changed her mind on the rally. I'll follow up with *The Alternative* to make sure, but my bet is she sent the fax, changed her mind, called them or faxed them to change it, then sent the email. Probably the last thing she did before she died. The kid found her just after 3:00, so that would put the time of death at somewhere between when she sent the email at 2:32 and, say, 3:05."

It did not feel right—the Newbury Street target was much more consistent with both Monique's personality and her strategy of choosing symbolic targets. But "it did not feel right" was not enough to change the course of the investigation. The detective said he would follow up with *The Alternative*, and that would have to suffice for now.

She met Bruce on the stoop a second time, explained what she learned, tried to convey her unease. "Monique wouldn't tell me where the second rally was going to be, but she kept dropping little hints about it. When I saw the fax message about Newbury Street, I said to myself, 'Of course!' It just made sense—she had been making fun of the wives and their shopping spree all week. I'm having trouble buying that she would choose Fenway Park instead. I mean, the protestors don't have tickets, they're not going to be able to get into the park. The delegates probably won't even know they're there. That's why the Newbury Street thing made so much sense—they could get right in the face of the delegates' wives, make it really personal."

Bruce studied her face, nodded. "Your unease is good enough for me." He broke into a broad smile. "Not to mention it's all we've got."

She cuffed him on the shoulder, took him by the arm and led him down the steps. "But seriously," he continued, "the detective's theory that Monique just changed her mind only makes sense if she was killed after 2:32. If it turns out she died before 2:32, then she couldn't have sent the email."

"Which would mean the killer sent it."

"Agreed. And that would be a pretty good clue, because it would give us a motive."

She thought for a second as they made their way down the slope of Beacon Hill to Cambridge Street. "But how would that explain the ad in *The Alternative*?"

"If the killer sent an email, they also could send a fax. Next time you talk to the detective, ask him how close they can get to time of death. If the police arrived at, say, 3:30, and the medical examiner came right over, they might be able to narrow the time of death down to before or after 2:32."

"If I'm right, then we still have to figure out the bigger question: Who would want the demonstration moved to Fenway Park so badly they would kill Monique?"

"If you're right, and it's still a big if, the obvious answer is that whoever killed Monique did so because they're planning a terrorist attack at Fenway and want to be able to use the demonstration as a cover. So they killed Monique, then sent out the email."

Shelby shook her head. "I don't know, Bruce. Like you said, that's the 'obvious' answer. But we're forgetting one variable: Rex Griffin. Things are never obvious when he's around. Maybe Griffin did it, as part of some plot to get his revenge on us." She sighed. "Or maybe the whole thing is just a diversion, and the real target is still the LNG tanker. Or maybe Fenway is the back-up target, if the LNG thing fails. Or maybe the murder is just random and has nothing to do with terrorism or Griffin or demonstrations at all."

Bruce waved down a taxi. "I think we have to assume the worst, that the murder is somehow related to a terrorist attack. Maybe Griffin is involved, maybe not. Either way, I'm thinking we should head down to Columbus Park, see what's going on there." He looked at his watch. "It's not even seven o'clock. We've got more than twelve hours until the rally at Fenway. But that LNG tanker could be getting ready to cruise into the harbor right now."

*   *   *

Shelby phoned her uncle from the taxi. She told him what she and Bruce had learned, then summarized their feeling that Monique's murder was not random but somehow related to a planned terrorist attack.

"You are probably correct," he demurred. "In any event, I believe the primary threat remains the LNG tanker. Reb Meyer is at Columbus Park now, with a team of operatives. Some are undercover, mixing in with the demonstrators."

"We are headed there ourselves."

"I assume you have forged relationships with Ms. Goulston's lieu-tenants? You will still be able to operate as our eyes and ears?"

"Yes." In fact, the *Herald* newspaper article had given Shelby a mini-celebrity status among the protest organizers.

"Good. I will instruct Reb Meyer to find you and brief you. He will be your liaison to Agent Ng. Also, remain in contact with the police detective and keep me apprised of developments in the mur-der investigation."

Less than five minutes later the cab dumped them off in front of Columbus Park. A number of demonstrators had camped out overnight in tents, and the park was already bustling with pre-rally activity: Burly men in green cover-alls unloaded Port-a-Potties off the back of a flatbed; a long-haired crew set up a performance stage and sound system; volunteers stocked a first aid tent; a couple of college students hung over-sized trash bags on tree limbs and light posts. The military-like precision that had gone into planning the event amazed Shelby. Monique enjoyed ultimate authority, but she had able lieu-tenants in place to make sure all the logistical issues were dealt with. But their relationship with Monique was professional, not person-al—they would mourn her for a few minutes, then focus on readying for today's events.

The burly figure of Reb Meyer emerged from under a tree, approached them slowly. He held a bagel in one hand and was wear-ing a multi-colored, tie-dyed t-shirt stretched tight over a red hood-ed sweatshirt. He looked like what a pre-schooler might come up with if asked to draw a peacock. Fearing Bruce would laugh in his face, Shelby stepped forward and greeted the ex-Mossad agent before he reached them.

"Good morning," she offered. "How did you find us so quickly?"

He scowled. "Hint one: You arrived by taxi—the other demon-strators arrived by chauffeured limousine." He took a bite of bagel, caught cream cheese on his finger and licked it clean. "Next time, walk or take the subway. Hint two: You guys look like you're dressed for the shopping mall." They were both wearing slacks and a sweater. He pulled a couple of t-shirts from his shoulder bag. "Here, put these on. You'll never blend in looking like models from a Gap ad." Which explained why Reb Meyer looked like a box of crayons. Shelby inspected the shirts. Hers was yellow with blue lettering: 'Housing Is for People, Not for Profits.' Bruce's was white with a red clenched fist on the front.

"What have you learned?" Bruce asked.

"The tanker is coming through today. Right now it's sitting in the outer harbor. The vessel is massive—it draws 36 feet—so they'll have to come in at or near high tide, a little after 11:00 this morning."

Bruce sighed, shook his head. "Do they really have to come in this morning? I mean, couldn't they wait until tomorrow?"

Reb Meyer looked like he had just bit into something rancid, spat out the words. "No. Today is the day." Then he seemed to catch himself, spoke in a more conciliatory tone. "Look, it's not that simple. The tanker has been anchored since last night. They don't like to leave it just floating out there, because then it becomes a stationary target. Plus tomorrow is supposed to be pretty windy, which makes it harder to maneuver under the Tobin Bridge…." He paused, as if considering whether to share the entirety of his knowledge with Bruce. The pause looked contrived to Shelby, an awkward attempt to win their favor by sharing his secret. "You know, I think you're right, I think they're crazy to bring that thing into Boston right now. But they've got a lot of manpower tied up right now on this, which means it's using up their overtime budgets. They want to get the tanker into dock and be done with it."

Shelby had a different take. "Isn't it equally possible they want to get the tanker through the harbor so they can redeploy the law enforcement personnel? Between the demonstrations and the summit and the Red Sox tonight, they could use the manpower in other places besides the Harbor."

Reb Meyer responded with an indifferent shrug, the digital camera hanging from a cord around his neck bouncing off his chest as he did so. He had grudgingly deigned to discuss security strategy with Bruce. But not with the girl. "Perhaps."

"Anything suspicious?" Bruce asked.

Reb Meyer's eyes scanned the park as he answered. "Nothing yet, but it's early. The crowd won't be coming in for another hour or so.

My people are spread around the park, trying to blend in. I've got one of them working on the sound system, another one's set up in an ice cream truck, the rest are just sitting on blankets waiting for things to get started."

Bruce, too, scanned the park. There were a few groups of people who had staked out spots near the stage, but the workers still outnumbered the demonstrators. "There cops here yet?"

"Of course. Most of the Homeland Security people are up in the hotel and in the condo buildings, trying to see from above. That's where Agent Ng is. The federal people are in charge, and the state cops are down here on the ground doing the dirty work. And there's also a bunch of Boston cops, too, but they're mostly around the perimeter. They're here for crowd control."

"My uncle said you'd brief us, tell us how we can help." Hopefully her rapport with Monique's lieutenants would allow her to perform her assigned task of providing logistical information about the rally. In the meantime, she and Bruce were available to assist in other ways.

Reb Meyer shrugged dismissively. "I've got my men in place."

Shelby had dealt with too many jerks over the years to let Reb Meyer get to her. "Fine, then you explain to Abraham why we left."

Reb Meyer coughed. "I suppose you could just blend in, walk around, keep your eyes open. Check in with me on my cell phone if you see anything." He waddled off.

Shelby turned to Bruce. "I don't trust him."

"Why?"

"Hard to articulate. Sometimes it seems like he wants our help, then it seems like he doesn't. Almost like he's got more than one agenda here today."

Bruce nodded. "I think he sees you as a threat. Like you're the boss' son coming in to take over the company. He probably sees himself as Abraham's heir apparent."

She grimaced. "The last thing I want to do is get more involved with *Kidon*. Let's just get through this weekend and be done with these people."

"Okay with me. So, what's the plan?"

She eyed the crowd. "Most of the people are here because they really care about this demonstration. Then there are people like us and Reb Meyer and the cops: We can wear our t-shirts and sit on our blankets, but we're never going to fit in. It's like at a rock concert, there's always some people who got dragged there by their friends. They try to look like they're having fun, but you can just tell they're not really into the music. That's what we look like."

"So what are you saying, we should leave?"

"No, I'm saying we should look around for other people who aren't that into the music."

*　　*　　*

Griffin watched as Shelby and Bruce spoke with Reb Meyer. The fat slob left, and the lovebirds pulled on their t-shirts. As Shelby did so, she raised her arms, revealing a telltale bulge in her midsection. So, the Dynamic Duo was soon to be three....

Griffin pulled out his cell phone, pressed the "1" on his speed dial. Abraham answered on the first ring.

"What is your report?"

"Pinnochio reporting from Columbus Park. *Bull* and *Shit* just arrived by taxi." He knew the old fool was too literal to pick up on the nicknames. But it was fun to push his buttons.

"Who did you say arrived?"

"You know, Bull and Shit, Bruce and Shelby. Come on, say it with me—Bull and Shit. I promise I won't tell the teacher—"

"Mr. Griffin." Abraham's impatience was showing. Good. "Continue your report."

"Oh, okay. They're talking to the fat pig who does your dirty work for you. He's wearing one of those shirts that looks like someone ate too much fruit salad and then barfed on it. Oh, and I had a muffin and some juice for breakfast. Bran, of course. Keeps me regular."

He heard Abraham take a deep breath. "Remember what you are working for, Mr. Griffin. I do not imagine that you desire a return to your previous residence." He paused, waiting for a response, then continued when none came. "Now, here are your instructions: Keep me apprised of Miss Baskin and Mr. Arrujo's movements. Follow them, but not so closely that they see you."

Griffin pushed the off button on the phone, imagined Abraham's gray eyes narrowing in anger as he realized he had been hung up on. Whatever the old man had in mind, it had to be more complicated than, "Follow them and keep me apprised." The puppet master clearly preferred to keep his puppet in the dark.

Not that Abraham's plans mattered—Griffin had his own agenda. If, as Abraham suggested, Griffin could somehow provoke Bruce into doing something reckless and stupid and dangerous, into doing something that would cause Shelby to throw up her hands and walk out of Bruce's life, that would be an acceptable victory. Not ideal, but acceptable. They had stolen his dreams; he would steal theirs. The stakes were not monetary; in fact, they were not even tangible. But both sides knew the game was on, and it was the victory more than the spoils that interested him. He would separate the Bull from the Shit, then find that island paradise that had eluded him a few years earlier.

And if that plan did not work, Plan B was not so bad either: Free himself from the tentacles of his puppet master, then find another way to torment and terrorize and eventually defeat his adversaries.

*   *   *

Less than two hours had passed since Shelby and Bruce arrived at Columbus Park, but somehow in that short amount of time tens of thousands of people managed to squeeze their way into the park area. The crowd simply appeared, as if magically materializing out of the storm drains and parking meters and pretzel-vending carts, all of these objects somehow transformed into futuristic people transporters for the day.

The ring of her cell phone interrupted her thoughts. She checked the caller ID—Detective Porras.

"Off the record, okay, Shelby?"

"Of course."

"Here's what I got. Best we can determine, time of death was somewhere between 2:00 and 2:45. Can't pin it down any tighter than that. But it does open up the possibility that Ms. Goulston was dead at the time that email was sent."

"I'd say *more* than a possibility. If she's already dead by 2:45, that's a pretty narrow window for her to send an email at 2:32...."

"Narrow, but it still could happen. But, like I said, it raises some questions. So I called Burt Ring, the publisher of *The Alternative*. I asked him about the ad. He said he got a fax, then he got another one, changing the location."

"Do you believe him?"

"It's easy enough to check. He must still have the fax sheets."

She smiled. "You didn't answer my question."

"Actually, he sounded a little skittish to me. But, I'll be honest, I made a mistake. I didn't realize he was Ms. Goulston's cousin."

Shelby's stomach tightened. What he really meant was that Shelby had made a mistake by not mentioning it. "Why does it matter?"

"Well, I assumed he didn't know Ms. Goulston was dead. I mean, none of the details had been released to the press yet. I figure he's not going to lie to me about changing the ad if she's alive to contradict him, right? But, knowing she's dead, now he's free to say anything he wants. If I had known he was her cousin, I would have called first thing, before word got out to the family."

In her experience, lawyers rarely apologized, even when they were wrong. She knew it was disarming when she did so. "My bad. Sorry."

"Don't worry about it. Things are moving pretty fast around here this morning."

"So what makes you think Ring is lying?"

"Just a gut feel. I wish I had driven out to interview him personally, but we're undermanned, what with the demonstration and all, and I've got to interview all these witnesses."

"So do you think Ring's the one who killed her?"

"That's getting a bit ahead of ourselves. All we know so far is that she *might* have died before that email was sent, and he *might* be lying about her calling and changing the message she faxed him. Not exactly a tight case. Anyway, like I said, we're pretty undermanned today. So any help you can give me, I'll take it."

"Okay, you got it."

"Oh, and Shelby?"

"Yeah."

"Be careful. It's no easy thing, squeezing the life out of another human being. Whoever did this, they mean business."

*   *   *

The crowd had long-since claimed every shred of grassy surface; tents and blankets and lawn chairs now also filled the paths and fountains and playground area. Demonstrators would soon overrun the flower gardens as well. There were some signs and banners you would not normally see, but otherwise the crowd had the multi-generational look of a Jimmy Buffet or Grateful Dead concert.

Shelby looked, listened, mingled, chatted. Best she could tell, she did not encounter many rabble-rousers—no surprise there, as Monique believed the anarchists would stay in hiding until later in the weekend. But the protestors she met were definitely liberals, unhappy ones at that, and they wanted change.

The organizers—Monique's lieutenants—erected the stage with its back to the harbor on a wide, paved walking path. Shelby leaned against a wrought iron railing, positioned near the waterfront at a sharp angle to the stage so she could alternately view the stage and scan the crowd. Bruce had taken up a similar position on the other side of the stage, their assumption being that the terrorists, if any, would arrive early and claim a spot close to the harbor's edge.

The question, of course, was whether they would recognize a terrorist if they tripped over one. Did terrorists wear name tags, carry badges? If they spotted something suspicious, they were to follow the chain of command and call Reb Meyer, who would contact Agent Ng or another security official.

The first speaker took the stage at about 9:30. A short, stocky woman with a wild mane of curly brown hair and a pair of wire-rimmed glasses. Monique, or one of her underlings, realized the importance of spending the extra money for a top-notch sound system; the speaker's words rang clear and sharp. "First of all, let there be no doubt: Our friend, our *comrade*, Monique Goulston, was murdered last night, killed because the people, the *men*, who run the global economy wanted her dead!" Shelby doubted it, but it made for good theatre. The woman surveyed the crowd. "That's right. They wanted her dead. She was a threat to them ... we all are a threat to them ... and they are trying to silence us! The men in the dark gray suits are trying to silence us!"

The crowd roared so as not to be silenced, then quieted as the woman raised her pudgy arms and continued. "But we will not be silenced! We will speak out against the injustices in the world! We will speak the words Monique can no longer speak, fight the fight Monique can no longer fight!"

The speaker sipped some water, began her assault against the evils of the North American Free Trade Agreement: "In the name of free trade, we get broken-down, pollution-spewing, head-on-collision-waiting-to-happen trucks crossing our borders, fouling our air, endangering our people. And we can't stop them, because NAFTA says so! I say, keep those trucks out of the United States!" The crowd cheered, then quieted as she continued.

"In the name of free trade, we get mercury-filled cans of tuna fish on our supermarket shelves, poisoning our children. And we can't stop them, because NAFTA says so! I say, keep that toxic tuna out of the United States!" The speaker was finding her rhythm, the crowd responding.

"In the name of free trade," boos now drowning the words 'free' and 'trade, "we get clothes made in the sweatshops of Latin American, made by children robbed of their childhoods and turned into slave laborers. And we can't stop them, because NAFTA says so!" She paused here and motioned to the crowd, imploring them to join her. "We say: Keep. Those. Clothes. Out. Of. The. United. States!" The crowd joined her in these last words, shaking their fists and cheering.

Unsafe trucks hurtling down our highways. Poisonous food on our supermarket shelves. Kidnapped children enslaved in textile sweat-shops. This was the message Monique had crafted and perfected, the talking points she and her group pounded home in rallies and in interviews and in op-ed pieces. If you supported safe roads and safe food and safe children, then you could not support liberalized global trade. Simple, concise, guttural.

Then again, you could support all these things and still drive like a jerk with your kid in the back seat gnawing on a Happy Meal. Shelby sniffed. Sometimes the world was more complicated than just a sound bite....

Reb Meyer rang her cell phone. "The tanker is on its way into the harbor. The escort boats and helicopters will soon be in sight. The tanker itself will be here in less than an hour." She was a bit surprised to be in the information loop.

She relayed the information to Bruce. "See anything?" he asked.

"There's a lot of groups with small tents, but nothing really suspicious."

"Same here. Stay where you are; I'll be right there."

The soft flutter of the baby's kick tickled the inside of her abdomen. When it first happened a few days ago, she thought she had indigestion. Now she recognized the popcorn popping as the movements of a little person. Bruce would, no doubt, try to get her to leave the Waterfront before the tanker arrived. She rested her hand on her belly. Maybe she should listen to him.

A rustle of activity. Three men trying to set up a tent in the middle area of the park were, apparently, blocking the view of a group of women seated behind them. The men were young, dark-haired, olive-skinned. One, wearing a black button-down shirt and a pair of acid-washed blue jeans, smoked a cigarette and argued with his neighbors, waving his arms imperiously and jabbing his cigarette in emphasis. The other two crawled on their knees, continued to erect the dark green camping tent. On the floor of the partially-erected tent, Shelby saw the outline of a large, long bag.

Bruce arrived; Shelby pointed out the scene. "Not to use stereotypes, but those guys look like they belong at a bazaar in Istanbul. I mean, who wears a black silk shirt to a rally?"

Bruce studied them. "They do look out of place. On the other hand, there are lots of Arab-Americans who are pissed at the Bush Administration."

Bruce was right, but that was the problem with this whole terrorism thing. In an ideal world, the practice of profiling was abhorrent—why should people be under heightened suspicion just because of their appearance? On the other hand, here in the real world, she could not take her eyes off the three swarthy men with the tent and duffel bag.

"Do you see that long bag on the floor of their tent?" she asked.

"Yeah."

"It's weird that they put it into the tent even before they finished putting the tent up."

"They're packed in pretty tight there. Maybe they had no place else to put it. It doesn't look like the people next to them are going to offer them any space on their blanket...." Like Shelby, he was trying not to jump to conclusions. His studied the men again, watched the man with the cigarette turn his back on, and then dismissively wave away, the women he was arguing with. Like Shelby, Bruce was losing the battle with his imagination. "I'm going to see if I can get a closer look."

Bruce hopscotched his way through the crowd, his feet landing on the slivers of grass protruding between the blankets and towels and coolers. The crowd seemed friendly and forgiving as he excused his way through them. Especially the women. Almost without fail, female heads turned to follow his progress as he edged his way along. A friend had once ogled Bruce in front of Shelby, then sheepishly asked if it bothered her that other women found him attractive. It did not then, and it had not since....

She long ago realized that if she were to lose Bruce, it would be because his soul strayed, not his heart. As Madame Radminikov observed, he possessed the soul of a warrior—he needed risk and action and danger the same way other men needed money or women or power. Shelby had made it clear that she had no interest in being married to—or the widow of—a warrior. His heart had agreed to her terms. But on days like today, when the smell of danger filled his nostrils and adrenaline coursed through his veins, would his soul be able to resist the call to battle?

Shelby followed the warrior's progress. He was now only a few blankets away from the green tent. One of the men was kneeling inside the canvas walls, while the other two sat in camping chairs in front of the opening. The man in the black shirt smoked a cigarette and spoke into a cell phone. Giving or receiving orders? Collecting surveillance reports? Just trying to get a date for tonight? His companion sipped on a bottle of water and stared out into the harbor. Watching for the tanker? Trying to identify security personnel? Just daydreaming? Whatever the case, neither of them seemed particularly interested in the speaker, who was now concluding her remarks with a call for a boycott of Nike and McDonald's and Wal-Mart and other large multinationals.

Bruce stopped near the tent, scanned the crowd as if looking for friends. He was more likely to spot enemies. Rex Griffin, almost certainly lurking and scheming somewhere in the mob. Perhaps Gregory Neary as well, hoping the anonymity of the crowd would give him cover for another shot at her. Reb Meyer, too; maybe not an enemy, but hardly a trusted friend. And Monique's killer, still at large and presumably vested in the outcome of today's rally. Factor in the anarchists hoping to loot the city and the terrorists hoping to blow it up, and Bruce was surveying one ugly, nasty crowd.

Bruce waved a greeting at an imaginary friend, crow-hopped his way in the direction of an invented destination on the far side of the tent. A long step, a stumble, an awkward drop to one knee a few feet from the tent's entrance. Bruce mumbled something—probably an apology—to the black-shirted man, lifted himself up, moved on.

A few minutes later he returned to Shelby's side. "I couldn't see much—the tent flap was mostly closed. But there's definitely some kind of long bag in there. Could be a grenade launcher. Could also be a camera tripod."

"Did the guy in the black shirt say anything to you?"

"No, he gave me a dirty look, but that could just be because I was such a buffoon." Bruce paused. "You should call Reb Meyer."

Shelby nodded, dialed the phone, described the men with the tent and duffel bag.

"Watch them," he grunted. "If they start doing anything suspicious when the tanker approaches, call me back. The tanker will be in view in about ten minutes."

She hung up. Bruce eyed her, chewed his lip. She heard the message even before he spoke the words. "I think you should leave."

"I know you do. And I understand where you're coming from. But I'm the one who can move this rally if we need to. They'll listen to me. They're not going to listen to Reb Meyer or Abraham or even Agent Ng. And definitely not you. But they trust me."

"But you're carrying our baby, Shelbs...."

His argument made sense—she should go, retreat to a distance where Sarah would be out of harm's way. Instead she was choosing the same sort of risky behavior she criticized him for. Hypocrisy, no doubt. Foolishness, perhaps, also. But how could she just run off and hide when she, alone, had the ability to save thousands of lives?

*   *   *

Shelby looked up, the whir of the assault helicopter announcing its arrival. The copter flew in from the direction of the tanker, low in the sky, nose downward. According to Reb Meyer's briefing, it would be first in the convoy of security vehicles escorting the tanker through the inner harbor. Unless something went terribly wrong, it would be alone in the sky. Logan Airport was now closed, and the airspace over the harbor restricted.

Bruce, too, followed the flight of the copter, then locked his eyes on Shelby. His pupils widened; there was both apprehension and excitement in his face. The apprehension was for her, the excitement for him. He took a deep breath, squeezed her hand. "I'm going to get closer to our friends in the tent." He kissed her on the mouth, lingered for a moment. A warrior preparing to do battle. "Please be careful, Shelby."

"You, too, my love."

A herd of small speedboats followed close behind the copter. The boats darted back and forth across the harbor channel, shooing away pleasure crafts and fishing vessels. A pair of Coast Guard patrol boats followed in the wake of the speed boats, each armed with machine guns mounted port and starboard. Uniformed men stood motionless on the deck of the patrol boats, binoculars to their eyes, scanning the office towers and apartment buildings and shoreline areas. Not surprisingly, more than a few of the binoculars were trained on

Columbus Park. The demonstrators stared back at the uniformed men, many with binoculars of their own. It was hard to say exactly who was in the fishbowl.

A half-dozen tugs, along with a fire boat, followed next in queue. Unlike the sleek speedboats and gleaming white Coast Guard patrol vessels, these ships were squat, cumbersome, gray. The tugs' job was to turn the tanker around and back her under the Tobin Bridge. *Unless she does not make it that far.* In which case the fire boat would be faced with a task comparable to extinguishing a forest fire with a garden hose.

Shelby glanced at the tent. Two of the men had retreated inside. They closed the flap, but she could see the canvas rustling from the movement within. Bruce had circled around, approached the tent from the rear.

She reminded herself to unclench her jaw, turned back toward the harbor. Last in the escort line, leading the massive blood-red tanker, was a 110-foot Coast Guard cutter, a cannon mounted conspicuously on its foredeck. Though the cutter itself was a sizeable vessel, it looked like a dingy next to the mother ship. The cutter, assisted by the assault helicopter, protected the tanker from any vessel that penetrated the outer rim of security and attempted a USS Cole-like ramming attack.

A similar flotilla safeguarded the tanker from behind. All in all, it was an impressive security ring, a significant investment in both firepower and manpower. And utterly powerless against a rocket-propelled grenade attack.

*   *   *

Abraham pressed his face up against the hotel window. His eyes were glued to a mass of blood-red steel, the hull of the tanker filling the entire panorama as it glided by. It reminded him of the times, as a boy, before the Nazis, when he pressed his nose to the window of a train and watched the tunnel walls speed by. If he stared long enough, and convinced his brain to go along with the trick, he could fool his body into believing the train was stationary and that it was instead the tunnel hurtling past him. Was there a young boy, someplace else in the hotel, watching the tanker go by and imagining instead that the hotel itself was in motion?

He had taken a suite on the fifth floor of the Long Wharf Marriott, the young boy now wearing an old man's gray business suit. The suite occupied the entire ocean-side end of the rectangular hotel, with a view of the harbor. At the moment, that view consisted entirely of the upper hull of the tanker, *Hoegh Galleon*. He sat in a wooden desk chair, his knees tight against the plate-glass window, a can of ginger ale resting on an end table next to him. Madame Radminikov sat next to him, but she knew not to interrupt his introspection with silly questions or inane conversation.

The muffled sound of the demonstrators—chants, cheers, an occasional high-pitched hum of electronic interference—echoed from Christopher Columbus Park below. He chose to keep the room's windows closed to the noise; he had heard it all before, and he was more interested in what he might see than what he might hear.

For months Abraham had observed the LNG tankers and their journeys through Boston. But never from such an intimate vantage point. At 900 feet, the tanker's height exceeded the length of any building in Boston. But the tanker's bulk was even more daunting. As it approached from the outer harbor, it appeared impossible for the tanker to squeeze into the narrow channel running between East Boston's industrial shoreline on the one side and the jagged wharves and piers protruding from Boston's waterfront on the other. Again the memory of the train kissing the edge of the tunnel walls as it sped past popped into his head. No wonder the tankers preferred not to navigate the harbor in times of heavy wind or low tide. And no wonder the authorities were so concerned about security.

*   *   *

Bruce crouched about ten feet behind the green canvas tent, focused on the would-be terrorist in the black shirt. Medium height, slope-shouldered, well on his way to a beer belly. Physically, no match. But he wore a dark blue fanny pack around his waist which, judging by the way it hung and swayed, contained a dense, heavy object. Too heavy for a cell phone or camera, too small for a hard-cover book. Could be a water bottle, could be binoculars. Or could be a gun. Funny how one gun neutralized thousands of push-ups and stomach-crunches.

The man raised a cigarette to his mouth, puffed at it in short, furtive movements. The sun had burned off the autumn morning chill, but it was still no more than 60 degrees, with a cool ocean breeze. Not hot enough for the shirt to be sticking to the back of a sedentary man. At least not one whose heart was not racing....

The black-shirted man leaned down, called into the mouth of the tent. "You guys ready yet?" The man felt for his fanny pack, tested the zipper, dried his hands on his pant leg. He pulled the pack around, positioned it over his right hip. Like a holster. "The camel is nearing the village."

Enough. Bruce pulled out his cell, phoned Shelby, turned away from the tent to shield his voice. "Something's going on. Guy's way too nervous. Asked his friends if they were ready yet. Mentioned something about a camel—probably code for the tanker. Plus I think he has a gun."

"Can you see into the tent?"

"No. Call Reb Meyer. Tell him I need help. Can't handle three myself. And try to get people out of here."

Bruce stared at the back of the tent, tried to guess what the men inside were doing. He raised his hand to shield his eyes from the sun....

The sun. Of course. He scampered to his left, now almost even with the side of the tent, positioned himself as the third point in a line made by the sun and the tent. The sun now backlit the men inside, their figures dimly outlined through the thick canvas. Hardly hi-definition, but enough to make out their movements.

The men kneeled, side by side, huddled over their task. Bruce dropped to his knees as well, hoping the new angle would give him a better vantage point. One man grasped a long pole-like object, the other made a twisting motion over it. Bruce's imagination filled in the blanks.

An announcement: "Ladies and gentlemen. Please evacuate the park." Bruce looked at the stage—the short, wild-haired girl held the microphone. Her voice shook. "We have had a report of a possible terrorist attack here in the park." *Way to go Shelby.*

The crowd surged to its feet—some stood frozen, yelling questions toward the stage; others turned and walked, briskly, toward the street; a few offered brave smiles and sat back down on their blankets. Bruce glanced back at the would-be terrorists. Their movements had become more frenzied, more frantic. They, like the crowd, were trying not to panic. But for different reasons.

His cell phone vibrated against his thigh. "I'm here."

"Bruce, I can't reach Reb Meyer. No cell."

Damn. Bruce stood, scanned the crowd as bodies bounced against him. "You seen him?"

"No, it's like he disappeared."

"Abraham?"

"Same problem, no cell."

"Weird...."

A movement in the tent. One of the men repositioned himself, turned toward the harbor, rested on one knee. The silhouette was clear: He was balancing a weapon on his right shoulder. "Shit," Bruce spat into the phone. "I can see a rocket launcher. Forget Reb Meyer, find a cop. Hurry!"

The tanker chugged along in plain view, a slow-moving wall of red blocking the entire span of water between Long and Commercial Wharves. Many of the demonstrators, still not sure whether to heed the warning, froze and followed the progress of the massive vessel. Others realized the danger the tanker brought and redoubled their efforts to flee the harbor area.

"Okay," the black-shirted man barked in a low voice. "It is time." He unzipped his pouch, rested his hand inside.

Bruce stood just to the side of the tent, about 10 feet away, the mass of fleeing bodies shielding him from the terrorists. The second man inside the tent raised himself to one knee; he, too, rested a rifle-like weapon on his shoulder. From inside the tent, the men had a clear shot at the tanker....

The black-shirted man shifted from foot to foot, studied the crowd around him. His eyes narrowed and his nostrils flared. Like an animal standing over its prey, he sensed danger, smelled a challenging predator nearby. Bruce crouched, edged away, using the tent as a shield.

Bruce glanced around, hoping to see the hurried approach of a policeman or undercover agent or even Reb Meyer. Nothing. He reached for his phone, pulled his hand away as the black-shirted man's words slapped at his ears. "Hosni, Mushin, now!"

Only one thing to do. Bruce charged, dove at the tent like a linebacker targeting a quarterback's ribcage. He spread his arms wide, then swung them forward as the tent gave way beneath him, hoping to knock the men over or dislodge their weapons. His left arm connected with something hard—either a head or a rocket launcher—and the man beneath him collapsed to the ground, Bruce atop him. But the other man remained upright on his knee, the tent pulled tight over him and the long weapon still on his shoulder. He looked like a sailboat, shrink-wrapped for the winter, its mast lowered and protruding off both bow and stern.

The black-shirted man's voice cut through the grunts and curses. "Hosni, shoot, shoot!"

Bruce rolled to his right, flailing at the man still perched on one knee. He landed an elbow; his adversary staggered, gasped a sharp intake of breath. The words, screamed in frenzy, echoed through the park. "Allah is great!" Then a dull thud, like the sound of a rock hitting a tree, followed by a high-pitched sizzle.

"Damn!" Bruce cursed. He had failed. The rocket had launched.

Bruce rolled to his stomach, flattened the front of the tent, searched for the flight of the missile. A blue-gray puff of smoke wafted from the launcher, obscuring his vision, but within a second or two his eyes found the rocket, streaking toward the tanker, low to the water, spiraling like a supersonic football. The terrorist buried beneath him in the tent canvas struggled to free himself, but otherwise the crowd was still and silent as all eyes focused on the deadly projectile.

A sharp thump, followed milliseconds later by a concussive blast, rolled in from the harbor. The rocket impacted, then detonated, against the hull of the tanker. Bruce waited for the explosion, the ball of fire. Already his mind raced—grab Shelby, sprint toward the subway, find shelter underground. And then the voice of the black-shirted terrorist, angry and desperate. "Too low, you fool! You aimed too low!" He spun toward Bruce, removed his gun from the fanny pack. Pointed it at Bruce's head. "You! Stay right where you are!"

Bruce allowed himself to breathe, forced back a smile. The missile had detonated, harmlessly, against the tanker's thick, steel hull. Not against one of the holding tanks. He had disrupted the terrorist's aim just enough to avert a fiery catastrophe.

Now all he had to do was deal with the gun pointed at his head. And do so without allowing the first terrorist to retrieve his launcher and take another shot at the tanker.

*　　*　　*

Shelby watched the missile hiss toward the tanker, edged away from the fireball that would soon roll across the harbor....

Instead, miraculously, the missile bounced off the tanker like an acorn off asphalt and fell harmlessly into the ocean. But already the tussle at the tent was on again. And again it was one of life and death. For Bruce. For tens of thousands.

She rushed toward the tent, shapes and forms and smells and noises mixing together into a collage of chaos. The world slowed. Events began to unfold like a series of snapshots, each full of detail and life, but each gone and replaced by another before she could fully view or comprehend the images....

A gunshot. She freezes, prays that the bullet is not for Bruce. The black-shirted man screams: "Get off him! Now!" The command is a response to her prayer. There is no need to shout orders at a dead man....

The gunshot is like a starter's pistol at a marathon. Thousands of people running, shouting. Panic. Screams, curses, commands, cries. Many running inland. Others moving deeper into the park toward the water, away from the gun. Marathon is now a stampede. Bodies cascade into and over and off each other. And her.

The terrorist re-aims his revolver at Bruce. Detective Porras' words echo: "It's no easy thing, squeezing the life out of another human being." The detective is right—the terrorist plots to kill tens of thousands, but has no stomach to put a bullet into Bruce's chest. At least not yet. Bruce rolls off the tent, stands. Sweat runs down the terrorist's cheeks. Gun-hand shakes. Free hand waves in a wide arc. "Everybody stay back," he commands.

The terrorist stands in an open area at the eye of the storm. Littered with blankets, coolers, backpacks. She scampers closer, uses the stumbling, cascading bodies as cover. The terrorist is about ten beach towels away. Fifty feet. She pushes against a tide of elbows and shoulders and chins.

The terrorist aims at the red fist in the center of Bruce's t-shirt. He barks an order. "Get up, Mushin. Fire the rocket! Hurry!"

Two bystanders spin around. Homeland Security agents? Heroes?

They take a couple of steps toward the tent. The terrorist spots them, shrieks: "Get away!" He fires a warning shot into the air. More screaming and frenzy. The would-be heroes duck, turn, retreat. The gun is aimed at Bruce again.

Mushin the terrorist crawls out from under the tent. Digs for rocket launcher under canvas. She is now 30 feet away. No sign of Reb Meyer.

A few uniformed police push toward the tent, making slow progress against the tide of a panicked mob. The police angle toward the wrong spot, fooled by the plume of blue-gray smoke wafting downwind.

It is up to Bruce, up to her....

Bruce has not spotted her. She does not yell to him—the terrorists will hear. She waves her arms, wills him to look her way. His jaw tightens. His eyes scan the crowd, lock onto hers in the swirl of bedlam. Just as hers always settle on the word 'Bruce' on a printed page. She holds up her cell phone and makes a throwing motion. He nods.

The black-shirted terrorist implores his colleague. "Now, Mushin, shoot now!"

Now it is. She reaches back. Years of catch with Dad, hours spent firing the ball from shortstop to first base. Dad's words: *Lock your eyes onto the target. Step toward the target. Point your fingers at the target.*

She finds the target, steps, throws. The phone hurdles end-over-end. Its metal and glass surfaces reflect the sun....

A dull thud as phone smacks against skull. The terrorist yelps in pain. Staggers. Reaches his left hand to his wound.

Bruce steps forward. Kicks at the right hand holding the gun. His kick is true, like her throw. Gun pops into air, arcs to ground, bounces onto beach blanket.

A thin man in a baseball cap scampers out of the crowd, grabs gun, retreats with it.

But terrorist Mushin has untangled his weapon. He hoists it onto his shoulder. Drops to one knee. Aims at tanker.

Bruce rushes him a second time. Crashes into him before he can fire. The two men tumble, roll, Bruce on top. The rocket launcher clatters to the ground. Mushin tries to roll away. Bruce twists his arm behind his back, pushes his face into the grass.

The other terrorist emerges from the tent. Hosni. The black-shirted terrorist barks another command. "Hosni, get the launcher!" Hosni runs toward the weapon. She moves to intercept him. The black-shirted terrorist steps into her path. But then he hesitates. Just as he cannot put a bullet into a man, he will not strike a woman. A gentleman terrorist.

She tries to run past him. He winces, shoves her. Not so gentle after all. She stumbles over a cooler, feels herself falling. She dips her shoulder, angles toward an uncluttered patch of ground, goes into a controlled roll. She lands cleanly. Back on her feet.

But Hosni is now free. Bruce remains tangled on the ground with Mushin. Still no police. No way Bruce can fight all three terrorists at once. If Hosni grabs the rocket launcher, he can fire the fatal shot.

"Bruce," she yells, "fire the rocket!"

Bruce sees Hosni coming. He karate chops Mushin in the back of the neck. Bruce rolls away, grabs the launcher off the ground, swings it onto his shoulder. Has he ever fired a rocket launcher before? Is there a safety lock? A pre-firing sequence? He aims at open harbor, far behind moving tanker. Squeezes trigger just as Hosni lunges for weapon.

The missile hisses, announcing its escape. Both men freeze, their heads fogged by blue-gray smoke. The rocket soars high into the sky above the harbor. It spirals as she counts. One. Two. Three. Four. Then it explodes over the open water.

Shelby breathes, watches as the missile debris wafts harmlessly down among the escort boats, like autumn leaves falling among the lily pads and water bugs in a blue-green pond.

*   *   *

Rex Griffin had been trailing Bruce and Shelby, had snaked his way to the edge of the cowering crowd and watched as Mr. and Mrs. Superhero saved the city. Perhaps he should have been thankful for their heroics—he had no particular desire to be char-broiled in Boston himself.

Griffin's cell phone rang, as it had been for the past few minutes. He ignored it—the puppet was out of commission for awhile. Broken string or something....

All eyes now followed the flight of the missile Bruce had fired high over the harbor. Griffin made his move. Crouching, he edged forward, leaned in toward the terrorist wearing the black shirt. He kept his voice low, almost to a whisper, spoke calmly. The serene tone would contrast with the screaming frenzy around them like the whimper of a baby in a packed cinema. "Hey, turn around."

The terrorist spun, his eyes frantic, searching for the island of serenity in the sea of chaos. Griffin smiled and nodded, reached into his pocket, withdrew the gun slowly and held it out like a man offering a nut to a squirrel. "I think you dropped this." A quick underhanded motion, and the black pieces controlled the chess board once again.

*   *   *

The sound of gunfire seemed puny and tinny after the explosion of the missile. But it was gunfire nonetheless. Bruce had no idea how the black-shirted terrorist had retrieved the gun so quickly, but there he was, the pistol pointed in the air yet again, screaming to his comrades. "Run, Cousins! Follow me!"

Bruce jumped to his feet to pursue the terrorists. There was something not right about this whole thing, about Reb Meyer disappearing and Abraham not answering his phone and the gun suddenly back in the terrorist's hand....

Shelby's plaintive cry slowed him for a split-second. "Bruce, no! He has a gun!" He shrugged off her warning. He needed answers. If the son-of-a-bitch had the balls to shoot him, he would have done it already. "Damn it, Bruce, no!" she yelled.

He thought her voice cracked as she called to him, but it was probably just the wind in his ears and the adrenaline in his veins. The terrorists ran toward Atlantic Avenue, three of many in the panicked crowd, hurdling coolers and dodging bodies. They had a head start on Bruce, but he was gaining, partly because he was a faster runner, and partly because they were clearing the trail for him.

Bruce ran past a pair of uniformed policeman, forcing their way into the park through the now-thinning exodus. As he ran, he surveyed the crowd—still no sign of Reb Meyer or Homeland Security. The two rocket-firing terrorists were pulling away from their paunchy little cohort. Bruce closed on him. He wanted all three of the scumbags, wanted answers. And wanted them to rot in jail for the rest of their lives. They had almost killed him, almost killed thousands of innocent people. Almost killed Shelby and their baby. *Motherfuckers.*

They crossed Atlantic Avenue, dodged cars stuck in the tide of humanity, headed toward the North End. But the crowd had slowed them down. If Bruce could find a cop to help subdue the black-shirted coward, he could then continue after the other two....

There. Bruce yelled, gestured, drew the attention of a young, rugged-looking policeman as they approached the far side of the intersection. This was no ordinary scattering of a mob, the cop seemed to sense. The policeman glanced quickly at something in his hand, then joined the chase himself, sprinting at an angle oblique to the path Bruce was taking. The black-shirted terrorist also saw the cop, veered away like the runt of the herd shying away from a fast-closing predator. Bruce, too, adjusted his path, angling away from the policeman.

Bruce was now only about a body-length away from the terrorist. Three or four more strides and he would be able to tackle the punk from behind. His prey seemed to sense his fate, slowed in resignation. Bruce reached out, ready to horse-collar the little maggot and drag him down....

Suddenly Bruce was airborne, knocked sideways by the policeman's flying tackle. *What?* The two men crashed to the pavement, the policeman on top, Bruce absorbing the force of both the impact with the asphalt and the weight of the man atop him. He skidded, his elbows and knees ripping apart. He tried to lift his head to keep his face from shredding as well. Even before the skid ended, the cop had pinned Bruce's hands behind him and was applying handcuffs.

Bruce fought to find his breath, coughed out the words. "Wrong guy. You got the wrong guy." He thought about fighting to free himself, but he could see two other officers running over, their guns drawn. *Idiots.*

The cop flipped him onto his back, pinned him down with a knee to the chest. He pulled out a digital camera from his pocket, shoved it in Bruce's face. "Sure looks like I got the right guy to me, Mr. Red Fist."

Bruce shook his head clear, focused on the small screen. There he was, a bright red fist emblazoned on his t-shirt, an RPG-7 perched on his shoulder, a puff of blue-gray smoke bubbling from the rear of the launch tube.

Bruce arched his head to the side, watched the black-shirted terrorist stagger around a corner to safety. And wondered: How did the cop end up with a digital camera shot of him firing the rocket launcher?

*   *   *

Rex Griffin pulled the hat low over his eyes, moved away from where Shelby might spot him. Many of the demonstrators had re-congregated in the park and were breathlessly exchanging near-death experiences. It had only been a few minutes since Bruce rode off into the sunset, fast on the heels of the bad guys. Shelby had implored him to stay—the danger was over, the tanker was safe, the threat had ended. Bruce had, deliciously, ignored her.

In a perfect world, the terrorist would use the gun to shoot Bruce in the chest. Actually, not perfect—it would not be as satisfying as Griffin actually killing Bruce himself. But there was not a huge difference between triggering the chain of events and actually pulling the trigger. And, this way, the puppet master could not blame him for Bruce's death.

In reality, the black-shirted terrorist probably did not have the guts to shoot a man. Griffin saw it in Vietnam—the terrorist had his chances to kill, and fired warning shots instead. A terrorist with a weak stomach. The wonders of the 21st century....

But even if Bruce did not die, the morning had been enlightening, perhaps productively so. Bruce ignoring Shelby's exhortations, chasing after the gun-wielding terrorist even after the danger had passed, highlighted the fault line in their relationship. In and of itself, Bruce's recklessness would not suffice to drive them apart. But Bruce's pattern of behavior was becoming habitual, and the lawyer in Shelby could disregard the evidence for only so long. Bruce was the drunk who stayed sober for a few months and then disappeared on a binge weekend, the gambler who stayed clean and then bet the mortgage on the Rose Bowl, the wife-beater who cried and begged for one more chance.

Perhaps, with a little help, Shelby would come to realize you could take Tarzan out of the jungle, and you could even send him to law school, but you could not take the law of the jungle out of Tarzan.

*   *   *

Madame Radminikov moved with Abraham from his suite overlooking the harbor to a second room of the hotel, this one on the sixth floor with a direct view of Columbus Park. Using binoculars, they witnessed the entire series of events—all in all, it went as well as an operation could go. Bruce and Shelby had stymied the attack. And Reb Meyer's men were in perfect position to intercede if they failed.

Abraham's cell phone rang, barely audible over the wail of sirens from both the land- and sea-based security vehicles. "Your report, Reb Meyer."

She leaned close to the receiver, smelled the familiar scent of menthol on Abraham's freshly-shaven face. "The attack has been averted. The terrorists have fled on foot from the park. Arrujo pursued them, but was intercepted." Reb Meyer's account was succinct, brisk. Almost curt, in fact, though Abraham did not seem to notice.

"Very well. I will expect a full report." Madame Radminikov would have liked more details, but, apparently, Abraham had more pressing matters.

He phoned an underling, an executive in charge of managing Continental Casualty's investment portfolio. "Execute the trades we discussed. Do so discretely, but do so quickly." The financial markets were closed, Abraham explained to her, but after-hour trading continued around the world. It would take at least a half-hour before word of the attempted terrorist strike hit the news channels and internet. In the meantime, Continental Casualty continued to load up, as it had done all week, on the stocks of companies in the business of fighting terrorism. The gains alone would not save Continental. But they would reverse many of the accrued losses.

Abraham sat on the front edge of a desk chair, continued to nurse the can of ginger ale he had carried with him from the harbor-facing suite. His right leg was bouncing up and down, a sure sign his anxiety level remained high.

"It's not over yet, is it Abraham?"

He focused his gray eyes on her, blinked. He responded to her query, but did not answer it. "In the overall scheme of things, the arrival of the tanker today was fortuitous. This cell of terrorists was going to attack the tanker at some point, and it was fortunate they did so while we were in a position to thwart them. And also to capitalize financially. There were risks, of course—the terrorists could have gotten a lucky shot off before being disarmed by Mr. Arrujo and Shelby. But life is not without risks...."

"No, it's not. But this was more than just an everyday risk, Abraham. We're talking about an explosion equal to 55 of Hiroshima's bombs."

He shrugged. "As you know, even if our operatives had failed, we had broken into the storage facility and adjusted the aiming mechanisms on the rocket launchers so they would fire well low of their targets. I was confident the attack would fail."

An easy statement to make, in retrospect. "You were confident. I see." And if the terrorists had mistakenly aimed high? "I wish my world was as black and white as yours." Abraham's world was all so scripted, so controllable. He managed every variable, knew every fact. Today, he knew the identity of the attackers, when they would attack, their target, their weapons, their escape plan, even who would foil the attack. Abraham was the maestro, and the players in the production unfolding beneath him a well-trained orchestra. They were trained professionals, and they would follow their conductor's lead.

He raised an eyebrow. "Some things are, indeed, black and white, Madame. Others are more chaotic."

Quite a concession from a man who took such pride in controlling events around him. "Chaos? Such as?"

"Such as the rest of this weekend. There are things happening I cannot explain. Who killed Monique Goulston, for example? And why did they want the demonstrations moved to Fenway Park tonight? And, perhaps most alarming, is any of this connected to the recent shipment of anthrax into Boston? Remember, we infiltrated only one terrorist cell, and these groups are notorious for running parallel operations—look at the simultaneous hijacking of the four September 11 planes, and the four bombs in the London subway. Our financial gains from today's events, extraordinary as they are, could just as quickly be lost if the terrorists succeed in attacking another part of the city."

"So you think there will be another attack?"

He nodded. "It is likely, I fear. Unfortunately, our ability to counteract such an attack has been severely degraded. With Miss Goulston alive, and Shelby our ally, we had the ability to maneuver the demonstrators as necessary, to contain them, to direct them. Now the entire herd of them is stampeding inland, away from the danger at the waterfront. They will wander aimlessly, then, like sheep, re-congregate in Kenmore Square at 7:00, as they were told to do."

"Really? Won't they be frightened off by the tanker attack and just go home?"

He shrugged. "Many will, no doubt. But, after the initial shock, many others—the young, especially—will feel euphoric, emboldened by having survived the attack. If anything, they will be more combative, more disruptive."

She nodded. Even if only half of them made their way to Kenmore Square, the crowd would still number 50,000. Plus another 35,000 for the Red Sox game.

He peered out the window. "From that chaos, the terrorists will strike again."

*   *   *

Gabriella sat in the dark blue SUV, disguised under a blond wig and tortoise shell glasses, idling on a side street near the mouth of the Callahan tunnel. She had opened the car windows, turned down the volume of the news radio station. Her ears strained for the sound of an explosion. She held her breath, then finally let it out. A few car horns voiced their dismay at her blocking a lane of traffic. But nothing else.

She checked her watch, resisted the urge to call Ahmad on his cell phone. He had phoned 12 minutes ago, tanker in sight, and requested final confirmation to proceed. She had taken a deep breath, surprised at the tightness in her chest, and gave the order to fire.

A siren in the distance, then another. She smiled; a tingle ran down her back. Then she caught herself: The sirens should *follow* the explosion, not precede it. She was only two blocks from Columbus Park; the nearby buildings would not muffle the sound of a tanker blowing....

She spun around at the sound of footsteps, watched Hosni and Mushin tumble into the backseat, sweaty and breathless.

"What happened? I didn't hear any explosion."

Hosni lowered his eyes, spoke in a low voice. "It was not Allah's will that we succeed today."

"Don't talk in riddles!" A pit formed in her stomach. "Tell me what happened! And where is Ahmad?"

Mushin offered little more. "A man interfered, and we missed the target. Ahmad was behind us, also running."

Gabriella opened the door, stood on the running board and peered over the roof of the SUV. There, a block away, the pear-shaped figure of Ahmad, arms pumping, ran toward them. He averted his eyes from her questioning gaze. She dropped back into the car. The old man's instructions were clear: *Even if the mission fails, do not alter the escape plan.* They would cross into East Boston before the police had time to set up area roadblocks. At the airport they would ditch the SUV in favor of another, and then drive to the woods of New Hampshire. From there the boys would cross the border to Canada. She would return to her life in suburbia, wait for the opportunity to train another cell of operatives.

She shifted the SUV into drive, began pulling away from the curb even before Ahmad closed the door behind him. She took a quick right, followed the down slope into the tunnel. Traffic was light. Not that they were trying to outrun a wall of fire anymore....

She flung the sunglasses onto the seat next to her, adjusted the rearview mirror until it framed Ahmad's sweaty face. "You failed, Ahmad."

He licked his lips, dried his face with a neatly-folded linen handkerchief, lifted his chin to defend himself. "We were interfered with, by a man and a woman. The man jumped on the tent, just as we were about to fire. Hosni's shot went low, probably because the missile had to pass through the canvas of the tent—"

"I told you that the shot must be unobstructed, or the aim would be thrown off—"

"Hosni is not to blame. It was my responsibility to keep bystanders away from the tent."

"And the second shot?"

"The man wrestled the launcher from Mushin and fired the grenade into the harbor."

Gabrielle sighed. They had failed. The details did not matter.

*   *   *

Abraham eyed the ginger ale, reached out, allowed himself a small sip, then set the can back on the hotel end table.

His cell phone rang. "Yes." He was expecting this call, had sent Madame Radminikov out of the room on an errand.

Reb Meyer spoke. "Confirming that three sheep and a shepherd have entered the cave."

"I expect they will reemerge in less than two minutes, yes?"

"This is correct."

He removed the photo of his family from his pocket, looked into the kind, trusting eyes of his mother and father. Wise in so many ways, yet so innocent. He took a deep breath. "Then proceed as planned. I will wait on the line." Abraham checked his watch. In approximately 100 seconds the curtain would come down on the first act of this performance. Rex Griffin, alone, had disappointed him— he was becoming increasingly insubordinate, unpredictable, difficult to manage. At some point the cost-benefit analysis might shift against Mr. Griffin, as it had with other assets....

Reb Meyer returned to the line. "We have visual confirmation. Three sheep and a shepherd have left the cave."

"Ensure that there are no other farm animals in the area, and then proceed."

"Confirmed. Hold the line."

Madame Radminikov had asked why, once Abraham had infiltrated the terrorist cell, he did not simply report the terrorists to the authorities. He had given her part of the answer: He needed the publicity of an attempted strike to raise insurance rates. But the rest of the answer he had hidden from her: Unlike the authorities, *Kidon* could dispose of the terrorists in a neat and final fashion....

A few seconds passed, then the rumble of an explosion filled the room. The sound came in stereo, first reaching his ears through the cell phone, then milliseconds later concussing across the harbor and into his hotel room. He chose not to picture the ugly event in his mind. Instead, he lifted the ginger ale can to his lips, tilted it back....

No. Death was never sweet. He spat the liquid back into the can, careful not to spill, and gently placed the cylinder, upright, into the waste basket.

CHAPTER 11

Sirens filled the air. Men and women in uniform ran about, shouted instructions and orders. Hundreds of them—rescue workers, policemen, firefighters—surrounded the mostly-empty, debris-filled Columbus Park. But they had no bystanders to rescue, no suspects to arrest, no fires to extinguish. The possibility of a second attack kept them alert. Otherwise, there was nothing but the cloying realization that they had been on the brink of a catastrophe, one that would have turned everything in their sight into a charred, ashy wasteland.

Shelby paced the perimeter of the park amidst the rescue workers, her heart both pounding from the near-miss of the terrorist attack and aching at the thought that Bruce might not return to her. He had sprinted off, in chase, 15 minutes ago. Nine hundred seconds. Nine hundred opportunities for some black-shirted zealot to pull a trigger and snuff out the life of the only person in the world she truly loved. And for what? So he could capture a terrorist who no longer threatened anybody? It was one thing to play the hero, to stop the attack. It was another to play the fool.

"Shelby!" Bruce called from across the street. Her head spun, her eyes found and drank his face. *Thank God.* He waved, bounded toward her.

"We did it! We stopped them." Euphoric, he embraced her, spun her around. Then dropped her quickly when he realized she was merely a rag doll in his arms.

He pulled back, furrowed his brow. "What's wrong? Are you okay?"

She sighed. "I'm fine. I was just worried about you, Bruce." The tears came; she raised her voice. "Damn it, it was over. We had stopped the attack. Why did you have to run after them?"

He looked at her wide-eyed, cocked his head. The fact that he was surprised she was upset made it even worse. How could she ever expect him to change when he had no clue he had done anything wrong? It was like being angry at a dog for chasing squirrels. You could try to train him not to, but, even if you succeeded, you'd never convince him it was the wrong thing to do.

He took her hands. "Listen, I understand what you're saying. You think I just ran after that guy for no reason, because I wanted to be a hero or something—"

"Like I said, it was over—"

"No. Here's the thing, let me explain. I don't think it was over. I think this whole terrorist thing is connected to Monique's death. And I think there's stuff your uncle isn't telling us. I wasn't just being a cowboy, I was trying to get information from that terrorist."

Maybe this was not just a dog chasing a squirrel. "What kind of information?"

"Didn't it strike you as odd that Reb Meyer and his team just totally disappeared? They've been working for months to stop this attack, they've got the terrorists in their sights, they've supposedly got men all around the park, and then, right when it's time for the attack, the boys from *Kidon* just vanish." He snapped his figures. "Puff. Where did they go? Where are they now?"

Shelby looked around. Cops, press, government officials. But no Reb Meyer.

Bruce continued. "So I'm chasing the terrorist, the one in the black shirt, and I'm just about to catch him, and some cop tackles me and puts me in handcuffs. He pulls out a digital camera—there's my picture in the little screen, me with the rocket launcher on my shoulder. Luckily there was another cop who saw the whole attack and knew that I was chasing the real terrorists." Bruce gestured to an older, uniformed officer standing a respectful distance away. "Lieutenant

Donato, I teach sailing to his kid. He vouched for me." The police no longer suspected Bruce, but Shelby knew you did not foil a deadly terrorist attack and then just walk off for a quiet lunch. They would need to give a statement and provide a description of the suspects and answer questions from the now-skittish Homeland Security folks.

Bruce kept his voice low enough so that only Shelby could hear him. "But how did the cop get the picture? There were no policemen around, and if there were, they should have been helping us stop the attack, not snapping photos, right?"

Shelby nodded. "Yeah...."

"So who took the picture? And why?"

"Shelby! Bruce!" interrupted their conversation. Agent Ng, her hair disheveled and her forehead dotted with sweat, jogged toward them. "Are you guys okay?"

They nodded.

"I was up there, I saw what happened." She gestured toward the Marriott hotel. "Thank God you guys were there. You were really heroic—"

Bruce cut her off. "Weren't we supposed to have some help down here?"

"Yes," she breathed. She lowered her voice, turned her back to Lieutenant Donato, who moved away politely. "Where is Reb Meyer? Where is his team?"

"No idea," Shelby answered. "We could ask the same of you—where is your team?"

Agent Ng dipped her head, shuffled her feet. She wore standard bureaucratic attire—blue work pants, white oxford shirt, black shoes and belt, a security badge hanging around her neck. "We screwed up. There was a commotion near the stage. Two of my men went over to investigate. By the time I got them on the radio, you had already disarmed the terrorists."

"You only had two people down here?" Shelby asked.

"No. Two others were on the far side of the park. They got caught up in the stampede. And we had a couple of others over by the Port-o-Potties, making sure nobody used them as a cover to fire from."

"Still, just six people…."

"Well, I thought I had Reb Meyer and his team also. Like I told you, we had most of our people along the shoreline and out on the water. That's where my superiors thought the attack would come from."

Agent Ng answered a call on her radio, then continued. "Look, things are crazy. Those terrorists are still on the loose. I'll catch up to you guys later." She started to trot away, then noticed the uniformed policeman ready to escort them. "I assume you're going to have to answer some questions from the FBI, right?"

Shelby nodded. "I don't suppose you want to tell us your real name."

Agent Ng smiled. "Uh, no. Like I said at the beginning, our meetings never occurred."

Shelby did not appreciate the agent hanging them out to dry. "It wouldn't be too tough for us to describe you—how many female Asian agents in Boston could there be?"

"True. But to what end? Look, you guys did a great job. In fact, better than we did." Agent Ng paused, hissed another response into her radio, turned back to Shelby and Bruce. "But I know how this works—the agency screwed up, so it's going to go into major cover-your-ass mode. If you start talking about our meetings, about how you and your uncle warned about this happening, some bureaucrat is going to see the chance to pin this all on somebody like me." She shrugged. "Look, I'm a big girl, I'll deal with it. But you should ask yourselves whether you really want to get in the middle of all this. At a minimum, you're going to be stuck in that interrogation room for the rest of the weekend. It seems to me like you have better things to do than help some paper-pusher save his career."

Agent Ng turned, began to jog off. "I know I do," she called over her shoulder.

"Talk about covering your ass," Shelby said.

"Can you blame her? She was right about this threat all along and they ignored her. Now she doesn't want to take the hit. And she is also right about getting stuck in that interrogation room. My vote is that we don't mention our meetings with her unless they happen to ask."

Shelby nodded. "Okay. And I give her credit for admitting she screwed up."

"I give her credit for making sure the Port-o-Potties were well-guarded," Bruce countered.

Shelby could not help but smile. Bruce was safe. The terrorists were disabled. Everything else was just a clean-up operation. Though, admittedly, a mountain-sized one. "So I guess that explains where Agent Ng's team was. But what about Reb Meyer? Where was he?"

"We know where he wasn't—he wasn't helping stop the terrorists. I'm wondering if he's the one who took my picture."

"What angle was the shot?"

Bruce looked into the distance, replayed the scene in his mind. "I was kneeling, facing the harbor. The picture was a profile, taken from off to my left. More than my face, you could see my t-shirt. That's how the cop identified me, that big red fist."

Shelby turned, faced the harbor. The park was slowly refilling as people returned to pick through debris, collect belongings. The police had cordoned off the area around the terrorists' tent. "We were there," she pointed. "Which meant the photographer would have been in that direction, near the trellis."

"Where was Reb Meyer last time you saw him?"

"I never saw him after we arrived. But the trellis would have been a good spot to hide and take a picture." Then a wave of anguish passed through her. "Wait. What about Griffin? Could he have taken the picture?"

Bruce shook his head. "I thought of that too. But taking the picture is only half the story. The person who took it also had to get it to the cop positioned along the route the terrorists were using to escape. Just handing it to some random cop wouldn't do any good. How would Griffin know where the terrorists would be running?"

"But it's the same thing with Reb Meyer, right? How would he know the terrorists' escape route any better than Griffin?"

"That's my point, Shelby." Bruce paced in a tight circle. "The whole thing doesn't add up, unless you turn it on its head and start to question your uncle. They've had the terrorists under surveillance, so they could know the escape route, right? And don't forget, Reb Meyer's the one who gave me the t-shirt."

"That's pretty flimsy, Bruce—a t-shirt and a cop standing on the right street corner."

"Maybe, but do you have a better explanation?"

"No." She tried to wrap her brain around his theory. "So you think Reb Meyer, or one of his men, takes a picture of you shooting the rocket launcher, then runs across the street while you're wrestling with the terrorists. He hands the camera to a cop, who happens to be standing along the terrorists' escape route, and he tackles you as you go running by. I guess it's plausible ... but why would *Kidon* want to help the terrorists?"

"They weren't helping the terrorists succeed, they were helping them escape. There's a difference."

"All right, but why? Why help them escape?"

He looked out over the harbor, searching for answers. "I don't know. But there's a lot of things happening today that don't make much sense."

She nodded. The reality of someone trying to send tens of thousands of innocent bystanders to a fiery death seemed somehow fathomable in light of what happened on September 11. The attempt was grotesque and monstrous and obscene, but her brain had accepted that this was the world in which they now lived. But someone killing Monique and then sending an email changing the location of the rally, and Reb Meyer disappearing just as the terrorists were in the process of blowing up half the city, and a cop ending up with a photo of Bruce firing a rocket launcher—these were events for which she had no rational explanation.

*   *   *

A handful of helicopters circled the area; occasionally, one dipped low over the mostly-empty park, scattering debris and buffeting security forces with concussive waves of air. Not much use for the copters now—they were like the fighter jets that scrambled and raced, too late, to the Twin Towers calamity.

They did, however, provide cover so Shelby and Bruce could speak privately while being escorted to the makeshift interrogation room set up in the ballroom of the Long Wharf Marriott. Bruce grabbed her arm. "We agree we're not going to mention Agent Ng, right?"

Shelby nodded. "Agreed." It had nothing to do with the attack, and it would just get them caught up in some bureaucratic witch hunt.

"Good. Next question: Are we going to mention our suspicions about your uncle? We've got about 30 seconds to decide."

"If you think he's involved with the terrorists, I don't see what choice we have."

"Here's the problem with telling them: I don't think they'll do anything about it right away. They have their hands full, and we don't really have any evidence against Abraham. By the time they follow up, it'll be too late."

She nodded. "Agent Ng is right about one thing: Half of them will be trying to catch the terrorists, and the other half will be trying to find someone to blame. I saw this stuff in the D.A.'s office when something big blew up."

"So, again, do we want to be wasting our time with them while your uncle is out there doing ... whatever?"

"Well, we have to tell somebody. We can't stop Abraham ourselves."

"I agree. How about this: We'll get out of here as quickly as we can, go talk to Detective Porras. We'll tell him what we know, see what he suggests, see what he's learned about the murder. If Abraham's still planning something, my bet is that it's somehow connected to Monique's murder. I think solving the murder is the key to getting ahead of your uncle. Then, if we need to, we can try to contact Agent Ng—"

"I have her cell number—"

"Good. Sounds like a plan."

The interrogation went quickly. Several people, including a few policemen, witnessed Bruce and Shelby's heroics, so nobody considered them suspects in the attack. One agent expressed some skepticism that Bruce just happened to be standing near the tent when he saw the back-lit silhouette of the terrorists inside, but the interrogators had little stomach for putting the screws to a guy who just saved thousands of lives. Including their own.

Two hours later they slipped out a loading dock entrance and into a waiting cab, away from the now-swarming press. Shelby gave the cabbie the Beacon Hill address. Hard to believe it was still mid-afternoon—more had happened in a half-day than in most months of Shelby's life.

*　　*　　*

Abraham paced in his hotel room, cell phone to his ear, listened to Grace Ng's report. "Baskin and Arrujo just left the hotel, jumped into a cab. I think we're okay."

"What is the basis for your conclusion?" he demanded.

"Two things. First, I don't think they suspect me of being an imposter. They believed my excuses why none of the Homeland Security forces was nearby to assist them. As you suggested, I focused the blame on Reb Meyer and his team, and on my superiors. They don't trust Reb Meyer, and I don't think they trust you, but they still trust me."

Abraham nodded. Bruce and Shelby would, understandably, question why they had been left to fight the terrorists alone. By blaming Reb Meyer and *Kidon*, Agent Ng took the focus off of herself and her team. It was the one variable in the whole operation that Abraham could not completely control—if Agent Ng's team's failure to assist during the terrorist attack caused Bruce and Shelby to suspect her of being an imposter, Homeland Security would quickly discover that one of *Kidon's* operatives was impersonating a federal agent. It would get ugly from there.

"And your second reason?"

"If the FBI had any suspicions about an imposter, there's no way Arrujo and Baskin would be let go so soon. They'd still be inside answering questions, retelling their story, working with a police artist on my picture."

"I agree. So far, at least, Homeland Security knows nothing about you, while Shelby and Mr. Arrujo do not suspect you are anything other than the federal agent you claim to be."

Abraham set high standards for *Kidon* members, but even he acknowledged that his operative had done an outstanding job. Logistically, it had been a simple operation—some office space, an untraceable cell phone, a couple of lunch meetings. And some false intelligence, carefully planted, to convince the real Homeland Security officials to concentrate their manpower against air and water attacks. But the operation required a skilled operative, one who possessed the ability both to master the details of a terrorist attack on an LNG tanker and to credibly impersonate a federal agent. Shelby would not have cooperated if she had not believed *Kidon* was working in conjunction with the federal authorities. "Your assignment is now complete, and you have performed it well. I expect you to be on a plane out of Boston within the hour."

*   *   *

The yellow police tape continued to flutter in the breeze, but otherwise the bustle of activity around the Phillips Street building had abated. No forensic teams, no ambulance, no police directing traffic. Shelby and Bruce pushed the door open, turned toward Monique's office.

Detective Porras, his back to them, sat in Monique's chair. He had drawn the shades; a single office lamp illuminated the room. Porras' fingers rested on the keyboard of her laptop, his eyes closed. Shelby pulled Bruce back by the elbow before he could enter the room. "Don't interrupt him. He's trying to relive the murder."

"Too late." The detective uncoiled out of the chair, turned to face his unannounced guests. "Actually, that's part of the problem with this whole murder. How could someone open the door and sneak up on the victim from behind without her hearing them? Or, for that matter, without anyone in the rest of the building seeing or hearing anything?" He shrugged, sighed, focused on the scrapes and cuts on

Bruce's hands and cheek. "What happened to you?" No concern, just curiosity.

Shelby recounted the attempted terrorist attack on the tanker. As she spoke, Porras' eyes—normally dark and recessed and brooding—grew wide in astonishment.

"Shit. I turned my radio off a few hours ago so I could concentrate. Guess I missed the whole thing." He reached down, clicked on his radio, listened to a few minutes of the post-attack chatter. "You guys really stopped a terrorist attack?"

Shelby shrugged, nodded. "It was mostly Bruce."

Porras stepped forward, offered his hand first to Shelby, then to Bruce. His handshake was firm but brief. "Well, good work. I've got a brother living in East Boston, wife and three little kids. Sounds like you probably saved their lives."

They exchanged awkward smiles, then Bruce spoke. "There's something that doesn't add up. We wanted to run it by you, but we need you to promise to keep it quiet for a while." Shelby had already explained to the detective that she had been working with Monique. She now took the story back further, omitting details of *Kidon's* more unsavory operations while explaining that her uncle was an insurance industry titan concerned about a terrorist attack and how he convinced Shelby to feed him information on the planned activities of the anarchist groups. "So, bottom line is that my uncle had a team of … I guess you would call them a private security force … down at Columbus Park this morning."

Porras nodded. "Yeah, these big insurance companies sometimes have their own guys, usually ex-cops and ex-military guys. Nothing unusual about that."

Bruce jumped in. "No, but they don't usually just disappear when things get rough, do they?" Bruce explained how Abraham and his team suddenly became unreachable by cell phone, described how the police ended up with a picture of him with an RPG-7 on his shoulder and a red fist on his t-shirt. "We think, for some reason, they wanted the terrorists to escape."

"Do you mean succeed and then escape, or fail and then escape?"

Bruce looked at Shelby, who responded. "It has to be fail. If they wanted them to succeed, they could have just kept us away from the demonstration. We wouldn't have been there if it weren't for my uncle, and we're the ones who stopped the attack."

Porras nodded, stared out the window for a few seconds. "It would seem that this Abraham guy somehow infiltrated the terrorist cell, which is how he knew their escape route. But there's only two reasons why he would want them to escape: Either he doesn't want them to talk, or he wants them to get away so they can attack another target."

Bruce began to respond, but chatter on Porras' radio caused the detective to raise his hand and silence him. He listened for a few seconds, furrowed his eyebrows into a shallow 'v', then excused himself and went into an adjoining room to make a phone call.

The detective strode back a few minutes later. "That's one mystery solved. A car blew up in East Boston a couple of hours ago. Four people dead, three men and a woman. They think it was your terrorists, probably killed by a remote-control bomb. Looks like we know why your uncle wanted to make sure they escaped."

*   *   *

Reb Meyer checked his watch, shook his head. The old man disappointed him. The operation had been neat and flawless—the girl and her boyfriend foiled the terrorist attempt, then *Kidon* eliminated the terrorists. But the plan lacked boldness.

Yes, he appreciated Abraham's strategy of strengthening *Kidon* by using a terrorist attack to raise insurance rates. And, of course, he also concurred with the plan to assassinate the terrorists—had they been captured, their connection to *Kidon* might have been revealed. But Abraham's plan settled for only half a loaf. They could have, *should* have, grabbed for the whole thing. Along with a few sticks of butter as well....

Under Abraham's plan, insurance rates would, indeed, rise after the failed attack, but not to the extent Continental and *Kidon* needed to guarantee permanent financial wellbeing. The attack would stay in the news for only a week or two, then fade away much as celebrity gossip and diet fad stories supplanted news of the original World

Trade Center parking garage bombing. As the story faded, so would the fear needed to justify continued and sizeable rate increases.

Kidon needed a more audacious move, something that would shock the country as September 11 had, something that would lead to rate increases in the 30-40 percent range and bring financial stability to Continental once and for all, but at the same time not cost it billions in claims. Yes, thousands might die. But the analysis was a simple one, faced by generals in battle for thousands of years: Was it better to kill a few now, so that many could survive later? Any answer other than a resounding 'yes' was nothing more than an admission of ineptitude.

Military strategy was clear on this point: An army must prioritize the survival of its people over all else. Only then could humanitarian concerns enter into the equation. It was no different than the United States dropping atomic bombs on Japan: In war, some people died so that others might live. It was really no more complicated than that.

The Jewish people were in a battle for their very existence. Nothing new here—the continuation of the Jewish bloodline had been in question ever since Biblical times. Simple arithmetic mandated that Jewish war strategy be particularly efficient and cold-blooded—in the Middle East, there were 50 Arabs for every Jew. A battle in which a Jewish soldier felled 10 opponents before succumbing would doom the Jewish people to certain annihilation.

Which was why *Kidon* needed strong, decisive leadership. Not some old man still haunted by the nightmares of his childhood. And definitely not some pretty-faced Polyanna with a law degree.

*   *   *

While Detective Porras tried to get details on the car-bombing of the terrorists, Shelby forced down a banana. She had totally forgotten about lunch, but a little kick in the abdomen and a wave of dizziness reminded her that she was now eating for two.

Porras finished his call, sighed through his moustache, looked at his watch. "Shit. Four o'clock. What a day. Feels like midnight already." He pulled a bag of pretzels from his briefcase, offered them to Shelby and Bruce before dropping a handful into his mouth. Like a Venus Fly Trap ensnaring a wayward insect....

He spoke between bites. "The car the terrorists were driving was stolen from an office park yesterday, so, unless we get lucky with some video surveillance, that's a dead end. The three guys are probably Arab; woman may be also, or she could be Hispanic. No I.D. on any of them."

Bruce turned to Shelby. "It's got to be your uncle. He made sure they escaped, then he made sure they died. Nice and neat."

"What's the motive?" Porras asked.

"Follow the money," Bruce answered. "He runs an insurance company—rates go up after an attack like this."

Porras nodded. "Makes sense. But why would he rely on you guys to stop the attack? If he wanted to stop it, and I guess we have to assume he did, why not just have his men do it?"

"He probably had his guys there as back-ups. But, this way, he doesn't have to have his people questioned by the police. Shelby and I are his buffers—with us in the middle, there's no way to link him to the terrorists."

"It sort of adds up, but not totally," Shelby interjected. "I mean, if he knew all about the LNG threat from the beginning, why would he go to the bother of recruiting us to spy on Monique? She's got to play into this somehow."

Bruce leaned back, stared at the ceiling. "You're right. There's something missing."

Shelby put down her water. "Figure out who killed Monique, and I bet we get some answers about my uncle."

"I agree," Porras said. "I'll keep working on the Monique murder. And I'll be heading over to Fenway—if you're right about that email message, whoever killed Monique wanted that rally moved. So something's probably going to go down there tonight."

"Are they still going to play the game?" Shelby asked.

Porras snorted. "Believe it or not, yes. The White House is treating this like a victory—Homeland Security foiled the attack, the city is safe, we're going to go about our lives. Apparently the President doesn't want to look weak with all the delegates here in Boston."

"Weak is one thing," Bruce said. "But he's going to look like a real idiot if something goes down at Fenway tonight."

Shelby couldn't help herself. "That's never stopped him before."

Porras smiled, then turned his bushy eyebrows from Shelby to Bruce and back to Shelby again. "Look, you guys have done a lot today, so I understand if you just want to go home and sit on the couch and watch TV. But you're the only ones who can get close to this Abraham guy, and, as far as we know, he doesn't have any idea you suspect him of anything. Why not give him a call, see where it leads?"

Shelby shook her head. "I have a better idea. I'm going to call Madame Radminikov instead."

*   *   *

An hour later, Shelby met Madame Radminikov at a bagel shop in Kenmore Square.

The butcher greeted her with a bear hug. "Shelby, I am so proud of you. You saved thousands of lives today." Shelby stiffened, then allowed herself to be embraced. She did not know if Madame Radminikov was complicit in the escape and then murder of the terrorists. But Shelby needed her help.

The woman released Shelby, beamed down at her, escorted her to a table in the back. "Is Bruce okay?" she asked as they sat.

"Yes, fine, just a few scrapes and bruises."

"Good. Now, what did you want to see me about?"

Shelby took a deep breath. "I assume my uncle is going to be at Fenway Park tonight."

"Yes. He's convinced there's going to be another attack." She rubbed her thick, calloused hands together. "I'm going with him. He seems to think we can help stop it."

Like you stopped the LNG attack? Shelby swallowed the words, took another deep breath. "Listen, a lot has happened today. I'm starting to think maybe my uncle is more involved than he's let on."

Madame Radminikov demurred. "What do you mean?"

"Well, for one thing, Bruce and I think he knew a lot more about the LNG tanker attack." Shelby waited for a denial, but the butcher instead buried her face in her coffee. "We also think he arranged for the terrorists to escape, and then killed them."

This time Madame Radminikov's eyes flew open. "He did what?" Coffee dribbled down her chin. The butcher was either not a murderer or an excellent liar.

Shelby explained the course of events that led to the terrorists eluding Bruce's pursuit. "It's circumstantial—we have no direct evidence that Abraham arranged the escape and murder. But the pieces all fit. It's a lot of coincidence to try to explain away."

Madame Radminikov stared out the window, weighed Shelby's argument. "I suppose it's possible...."

Halfway there. The whys would come later. For now, Shelby just wanted facts. "We also think he was involved in Monique Goulston's murder."

Madame Radminikov arched her head. "Why would he want to kill Monique Goulston?"

"I was hoping you could help us on that one. We think whoever killed her did so because they wanted to move tonight's rally to Fenway Park." Shelby explained the fax and email sent around the time of her death, changing the location of the rally. "So, the question is, who stands to gain by moving the rally?"

Madame Radminikov shrugged. "I truly have no idea, Shelby. But I don't think Abraham did it. We needed Monique to be alive—she was our circuit breaker. If things got overheated, we expected that you could convince her to call things off, or move the rally. That's why Abraham was so desperate to have your full cooperation. But with Monique dead, there was no way for him to shut things down."

It made sense. Abraham had fought for months to enlist Shelby's aid. But her value to him was pretty much limited to her ability to influence Monique. Why recruit a pilot if you knew the plane would soon be grounded? "All right. So Abraham didn't kill Monique. But the question still remains: Who did? And why?"

The butcher sighed. She pulled out a pair of tickets from her purse, handed them to Shelby. "I have a feeling you're about to ask for these, right?"

Shelby nodded.

"I really don't know what Abraham did do or didn't do or might do. I'll try to keep an eye on him, and I'll dig around a bit. I understand why you and Bruce think you should be at Fenway tonight. You should try to get the police there also. You think whoever killed Monique did so because they wanted the demonstrators to rally there. Abraham believes the terrorists are going to attack. Either way, someone has got to stop this nonsense before more people get hurt." She glanced at Shelby's midsection. "Just be careful, okay?"

*   *   *

Shelby phoned Bruce as soon as she and Madame Radminikov left the Kenmore Square bagel shop, described Madame Radminikov's reaction to the assassination of the terrorists. "She didn't know about the car bomb—Abraham kept that from her."

"Smart move by your uncle. My guess is she wouldn't have approved."

"I agree. But the good thing is that now she doesn't totally trust him."

"What about Monique's murder?"

"I don't think she knows anything about that either. But she did say Abraham is worried about another terrorist attack tonight, maybe at Fenway—"

"Makes sense. I've been hanging around Monique's office with some of the organizers—a bunch of people came back here after the tanker attack—and I'm hearing that the anarchists somehow got tickets and are going to be raising hell at Fenway."

"Speaking of Red Sox tickets, I got a pair from Madame Radminikov. She and Abraham will be there also."

Shelby readied herself, knowing Bruce would try to talk her out of stepping into another dangerous situation. But he would insist on going himself. The whole argument was getting old. Hadn't she proved herself at Columbus Park? She stopped; she was arguing with herself. Bruce had not asked her to stay home. In fact, he was making a joke.

"You know me—I just love baseball. Who's playing again?"

Shelby laughed for the first time since seeing Reb Meyer waddle over in his multi-colored t-shirt this morning. Which seemed like weeks ago. "Very funny." Maybe they would make it, Bruce and she. Assuming they did not get caught in tonight's crossfire....

He continued. "I've been trying Agent Ng's cell phone, but no luck—"

"Not surprising. She's probably still investigating the tanker attack."

"Right, but she should be at Fenway tonight. I'll keep trying. Also, the people here are mostly talking about the tanker attack, but a couple are still really freaked out about Monique's murder—"

"Probably because they were sleeping in the next room—"

"Yeah, but listen. This one college girl was talking about a creepy old guy who owns the building, said he used to be a Weatherman. She thought he might have killed Monique, figured he had all the keys. But check this out: Her friend said to her, 'No, Rex is harmless.'"

"*Rex?*"

"That's what I thought. How many old guys named Rex could there be in one office?"

"They said he owned the building?"

"Right."

"That makes absolutely no sense at all."

"Agreed. I went on the city's web site. The property's owned by some trust using a post office box in New York City as its address."

"In other words, someone who doesn't want the world to know their business."

*   *   *

The 8:00 start time for Game 7 was still almost two hours away, but already the Kenmore Square area overflowed with pedestrians. Griffin studied them. Rather than unnerving the populace, the foiled attack on the LNG tanker seemed to embolden it. Festive relief, rather than nervous foreboding, filled the evening air. The terrorists took their best shot, and Boston swatted it right back at them. Of course, the press did not have the real story yet, had not yet reported how close the missile came to obliterating the city.

He wandered among the swarm, looking, listening, smelling, tasting, feeling. The World Series contest would be the least interesting of the many games played around Fenway Park tonight.

The crowd comprised a cross-section of America. There were plenty of suitless suits, men and women who during the week worked in the windowed offices of Boston's power towers. Tonight they had traded their worsted wools for windbreakers, their button-downs for blue jeans, their red silk ties for Red Sox hats. Plenty of blue-collar guys also; some had tickets, but most were hoping to score one from a scalper. And thousands of demonstrators as well, some of them college kids waiting for a frat party to break out, others hoping to get in the face of the summit delegates rumored to be attending tonight's game, none of them wearing Red Sox paraphernalia. The demonstrators gravitated together on the sidewalk in front of what used to be the grungy Rathskeller bar, as if drawn to the counter-culture haven by the ghosts of radicals past. The space now housed a Yuppie bistro advertising *fois gras* and flavored vodkas.

Griffin mingled among the demonstrators. Most of them had either the stoned, droopy-eyed look of a serial partier or the wide-eyed, flush-faced countenance of a young idealist. He also spotted the occasional pair of steel-like eyes set over a pursed mouth. These were the hard-core, veteran anarchists.

Just as the demonstrators segregated themselves from the baseball crowd, the anarchists formed a subgroup among the demonstrators. Griffin edged toward them, adopted their slouched posture, mimicked their furtive eye movements, stuffed his hands into the pockets of his windbreaker as they did.

A jostling to his left caught his eye. A tall Asian woman leaning against a wall distributed bookmark-sized slips of paper to the anarchists gathered around her. Griffin shouldered his way forward. He reached his hand into the vortex. A set of strong fingers closed vice-like onto his wrist.

"Hey, who's the old dude?" The fingers tightened, pulled him into the tight mass of bodies.

A gaunt woman with smudged glasses and a mustache that would make some soldiers proud came to his defense. "He's cool. He was working down at headquarters. Give him a ticket." She reached down, pulled up his pant leg and exposed the ankle monitor. "Look, the cops already put a tracking device on him. Fucking Nazis."

The Asian woman nodded, handed him a ticket, whispered instructions: "We make our move when the crowd stands for the seventh inning stretch."

Make our move? He nodded and slipped the ticket into his pocket. The woman with the facial hair saddled up to him. "My name's Hazel." Hazel was pushing 60, sallow, almost sickly. Likely a leftover, or a hangover, from the Sixties. With a name like Hazel and a face like a Chia Pet, it was no wonder she was an anarchist. Trying to change as many rules as she could. She gestured to a slouching young man with baggy pants and a black hooded sweatshirt. "This is Gregory."

Griffin eyed him. It was the same punk he had seen following Bruce and Shelby. He swallowed a smile. Might be a good idea to stick close. "I'm Rex," Griffin said. Gregory, like Griffin, had probably latched onto Hazel because she seemed to be part of the anarchist hierarchy. The anarchists did not believe in authority, yet a core cluster of them seemed to be making the decisions for the rest. Sort of like *Animal Farm*—all the pigs were equal, but some pigs were more equal than others. Apparently the group considered Hazel one of the uber-equal pigs.

"You with a team yet?" she asked.

He had no idea what she meant. "No, not yet."

"Okay, then, you're with me and Gregory." She grinned. "We're just Mr. and Mrs. Apple Pie taking our college kid to the game."

Griffin forced a smile. "So, what's the plan?"

"We're going after the delegates. If not them, then the local big shots. Look for suits, guys with foreign accents, women with gaudy jewelry. They should be down by the field in the box seats, or else up in the roof boxes."

Gregory chimed in. "Then we get in their face."

Griffin played along. "Sounds good to me."

Hazel had raised her bony arms high in the air in response to Gregory's comment. Arms still in the air, she bent her wrists forward and now pointed her hands toward the ground and waved them back and forth, like a 2nd-grader portraying a wind-blown willow tree in a school play. Apparently anarchists did not interrupt each other; instead, hands down expressed disagreement, hands up indicated concurrence.

Their silence cued Hazel to speak. "The plan is much more specific than just getting in their face." She dropped her arms. "Did you guys see what we did in Edinburgh, when our comrades kissed the shields of the riot police and left bright red lip marks? Those pictures were in every newspaper in the world. That's what we want! We need something more symbolic than just a riot or looting or broken windows. We need a good *photo op.*"

Griffin tried not to smile. Next, the anarchists would hire a P.R. firm to offer spin for the evening news. "So, like I said, what's the plan?"

Hazel grinned, showing a crooked set of yellowed teeth. It was a strange combination of utter joy and repulsive ugliness. "You'll have to wait and see."

*   *   *

This was not Gregory Neary's scene. At the Holocaust protest, he had hooked up with some dude from something called the Black Tea Society—they were protesting Israel's treatment of the Palestinians. He suggested Neary come down to Columbus Park and check out the protest against globalization. "If you hate the Jews," the guy said, "then you also got to rage against the global economy—it's all controlled by the Jews."

Neary went to the Columbus Park rally, but he did not stick around long—too many foreigners and fags and freaks. And way too much singing and holding hands. He was just about to leave the rally when the three greasy towel-heads tried to take out the tanker. Motherfuckers would have succeeded if the Shelby bitch and her boyfriend did not stop them. Probably saved his life. Maybe he would go a little easy on them down the road. But not the fat fuck who stuck him with the stun gun. And not the old man or any of the rest of them....

Speaking of the fat guy, he was at the rally also, wearing some retarded t-shirt and talking to the cops. Neary had followed him, gotten close enough to hear him on his cell phone talking about meeting in Kenmore Square at 7:00 tonight. Sounded good to Neary—he wanted to take out the fat guy and the old man, and he needed to do it when they were not surrounded by a bunch of their soldiers. Maybe he would get the chance tonight. He had a shiv tucked in the hollowed-out part of his boot which could put a nice hole in some Jew if he got the chance....

Somebody also said they expected some action tonight, something more than just sitting around listening to music. He did not know much about this whole globalism thing, but it made sense—the Jews ran all the big companies, and they were the cheapest motherfuckers on the planet. Why should people have to work like dogs just so the Jews could sit by their pools in Florida?

He checked out the crowd: The people around him definitely were hard-core. They talked about battles they had fought in Seattle, Quebec, Edinburgh. Even the ugly know-it-all with the mustache and the skinny guy who looked like a hamster had that "Don't fuck with me" look in their eyes. They knew what had to be done, and they were prepared to do it.

They knew banging heads won wars, not holding hands.

*   *   *

Shelby paced in front of the window overlooking Commonwealth Avenue. The last few minutes of the day's sunlight reflected off the Hancock Tower. She reflected on the letter from her mother which had started this whole adventure five months earlier.

Her mother's voice had been surprisingly silent today, amidst all the excitement...

I'm still here, darling. I'll always be here.

Shelby sighed, rested her hand on her abdomen. It was not true—

her mother was not really here. Nor was her father. What did Woody Allen say, that 90 percent of life was just showing up? Well, her baby would be born with grandparents who could not even show up. She and Bruce owed it to the child to at least make sure the kid had both parents....

The phone interrupted her melancholy. Porras. "I can't get near your apartment." He was supposed to pick them up in 10 minutes. "Kenmore Square is packed with demonstrators, and the roads all the way through the Back Bay are a parking lot. Same with the subways—nothing's moving, in or out of the city. I'm going to ditch the car and walk over."

"We'll meet you out front."

"Great. I'll be there in about 20." That cut it close. They still had to walk to Fenway, and it was already 6:45. "Oh, one more thing. I called a friend who works at City Hall, told him what Bruce learned about the owner of the Phillips Street building, asked him to dig around. Turns out there are a bunch of real estate trusts with New York City addresses that own buildings on Beacon Hill. The trusts all have different names, different trustees, and even different P.O. boxes as their address. But I did some digging—all the P.O. boxes for these trusts are from the same post office in Manhattan. I'll let you legal eagles mull it over...."

Interesting. Shelby thought back to her tour of Beacon Hill with Abraham and Mr. Clevinsky—the Phillips Street building was not one of the ones he showed her, but....

She pulled a Boston map out of the bookcase. She traced the route they had taken, starting at Revere Street and winding their way toward Charles Street, then veering off down the alleys toward Cambridge Street. The back of the Phillips Street building shared a narrow alley with one of Abraham's properties. The pieces were beginning to fit together....

Bruce was bandaging his wounds. She called into the bathroom. "Porras just called. Looks like the Phillips Street building is owned by my uncle. I think the killer came through a hidden door in Monique's office—that's how he got in without anyone seeing or hearing him."

"Did anyone find a hidden door?"

"Nobody has looked yet." She told him what Porras said about the city being jammed.

"I could take my bike over, check it out."

"No time. Porras is going to be here in a few minutes, and we need to get to Fenway...."

"Can't Porras get a guy to go over?"

"Every free cop in the city is in Kenmore Square. Plus, he put a padlock on the door, and he has the key."

"Wait, I have an idea. You said streets and subways are closed, but you didn't say anything about the river. Can you grab my cell phone?"

He found a number in memory, dialed. "Anthony, it's Bruce. Where are you?"

Shelby could barely make out the boy's tinny response. "I'm out on the river—wind's great today. Why?" The city was on the verge of exploding around him, and, like a true teenager, he was out enjoying the day.

"Listen, I need a favor. An important one. Head over to the Mass. Avenue bridge, Boston side. I'm going to be there in about fifteen minutes with a key. Then I need you to bust your ass back to dock, then go up to Phillips Street on Beacon Hill and look for a hidden passageway...."

Shelby's mind raced as Bruce gave Anthony instructions. She had no doubt what the boy would find. But what did it mean?

*   *   *

Detective Porras arrived in front of Shelby and Bruce's apartment. He shook his head. "I still can't believe they're letting 'em play this fucking game tonight. Half the city almost turned into that crud you scrape off your gas grill, but, hey, the show must go on...."

"Who made the final call?" Shelby asked.

"The mayor wanted the game postponed until tomorrow, but the cowboys in the White House don't want to make it look like we're afraid of the terrorists. Especially with all the foreign delegates here.

They say the terrorists are dead, and the LNG tanker made it to dock, so there's no reason to postpone. But Fenway's going to be crawling with Secret Service, I can tell you that."

Bruce described his plan to Porras.

Porras responded, "You said this kid's father, Donato, is a police lieutenant?" He shook his head, eyebrows and mustache brushing the air. "What the fuck. I've already practically deputized you guys. And I guess we need to look in that closet...." He flipped Bruce the key.

"Great. You guys start walking. I'll run down to the river and meet you in front of Waterman Funeral Home in ten...."

Bruce rejoined Shelby and Porras on Commonwealth Avenue; together they pushed ahead another half-block, then hit a wall of people massing in Kenmore Square. Some were Red Sox fans trying to navigate their way to the game, but most were content just to gather in the street, link arms and chant anti-capitalist slogans into the news cameras. A couple of people had set up a makeshift stage atop an old van and were rallying the crowd. The police seemed content to stay back and wait. Bruce pointed out Anthony's father in the distance, speaking into a two-way radio.

"Looks like all the same people from this morning. Even the same cops," Bruce observed.

"More of them," Porras responded, his impatient eyes darting back and forth, searching for a path through the crowd and to Fenway. "Everyone with either a badge or a gun is on duty tonight." The game started in less than an hour. "Follow me." They cut up a side street, turned right on a narrow stretch of Newbury Street that bordered the Massachusetts Turnpike. The block was loud, dirty, desolate—nothing more than an alley with a ritzy address, a Rockefeller on skid row. But it was empty.

They jogged the block, emerged at Brookline Avenue just before it crossed over the Turnpike. This was the bottleneck point for getting to Fenway Park, the only route to the park from the Kenmore Square subway station and for anyone coming from the Back Bay. Many demonstrators—not nearly as many as in Columbus Park, but still numbering a few thousand—had marched up from the square and now gathered with signs and banners; the same autumn wind that propelled Anthony across the river threatened to rip the placards free and sail them onto the Turnpike below.

"Eat the Rich," read one. Another read, "Star Spangled Blindfold." Porras shouldered his way past an "Our World Is Not For Sale" sign. Bruce took Shelby's elbow, pulled her close to him, followed in Porras' wake. Uniformed police lined either side of the bridge, eyed the protestors warily. It had been a long day already; they feared an even longer night.

Shelby recognized one of Monique's lieutenants. "Are the cops bothering you?" Shelby asked, stopping. Bruce caught up to Porras; together they waited out of earshot.

It was the same stocky woman—wild mane of curly brown hair, wire-rimmed glasses—who delivered the anti-NAFTA speech at Columbus Park. She shook her head. "No, they're leaving us alone. So far. But they look nervous, like they're waiting for something to happen."

"Is it going to?"

She shrugged. "Who knows? I saw a bunch of the hard-core types huddling together down in Kenmore Square. So, yeah, probably."

She turned, began to walk away. Shelby called to her. "Hey, be careful, okay?"

The woman shrugged again. "Whatever."

Shelby rejoined Bruce and Porras. "Only a half-hour until the game starts," she announced. A half-hour to figure out who killed Monique, then figure out why they wanted the protest moved to Fenway, then stop the terrorist attack. Great.

They broke free of the swarm of protesters, quickly became engulfed in an equally dense crowd of people trying to enter the park. Bruce questioned the detective. "There's no way everyone with a ticket is going to get into the park by game time. Any chance they'll delay the start?"

Porras turned his head. "No way. First pitch is at 8:18, no matter what. The networks pay big bucks for this, and it's all set up to lead into the 11:00 news."

"One failed terrorist attack, one World Series game. Hopefully that'll be all the news for tonight," Bruce said.

Shelby peered at the mass of ticket holders slowly pushing their way toward the stadium entrance. Uniformed security personnel herded them through a security gauntlet—metal detectors, dogs sniffing for explosives, even temporary phone booth-like enclosures erected for strip searches. "Orders from Homeland Security are that, for people coming into the park, it's no different than getting on an airplane," Porras explained. "You can bring a few personal items in a small bag, but nothing that could be used as a weapon."

A trio of helicopters appeared from behind them, flying in from the direction of Cambridge. The copters descended over the ballpark wall and into Fenway Park, presumably landing on the field. The demonstrators quickly understood what was happening—the delegates were flying in, over the heads of the riff-raff and citizenry. As the realization spread, the demonstrators, gathered about 100 yards away, whistled and booed and shook their fists at the copters. A number of ticket holders joined in the jeering from within their cattle corral. Not that the delegates could hear anything.

The first three helicopters lifted out of Fenway, and another three crested over the buildings behind them. Porras nodded. "They'll definitely start on time now. All the important people are here."

*   *   *

Detective Porras flashed his badge, tried to escort Shelby and Bruce past the security phalanx. An unsmiling female State Trooper, watched over by an equally dour man wearing a blue suit and white shirt, shook her head. "Sorry. Nobody passes through unchecked." The trooper gestured with her head toward a security team patting down an overweight man in a wheelchair wearing an oxygen mask. Shelby had no interest in being poked and prodded. But she appreciated the tight security.

Ten minutes later they rejoined Porras. "I've been walking around," he reported. "Lots of Secret Service, especially down near the box seats and up in the luxury boxes. That's where most of the VIPs must be. And also lots of uniforms."

"So, if you're a terrorist, what would you do?" Bruce asked.

Porras' eyes moved upward. "Well, it'd be tough to get weapons in here, unless it was an inside job. So maybe an attack from the air, a suicide plane or something."

"Air space must be closed," Shelby said.

"Agreed," Porras responded. "So maybe a small bomb, something the dogs wouldn't have detected."

"Radioactive?" Bruce asked.

Porras nodded. "Sure, otherwise you'd only be killing a few dozen people. So a dirty bomb makes sense."

"I don't know," Shelby said. "From what I've read, unless you had a really big bomb, with lots of radioactive material, it would disperse too quickly to really do much damage. I'd be more concerned with some kind of biological or chemical weapon." Smallpox, anthrax, the plague, ricin, botulism, mustard gas—with enough expertise, and enough money, a group of terrorists could unleash any of these scourges. "They'd be easier to smuggle into the park."

"But how would you disperse them?" Porras asked. "Those things work best if you get them into the air ducts of a building, or in a subway station, where the air is contained. I'm not sure how you'd spread something like that in an outdoor baseball stadium."

"Maybe through the concession stands?" Bruce suggested. "Get something in the hot dogs, or the water they steam them in. Everybody eats that crap."

"Again, now you're probably talking about an inside job," Porras said. "Otherwise how do you disperse the agent throughout the entire stadium, into all the snack bars? And if you have an insider, you might as well just use conventional weapons, right?"

Shelby shook her head. "Look, under our theory, the terrorists are somehow using the demonstration as a cover. So that rules out an inside job." She sighed. "Probably." In the end, they really had no clue what the terrorists planned. They were just guessing. "Guys, I think we're back to square one: Somebody killed Monique because they want the demonstrations moved to Fenway Park. If we can figure out who killed her, we might be able to figure out who the terrorists are. And what they're planning."

"I say we go find Abraham," Bruce said. "He's the nexus between

the terrorists and Monique. So he's our best lead. At least until
Anthony calls and tells us what he found in that closet."

They found Abraham and Madame Radminikov in Section 14,
under the overhang about 30 rows off of first base. Abraham spoke
without greeting them. "I chose these seats because I wanted to be
high up, to give us a better vantage point. Similar to gaining the high
ground in battle."

"I see," Shelby said. Like the players, Abraham was in uniform—
dark suit, red tie.

Bruce's cell phone rang. He turned away, spoke in a low voice.
Shelby introduced Abraham and Madame Radminikov to Porras.
"Detective Porras is investigating Monique Goulston's murder." She
left it at that, watched Bruce finish his call.

Bruce took a deep breath, spoke to Shelby and Porras while looking directly at Abraham. "That was Anthony. He found a hidden
door in the closet of the room where Monique was murdered.
Whoever killed her probably came in that way."

Shelby and Porras now turned on Abraham as well. Even Madame
Radminikov swiveled in her seat and gazed at him expectantly. He
nodded, met their glances without a single blink of his ice-gray eyes.
"I suggest we go someplace more private to talk."

*   *   *

They huddled in a cement tunnel, deep in the bowels of the old
ballpark. Shelby remembered being in the same tunnel once before,
perhaps a decade ago, during a rain storm. The tunnel had flooded,
as had much of the rest of the park, and fans and squirrel-sized rats
competed for a foot-wide edge of dry walkway as they fled to higher
ground. The tunnel had been painted, and new light fixtures
installed, but the dank smell of basement still hung in the air, only
partially obscured by the aroma of popcorn and spilled beer. At least
the urine smell was gone....

Shelby shook the memories away. Somehow the pregnancy had
heightened her sense of smell. And also the memories tied to smell.
She often found herself flashing back to a distant event, sparked by a
waft of some random scent....

The prosecutor in her spoke, confident and sure, connecting the dots, piecing together the jigsaw. She extended her index finger, jabbed at her uncle. Cold, flat, accusatory words. A prosecutor's words. She half-expected her mother to scold her, but even Mom was outraged by the actions of her brother.

"You knew a lot more about the terrorist attack on the LNG tanker today than you let on. You arranged for the terrorists to escape, and then assassinated them. And you snuck into Monique Goulston's office through a hidden door connected to other buildings you own, and you murdered her. You did it because you wanted the demonstrators to rally at Fenway Park tonight. What I don't know, is why."

Abraham listened impassively as Shelby set out the case against him. When she finished, he responded. "Guilty. Guilty. Innocent. Innocent."

Detective Porras' eyebrows raised. He edged around, blocked Abraham's path to the exit. "Sir, I must advise you that you have the right to remain silent—"

Abraham chopped his hand. "Please, Detective. Stop the theatrics. Thousands of people are in danger. And I'm an old man who can afford a squadron of lawyers—I'll be dead long before you can put me in jail." He turned to Shelby. "As I said, I am not responsible for the death of Monique Goulston. But I believe I know who is. And this information will assist us in stopping the terrorist attack."

"I'm listening," Shelby said. The bastard had been lying to them all along. She held her anger in check, resisted the impulse to urge Porras to put the cuffs on him and parade him off to jail.

Abraham turned to Madame Radminikov, placed his hand gently on her elbow. "I am sorry, Leah. I truly am."

She looked at him quizzically. "For what, Abraham? What are you saying?"

"This revelation will shock you, but your friend Myron Kline killed Monique Goulston."

"What?"

Abraham explained Myron's activities as a local bookie, laid out the imbalance on Myron's books. "Years ago, Mr. Kline stayed in the property connected to the building in which Monique was killed. He knew about the secret door. It is a simple matter of deductive reasoning: Last night Mr. Kline came through that door and strangled Miss Goulston."

"But why?" Madame Radminikov blustered.

"Once the Red Sox won the sixth game of the World Series, he needed some way to make sure they did not win the seventh game as well. Since there was no way for him to affect the on-field action, he did the next best thing: By creating a large-scale demonstration, complete with a terrorist attack, he ensured that the game itself would not be played. My prediction is that the attack will take place here in the park, and will somehow involve the players themselves. After all, if there are no players, there can be no game; without a game, there can be no winner."

Detective Porras whistled. "Holy shit."

Madame Radminikov slumped, tears welling in her eyes. "Oh my God. I knew Myron was in trouble, but I never would have expected *this.*"

Shelby paced off to the side, away from the others. If Abraham was correct, there would be an attack here in the stadium, on the players, tonight. But Abraham's theory did not feel right. In fact, the whole scene—her accusing Abraham, him accusing the bookie—was beginning to feel like a real-life version of the parlor game, *Clue. The bookie, in the office, with the garrote.* She fingered Abraham because he had motive, means and opportunity. But perhaps also, subconsciously, because she did not like him. Abraham, in turn, fingered the bookie, who also apparently possessed the requisite motive/means/opportunity. But could it also be that her uncle was predisposed against Myron, perhaps even jealous of the time he spent with Madame Radminikov?

Shelby put on her defense attorney hat. "Hold on a second. There's a hole in your theory: How would this Myron guy even know who Monique is? And even if he did, how would he know enough to send an email out changing the time and place of the demonstration? We know about it," she said, making a hand gesture that encompassed Madame Radminikov, Abraham and Bruce, "because we were spying on her. But how would he?"

"He and Madame Radminikov are close friends," Abraham responded. "I assume she mentioned something to him in passing." He turned to his companion. "No offense, Madame. I am sure it was inadvertent."

Madame Radminikov's face flushed. "Offense *taken*. I never discuss *Kidon* matters with outsiders." She took a deep breath. "I think you are mistaken, Abraham. There must be another explanation—"

Porras' phone rang. He scribbled some notes, nodded a few times, hung up. He turned to Abraham and Madame Radminikov, studied them, finally sighed. "I guess there's no harm in you two hearing this. They just identified one of the terrorists' bodies. A woman, probably driving the car. Her name is Gabriella Garcia-Ring."

Madame Radminikov gasped, turned on Abraham. "You never told me that *she* was the head of the cell you infiltrated." She stared at a point deep beyond the cement tunnel wall, her mind apparently searching for patterns in the chaos. She raised her chin. "It all makes sense now. Gabriella's husband, Burt Ring, is behind all this. He's the one who killed Monique."

Another clue, another motive/means/opportunity ring drawn around yet another suspect....

Abraham furrowed his brow. "I do not follow your reasoning, Leah. Why would he kill his own cousin? To what end?"

"Don't you see, Abraham? You thought you were manipulating him, but he was manipulating you—"

Shelby interjected. "Wait. Hold on. I'm not getting this."

Madame Radminikov took another deep breath. "All right. Here's the story." She explained how Burt Ring owned *The Alternative* newspaper and nightclubs adjacent to Fenway Park. "For years he has been fighting the Red Sox, trying to keep them from expanding in the neighborhood. But he's not stupid—if the Red Sox win another World Series, he knows the city will let them take all the land they want, including his nightclubs. His only hope is to unify the neighborhood against the Red Sox. Well, what better way to rally the neighbors than by having a bunch of anarchists rioting in the streets, breaking windows and burning cars? He figures if they do enough damage, the neighbors will stand up to the Red Sox."

She turned to Abraham, continued. "He was using you. You thought you were using him to plant your spy in Monique's offices. In reality, he was using your spy to get information for himself."

Abraham's normally pale complexion turned even more ashen. "What information?"

"The same information you wanted—details about the demonstrations. Once he learned Monique was going to announce the demonstrations via an email chain, he killed her and sent the email himself, with a new demonstration destination."

Porras nodded. "That explains how the killer was able to sneak up on her. He's her cousin … maybe he calls a hello as he enters … so she probably doesn't even turn around as he walks in. He throws the garrote around her neck before she knows what's happening."

He looked around, waited for someone to offer a rebuttal. None came.

"If that's the case," Shelby observed, "then Monique's murder has nothing to do with a terrorist attack. Burt Ring killed her because he wanted the anarchists to riot around Fenway Park, not because he wanted to provide cover for a terrorist attack."

"Shelby's right," Bruce said. "This is about a riot, not about terrorism."

"Not necessarily," Abraham responded. "Remember, Ring's wife led the terrorist attack on the LNG tanker. Do you find it plausible that she did all this without her husband's support?" It was an old-fashioned way of looking at things. But probably not far off the mark. "I believe they are working together. Saving his nightclubs is not Ring's only agenda—he, like his wife, is likely a terrorist. And Fenway Park is his target."

Shelby took it one step further. "Even if Ring has nothing to do with the terrorists, it's still likely they'll strike tonight. If their plan was to use an anarchist riot as cover for their attack, that plan is still viable. It doesn't matter to the terrorists whether the riot is at Fenway Park rather than on Newbury Street. A cover is a cover."

Porras looked at Abraham, then at Shelby, then nodded. "Good points. Both of you." He stroked his mustache with his thumb and forefinger. "I'm gonna make a call, have Burt Ring picked up for questioning. That is, if he hasn't already been dragged in to talk about his wife. I'm going to squeeze him hard—if he knows anything about an attack tonight, I'll get it from him."

He began to jog away, called back over his shoulder to Abraham. "Normally, I'd arrest you. But I don't have time for that tonight. There'll be plenty of time to answer questions about a few dead terrorists later. Just don't leave town."

Abraham nodded. "Understood."

Shelby watched the detective jog away, up the concrete ramp. There were still more questions than answers. They seemingly had solved the mystery of Monique's murder. But it did not feel right, someone murdering his cousin just to save his nightclubs. But that was the thing about murder, the recurring theme she found in her years in the D.A.'s office. It never felt quite right, because it never seemed like anything could be worth it.

*   *   *

Hazel took Griffin's hand, linked her cold fingers tightly into his like a Redback spider preparing to consume its mate. He turned away just as she flashed another of her hideous grins. "Just trying to blend in, Rex baby. Gotta look like we're just here for the game."

They, along with Gregory, shuffled along in a winding line outside Fenway Park's main entrance, Gate D. Grim-faced, uniformed men and women checked a baby bottle for booze, patted down a nun, confiscated an army knife from an old geezer in a wool suit.

Hazel dug around in a plastic bag she was carrying. "Here, wear these. It'll help you blend in." She handed them each a dark blue Red Sox cap. Gregory put his on backward.

It was well past 8:00 now, only minutes until game time. Griffin looked around, hoped to spot Bruce and Shelby. Where else would a couple of Superheroes be? He half-expected them to come out and sing the National Anthem....

They reached the turnstiles. Even with Hazel clinging to his hand and Gregory shuffling dutifully behind, they hardly looked like the all-American family—they each had something in their faces, a hardness, that even the most poorly-trained security screener would sense. The screener made them empty their pockets, studied their tickets, called a supervisor over to examine Griffin's ankle monitor. He only gave up when, while being patted down, Hazel raised her arms high in the air and practically knocked him unconscious with the stench.

"We're in," Hazel crowed. "Now I can tell you the plan." She pulled them into a private huddle, paused for dramatic effect. "There's about 80 or 90 of us in the park. During the seventh-inning stretch, we're going to take bagfuls of cash and dump them over the heads of any capitalist we can find. We're going to give dollar showers to the dollar lovers."

"That's it?" Gregory protested.

She continued. "Our main target will be the summit delegates. But even if we can't get to them, just look around—the park is full of bankers and lawyers and stockbrokers and politicians. They're all targets. We're trying to win the P.R. battle here—if we riot and turn over cars and light fires, it'll just be page 5 of the papers. Been there, seen that. But the dollar showers are great symbolism, perfect pictures for the front pages all over the country. What we're trying for is *a clever brand of chaos*. I came up with that term myself; pretty good, huh?"

She slapped Gregory on the back. "Now, no long faces from you. Here's the good news: Everyone's working in teams of three, so there'll be plenty of chances to stuff a few bills down some throats and into some ears if you want...."

Gregory smiled, nodded. "Now you're talking."

Griffin, too, smiled. In addition to its symbolic value, the plan was ingeniously strategic. The bills flying around the stadium would lead to chaos as fans descended from the upper seats to scoop up free cash. The whirlwind would provide perfect cover for the anarchists, shielding them from security personnel.

Just one problem: There was no way anyone could sneak bags of money into the park. "So where's the cash?" he asked.

She placed a finger on the lens of her eyeglasses and pushed them back up her nose, leered at Griffin. "Typical husband, always freeloading off the wife. Lucky for you you're so good in the sack." She elbowed him playfully, then stuffed a hand into the side pocket of her

baggy black jeans and pulled out a thick roll of $20 bills. She hand-
ed a stack to each of them. "Here you go. Start buying things and getting change. Obviously, get as many singles as you can. By the time
we're done we should each have three or four hundred singles."

Gregory asked the obvious question. "How we gonna carry it all?"

"I'll tell you in a minute. First, we need to go to our seats and sit
there for a while. In case we're being watched, it'll look suspicious if
we don't even take a peek at the game." They wandered far down the
first base line, turned left up a runway, emerged deep in the right field
grandstand. They found their seats—two of which were behind a
pole—and watched the game for half an inning.

Hazel leaned into Griffin. "Come on, lover boy, you gotta cheer a
bit. Make it look like you care...."

When the inning ended, Hazel stood. "Okay. Follow me."

They walked back down the runway, doubled back to the main
entryway area and entered the cavernous main concession concourse
behind home plate. "Gregory asked how we're gonna carry the
money. Well, we've got one guy that smuggled in garbage bags, somebody who looks less suspicious than us. He'll be near the concession
stand behind home plate, sitting in a wheelchair wearing a baseball
hat with a dollar sign on the front." She laughed. "Nice touch, huh?
A bill on his bill...." She gestured with her chin toward a condiment
table. "There he is."

Griffin looked to his left, focused on the form of an overweight,
middle-aged man in a wheelchair. An oxygen tank was mounted on
the back of the chair, and the man wore an oxygen mask, connected
to the tank by a clear plastic tube, over his mouth. The man carefully spread mustard on a hot dog. An excellent choice for a courier—
nobody would harass a sick man in a wheelchair.

As they approached, the man turned. Griffin swallowed a gasp. He
recognized him immediately—Abraham's henchman, the one they
called Oscar Meyer behind his back. *Excellent.* If Abraham's team was
here, that made it more likely that Shelby and Bruce were nearby as
well. Griffin's face remained impassive—the fat man would not blow
his own cover by confronting Griffin. And it served Griffin no purpose to blow his cover for him.

But the fat man did not even seem to notice Griffin. Instead, his eyes locked onto Gregory's. Griffin glanced over. Gregory's jaw was set, his fists clenched at his sides....

Hazel greeted the fat man, oblivious to the stare-down occurring only inches from her. "Nice hat, Bill." She laughed—apparently Bill was Oscar Meyer's *nom de guerre*, another pun to go along with his hat. Apparently, Abraham's man had infiltrated this group of anarchists, won their trust. Then again, it was not that difficult—Griffin just showed up a couple of hours ago himself, and they already called him *comrade*. The fat guy must have been around longer than that in order to be part of the planning team, but Abraham and his gang seemed to be adept at this type of thing.

Hazel reached into a gym bag on the floor at Oscar Meyer's feet, grabbed a couple of scrunched-up, kitchen-size, white trash bags. "Here, Gregory, take one of these. Stick it in your pocket until you need it to carry your bills. Rex, you stay with me, share my bag." She giggled, even blushed a bit at the racy implication of her suggestion. Griffin tried to keep his face from displaying the revulsion he was feeling. She turned back to Gregory. "Once you've made your change, walk around, try to find good targets for the dollar shower. Then the three of us will meet in the sixth inning at the first beer stand you come to going from here up the first base line. We make our move during the seventh inning stretch, right when they all stand to sing *Take Me Out to the Ballgame.*"

A few other groups of anarchists milled about, trying not to draw undue attention to themselves or to the fat man with the garbage bags. Oscar Meyer rolled away from the condiment table, checked his watch as if waiting for a friend. Hazel motioned for Gregory to join her as she spotted Griffin.

"Okay, boys, let's go!" she commanded.

"I'll catch you guys later," Gregory announced. "I need to take a piss first."

*   *   *

Gregory Neary slipped into a men's room stall, lifted his right foot onto the rim of the toilet. Using a fingernail, he pried a thin rectangular plug from the sole of his Dry Duck leather work boot. He lowered his foot to the ground, then kicked the bottom of the toilet bowl. The steel toe impacted, jarring the boot and sending the contents of the hidden void in the sole clanking to the floor. Neary picked up the narrow metal shiv, slid it up the sleeve of his sweatshirt.

What the fat motherfucker was doing out there in a wheelchair, Neary had no idea. But no doubt it was him. Alone and just sitting there.

Neary put on a pair of sunglasses, shrouded his face with the hood of his sweatshirt, held the hood in place with the baseball cap. He checked the mirror: His chin, mouth and nose were still visible. Not good enough....

He left the bathroom, ambled over to a long line at a nearby concession stand. Ten minutes later, one of Hazel's $20 bills bought him a box of popcorn. "Can I have all ones for change?" he asked. Just in case he ran into Hazel or that Rex dude, he wanted it to look like he had been on the job. He stuffed the singles into the white garbage bag, shoved the bag back into the front pocket of his sweatshirt.

Neary positioned himself behind a steel support stanchion, peered out toward the main concession area. He glanced up at a monitor—the game was moving quickly, already into the fifth inning. The Red Sox got a cheap hit, loading the bases, sending streams of fans out of the concession area and back to their seats.

About fifty feet away, the fat guy sat near the condiment table, checked his watch and nursed his hot dog. Surprisingly, the hot dog was still whole—the fat fuck had not even bothered to remove the oxygen mask to take a bite. A few more anarchists moved in, dug deep, took garbage bags from the gym bag. Once the garbage bags were gone, the fat guy would probably bolt. Neary would have to make his move soon.

He edged toward the fat man, shielding himself behind a few stray fans, and closed to within ten feet. He settled behind another support stanchion and studied his prey. The guy seemed to have a pattern: Check his watch, roll away from the condiment table, peer toward the runway descending from the main gate, shake his head in agitation, return to the table, add a little mustard to his hot dog, and then start the cycle all over again. Anal motherfucker did not even bother to change the pattern....

Neary took a deep breath, lifted the popcorn box to his face and held it there with his left hand. He buried his face in it, like a dog eating from its bowl. He shook his right arm, allowed the shiv to slide down over his wrist and into his hand. He kept his right arm close to his pant leg, hiding the blade from view. The fat man did the agitated shake of the head thing, returned to the table, picked up the mustard....

Neary spun from behind the support stanchion, dashed toward his quarry. The fat man heard the heavy footsteps, turned his body toward him just as Neary arrived. Neary swung his arm forward and thrust the knife deep into the man's soft belly. A gasp of hot, rubber-scented air escaped from behind the oxygen mask as his eyes widened in recognition.

"I told you I'd kill you, motherfucker!" Neary pulled at the blade. It caught on contracted muscle or cartilage or maybe just blubber. The fat man grabbed at the knife and, for the first time, Neary realized the anal freak was wearing clear latex gloves. Not that it mattered. Neary yanked a second time, overpowering his weakened prey. The knife came clean; he rammed it in again. Another gasp of air, and this time the fat man toppled out of the chair and slumped to the floor. Neary dropped to one knee, pulled him up to a sitting position, and worked the knife around inside his abdomen, slicing and carving and cutting. As he did so, the wheelchair rolled away, clattering like a supermarket carriage in the parking lot, the oxygen mask trailing behind. A few bystanders noticed the crash, turned to see Neary kneeling by the man, blood pooling on the floor. Time to beat it.

"Live by the knife, die by the knife, you fat bastard!" Neary crowed.

The fat man lifted an arm, swung a fist feebly at Neary in an attempt to swat his assailant away. Neary merely laughed, gave the shiv a final, violent thrust.

Neary stood. The fat man gasped a final, garbled rebuke. Neary raced toward the exit, burst through an emergency door out onto the street. Only then did he realize what the dying exclamation had been. The message did not make a lot of sense, but for some reason the words echoed inside his head as he jogged toward the safety of the crowd of demonstrators.

"You're dead, too," the fat man had mumbled. And then he had smiled.

* * *

Shelby scanned the crowd, looked for something out of the ordinary, something that did not quite fit in. Abraham, next to her, also studied the stadium, his gray eyes sharp and alert, his nose sniffing for danger. They had returned to their seats under the overhang along the first base side because it gave them a good vantage point to survey the stadium. The problem was they were trying to stop a terrorist attack they did not know anything about—was she looking for a team of men with conventional weapons, or merely a single terrorist with a vial or test tube? Unlike with the LNG tanker, none of them—not even Abraham—had any idea what the terrorists might target.

Bruce shifted in his seat, his knee bouncing beside her. He punched redial on his cell phone, cursed as he reached Agent Ng's voice mail for the umpteenth time. "Shit. Where could she be? Maybe I should go out and find Lieutenant Donato."

She put her hand on his knee. "And tell him what? That we think there's going to be another terrorist attack? They know that already—they're on heightened alert, they've got cops everywhere. If we had something specific to tell them, sure, they could do something. If Porras gets anything from Ring, I'm sure he'll spread the word—"

"Well, we can't just sit here," Bruce said. "We've got to do *something.*"

"Patience, Mr. Arrujo," Abraham said. "I fear there will soon be plenty for us to do."

Shelby's cell phone sang out. It was Porras. "I just heard on the radio that somebody got stabbed at Fenway, over behind the home plate concession area."

"When?"

"Less than a minute ago. Call just came in."

Shelby leapt from her seat, bound down the concrete aisle toward the runway. Was it possible the anarchists were rioting inside the park? "Come on. Follow me." Bruce was right on her tail, Abraham and Madame Radminikov further behind. Bruce caught her, took her hand, listened as she relayed the detective's call. Together they ran through the stadium tunnel, toward the home plate concourse.

Bystanders were gathered in a circle near a condiment table. Bruce pushed through, dragged Shelby with him. A heavyset man was propped against the leg of the table, a uniformed policewoman applying pressure to a wound in his stomach. As the man lifted his head, Shelby gasped. "Reb Meyer!"

He blinked a couple of times, eventually focused on her face. He was ashen, slumped.

"What happened? Who stabbed you?" she asked.

He shook his head, closed his eyes.

Abraham and Madame Radminikov appeared at her side, panting. Abraham's voice was strong despite the exertion. "Reb Meyer. What are you doing here? And what is that ridiculous hat you are wearing?"

Her stomach lurched. She turned to Abraham. "He's not supposed to be here?"

Abraham glared at his lieutenant. "He is *not*." He lowered his voice. "His orders were to maintain surveillance outside the stadium." In Abraham's mind, insubordination was a far graver matter than a potentially fatal knife in the gut.

Shelby was focused on an even graver matter. A pattern was beginning to form....

She turned to her uncle, spoke in a hushed voice. "Earlier I accused you of knowing more about the terrorist attack on the LNG tanker than you let on. You admitted it. But you never said why."

"Tell them, Abraham," Madame Radminikov commanded. Abraham nodded, pulled them away from the crowd and quickly summarized Continental Casualty's financial predicament and his plan to raise insurance rates through a high-profile terrorist attack.

"Did Reb Meyer know of this plan?" Shelby asked.

"Of course. He was a key part of it. In fact, he had a team of men in place—snipers and whatnot—to stop the terrorists if you and Bruce had failed."

She took a deep breath. "Is it possible that he wanted things to go further, that he wanted a *successful* attack—something really dramatic, like 9/11—so that rates could be raised even higher?"

Abraham focused his gray eyes on a distant point. A few seconds passed, then Madame Radminikov answered for him. "Yes, Shelby. That is exactly how Reb Meyer would see things. He was not a patient man."

Abraham now spoke. "This is a fruitless line of reasoning. Reb Meyer understood perfectly well that an LNG tanker explosion would bankrupt Continental because of the massive property damage claims. So of course he wanted the attack to fail. As it did."

The EMTs arrived, slipped an oxygen mask on Reb Meyer and rolled him onto a gurney. One of them turned to the policewoman. "We're going to have to treat him here. We have an ambulance here at the park, but no way we can get through the demonstrations going on outside. We've got a doctor on his way."

In the background, the crowd begin to sing *Take Me Out to the Ballgame.* Somehow the game had moved all the way into the seventh inning.

The policewoman's radio cackled. "All available officers report to the box seat areas. We have multiple disturbances in the stands."

Bruce reacted quickly. "Keep your cell phone on. I'm going to see what's happening." He raced toward the nearest ramp, turned after a few strides, yelled back to Shelby. "Whatever you do, don't let them take Reb Meyer away."

*   *   *

Hazel let out a battle cry, sprinted down the aisle toward the box seats next to the Red Sox dugout on the first-base side. "Come on, Rexie-boy, it's party time!" She threw the white garbage bag filled with cash over her shoulder; it bounced against her hip as she ran. Griffin looked around: Across the stadium, dozens of other white-bagged, would-be Santas were rushing to deliver gifts of their own.

He followed behind in a slow jog, caught Hazel just as she pounced on a couple of middle-aged men in business suits.

"Capitalist pigs!" she shouted. "Take a dollar shower! Scrub your-selves green with greed!" She reached into her bag, withdrew a hand-ful of cash, threw the bills into the air above their heads. The men leaned away from her, a mix of fear and surprise and wonder in their eyes. Cash fell on their heads, their shoulders, their laps. They sat frozen, not sure if the crazy, bearded lady was an actual threat or merely a kook.

She turned to Rex, whooped, pointed at a row of well-dressed men and women a few rows further back. "Those are capitalist pigs also. Watch me give them a shower, Rex!" She reached into her bag again, threw the money high into the air, rubbed a few bills along the scalp of a wide-eyed blond woman in a black leather coat.

Griffin made his way back up the aisle. The bills from Hazel's bag were scattering haphazardly like the white fuzz of a dandelion blow-ing in the breeze. Fans in the upper sections saw the mini-eruptions of dollar bills in the box seats and poured down from above. Griffin fought through them, his instincts telling him to distance himself from Hazel and the other anarchists. Near the runway leading to the concourse area, a tall, well-built man stepped into his path.

"Rex Griffin. Somehow I'm not surprised to see you here."

He responded without looking up. "And I'm not surprised to see you here either, Mr. Arrujo."

"But I am a bit surprised you have a girlfriend." Bruce gestured toward the screaming Hazel. "Couldn't help but noticing how cute you two look together."

* * *

Shelby's cell phone rang within a minute of Bruce dashing off. "Wild stuff out here," Bruce said. "A bunch of people are running through the stadium with white garbage bags full of money. They're dumping cash on fans' heads...."

White garbage bags? Among the crazy details of Bruce's account, in a weekend full of wild, unforgettable events, why did the gears of her brain catch on the words *white garbage bags*? Shelby looked around, stumbled upon the answer. A gym bag, on the floor not far from Reb

Meyer, half-opened, a white garbage bag protruding....

"Shelby, you there?"

"Sorry, yes." The pieces were tumbling into place now. "Bruce, is it the anarchists doing it?"

"I think so. They're yelling anti-capitalist stuff, seem to be targeting people in the box seats. Looks like one of their off-beat ways of getting in peoples' faces—'dollar showers,' they're calling it. Oh, and one more thing: Rex Griffin is helping them."

Griffin? Another piece of the puzzle. "Is he near you?"

"Yup."

"Try this. Tell him we've been following him ever since he picked up his garbage bag from the fat man."

"Could you repeat that?"

She did. "I'll hold. Use my exact words. I want you to tell me his reaction."

She waited. Bruce's voice was barely audible in the background. Reb Meyer was barely alive on the gurney.

Bruce returned. "He just nodded and said, 'Am I supposed to be impressed by that?'"

"But he nodded, right? So, in his mind, if we had been following him, that's what we would have seen—him getting a garbage bag from the fat man, right? This is important, Bruce. I need to know if he got his bag from Reb Meyer."

There was a slight pause as Bruce pondered the question. "I understand what you're saying exactly. He doesn't have a bag himself, but, yes, the person he's with got the bag from Reb Meyer. What's going on?"

She took a deep breath. "I'm not exactly sure, but I think we've got a huge problem. Forget Griffin. Get back here as quick as you can."

Abraham and Madame Radminikov waited for an explanation. "I think we were wrong about Burt Ring."

"Why?" they asked together.

"Well, for one thing, the anarchists are rioting *inside* Fenway, not outside. That doesn't help Ring at all. Why would he go to all the trouble of murdering his cousin if he couldn't somehow control the rioters?"

"Because he's a terrorist," Abraham countered.

"Actually, he's not. But I know who is."

She forced her way closer to Reb Meyer, addressed the police-woman. "I know you don't know me, but I used to be an Assistant District Attorney, and I've been working with Detective Porras all day on a murder, the one over on Beacon Hill. I think this man has some information we need. I just want to ask him a question." The police-woman sensed the urgency in Shelby, motioned to the paramedics to move aside. Shelby leaned in, kept her voice low. "You have to tell us what's going on. I know you've been helping the anarchists, I know you're part of this whole dollar shower thing. But why?"

He shook his head, turned his eyes away from her. Shelby leaned over him, her face again in his field of vision. "There's more going on here than a bunch of anarchists throwing money into the air, isn't there? Something lethal, right?" He continued to ignore her. "I think you want a *successful* terrorist attack, don't you Reb Meyer? Something spectacular and horrible and grotesque that will shock the country but won't bankrupt Continental with damage claims." She studied his face, searched for a reaction. She raised her voice. "I think you're trying to commit mass murder."

His ashen face flushed a little, and his eyes flicked back to her face. The anger swelled inside her, the rage ready to erupt. "You all claim you are fighting for the Jewish people." She turned on Abraham and Madame Radminikov, included them in her condemnation. "But you've lost all sense of what it means to be Jewish. Our faith, our cul-ture, is based on peace, compassion. Not on anger and hate and tor-ture. And definitely not on mass murder. How can you possibly think that you can save our people by destroying everything about us that is good and pure?"

She waited for an answer. Madame Radminikov stared at the floor, shuffled her feet. Abraham's gray eyes rested on Reb Meyer, refusing to meet hers. Only Reb Meyer turned in his death bed, accepted her admonition.

Shelby knew this was her last shot. She spat the words into Reb Meyer's ashen face. "You're no better than the Nazis. You claim to hate them, but you've actually become one yourself."

The words jolted him like the stun gun he had used on Gregory Neary. His whole body trembled, his eyes now wide in desperation. He reached up, pushed the oxygen mask off his face, opened his mouth to speak. A gurgling sound leaked out, along with a bloody drool. But no words were able to fight their way through the nasty mess of bodily sludge that now filled his lungs.

Shelby leaned closer, smelled the death escaping from between his lips. "You must tell me how to stop this. You must not let this happen. You are better than this. Tell me the plan."

She read his eyes. She had reached him. He lifted his right hand off the gurney, opened his palm to her as if in a wave goodbye, held it there for a few seconds as his arm quivered and his eyes implored her to understand. Then the arm fell. His body seized in one last spasm, and he was dead.

Madame Radminikov rushed at the bed, dropped to her knees, pounded on Reb Meyer's shoulder with her meaty fists. "You have the chance to stop this madness and you wave goodbye? On your deathbed you commit mass murder? May you rot in Hell!"

Shelby reached down, lifted the woman to her feet. "Actually, I don't think he was waving goodbye. I think he was showing us the latex glove on his hand."

*   *   *

Bruce sprinted toward them just as Shelby guided Madame Radminikov away from Reb Meyer's gurney.

"What's going on?" he panted.

"I hope I'm wrong, but listen to this." She recounted the scene with Reb Meyer. "Tell me what you think." She had reached a conclusion, a horrific one, but wanted confirmation before panicking 35,000 people. "He couldn't talk, but my sense is he wanted to tell me something. I think he was showing me the glove as some kind of deathbed confession, not waving goodbye."

Bruce's eyes widened, followed the path the clues illuminated. "Holy shit. Reb Meyer killed Monique because he wanted the anarchists here, at Fenway. He put something in those garbage bags—

anthrax, smallpox, ricin, something."

Abraham spoke, his voice still matter-of-fact. "Reb Meyer is ... was ... an expert on anthrax."

Anthrax. Shelby nodded; her shoulders slumped. "I was hoping I was wrong...."

Bruce began pacing, his body's response to the adrenaline coursing through him. "The fat bastard laced those garbage bags with anthrax—he's using the anarchists to spread it all around the stadium—that's why he was wearing the gloves, so he wouldn't contaminate himself—"

Another stray image popped into Shelby's mind. She looked around, found the wheelchair with the oxygen tank and mask resting askew against a cement wall. "Look," she said, pointing. "He was probably using the oxygen mask to protect himself from the anthrax."

Bruce shook his head, clenched his fists. "That motherfucker is trying to kill thousands of people. And the anarchists don't even know what they're doing out there. Anybody who touches that money will probably die."

Shelby's body tingled in fear. "Bruce, we have to do something. Those bills are blowing all around the park."

They ran back up the runway, watched in horror as the money continued to fly around the stadium. The wind had blown much of it onto the playing field, and hundreds of fans—mostly kids and young adults—were on the field, chasing dollars across the lush, green Fenway lawn.

"What a nightmare," Shelby whispered.

Dozens of horse-mounted police emerged from underneath the center field bleachers, began to ring the playing field. Meanwhile, uniformed officers on foot, accompanied by Fenway security personnel, rushed onto the field in an effort to corral fans and force them off the playing surface. A few dozen of the anarchists joined the melee on the field and charged at the horses, trying to spook them. Some still had money in their bags and tossed cash into the air as they pranced about, the bills fluttering and tumbling and spreading death in the breeze.

Madame Radminikov appeared at Shelby's side. "I know a little about anthrax from working with meat. There are some strong antibiotics you can use to treat it, but it's deadly if you don't start treatment right away."

"How contagious is it?" Shelby asked.

"It depends on how Reb Meyer prepared it. But I think we have to assume the worst, which is that anyone who touches the money or breathes air near where the money is thrown will be infected. All you need is one little spore to get into your lungs…."

"All right, then," Shelby declared. "The first thing we have to do is contain the outbreak. We can't let the contaminated bills or people out of the stadium." As she spoke, the police were making dozens of arrests—both anarchists and fans who had run onto the field. If they brought those people out of the stadium, and if their hands and their clothes and those dollar bills began to circulate….

Shelby took a step up the runway. She needed to get down to the field, to warn the police. Madame Radminikov grabbed her by the elbow, pulled her back down the runway. "You can't go out there. The antibiotics for anthrax are very strong—they're not safe for a pregnant woman." She paused. "You didn't get close to any of the garbage bags, did you?"

"No."

"Good. And you've been down here in the concourse the whole time, so you haven't been exposed to the anthrax flying around the stadium. Yet. Now go someplace safe. Abraham and I will stay and help Bruce…."

She began to argue, then felt a gentle kick from the baby. Bruce saw the conflict in her face. "Madame Radminikov's right," he said. "Get outside of the stadium, away from the anthrax. See if you can find someone in charge, someone who can seal the gates and keep this from spreading. Maybe Porras can help you. I'm going to try to find Lieutenant Donato."

Shelby nodded, turned to head back down the ramp. Unlike the situation at Columbus Park, she could be just as useful out of the park as in. There was not anything physically they could do now to stop the attack—the money was out there, people had been contaminated. At best, they could contain the outbreak and make sure the victims received treatment. Hopefully the local hospitals had enough of the right antibiotics. She pulled her cell phone from her pocket to call Porras, began to jog toward the exit....

A man edged out from behind a stanchion, stepped into her path. "Not so fast, Miss Baskin." Rex Griffin offered one of his feral smiles. "We have some unfinished business."

*   *   *

Griffin wrapped a metal wire around Shelby's neck, yanked her into a darkened corner of the stadium bowels, away from the concession stands and restrooms and foot traffic. "Just so we understand each other," he hissed, "if you scream, or if you fight me, or if you try to run, I will twist this wire and sever your windpipe. Based on what a wire like this did to your friend Monique Goulston, you'd have to agree this would be an unpleasant experience. You may survive, or you may not. But, either way, your baby will be oxygen deprived for quite a long while. Probably not the best thing for the little rug rat, eh?"

Shelby tried to turn away from his fetid breath, but even the slightest movement caused the wire to slice into her skin. A few drops of blood trickled toward her chest. She tried to keep her voice steady. "What do you want?" He was behind her, the wire binding her to him.

He turned theatrical, tapped his chin with his forefinger, the gesture barely visible out of the corner of her eye. "Justice, I suppose. I want to avenge my prior defeat. I want to make Mr. and Mrs. Perfect as unhappy as you have made me these past couple of years."

"Cut the melodrama, Griffin. What, specifically, do you want?" *Buy some time. Help will come.*

The pressure on the wire tightened for an instant in response to her insolence. She jolted back, then he regained his self-control and moderated the tension. It was a button she could push on him—he hated being disrespected. Not that she wanted to push that button as long as it was attached to the piano wire....

He ignored her inquiry, instead reached into the back pocket of her pants. She tensed, turned her hips away from him as his fingers worked down her cheek. "Don't flatter yourself," he sneered as he pulled her cell phone out of her pocket.

He scrolled down her call list, quickly found Bruce's number, punched it in. "Black captures White's queen," he declared. "Your move."

She heard the intake of air on Bruce's end, then his voice. "Where are you, Griffin?"

His voice remained calm, even playful. "I'm in the concourse, under Section 16 on the first base side. I expect you and the old man and that Neanderthal butcher here in 30 seconds. And a box of Cracker Jacks would be nice, if you can find one...."

Griffin began his count. The pounding of footsteps echoed off the cement walls at the count of 22....

Bruce rounded the corner, stopped short. "Another step, and I twist the wire," Griffin snarled. "And now that I think of it, move back about five steps."

"You hurt her, and I'll kill you," Bruce snarled.

Griffin shrugged, an exaggerated motion that caused the wire to slice deeper into her neck. "Ah, yes, the Superhero is here. Save the damsel in distress, maybe even save the World Series."

Shelby suddenly realized Griffin knew nothing about the anthrax. If he did, he would have commented on Bruce saving thousands of lives rather than Bruce saving the World Series. In Griffin's mind, the events at Fenway were all about the anarchists wreaking havoc, not about terrorism. She spoke before Bruce—or Abraham and Madame Radminikov, who had now joined him—clued Griffin in. If Griffin knew there were thousands of lives at stake, he would quickly leverage that knowledge, and that danger, to his advantage.

"That's right," she said, trying to keep her neck from pulsing. "We're trying to stop the anarchists from ruining the World Series." She raised her eyebrow at Bruce—he nodded imperceptibly, acknowledging her message.

"How noble of you all." Griffin turned toward Abraham. "Though my guess is that at least some of you have ulterior motives, perhaps something to do with insurance rates." He smiled at his audience. "So, the moment you've all been waiting for: Here's what I want." He turned to Abraham. "From you, I want that silly monitoring device. Come now, give it up."

Monitoring device? Shelby gasped, coughed as the wire gagged her. "You bastard," she spat at her uncle. He had begged for her help and then, when he failed to persuade her to assist him, coerced her collaboration by unleashing a demon to torment her. "Did it ever occur to you that the reason I wasn't helping you is because you're a delusional, paranoid psychopath?" He stared back at her, impassive. But for the first time, she saw a flicker of blue doubt in his gray eyes.

Not that it mattered. She could accept this type of duplicity from her uncle because she expected little more. But not from Madame Radminikov. They were supposed to be friends. She turned to the large woman, her eyes firing a silent accusation. She was hoping for a look of surprise or a shake of the head or even a shrug of her shoulders. Instead the butcher stared down at her feet, stammered a response to her silent accusation. "I'm sorry, Shelby. We made a horrible mistake."

Griffin cackled. "Yes. Dear Uncle Abraham and his band of merry men have betrayed you, Shelby. He freed me, brought me here, used me as his puppet. Just as he has used you. And did you know that Agent Ng is his operative as well?"

Shelby looked from her uncle to Madame Radminikov, waiting for the denial that never came. "You are truly contemptible!" she hissed through the wire. "Half of Boston could have been destroyed, hundreds of thousands of people killed. What is wrong with you people?"

Griffin pressured the wire, choking off Shelby's words. "But enough of that—you can settle your little family squabbles later. If you're still alive." He motioned to Abraham. "Now, the monitoring device, if you please."

"Need I remind you of our agreement, Mr. Griffin?"

"Our agreement has changed, in case you haven't noticed."

"No. Circumstances have changed. Our agreement has not."

Griffin guffawed. "That's like Stalin believing his treaty with Germany would preclude Hitler from invading. There may be honor amongst thieves, Mr. Gottlieb, but not among tyrants like Hitler and Stalin. And not among men like you and me." He pulled Shelby closer to him. "Now do as I say or I'll kill your niece."

Abraham reached into the pocket of his suit coat, withdrew a rectangular device that resembled a cell phone. He held it out. "Put it on the floor," Griffin ordered. "Kick it over to me." Abraham pushed at it stiffly with his toe, as if kicking a dog turd off his walkway. The monitor slid a few feet toward Griffin, well short of its goal. "That's the best you can do?" Griffin mocked. "Now I want you to get on your hands and knees and push it over with your nose."

Abraham's ice-gray eyes bore into his adversary. "I will not."

"Oh, I think you will," Griffin responded. He tightened the tension on the wire. Shelby's knees began to buckle. A soft gurgle escaped from her lips.

Abraham froze, but Madame Radminikov dropped to her hands and knees, began to crawl toward the monitor. "I'll do it."

"No, Madam!" Abraham shouted, reaching for her elbow and yanking her to her feet. "I will not allow it." His gray eyes turned almost white with anger. One eye twitched, and his top lip pulled back in a wolf-like snarl, exposing his yellowed teeth. "My people— the Jewish people—do not drop to our knees for *anyone.*"

Griffin seemed immune to Abraham's rage. Rather, dealing with the darker sides of human nature seemed to calm him, to give him confidence. "Please. Do not insult me." Griffin's voice was matter-of-fact. "There are exceptions to every rule. Now, you will either push that monitor over to me with your nose, or your niece will die. It really is a simple equation."

Abraham's head tilted back, and his mouth opened in a silent howl of protest. Suddenly the hatred Shelby felt for him only moments earlier turned to pity. This proud man, who endured so much at a young age, was enduring yet another humiliation. She was being strangled, but it was he who truly suffered. Not that he did not deserve it....

He closed his eyes, clenched his fists. With a final anguished gasp of air, he allowed his knees to fold. He dropped violently to the ground, his knees slapping against the concrete, his dark suit pants contrasting with the mustard-stained floor of the old stadium. Shelby felt a pang of admiration for the old man's unwavering sense of duty, misguided and perverted though it was. The wire loosened slightly, allowing another trickle of air to reach her lungs.

On his knees, his back rigid, Abraham focused his ice gray eyes up at Griffin.

Madame Radminikov reached down, rested a hand on Abraham's shoulder. He looked up at her in confusion, drew away, tried to place her face. A couple of seconds passed, and then his eyes widened in recognition. "Leah," he breathed. He gently removed her hand, took a deep breath. "Not to worry, Madame. I have been subjected to far worse." He placed his hands on the floor and, ignoring a puddle of spilled beer, lowered his face and began to push at the monitor with his nose. He did so almost violently, like a wild animal shoving its snout into the brush in search of prey.

"Splendid!" Griffin cackled after Abraham moved it a few feet. "That's far enough." He loosened the wire tension again, even as Abraham gave the monitor a few extra pushes.

Shelby sucked at the air, filled her lungs. She had been a long way from death, but even the few seconds of strangulation had been horrific. Monique must have suffered miserably at the hands of Reb Meyer....

Griffin turned to Abraham. "Now. Here's what we're going to do." He reached into his pocket, pulled out a piece of paper, crumpled it up and tossed it like a dart at the old man. Abraham cupped his hands, trapped it against his chest, stood. "That's an account number at Deutsche Bank in Jakarta. Jakarta, you may know, is the capital of Indonesia, which has no extradition treaty with the U.S. I want $10 million wired there, no later than tomorrow. If the money is not there, or if I get arrested, I'll tell the press about your extra-curricular activities. Understood?"

Abraham nodded. *Thank God.* Shelby prayed that nobody would oppose Griffin's terms. More important than the chokehold he had on her was the figurative noose he held over the necks of the 35,000 fans at Fenway Park. Few people, if any, had left the park. But the more time they wasted here with Griffin, the more difficult it would be to contain the anthrax outbreak.

Griffin continued blabbering, enjoying his victory. "I'd say you're getting off cheap, my puppeteer. I'm sure you made a hundred times that going long on defense industry stocks yesterday. Profits that would quickly be disgorged if I went to the press."

Abraham merely glared at him.

"And don't try anything stupid, like assassinating me. If I die, your story goes public." Griffin shrugged, addressed them all. "That's it, then. I'm going to walk over to that emergency exit. You're all going to stay where you are, except for Miss Baskin, who's going to escort me to the door. Then I'm going to lose myself in the crowd of demonstrators and find my way to Indonesia. I may return, I may not." He offered a one-note laugh, then paused and turned to Bruce. "Oh, one more thing, Arrujo. Black says *check*. Your move."

Griffin sidestepped to the exit, dragging Shelby with him, then shoved her away and leaned into the steel door to make his escape....

Suddenly Griffin's back arched, his body convulsed, his jaw clenched. A buzzing sound echoed off the walls. Shelby watched as Griffin fell to the floor, twitching. A line of drool dribbled over his bottom lip and down his chin. The steel door swung closed, echoed.

They all stared at the fallen demon, then turned their eyes toward Abraham. He held a key fob-sized device. He answered their unasked question. "When we put the ankle bracelet on Griffin, we also inserted a number of microchips under his skin. They allowed us to monitor his whereabouts. But they also allowed us to deliver an electric charge to his body." He gestured toward Shelby. "I could not risk shocking him while he was holding you. The charge may have damaged you or your baby."

Now, all of a sudden, he cared about her well-being? Bruce took her hand, squeezed it, gave her a hug. "You okay?

She nodded. "Yes, fine." She glared at her uncle, at Madame Radminikov. The confrontation with them would come later.

Bruce continued. "I was following Griffin for a while, and I didn't see him near any garbage bags or bills, so I don't think he passed any anthrax spores to you when he grabbed you."

"Good." She gestured at Griffin. "What should we do with him?"

"I will deal with Mr. Griffin," Abraham responded.

Bruce took charge. "Whatever you do with him, do it quickly." He turned to Shelby and Madame Radminikov. "We need to seal this stadium. I'll try to find Lieutenant Donato. Shelby, stay in the concourse area, away from the anthrax. Try to call Porras. Abraham and Madame Radminikov, you must know people who can get hold of the Secret Service guys stationed inside the park. We need to make sure everybody who's in the park stays here, then gets treated."

"Madame, you know who to call," Abraham responded. "As I said, I will deal with Mr. Griffin, and then join you." He bent down, checked for a pulse, put a finger under Griffin's nose to feel his breath. "He should be okay when he regains consciousness. I will find some rope and restrain him. You three go."

They started to move away, then Bruce stopped, turned and faced Griffin's fallen body. "White captures Black's knight. Black's move."

                              *   *   *

Abraham reached into Griffin's pocket, retrieved the monitoring device he lost only minutes earlier. He dragged his unconscious adversary behind a steel stanchion, propped him up....

He should kill the demon now, before he did any more damage. But he had no way to dispose of the body, and Shelby would not allow such a crime to go unreported. Nor was murder something he could make go away with a few phone calls.

He made a quick decision. He turned, walked back a few hundred feet to where Reb Meyer had been stabbed. There were a couple of police milling about, questioning witnesses to the stabbing, but the duffel bag with the anthrax-laced garbage bags had been kicked aside and sat unnoticed against a garbage can. Abraham strolled over, bent to fix his sock, pulled a white plastic bag from the duffel. Careful to keep the bag closed, he rolled it up and tucked it into his jacket pocket.

He returned to Griffin, toppled him to the ground, and dropped the plastic bag next to him, the open side only inches from Griffin's face. He gently fluffed the bag to fill it with air, then stepped back and stomped on it. A white, dusty mist escaped from the bag's opening, enveloping Griffin's head.

Abraham edged away, waited a minute for the mist to settle. He then returned, quickly rolled up the garbage bag and buried it deep in an overflowing trash barrel. When he finished, he hid behind a pole, waited. A few minutes later Griffin awakened and dragged himself to his knees. He shook his head clear, staggered toward the exit.

Abraham made sure the steel door closed tightly behind Griffin, then found a bathroom. Using his elbows to open doors and turn on faucets, he washed his hands with hot, soapy water. That was as careful as he could be. In all likelihood the anthrax had infected his lungs just as it infected Griffin's—a single spore was sufficient to kill a man. The difference was that Abraham knew enough to immediately take antibiotics, whereas Griffin would be near death by the time he stepped off the plane in Jakarta.

*   *   *

Shelby jogged halfway up the runway, careful not to touch the iron railings, torn by the danger to her baby on the one hand and the possibility of thousands of people dying on the other. She phoned Detective Porras, reached his voicemail. "It's Shelby. We've got big problems here. Please call back ASAP." Her next call, or even her first, should have been to Agent Ng. But she was a fraud. Shelby suddenly felt alone—until now, she assumed that the full power and resources of the Homeland Security department were fighting alongside Bruce and her. It was one thing to be a soldier. It was another entirely to have to be an entire platoon.

She stood for a few seconds, unsure what else she should—or could—do. Short of running through the aisles and screaming that everyone was infected with a deadly bacteria, which would do no good at all, there really was not much to do....

A brown-haired girl, perhaps 11 or 12, a blue Red Sox cap perched off-center on her head and an orange *Westford Softball* jersey hanging loosely off her frame, ran by her up the ramp, racing to view the field before she missed a single pitch. Her father's voice called out to her.

"Slow down, Honey, your old dad can't keep up." The girl leaned against a railing and flashed her braces back at him. Shelby's heart throbbed—did the simple act of leaning against the railing expose the girl to the anthrax? Would a young girl's dream outing, the seventh game of the World Series with her dad, become a fatal excursion?

Shelby took a deep breath, edged a few more steps up the ramp. Standing on her tip-toes, she craned her neck, focused on the electronic scoreboard high above the left field stands. Eighth inning, game tied 1-1. The game had resumed, which meant that the anarchists had either been gathered up and placed in some holding cell someplace or, more likely, simply melted back into the crowd. The good news was that the score was tied—if the game got out of hand, people would start leaving before the authorities could seal the exits.

Madame Radminikov's figure appeared at the top of the runway just as the girl and her father moved on. "Shelby, we have a problem," she yelled over the cheering of the crowd. She pointed a heavy arm toward the box seat areas. "The Secret Service is starting to evacuate all the VIPs. They think it's too big a security risk to let them stay." They had it backwards. The real risk was letting them leave.

Young, fit, blue-suited men escorted dozens of older, not-so-fit, gray-suited men toward the exit runways. Fortunately, not all of the VIPs were cooperating, which slowed the process. A couple of the delegates sported bloody noses or split lips courtesy of some overzealous anarchists, but for the most part the dollar showers left them unharmed. Other than the microscopic anthrax spores boring their way into their lung membranes....

In all likelihood, the Secret Service planned to herd all the VIPs together, then arrange for a police escort to fight through the demonstrators. "These are the people who are most contaminated with the anthrax," Shelby said as she and Madame Radminikov descended back into the relative safety of the stadium's bowels. "The spores are on their clothes, in their hair, on their hands. Even the Secret Service guys escorting them are getting infected just from touching them. If we let them leave, the spores will spread all over the city."

"I know, I know. I've been on the phone, trying to get hold of the

White House. Abraham is now trying also." She grabbed Shelby's hand. "Come with me."

Madame Radminikov pulled Shelby deep down the right field line into a lesser-used area that housed some of the stadium's infrastructure and maintenance operations. For some reason Shelby's anger toward the butcher was fading—she did Abraham's bidding, followed him almost blindly. Like the soldier who followed an illegal order. Still culpable, but not necessarily evil.

While they half-jogged, Shelby phoned Bruce. "Any luck finding Lieutenant Donato?"

"Not yet. One of the cops said he was out on Brookline Ave., probably getting ready for the rioting if the Sox win. I'm on my way there now, but it's slow going because of all the police barriers." The crowd roared, drowning her words.

Abraham stood ramrod straight along a cement wall. One hand over his ear, he tried to communicate over the chanting and cheering and foot-stomping of the thousands of people in the stadium above who had no idea their love for the home team had put them at death's door. He covered the mouthpiece, timed his words to fall between the "Let's go Red Sox" chorus that filled the old ballpark. There was a frustration in his voice Shelby had never heard. "I am on hold. Again. First, they put me through to the office of Homeland Security. But Homeland Security sent me back to the White House—"

He removed his hand from the mouthpiece. "That is correct ... Anthrax at Fenway Park ... I am certain ... Yes, I know they are evacuating the delegates right now ... Affirmative. I am at the stadium now ... G-O-T-T-L-I-E-B, Abraham, the Vice President will recognize the name...."

He looked back at Shelby and Madame Radminikov, spat out the words. "There is only junior staff at the White House tonight. Between the LNG attack this morning, and the anarchists rioting here in Boston, the chain of command has been stretched thin. I am unable to find someone in a position of authority willing to make a decision—"

He returned to his telephone conversation. "Yes ... I understand."

He recited his cell phone number, said goodbye, shook his head. "I fear I have failed." His gray eyes focused on some distant point behind a gray wall. He blamed himself—Reb Meyer was his charge, and he had somehow evolved, or devolved, from loyal soldier to mass murderer. Shelby resisted observing that the fish rotted from its head.

Madame Radminikov watched Abraham for a second, then set her chin and marched back up the nearest runway. Of course, she felt responsible also. *Kidon* was her life's work; these were her friends and family and work colleagues rolled into one. And one of them had betrayed the others. She reported back. "The Secret Service is continuing to round up the delegates. Some aren't very happy about leaving, but the guys in blue suits are pretty persuasive."

How were they going to get the Secret Service to stop the evacuation? Shelby thought back to a course she had taken in college about bureaucracy and the decision-making process. "The problem is that nobody wants to put their neck on the line and reverse the decision. This is the Secret Service. Their mission is to protect the delegates. They've decided this is an unsafe environment, so they're evacuating them. Then Abraham calls and tells them it's not just unsafe, but it's *really* unsafe. If anything, all we've done is add urgency to the evacuation. We need to counterbalance that somehow...."

The seed of an idea took hold in Shelby's mind. *It just might work.* She spotted a young, uniformed policeman near an exit, trotted toward him. "I'm looking for Lieutenant Donato. It's urgent. Do you know where he is?"

The cop looked at her funny. He had chocolate skin, spoke with an island accent. Maybe Haitian. "Aren't you the lady who stopped the LNG tanker attack this morning?"

"Yeah." She shifted on her feet.

He grinned, shook his head. "Crazy day, huh?"

"Lieutenant Donato. Please."

"Yeah. Hold on, I'll check." He made a call on his radio. "He's outside the park, in the command truck."

"Listen, I really need to talk to him. Can you tell him that Shelby Baskin has some important information." She paused, look hard at the young man. They were running out of time, and he was her only link to Donato. She put her hand on his elbow. "I think there's going to be another terrorist attack."

The young officer's big brown eyes widened further. He licked his lips, returned to the radio. His forehead glistened with sweat as he fought his way up the chain of command, finally reaching Donato. With a triumphant grin, he handed her the radio.

"Donato here. Is this really Shelby Baskin?"

"Yes, Lieutenant. Listen, we have a big problem." She edged away from the young cop, explained the anthrax-laced dollar showers.

"No offense, Ms. Baskin, but you're a regular angel of death."

"Tell me about it. Anyway, now the Secret Service is escorting all the big shots out of the stadium. But they're covered with anthrax, and they're going to spread it all over the city. We need to seal the doors, keep everything contained here in the park."

"And then what?" There was a hint of panic in the lieutenant's voice. "This stuff is deadly, right?"

"Not if it's caught early enough. Once we seal the stadium, we can decontaminate everyone and get them on antibiotics."

"And if we don't?"

"Then the entire city gets contaminated. We're talking hundreds of thousands of deaths."

He coughed. "You can't be serious."

"I am. If this stuff spreads into the subway system, into the bars and restaurants, into the dorms and apartment buildings...." She shook the nightmare away. "Remember, even a single spore can kill. Once the anthrax leaves the stadium, it's over."

"Unbelievable." He sighed. "I hear what you're saying, but those Secret Service guys don't give a shit ... pardon my French ... about anything beside protecting the delegates. Including innocent bystanders. If they've decided to get the delegates out of the stadium, I don't know how we're going to stop them, short of shooting them in the back."

Shelby took a deep breath. "I do."

"You know a way to get those Secret Service prigs to change their mind?" Donato offered a cautious laugh. "Why am I not surprised? All right, I'm listening."

She explained Abraham's previous call to the White House. "He didn't get very far. If anything, it made them even more anxious to evacuate the park. But they're on notice of some kind of anthrax problem, so they're on high alert. What if we tell them the anthrax is *outside* Fenway, not inside?"

"You mean lie to them?"

"Well, yes, that is what I mean." He was worried about his career. "If you want to cover your ass, you can tell them you've learned that the demonstrators have anthrax, and that they've surrounded the stadium, and that they've targeted the delegates. You'd be telling the truth on all three counts. If it weren't for this phone call, there's no way you could know that it was the demonstrators inside the stadium who had the anthrax, not outside."

"So, once I hang up, this phone call never happened?"

She smiled. She did it. "Sure it happened. I'm the one who told you about the demonstrators having anthrax outside the stadium."

*   *   *

Madame Radminikov stood at the top of the runway with a pair or binoculars. She alternately peered in toward the box seats, then yelled her report down to Shelby.

"All of a sudden, a couple of dozen blue-suited guys stopped in mid-stride, held their hands to their earpieces, and nodded. Then they spun around and escorted the VIPs right back to their seats." She laughed. "Like some line dance at a wedding."

Shelby exhaled. "I guess Lieutenant Donato was able to get hold of the right people. Thank God."

Abraham had been trying to get them to not flee from a known danger—she doubted anyone had established a standard operating procedure in response to intelligence of that sort. But Donato's message—that a security risk existed outside the stadium—spurred a simple and well-rehearsed reaction: risk avoidance.

She called up to Madame Radminikov. "I'll be right back. I'm going to try something." She spotted an emergency exit, strolled toward it, pushed open the metal door. A uniformed man on the other side gently pushed it mostly closed, leaned his round, freckled face in to speak with her. "Sorry, Ma'am, the stadium is in a lock-down. Nobody gets in or out."

"What? Why? You can't do that! I demand to be let out of here!"

He shook his head. "All I know is I can't let you out. Orders came straight from the White House. Sorry." He pushed the door closed. She had never been so happy to have a door slammed in her face.

*   *   *

The announcement came in the bottom of the eighth inning, with the score still tied. "Ladies and gentlemen, boys and girls, your attention please. We have received credible reports that Fenway Park has been contaminated with a hazardous biological agent." The words echoed through the stadium, their impact heightened as they hit ears twice and even three times. "Tonight's game has been suspended. The Boston Red Sox and United States Homeland Security Department request your full cooperation with the following measures designed to ensure the safety and well-being of the entire Fenway Park population. First, everybody in the stadium must go through a decontamination process...."

Shelby paced in the concourse area of the stadium, watched the crowd on the television monitors. She half-expected to see a stampede toward the exits, but people remained in their seats and listened to the decontamination process explanation. Unlike a fire or a bomb or a man with a gun, there was no way to run from a fine, white powder. Information was the best weapon against the anthrax, and the fans seemed to realize that.

She phoned Bruce, explained how Donato convinced the Secret Service to seal the park.

"Great work, Shelbs. Way to go. I couldn't get near Donato—it was like trying to get to the Pope."

She also explained that Griffin had escaped—according to Abraham, by the time he found some rope, Griffin was gone. Presumably on his way to the airport, then to Jakarta.

"Too bad about Griffin. But at least he's out of our lives."

"Well, anyway, you need to get back here and get decontaminated."

"Actually, they're stopping everyone outside the park, asking if we were inside. They've already set up a decontamination tent for us. So I'll just wait for you outside the stadium."

"I have a better idea. As soon as you're done, come to Gate B, over on Yawkey Way. You won't be able to get in, and I can't get out yet, but I need to talk to you about something and there's some metal bars we can talk through. Call me when you get there."

It was somebody's job, somewhere, to plan for this kind of event. So the protocol was set: Decontaminate the crowd, then evacuate everyone, then distribute the Cipro (apparently arriving via a Pentagon airlift), then decontaminate the site. But she doubted that anybody planned on 35,000 potential victims....

But they somehow managed to set up a workable system. Scores of men and women in white hazmat suits entered the stadium and set up dozens of portable showers in the concourse areas, near the exits. Other teams pushed past the crowd, into the stadium, and began scouring every exposed surface with a bleach-based solvent. Shelby lined up with thousands of other fans, snaked her way forward. Because she was already in the concourse, she was in the front of the line. Normally she would have given up her place in line to a family with children or to some other hardship case. But not this time, not with her baby at risk.

After about an hour, the line divided. Men one way, women another. A tap on her shoulder. Madame Radminikov. "I wanted to apologize. I don't know if I'll ever see you again." She sniffled, pulled a handkerchief from her purse. Shelby folded her arms in front of her chest, remained silent. "I just want you to know that I feel terrible about lying to you about Agent Ng, terrible about unleashing that monster Griffin on you. I know you'll never forgive me, never forgive your uncle, but you have to know that we did it because we truly believed it was the right thing—"

Shelby interrupted, not really caring that she was being rude. "You know, Oliver Wendell Holmes said something once that you and Abraham might want to think about: *To have doubted one's own first principles is the mark of a civilized man.* Maybe you guys should consider the possibility that this whole *Kidon* thing is misguided."

The butcher weighed the words for a few seconds, sniffled again, then broke into a smile. "I like that. You may have a point." She stuck out a fleshy hand. "If it's still possible, I'd like to be friends."

There was both kindness and sadness in the woman's eyes. Shelby surprised herself, reached out, grasped the butcher's hand. Perhaps the baby would have a forgiving heart. "Okay, Madame Radminikov. Friends."

The large woman smiled. "Please, Shelby, can you call me Leah?"

Shelby's cell phone interrupted. She answered—Bruce was waiting for her outside the metal bars. "Can you hold my spot in line ... Leah? I need to talk to Bruce about something."

"Of course, darling."

Shelby found Bruce and, invoking the name of Lieutenant Donato, convinced the policeman stationed near the exit to give them a few minutes, provided she stay at least 10 feet away from the bars.

"You all clean?" she asked with a smile.

"A little raw," he laughed. "Add some bleach, and those cuts sting like crazy." His smile faded as he noticed the turmoil in her eyes. "What's up, Shelby? Something's on your mind."

She took a deep breath. "Bruce, you've got to go after Griffin. Find him, warn him about the anthrax. He's probably at the airport—"

"Go *after* him? Why would I do that?"

Shelby raised her voice. She was afraid he would react this way. "You would *do that* because he is infected with anthrax and doesn't know it. You would *do that* to save his life. You would *do that* because you're a fellow human being."

Bruce met her frustration with incredulity. "I can't believe I'm hearing this. This is *Rex Griffin* we're talking about here. The guy almost strangled you, and you want me to chase him down and make sure he gets to a hospital? Do I have to buy him an ice cream cone, too?"

"Fine, Bruce." She spun away from him. "I'll go after him. As soon as I get out of here."

"That's not fair. You're carrying my baby, too. If he sees you chasing him, who knows what he might do? You have no right to put our baby in danger."

She turned back, fire in her eyes. "That's bullshit, Bruce. We've been in danger all day—"

"Yeah, but that was different. We were trying to save innocent people."

The moisture began to pool in her eyes. *Damn hormones.* "Why do you think it's okay for you to decide who's life is important enough to save, Bruce? The terrorists decide it's okay to kill Americans. Abraham decides it's okay to kill the terrorists. Reb Meyer decides it's okay to kill Monique. Now you decide it's okay to kill Griffin. You're as bad as they are, Bruce...."

She sniffled, turned to go, took a few angry steps. His words stopped her. "That's not fair. Just because I don't value Rex Griffin's life, that doesn't make me a murderer."

"No, Bruce, it doesn't. But it makes you something almost as bad—complicit. You're not a Nazi, but you're the German guy who stood by and watched the Nazis drag the neighbor's kids off to the concentration camps." She regretted the words as soon as they escaped her mouth. They were unfair, and she knew it, but something kept her from taking them back. She had to reach him, had to make him understand....

A hint of comprehension flickered in his eyes. "I understand your argument on an intellectual level, Shelbs. I really do. But I'm having a little trouble with this moral absolutism you're pushing on me."

She stayed with him; she was getting close. "I know it's not that black and white, and I know the Nazi comment wasn't fair, but damn it, Bruce, why can't you see this? You say you don't value Rex Griffin's life, so it's okay to let him die. Well, that's what the al-Qaeda say about us, and that's what Abraham says about Neary and the terrorists, and that's what Reb Meyer is saying about all those people in the park. If you start picking and choosing whose lives you value and whose you don't, you're no better than the terrorists. That's the whole basis of our Judeo-Christian culture—*all* lives are equally valuable. We don't get to pick and choose who has rights and who doesn't."

She moved toward him, looked through the bars, deep into his eyes. "When you make the decision, all by yourself, that it's okay to let the Rex Griffins of the world die, you're actually killing everything a civilized society stands for. So don't lecture me about putting our child in danger." She turned again to leave. This time not in anger, but in sadness.

*   *   *

Bruce clenched the metal bars, watched Shelby retreat back into the stadium. Her words echoed, resonated. They were powerful words, heartfelt words. Part of him even agreed with them. But the world was a complicated, dirty, ugly place. Sometimes, despite what Shelby believed, it was okay to let the Rex Griffins die....

But perhaps now was not one of those times.

Not if it meant losing his fiancé and his baby. Rex Griffin could live, or he could die. He did not really care. What he cared about was keeping his family together. A maggot like Griffin was not worth destroying his family over.

He took a deep breath. "Shelby, wait. I don't agree with you on this. But I know how strongly you feel about it. So I'll go chase down Griffin."

She turned her head, nodded, offered a sad, half smile. "I appreciate that. I really do. But it seems like we're barely able to meet in the middle on this stuff, Bruce. It's hard...."

"I know." He wanted to run to her, embrace her, hold her tight. He wanted to explain to her that none of this—not Griffin, not Abraham, none of it—meant more to him than she did. Instead he offered a muted response. "But barely is a lot better than not at all."

*   *   *

Griffin strolled away from Fenway Park, a bottle of the antibiotic Cipro clenched in his hand.

He laughed aloud. The whole scene with him holding Shelby Baskin prisoner had been hysterical. It was all he could do to keep a straight face. The loyal servant Madame Radminikov, dropping to the ground, trying to protect the dignity of her master. The puppeteer Abraham, on his hands and knees, reduced to a puppet himself. The haughty warrior Bruce, powerless to rescue the fair maiden. And the brilliant Shelby, winking and nodding at Bruce, deluding herself into believing that he, Rex Griffin, had not already figured out that the dollar bills were laced with anthrax. If her delusion had not been so damn insulting, it would have been comical. The reality was he knew something was up as soon as he saw Reb Meyer handing out the trash bags. Which was why he had not touched any of them.

Yes, in the end the old wolf Abraham played his trump card and immobilized him. But that was a mere border skirmish amid a larger battle. He had escaped, free from the monitoring device, free from his captivity in the hospital, free to buy a new identity and a new life. And, if victory escaped him today, free to return later to exact his revenge on his enemies.

*   *   *

Shelby watched Bruce jog off, wondered how diligent he would be in tracking the man they both hated, just to save his life. Actually, that was not fair—when Bruce agreed to do something, it got done.

She returned to her spot in line with Madame Radminikov.

"What's wrong, darling? You look troubled."

She shrugged. "It's actually pretty petty, in light of everything else." She explained the disagreement about whether to chase down Griffin and warn him about the anthrax.

"So Bruce refused to go after him, huh?"

Shelby lifted her eyes to the butcher. "No, actually, he went. But only because I wanted him to. He didn't agree with it. He would have let Griffin die."

Madame Radminikov raised her eyebrows. "No offense, Shelby, but you're upset about this? My God, what more can you ask of a man, of a partner? You're not always going to agree on everything—we talked about this before. But you've got a man who listens to you, respects you, often even defers to you. Short of a pet, that's about as good as you're ever going to find. If you don't want him, I'll take him!"

Shelby would not normally have solicited advice on her love life from a middle-aged widow. Especially one infatuated with her psycho uncle. But Madame Radminikov was able to cut right to the heart of matters of the heart. She actually made Shelby feel a little foolish. Which was fine, because she preferred foolish to miserable.

She smiled. "Thanks, Leah."

A few minutes later, they reached a holding area—a makeshift nylon tent with a flap to enter and exit on either end. Shelby stripped, handed her clothes to a woman in one of the astronaut suits. The woman also took her jewelry, wallet and cell phone. She sealed them in a plastic bag and wrote Shelby's name on the outside. Shelby stared at her engagement ring, swallowed. "Your old clothes will be burned," the woman explained through her mask. "And the stuff in the bag will be irradiated and returned to you in a few days."

Shelby thanked her, pushed through the back flap of the tent, entered a canvas tunnel leading to another, larger tent-like structure. This structure housed a portable shower, and another Hazmat woman emerged from the shower area and motioned Shelby toward her. She handed her a bar of soap and some shampoo, explained that a mild amount of bleach had been added to the shower water. "If you have any open cuts," she said, "I can cover them with a band-aid so they don't sting." She looked down at Shelby's stomach. "And don't worry, the shower won't hurt your baby. But you will want to talk to one of the doctors about the antibiotics."

Shelby showered and scrubbed her body, her skin turning red and raw from the bleach and harsh soap. She had planned on washing quickly anyway, aware of the long line behind her, but the bleachy water ensured she did not dawdle. The entire shower took less than 60 seconds.

She pushed through another flap, into another sterilized holding area. Makeshift shelves had been set up; piled on one side were towels and on the other sets of clothes—sweatpants and sweatshirts divided into medium and extra-large sizes. A bin with flip-flops stood in the corner. She dried off, stepped into some sweats, found a pair of flip-flops that fit, and pushed through yet another flap. The memory of an old sitcom involving Maxwell Smart popped into her head....

This last flap separated the stadium from the street. As she stepped onto the sidewalk, a young doctor with a sing-song voice—Indian, she guessed, though possibly Pakistani—greeted her. "I am Doctor Kapadia." He stood under a streetlight, in front of a white medical van.

She looked around—there were hundreds of people packed onto Yawkey Way, waiting for friends and loved ones to emerge from the ballpark. Based on the line, some would be waiting until dawn. At least the demonstrators had cleared out.

She addressed the doctor. "You should know that I'm pregnant."

The doctor nodded. "In that case, we want to be careful about prescribing the Cipro. It will depend on how much contact you think you may have had with the anthrax. Specifically, were you near the money that was being thrown around the stadium?"

"No. And I was in the concourse area most of the game." Madame Radminikov emerged from the park, gave Shelby a quick hug, ambled off to find Abraham. Shelby wished she could follow, just for the chance to see her uncle in sweats and flip-flops.

"Good," the doctor responded. He handed her a bottle of the antibiotic, recommended she head over to Beth Israel Hospital to meet with a team of medical experts being assembled from around the country. "They can tell you whether you should begin to take this or not. But if you start getting cold symptoms, that should be a red flag for you that you might be infected."

A figure emerged from the crowd, pushed toward her. Detective Porras. His mustache moved as if he had smiled at her, then addressed the doctor. "Without this lady, Doc, all these people would have gone home tonight and we never would have known about the anthrax."

The doctor's eyes widened. "Truly? If that had happened, tens of thousands would have died. Probably even more."

Porras nodded, then pulled her aside. "Hey, turns out Burt Ring knew nothing about his wife being a terrorist. Passed a lie detector with flying colors. Poor guy's pretty devastated." He shook his head. "I thought you'd want to know."

"Thanks."

He stepped back. "Now, I don't suppose you know anything about the fat guy who got stabbed, do you?"

Sarah kicked. "If you give me a lift over to Beth Israel, I'll tell you the whole story."

He nodded. "Deal."

*   *   *

Bruce jogged down Yawkey Way, pushed through a handful of demonstrators still chanting outside the stadium, angled right onto Brookline Avenue. He would catch a cab, head for Logan Airport.

Then what? Time to think like Rex Griffin. Not the plotting, scheming, lurking in the alleys and shadows and gutters Rex Griffin. But the recipient of both a Get Out of Jail Free card and $10 million wire transfer Rex Griffin. He would be walking tall, ankle bracelet cut away, on his way to a new life. He had probably deduced that Abraham would make the $10 million payment: It was short money compared to the damage to Continental if the press ran with the story. And no doubt Griffin knew the plane schedules, had somehow procured a passport....

Bruce flagged a cab, dropped three twenties through the window onto the front seat. "Logan Airport. Beat the traffic."

Bruce spent the twelve-minute ride on the phone with the airlines. Too late to catch a flight tonight. The first flight out in the morning that connected with Jakarta was on United, via Toronto. "United Terminal," he directed the cabbie.

At the terminal, he jumped from the taxi, pushed through the revolving doors. The terminal was largely abandoned, other than a few people waiting for an arriving flight. He hopped on an escalator, entered a concourse leading to the boarding areas. In the distance, leaning against a railing in front of a large window, stood a solitary figure, its hamster-like profile tinted red by the brake lights of an airport vehicle.

Bruce moved toward him slowly, as if approaching a rabid animal. He got within 50 feet, then the figure tensed, his head moving in jerky motions as his ears tried to locate the source of the intruding predator. Or prey.

The head rotated toward Bruce, a pair of raisin-like eyes settling on him. His shoulders slumped momentarily, then the raisins shrunk in size and he bared his yellow teeth. "What do you want, Arrujo?"

"Relax." Bruce jogged to a stop a few feet away. "I'm actually here to save your life."

Bruce expected to see surprise, or curiosity, or even apprecia-tion in Griffin's eyes. Instead there was only anger. Griffin took a deep breath, spat out the words. "You're such a smug S.O.B., Arrujo. I really hate people like you."

Bruce's muscles tensed. He promised Shelby he would warn Griffin about the anthrax. But he did not agree to let the little rodent insult him. "Hey, what's your problem?"

Griffin glared at him, both hands held in front of his stomach, fin-gers curled in a claw-like posture. For the first time, Bruce noticed the long, yellowed fingernails. "I know all about the anthrax," Griffin growled.

Bruce stepped back. "What? How?"

Drool pooled on Griffin's lower lip. "Same as you—I figured it out." He shook his head disdainfully. "Your problem is that you and Little Miss Perfect think you're smarter than everyone else. Well, guess again."

Bruce stared back at the twitching, feral man-beast. Suddenly he had the urge to end this encounter.

"All right then, whatever. Message delivered, I'm out of here."

Bruce turned to go. Griffin's snarl stopped him. "You're a fool, Arrujo. It could have been over between us—you were supposed to let me die, which would have distressed Wonder Woman to no end."

How did he know that?

Griffin read the surprise in Bruce's eyes. "Oh, yes, I knew you'd fight about that, I knew she'd want to save me and that you'd rather let me die. I've been *studying* you, Arrujo. Like rats in a cage."

Griffin spat. "But you blew it. This was to be my final victory over you. I had the letter already drafted in my head: *Dear Shelby and Bruce: I am writing to tell you I am near death, the victim of a deadly and vicious disease that you could have prevented. Instead, I lie here, my lungs filled with pus, my every breath a painful, choking reminder of how little life I have left in me. I have just one question: Why did you not save me when you had the chance? A simple word of warning is all that was needed. My death is on your hands, blah, blah, blah."* He cackled. "I'm sure that would have gone over well—Little Miss Perfect would have been guilt-ridden at the thought of causing my death. She may even have left you. And that would have been my victory—I would have ruined your lives as you ruined mine. But you had to be a superhero, had to come warn me."

Bruce's heart pounded. The demon had read them correctly—Shelby might indeed have left him after reading such a letter. "And if she hadn't left me? If we had worked through it?" He could not resist asking.

Griffin curled his lips, bared his teeth. "Well, then we'd be where we are right now: I still owe you one, Arrujo. My thirst for vengeance has not been sated. And I have ten million dollars to devote to my cause. I'll be back."

"You're a sick bastard, Griffin. Most people would thank me for trying to save their life."

Griffin crouched, almost as if ready to leap. He held his hands, still clawed, in front of him. Bruce tensed, watched his adversary's empty eyes. Griffin lifted his chin, released a short, bark-like laugh from behind wet, sharp, yellowed teeth. "My life? I'll worry about my life once I've ruined yours." He glared at Bruce again, then scurried away from the boarding gates and disappeared into the shadows of the abandoned terminal.

*   *   *

Shelby called Bruce's cell. Their argument still bothered her—maybe Madame Radminikov was right, maybe she should not expect him to accept her moral code as his own.

"Hi, Shelbs." He seemed excited to hear from her. She found herself smiling.

"So, did you catch Griffin?"

Bruce snorted. "Yeah. The maggot knew all about the anthrax already."

"Really?"

"Claims he figured it out before we did. Anyway, it's actually good news. If he knew about the anthrax, he knew enough to stay away from it. Which means you're probably not infected. Don't forget, he had his hands on you...."

She shivered. "I won't forget that for a while."

"Anyway, I'll tell you all about it later. You go through decontamination?"

"Yeah, I'm actually on the way to Beth Israel for a full exam. Porras is taking me." She turned away from the detective. "I'm going to tell him about Reb Meyer killing Monique, and Reb Meyer releasing the anthrax, and my uncle blowing up the terrorists. Everything."

"Griffin too?"

She pondered the question. "No, not that. All he did was threaten to strangle me." She laughed. "He's practically the good guy in all this."

"It's good to hear you laughing, Shelby."

She sighed. "All right. I'll talk to you later...."

"Wait, Shelby. One more thing."

"Yeah?"

"It's been quite a day. If we can make it through this, we can make it through anything, right?"

The baby kicked and rolled. She lifted her hand to her belly, then recoiled at the sight of her naked ring finger. She had worn the ring only five months, but already her hand looked barren without it. Things were not perfect. But the thought of never wearing Bruce's ring again made her eyes pool, her chest ache. She took a deep breath. "We're good, my love. We're good."

CHAPTER 12

[November]

It was a cool, rainy Sunday morning. Red and yellow and orange leaves—only recently the objects of much admiration—now covered the sidewalks and walkways of the Back Bay in a slick, gritty carpet, obscuring even the confetti and dried beer from the Red Sox victory celebration. The streets were empty except for Bruce and Shelby, hand-in-hand, sauntering down Commonwealth Avenue.

"Remember our first date, we walked for hours in the rain?" Shelby asked.

"Of course I do," Bruce sniffed. "How could I forget—I did that on all my first dates. Still do."

She elbowed him in the ribs, felt the tightness of his abdomen muscles. They had just worked out together in the gym—she intended on fitting into her wedding dress despite the pregnancy....

As they approached their apartment building, a dark sedan pulled up in front and double-parked. The driver's side door opened, and a short man in a dark suit and hat hopped down to the street and walked toward them.

Shelby could not help but smile. Partly because she was happy. And partly because the little old man with the big smile and wrinkled face was—unlike many of his associates—so endearing. "Hello, Mr. Clevinsky," she called. She was half-expecting some kind of communication from her uncle and his crew. Two weeks had passed since the LNG tanker and anthrax attacks—Bruce referred to the day as "Stay-Out-of-the-City-Saturday"—and, other than a call from Madame Radminikov to make sure they did not exhibit any signs of anthrax sickness, and to tell her Gregory Neary was in intensive care with anthrax poisoning and had been identified by a surveillance camera as Reb Meyer's killer, Shelby had not heard anything from the *Kidon* contingent.

Mr. Clevinsky's smile broadened, and he nodded first to her and then to Bruce. He reached into his jacket pocket, withdrew a sealed envelope, and handed it to her.

She accepted it. The sender had addressed it in a flowing script: *Ms. Shelby Baskin and Mr. Bruce Arrujo.* She resisted opening it right away. Instead, she smiled again at Mr. Clevinsky. "Wait, isn't this how we met back in June?" She offered the letter back to him. "I don't think I want to read this one. You guys are bad news."

His eyes twinkled through the rain as he folded his hands behind his back and refused her tender. Something in his face told her that it was safe to open this missive. Even her mother agreed. *This one's not from me, darling.*

She looked at Bruce, who nodded, and she dug her finger into the envelope flap and pulled it open. Inside she found a single sheet of heavy, gray business paper, folded in thirds. She flipped it open, leaned over it to shelter it from the rain. Bruce's warm breath caressed her cheek as she read:

> *Dear Shelby and Bruce:*
>
> *Please join Madame Radminikov, Mr. Clevinsky, and myself for dinner tonight. Others will also be attending. We will be dining at 7:00 p.m. at Mama Maria's in the North End.*
>
> > *Sincerely,*
> > *Abraham Gottlieb*
>
> *P.S. Perhaps Oliver Wendell Holmes had a point. I hope it is not too late to doubt my own first principles.*

Shelby looked at Bruce, who was clearly puzzled by the postscript. "I'll explain later." She turned to the messenger. "Thank you, Mr. Clevinsky. We will be there."

*   *   *

Shelby loved eating at Mama Maria's. It combined the best in Italian cuisine with a quaint, 19th-century brick rowhouse setting. It was the type of place that was so comfortable, and the food so tasty, and the wine so smooth, that it made her want to linger when dinner was over. She wanted to play a board game, sit in front of the fire, chat with other diners.

She and Bruce arrived a few minutes after 7:00. Normally, this would have been perfectly acceptable for a 7:00 dinner, but apparently Abraham and his penchant for punctuality preceded him: The private room he had secured was filled when they arrived.

Shelby scanned the room, looked for familiar faces among the guests milling around the large table. Abraham and Madame Radminikov were there, of course, as was Mr. Clevinsky, all of them in dark business suits. Shelby also recognized Dr. Walters. She leaned in to Bruce. "That's the guy who did the Neary castration. Don't let him sit next to you at dinner, especially if he has a steak knife."

Bruce crossed his hands in front of his crotch. "Agreed."

The other guests—numbering about a dozen—all seemed to recognize her. Every time she looked up she found a pair of eyes studying her. Was it because she had helped foil the terrorist attacks? Or was it instead because she had ratted-out Abraham to the authorities? Not that the latter seemed to matter—apparently, somewhere, at the highest levels of government, it had been decided that the unexplained death of the four LNG terrorists would remain just that, unexplained. It made sense from a political perspective—a public trial, exposing the shortcomings of the Office of Homeland Security, did not serve the Administration's best interests. Officially, the terrorists died when one of the bombs they carried detonated prematurely. The end result was that the assassination was a non-event to everyone except the dead terrorists. Abraham still ran a multi-billion dollar insurance conglomerate, presumably still funded *Kidon*, and still presided over dinners at fancy restaurants where his minions revered him.

Abraham cleared his throat, and the room instantly fell quiet. Shelby wondered what would happen if he asked them to all sit in a circle and drink Kool-Aid. "Ladies and gentlemen, please be seated." Shelby and Bruce began to take seats at the far end of the table, but Madame Radminikov motioned them forward. Abraham sat at the head, with Madame Radminikov to his right and Mr. Clevinsky opposite her. Shelby sat next to the butcher, Bruce next to Shelby.

"Thank you all for coming tonight," Abraham began. "As you know, I am not one for long speeches. So I will merely say this: I fear that I am no longer the best person to lead *Kidon*. As many of you are aware, I have made a number of poor choices over the past few months, choices that have put the lives of many innocent people in danger, choices that have put the future of *Kidon* in question."

He took a sip of water, continued. "I have been reflecting recently on a quaint American saying about throwing the baby away with the bathwater. All of us here tonight believe in our hearts that the future of the Jewish people must be safeguarded." He paused again, smiled at Shelby. "But my niece, Shelby Baskin, asked a question a few weeks ago that I fear I had not asked myself in many years: Is it worth saving the Jewish people if, by doing so, we are sacrificing everything that is good and noble about being Jewish? If we choose to lie and cheat and steal and ... yes, even kill ... to save ourselves, are we truly worth saving?"

Was this really her uncle speaking? Apparently the actions of Reb Meyer had shaken his world....

Abraham scanned the room with his gray eyes, inviting anyone to challenge his words. Most were probably too shocked to say anything. He continued. "I feel that *Kidon* needs fresh leadership." He glanced down to his right, smiled. "Someone younger and less jaded than I." A few eyes turned toward Shelby. "Someone not haunted by the nightmares of the Holocaust. Someone who will build bridges rather than dig moats. Someone less focused on business and politics and instead more in tune with the human condition." By now, most of the diners were shifting their gaze back and forth between Abraham and Shelby, like spectators at a tennis match. "In short, someone who understands that the best way to ensure the survival and well-being of the Jewish people is by promoting the Jewish values of justice and fairness and generosity and compassion."

Shelby took Bruce's hand, leaned into him and whispered into his ear. "Watch this. I think my uncle is finally turning into a *mensch*."

"What's a *mensch*?" he asked.

She smiled. "You'll see."

The timbre of Abraham's voice had changed, become more impassioned. He lowered his voice. "Yes, going forward, there will still be times when we need to defend ourselves, with force if necessary. But *Kidon's* new leader will show restraint during these times of crisis. *She* will—"

Everyone was staring at Shelby now. Even Bruce looked at her quizzically. "Just watch," she whispered.

Abraham waited until the buzz died down. "She will," he repeated, "use *Kidon's* considerable resources not as swords but as shields, not to destroy our enemies but to nurture our allies."

Abraham extended his right arm. "I present *Kidon's* new leader: Madame Leah Radminikov."

The room fell silent for a few seconds, then Madame Radminikov stammered a response. "But, Abraham, are you sure? What do I know about leading *Kidon?*"

His gray eyes bored into her. "Everything, Madame. Absolutely everything."

Shelby leaned into Bruce again. "Now you know what it means to be a *mensch*."

"I see," he responded. Madame Radminikov rose from her seat and enveloped an unsuspecting Abraham in a bear hug. Bruce slipped his arm around Shelby, pulled her near. "Looks like fun," he smiled. "Can I be a *mensch* too?"

She kissed him gently, rested her forehead on his. "Anytime you want."

ACKNOWLEDGEMENTS

I could not have written this book without the assistance of a number of members of the Massachusetts State Police force. For security reasons, they do not wish to be named here, but they know who they are, and I am grateful for their assistance. They are skilled, dedicated law enforcement professionals—with men and women like them on the job, the fictional accounts of terrorism in this book will, hopefully, remain just that: fiction.

I also want to thank the following individuals for their efforts in critiquing this story during its various stages of completion. Someday I will write a novel in which the first draft is of publishable quality. Until then, I rely, with much gratitude, on my team of readers: Jeanne Scott, Richard Scott, Spencer Brody, Jeffrey Brody and Eric Stearns. Gold stars (and a fresh box of red pens) for each of you.

Many thanks as well to the crack publicity team, Kelley & Hall Book Publicity. Jocelyn and Megan, you have been great to work with. Your passion and creativity are directly responsible for this book's success.

Lastly, extra special thanks go to two individuals. Without them, this novel never would have reached its full potential. To Richard Meibers, of Martin and Lawrence Press, who spent countless hours reviewing, editing and critiquing (not to mention cajoling and even blackmailing). Richard's ability to grab an unruly plot by the horns and wrestle it into submission is truly remarkable. And to my wife, Kimberly Scott (also an author), for her skillful navigation between insightful critic and supportive spouse. Kim knows when to challenge, and knows when, instead, to smile and crack open a bottle of wine.

ATTRIBUTIONS

"It is better to be boldly decisive and risk being wrong than to agonize at length and be right too late."
—Marilyn Moats Kennedy, *Across the Board*

"The bible tells us to love our neighbors and also to love our enemies, probably because they are generally the same people."
—G.K. Chesterton

"If youth only knew; if age only could."
—Henri Estienne

"Each of us is the accumulation of our memories."
—Alan Loy McGinnis, *The Romance Factor*

"To have doubted one's own first principles is the mark of a civilized man."
—Oliver Wendell Holmes, Jr.

"He who never made a mistake never made a discovery."
—Samuel Smiles